# The
# Dover Café
## *under* Fire

Ginny Bell went to school in Dover, never realising at the time what a fascinating and crucial role the town played in the Second World War. She is a freelance editor who lives in London with her three children.

**Also by Ginny Bell:**
*The Dover Café at War*
*The Dover Café on the Front Line*

# The
# Dover Café
# *under* Fire

## Ginny Bell

**ZAFFRE**

First published in the UK in 2022 by
ZAFFRE
An imprint of Bonnier Books UK
4th Floor, Victoria House, Bloomsbury Square, London, England, WC1B 4DA
Owned by Bonnier Books
Sveavägen 56, Stockholm, Sweden

This is a work of fiction. Names, places, events and
incidents are either the products of the author's
imagination or used fictitiously. Any resemblance to
actual persons, living or dead, or actual
events is purely coincidental.

A CIP catalogue record for this book is
available from the British Library.

ISBN: 978-1-83877-609-1

*Also available as an ebook and in audio*

1 3 5 7 9 10 8 6 4 2

Typeset by IDSUK (Data Connection) Ltd
Printed and bound in Great Britain by Clays Ltd, Elcograf S.p.A.

MIX
Paper from
responsible sources
FSC® C018072

Zaffre is an imprint of Bonnier Books UK
www.bonnierbooks.co.uk

*For my extraordinary sister, Sandy.*
*The purest soul, the kindest heart. And the most determined, stubborn and inspirational person I will ever know. Fly safe, my love.*

# Character List

## The Market Square

### Castle's Cafe
*Nellie Castle* – Opinionated matriarch of Castle's Cafe
*Donald Castle* (died in 1927) – Nellie's husband

### Nellie and Donald's children:
*Rodney* (30) – Officer in the navy, works at Dover Castle
*Marianne* (29) – Best cook in Dover, lives and works at Castle's Café
*Jimmy* (24) – Private in the army, currently stationed at Drop Redoubt on Western Heights
*Bert* (22) – Also at Drop Redoubt
*Edie* (20) – Works as a mechanic at Pearson's Garage
*Lily* (18) – A trainee nurse at the Casualty Hospital
*Donny* (11) – Marianne's son
*Polly* – Talkative parrot

*Jasper Cane* – Donald Castle's best friend and surrogate father to the Castle children.
*Gladys* – Works at Castle's Café. Nellie took her in after her husband was killed in WWI
*Alfie Lomax* – Marianne's husband and stationed with Jimmy and Bert at Drop Redoubt
*Dr Charlie Alexander* – Lily's boyfriend, a doctor in the Royal Medical Corps
*Marge Atkinson* – Good friend of Marianne's. Is in the Wrens and stationed at Dover Castle. In love with *Rodney Castle*
*Hester Erskine* – Brothel madam from Folkestone. Left Dover age sixteen when she found out she was pregnant

### Turner's Grocery
*Ethel Turner* – Good friend of Nellie's
*Brian Turner* – Ethel's husband
*Reenie Turner* – Ethel and Brian's niece, works in the shop and also runs the Dig for Victory Campaign in the allotments near Western Heights. Good friend of Marianne's. Currently walking out with *Jimmy Castle*

## Perkins' Fish

*Phyllis Perkins* – Good friend of Nellie's
*Reg Perkins* – Phyllis's husband
*Wilf Perkins* – Phyllis and Reg's son. Works on the lifeboats. Has lived with his parents since his wife, *June Turner* (*Reenie*'s sister), died many years before
*Freddie Perkins* – Wilf's son and Donny's best friend

## Bakery – The Guthries

*Mary and Jack Guthrie* – Run the bakery
*Colin Guthrie* – Mary and Jack's son, missing since Dunkirk. Best friend of Jimmy Castle
*Susan Blake* – Mary's niece

## The Royal Oak

*Mavis Woodbridge* – Proprietor of the pub
*Derek Woodbridge* – Mavis's husband
*Stan Woodbridge* – Mavis and Derek's son, invalided out of the army after Dunkirk. He left Dover with his baby daughter, Marguerite
*Daisy Woodbridge* – wife of Stan, good friend of Marianne's

## Pearson's Garage

*Clive Pearson* – Edie's boss
*Bill Penfold* – Mr Pearson's nephew and newly qualified pilot with the RAF
*Walter Penfold* – Bill's father, a chauffeur

## Other Characters

*Muriel Palmer* – Runs the Dover WVS
*Dr Palmer* – Muriel's husband
*Lou Carter* – Runs whelk stall in Market Square. Local gossip
*Terence Carter* – Lou's son. Wheeler-dealer on the black market
*Mr Wainwright* – Local solicitor who has helped both Marianne and Lily
*Padre Philip Sterling* – Army chaplain at the castle, very keen on *Marge*
*Greg Manning* – Canadian Pilot, stationed at Hawkinge. Edie's boyfriend
*Ernest Fanshawe* – Owner of Folkestone brewery
*Henry Fanshawe* – Donny's father. Son of *Ernest*
*Elspeth Fanshawe* – Henry's wife
*Rupert Fanshawe* – Ernest's other son
*Roger Humphries* – Local constable. Was in love with Marianne
*Reverend Johnson* – Vicar of St Mary's Church
*Adelaide Frost* – Member of Market Square community
*Mr Gallagher* – Runs the news-stand
*Tom Burton* – The cobbler
*Dot* – Trainee nurse and friend of Lily
*Vi* – Trainee nurse and friend of Lily
*Mr Evans* – WWI veteran, has lived in Barwick Caves since shelling began

# Prologue

## 27 December, 1927

A loud bang made Edie sit up. 'Marianne? Lily?' she croaked. But her sisters weren't in their beds. Then she remembered: they'd gone tobogganing with her brothers and Jasper, but she'd had to stay home because she had a cold. She sniffed and wrinkled her nose. But she felt better now. She'd go and find them, she decided. Maybe she could get Daddy to come too. It might make him happy.

She stood up on the bed and peered out of the window. Snow was falling heavily and she could see people on Castle Street throwing snowballs at each other. She looked up towards the castle, but it was almost obscured by the flurries of snowflakes. 'Like fairies,' she whispered to herself.

Jumping down to the floor, she started to dress, struggling with the buttons on her skirt. She'd just managed to do them up when a loud scream made her jump.

Startled, she went out onto the landing. 'Mummy?'

'Get back in your room, Edith!' her mother called. Her voice sounded strange – high-pitched and shaky.

'Why did you scream? What was that bang?' she called back.

'GET BACK IN YOUR ROOM!'

Her mother's fierce tone frightened her and she started to wail.

Suddenly her mother's friend Gladys was beside her, pale and shaking. 'It's all right, love. Just go back to bed and I'll bring you a

1

nice hot drink.' She put her hands on Edie's shoulders and urged her back into her room.

'Why's Mummy cross?'

Gladys kissed her hair and pulled back the blankets. 'She's not cross. She just banged her head.'

Lying down, Edie stared up at the woman curiously. 'Are you cold?' she asked.

'No, of course I'm not. It's nice and toasty inside.'

'But your hands are all shivery.' Edie caught one of Gladys's hands in hers.

'I'm fine. Now stay here and I'll bring you some of my special tea.'

Gladys's tea always made her feel better, so Edie nodded.

But no sooner had Gladys shut the door than she heard the muffled sound of her mother crying.

Mummy never cried, Edie thought in alarm. She got up again and eased the door open.

'Don't let her come down here!' she heard her mother sob.

'God have mercy on you, Nellie Castle,' Gladys's tone was equally strained. 'What have you done?'

'I don't know . . . He just . . . Oh my God! What are we going to *do*?'

Really worried now, Edie's heart started to beat faster. She wanted to go down to make sure they were all right, but she didn't want to make her mother any more angry – she was scary when she shouted.

But she could hear the distress in the hushed voices and she needed to see what had happened, so she tiptoed down the stairs, hanging on tight to the bannister.

Then, poking her head around the sitting room door, she took in the scene and started to scream.

# Chapter 1

*27 December, 1940*

The dawn had yet to break when Edie Castle woke from a troubled sleep. She lay for a moment, staring into the dark, listening to her sister Lily's soft breaths in the bed beside her as snatches of the dream came back to her: a bang, a scream, a splash of red on the wall. Her stomach clenched and she swallowed hard, willing the nausea away. She'd been having the same dream for thirteen years, and the details were as insubstantial now as they had always been.

She knelt up on the mattress and stuck her head beneath the blackout curtain, peering out of the large dormer window that over-looked Castle Street. But it was as if she were looking into a deep, black hole, with not a speck of light to be seen. Usually searchlights criss-crossed the sky, lighting up the castle and making it look otherworldly, a place haunted by ghosts and demons. But there were no lights today and the castle was hidden by the dark, velvet cloak of night. It seemed appropriate somehow.

Quietly, she slipped out of bed and pulled on some warm clothes. Beside her Lily stirred. 'Is it time to get up?' she asked sleepily.

'Not yet. Go back to sleep.' Edie left the room quietly, ignoring the muffled, 'Where you going?'

Outside the back door, she stopped and breathed in the freezing air. The sun wouldn't rise for a couple of hours yet and cloud covered the stars and moon, so there wasn't a pinprick of light to see by. But it didn't matter. She could have made the short walk to the churchyard blindfolded. With her torch pointing at the ground, she crossed the small concrete yard and slipped out of the back gate, making her way down Church Street towards St Mary's churchyard. Even in the dark, she knew where her father's grave was and she counted the stones, her hand resting briefly on each. She paused at one. 'Rest easy, Daisy. All's well with Stan and Maggie,' she whispered, touching the newly erected gravestone for her sister Marianne's friend, who'd been killed during a shell attack just three short months ago.

She moved on until she came to the plot she knew so well. In her mind's eye she could see the simple headstone, dirty now, but she remembered when it was a bright white; how the sun shining on it used to blind her, so she had to turn her face away.

She knelt down and ran her fingers over the words, invisible to her eyes, but she knew them by heart.

*Donald James Castle. 3 October 1888–27 December 1927.*
*Loving husband to Nellie. Father to Rodney, Marianne, James,*
*Albert, Edith and Lily.*
*To live in the hearts of those we love is not to die.*

She huffed. Her mother was such a liar. She hadn't loved her husband when he died. And she didn't love his memory. In fact, she seemed to have done all she could to erase him from their lives. And after the revelations of earlier in the year, she had come to understand that her parents' love had died long before her father had.

'Hello, Daddy,' she said. 'I wasn't sure I'd come this year because I've been so angry with you.' She paused, thinking about the events of last summer. 'He came looking for you, you know,' she said eventually. 'Your son – our half-brother. And he was a hateful man. Angry and bitter and dangerous. He could have harmed us all and it would have been your fault. How could you be so cruel and just abandon him and his mother? No one deserves that.'

She sat down on the frosty grass, crossing her legs and leaning her elbows on her trousered knees. 'I've found it hard to forgive you. Like I find it hard to forgive Mum for doing the same with Jasper. Did you know that Lily wasn't yours? Is that why you never spoke to her? It wasn't her fault, you know.' She sighed. 'I'm sorry. I didn't come here to argue with you, but I needed to say it. And despite everything, I still love you. I'm still your little Edie. I still think of you every day and wonder why you killed yourself. What happened, Daddy?'

She'd put the torch on the ground beside her and its dim beam showed something had been left on the grave. She didn't need the light to tell her what it was. A single stem of blue hydrangeas.

She picked it up and twirled it round, instinctively giving it a sniff. It smelt of springtime and the promise of better days to come. Every year, no matter what time she visited the grave, there was always a single stem of hydrangeas lying in front of the gravestone.

'Who leaves this, Daddy? Please don't tell me there's *another* brother or sister out there bent on revenge.' She laughed slightly. 'I mean, I love you, but after everything we found out, I wouldn't put it past you.'

The steady drone of planes interrupted her and she sighed. It looked like Dover was back to normal after the quiet over Christmas. As though to confirm her fears, the siren started to wail and a distant boom rumbled towards her from the direction of the sea.

She stood up, then jumped as a figure loomed out of the dark towards her.

'I thought I'd find you here,' Reverend Johnson shouted above the noise. 'Come inside.' He turned and started to jog towards the church, Edie beside him.

Once inside they sped down the aisle towards a door set into the wall near the altar. The vicar opened it and they ran down the stone steps into the crypt. Edie wrinkled her nose at the smell of damp as she waited at the door for Reverend Johnson to light an oil lamp.

Finally, with the lamp lit, she sat down and wrapped one of the blankets that was kept down there around herself.

5

'Deary me,' the reverend said mildly. 'What a way to start the day. How are you doing, dear?' he asked kindly, examining her face carefully.

Edie shrugged. 'I'm just a bit ... sad, I suppose. Thank you for stopping by, Reverend.'

'I never forget, Edie. Not since I found you nearly frozen solid that morning when you were just a little girl. I will always come to stand memorial with you.'

'I'm glad it's not just me.' She twirled the flower, which she'd grabbed as she ran away, between her fingers. 'But then I suppose I shouldn't be surprised. The others don't seem to care that he's dead, and as for Mum ... I reckon she was glad when he died.'

'I don't think that's true, Edie. Although your father was very difficult towards the end.'

'Not with me, he wasn't,' she said sulkily. 'I loved him, you know. I think I may have been the only person in my family who did. I know he was awful a lot of the time, but I remember other things about him.'

'No one is completely bad and it sounds to me like you gave your father happiness.'

Edie smiled. 'I hope so. He was so rarely happy,' she said wistfully. She held up the flower. 'I found this on Dad's grave again. It's strange don't you think? Every year, without fail, someone leaves the same thing, yet neither you nor I have ever seen who.'

The vicar nodded. 'It is strange. But it shows you that you aren't the only one to remember.'

'But who could it be?'

He shrugged. 'If they wanted you to know, then I'm sure they'd have found a way to tell you. Blue hydrangeas signify apology. Did you know that?'

Edie shook her head.

'And maybe whoever leaves this has their own reasons for hiding their identity.'

'But what shame could there be in remembering someone? Unless it's another woman—' She stopped abruptly, suddenly aware that

6

she shouldn't say any more, even though she knew the vicar would never breathe a word. But it was private family business and should probably stay that way.

'Is there anything else on your mind, dear?' he asked.

Not wanting to go into the events of the summer when they had discovered the existence of a half-brother who seemed intent on revenge, Edie said, 'I used to have nightmares. For years after Dad died, I'd wake up screaming. It used to drive Mum mad. Then they stopped. But recently they've returned.'

The reverend didn't say anything, but his steady gaze never left her face.

'I think I'm dreaming about the day my father died. I wake up and I'm so scared and angry. Sometimes it makes me sick.'

His brow furrowed. 'I didn't know you were there when he died.'

Edie shrugged. 'I don't know for sure that I was. Mum will never talk about it. Lily told me that sometimes people forget things that are too hard to bear. Do you think that could have happened to me?'

Reverend Johnson sighed. 'Yes, I've heard of that happening before. But if you did see anything, then it's a blessing that your mind has wiped it from your memory. God only gives us the troubles we can bear.'

Edie snorted, then glanced up at the vicar apologetically. 'Sorry, Reverend, but I find that hard to believe. Especially as there are so many millions suffering because of this horrible war! I mean, look at us, hiding away in a basement like rats.'

He inclined his head. 'We all have our own beliefs.'

Just then the all-clear sounded. 'That was quick,' Edie remarked. 'Must have been a false alarm.' She stood up. 'I'd better get going. Mr Pearson's expecting me at the garage early this morning, and to be honest, I'll be glad to get back. Living with him is so much more peaceful than being at home.'

Reverend Johnson chuckled. 'Yes, your family has always struck me as rather . . . lively.'

7

'That's one way of putting it,' Edie laughed as they walked up the stairs and back through the church.

'You know you can talk to me any time,' the vicar said kindly as they stood on the church steps.

'I know. Thank you.' Impulsively she leant forward and kissed his cheek.

'Take care, dear.' She could hear the smile in his voice, then he turned and in the beam of her torch she could vaguely see his white collar bobbing back to the church.

She looked out over the small graveyard. 'Bye, Dad. Sleep tight.'

It was time to put her sadness aside and get on with what needed to be done. Thank God Christmas was over and they could all go back to normal. Although, she thought, as she heard the drone of aircraft, the first they'd had for a few days, back to normal wasn't necessarily a good thing.

This time the planes were flying back the other way, and she stopped and looked up at the dark sky. Was that Greg? she wondered, feeling a little sick as she remembered how Lily had discovered her and the Canadian pilot, naked and fast asleep in the basement on Christmas morning. She shuddered with self-disgust.

She should never have slept with him. He was handsome and she'd enjoyed his company, but she was uncomfortably aware that on both occasions they'd been together, she'd not been entirely willing. Somehow, though, he always managed to persuade her. But never again, she promised herself. She wasn't ready to risk her heart again.

# Chapter 2

It was six fifty-five in the morning and Nellie peered down at the market square from the sitting room window above Castle's Café. There wasn't much to see on this cold, dark December morning, but she could hear the murmur of voices and see the glow of several cigarettes, bobbing through the darkness like fireflies.

She tutted. Where was the ARP warden when you needed him? If Jasper were here, he wouldn't stand for that. But then, he wasn't here, she thought glumly. And who knew when he would be again. He might be awake after three long months in a coma, but there was a long road ahead before he'd be back to his old self – if he ever would be.

Throwing open the window, she shouted down to the crowd, 'Ciggies out, please. Amount of light coming from your fags, the entire Waffa'll be flyin' over quicker than Lou Carter can polish off a pint of whelks.'

'Oi, watch your mouth!' a woman's voice shouted.

'We've all seen you, scoffing 'em down, Lou. It's a wonder you've got anything to sell the amount you eat.'

'Aw, come on, Mrs C, open up. It's brass monkeys out here!' a man called.

Just then the air raid siren wailed around them.

'See?' Nellie screeched. 'Now we're gonna be stuck in the basement and all because you couldn't wait to light up.'

Hastily picking up a bird cage, inside which sat a green parrot with bright red tail feathers, Nellie ran downstairs and, leaving the cage on the counter, she went and opened the front door, allowing the small crowd outside to run through the café and into the kitchen, where Marianne, Nellie's eldest daughter, was busily pouring water into a large teapot.

'Bring us down some grub, love,' Lou Carter said as she swept past and Marianne sighed as she went to the pantry and took out a tin of currant buns she'd baked the night before. If her mother couldn't get hold of more supplies soon, they'd have to stop feeding everyone who sheltered in the basement.

The back door opened and a tall thin woman with grey-streaked blonde hair rushed in.

'Mornin', Gladys,' Nellie said brightly. 'No need to hurry, love, God'll look after ya.' She chortled at her own joke.

'It's not me I'm worried about,' she retorted. She gave Nellie a hard look.

Ignoring her, Nellie turned away to usher the customers down the stairs.

'Sounds like a false alarm to me,' someone was saying as Marianne walked in to the large basement, the tin of buns under one arm.

'You could be right,' Nellie replied, cocking her head. 'What do you reckon? Shall we risk it?'

'I'm not sure, Mum,' Marianne said. 'I heard an explosion.'

'But the walls didn't shake. I'd lay money on this bein' one of them damn precautionary sirens,' a man in army uniform commented irritably.

'I agree. What say we go back up and get on with the day,' Nellie replied. 'Any who don't like it can stay put.'

As everyone filed back out, Marianne caught her mother's arm. 'We're running low,' she whispered.

Nellie huffed. 'What do we need?'

'Everything.'

'But I only got stuff a few weeks ago.'

'And it's all gone to the tea stand in the caves.'

Nellie sighed. 'Fine, I'll see what I can do. But reuse the tea leaves, for gawd's sake. Amount we get through, anyone'd think we bathed in the stuff.'

'Oh, silly me, why didn't I think of that?' Marianne said sarcastically.

Nellie frowned. 'No need for that tone, my girl. I said I'd do my best, didn't I?'

As they went back into the kitchen, Lily, Nellie's youngest daughter appeared from upstairs, dressed in her nurses' uniform.

'Shouldn't you be sheltering?' she asked, picking up her cape and swinging it around her shoulders.

'I could ask the same of you, young lady,' Nellie said disapprovingly.

Lily shrugged. 'Matron'll kill me if I'm late, and it sounds like a false alarm to me.'

'Get off then, but keep an eye out. Oh, and I'll be up later to see Jasper,' Nellie told her.

'Maybe not today, Mum. Charlie's coming in to examine him—'

'Charlie?' Marianne turned from the range. 'Won't that be a bit difficult after you dumped him on Christmas Eve?'

'I didn't dump him,' Lily muttered defensively. 'I just said I wouldn't marry him. He's still my boyfriend.'

'Boyfriend, my foot!' Nellie snorted. 'You turned down a proposal from a doctor who also happens to be an officer!' She regarded her youngest daughter sternly. 'And here was me thinking you were the brains in the family.' She tutted. 'Anyway, like I said, I'll be up later.'

'No, Mum! Jasper needs rest and you're not very restful.'

'Stuff and nonsense,' Nellie responded briskly. 'What Jasper needs is to be cheered up and fattened up. Here, Marianne, stick a few of them left-over mince pies in a tin, love, and I'll take 'em up to him.'

As she went back into the café, Lily rolled her eyes at her older sister. 'Why won't she listen to me?'

Marianne laughed, pouring out a cup of tea and pushing it across the large table in the centre of the kitchen. 'Is that a serious question?'

Lily chuckled. 'No.' She picked up the cup and took a gulp.

Marianne eyed her curiously. 'Won't it be awkward seeing Charlie today?'

Lily sighed. 'Maybe. I still don't know if I did the right thing. But . . .'

'But?'

'But like I said, he's still my boyfriend.'

'Is he?'

'Yes! Of course he is. He loves me and I love him.'

'Just not enough.' Marianne turned to the range and flipped the sausages over.

'That's not fair! I've got stuff I want to do with my life, that's all. And marriage would put an end to all that.'

'Well, I'm sure you know what you're doing,' Marianne said non-committally.

'Any sign of Edie?' Lily asked. She didn't want to talk about Charlie anymore. She'd been driving herself mad over Christmas, asking herself if she'd done the right thing and missing him so much, her heart hurt.

'No. You know where she's gone, though, don't you?'

Lily wrinkled her brow.

'It's the twenty-seventh of December. Thirteen years since Dad died.'

'Oh,' Lily said. 'I'd forgotten . . . But then, seeing as he wasn't my dad, and I barely remember him, I don't think about him at all.'

'Aren't you the lucky one,' Marianne muttered. In truth, though, her own feelings were conflicted. On the one hand, she felt she ought to stand remembrance with Edie, but on the other . . . She had nothing but bad memories of her father and since they'd discovered the existence of a half-brother, she'd decided he didn't deserve her loyalty. As far as she was concerned, Jasper was their father in every way that counted.

# Chapter 3

When Edie returned to the café, the three rows of dark wood tables were crowded and the place was humming with chatter, the air thick with cigarette smoke and the smell of fried food. Most of the customers were dressed in khaki or navy blue, and while some had just finished their night shifts, others were getting ready for another long day of trying to keep the enemy at bay.

Edie put the hyacinth stem in a glass of water and placed it on the small table at the side of the kitchen.

'Another one?' Marianne asked as she turned from the range to slide eggs on to a plate.

'Yup. And today Reverend Johnson told me that blue hydrangeas signify apology. Do you think maybe Mum . . . ?'

Marianne studied the flower for a moment, then shrugged. 'Maybe,' she said. 'But why would she keep it so secret?'

'Well, as we've discovered, Mum's quite good at keeping secrets. Which is odd, considering she's always shouting her mouth off,' Edie said snidely.

'It's strange, though. Every spare bit of land's been dug up to plant veg, so where did she get it?'

Just then, Gladys bustled in. 'You look like you've lost a pound and found a penny,' she said as she picked up the plates Marianne had just filled.

'You've forgotten as well, haven't you?' Edie said.

13

Gladys stilled. 'No, I've not forgotten. Hard to forget something like that.'

'You were there when Dad died. Can you tell me what happened?'

Gladys shook her head. 'Nothing to tell, love – he shot himself with his service pistol. Go and sit down and I'll bring you something to eat.'

Gladys hobbled out of the kitchen and Edie sighed as she followed her and sat down at the table by the counter – Jasper's table. Gladys was as tight-lipped as her mother when it came to discussing what had happened that fateful day.

'Won't be a minute, love,' Gladys called over to her. 'Tea and toast, is it?'

'Let her get it herself,' Nellie called. 'Unless she fancies paying?' Nellie gave her middle daughter a challenging stare.

Edie glared back, her eyes running over her mother's lime-green jersey, red skirt and bright pink pinny. Since Jasper had been injured three months before, she'd been wearing more sober clothes, but today it looked like she was back to her old colourful self. 'Nice outfit, Mum,' she said sarcastically. 'The anniversary of your husband's death, and here you are, dressed for the carnival.'

Nellie crossed her arms over her chest. 'I can dress how I like. Not as if it makes any difference to him, is it?'

Gladys hurried back into the kitchen, returning with Edie's break-fast. 'That's enough, you two. God knows what's in our hearts, and it's not for anyone else to judge.'

'I bloody hope God don't know what's in my heart,' Nellie said.

Gladys looked at her friend. 'As do I, Nell,' she said quietly. 'But rest assured, he does.'

Nellie looked away. 'Oh, shut up. Your God-botherin's been getting worse since the war started. What you do in your own time is nothing to do with me, but don't bring that nonsense into my café!'

Gladys turned and went to take an order without another word.

'How can you be so rude to her? She's one of your oldest friends, and you couldn't manage without her.'

14

'Me and Glad understand each other.'

Edie felt the familiar anger with her mother fizz in her stomach, but there was no point continuing the argument. Especially not in front of so many people.

The bell over the door tinkled and another soldier walked in, rubbing his hands against the cold. 'Land's sakes, Mrs C,' he exclaimed as he walked up to the counter, shielding his eyes. 'You could have warned us.'

Nellie raised an eyebrow. 'About what exactly?'

The man's eyes ran over her, then he shrugged. 'Nuffin',' he muttered, sticking his fingers through the bars of the birdcage that sat by the cash register. 'All right, Polly. How's Hitler these days?'

'Bloody man!' the parrot responded, turning full circle on her perch and flapping her wings.

The soldier grinned and sat down. 'By heck, it's good to be back,' he said. 'Colours, parrot and all. Mornin's aren't the same without a good nosh-up at the caff before work.'

'Café,' Nellie responded. 'This is a café, and please don't forget it.'

He gave her a brief salute and Nellie smiled in response, before picking up a teacup, which she tapped loudly with a spoon. 'Listen up, everyone. I have an announcement to make!'

Edie sighed. What now? she thought moodily. On the one hand she was pleased her mother had returned to her usual snippy, colourful self, but on the other . . . God, she drove her round the bend!

Lou Carter groaned loudly. 'Can't it wait till after I've got me grub, Nell?' she said. 'I'm bloody starvin'.'

'Feel free to leave if you don't want to hear it, Lou. No one's forcin' you to come in here every single bloomin' day!'

Lou grimaced at her. 'Nor I wouldn't, if not for Marianne's cookin'. This place'd be nothin' without her.'

Nellie ignored her and continued, 'So no one's interested in how Jasper is? The man that's saved a fair few lives and helped most of you at some point.'

15

'Is he awake?' Lou asked.

'He is!' Nellie's face broke into a broad grin. 'Woke up Christmas Eve while you lot were all singing along to Vera Lynn at the Oak. It'll be a long road to recovery, but I'm happy to say that hopefully soon the market square will have its ARP warden back so you, Mr Bulger' – she pointed at a tall thin man with grey hair and a bushy moustache – 'can get back to your normal rounds.'

'Thank gawd for that,' Mr Burton the cobbler called out, then shot a wary glance at Mr Bulger, whose moustache was bristling with outrage. 'No offence, but life's not been the same without Jasper.'

'You should be grateful there's folk willing to do the job!' Mr Bulger exclaimed bad-temperedly. 'There's some I could mention what don't do anything to help the war effort.'

Mr Burton looked outraged. 'I'll have you know, I spent Christmas night fire-watchin'.'

'The fact is' – Nellie raised her voice and shot a warning look at the two men – 'Jasper will soon be back where he belongs, sitting at his table and enjoying his grub.'

Edie shook her head. Aside from the fact that he was blind, she wasn't convinced that Jasper would want to come back to the café. And frankly, she wouldn't blame him if he never set foot in here again, after the way her mother had suggested he wasn't part of the family.

'I'm not so sure,' Edie hissed as she stood up. 'Not after the way you treated him.' She picked up her plate and cup and saucer and went through to the pantry where she dumped them in the sink with a clatter, then took her coat off the hook by the back door.

'I don't know how you stand it,' she said.

Marianne looked surprised. 'What?'

'Mum going on day in and day out. And now she's just pretending that nothing happened between her and Jasper before he got hurt.'

'Oh, stop it,' Gladys hissed. 'Believe me, just cos she don't show it, today's no picnic for her either.' She slammed the empty tray she was carrying on the table. 'Two more porridges if you please, Marianne.'

16

She pointed a skinny finger at Edie. 'You have no idea what that woman has done for you. For all of you. It ain't been easy, bringin' you six up on her own and keeping this place going, so in future, maybe you should think about that before you have a go at her!'

'Sorry,' Edie replied, feeling ashamed. 'You're right, as usual, Gladys. I'll try to be nicer. But she makes it so hard sometimes. Anyway, I've got to get to work. Tell Mum I'll be back New Year's Eve.' She put her tin hat onto her head, picked up her gas mask and stomped towards the back door.

Gladys stared after her with a frown. 'Why can't you tell her yourself?' she called.

'Because I don't want to,' Edie called back, slamming the back door shut behind her.

# Chapter 4

Determinedly pushing all thoughts of the morning and her mother from her mind, Edie walked up Castle Street, keeping her eye out for a bus. But as she passed the umbrella factory, her attention was caught by a woman on the other side of the road wearing a brown fur coat and red high-heeled shoes who was struggling down the road with what looked to be a very heavy suitcase.

'Need a hand?' Edie called.

The woman stopped and squinted over at her. 'Wouldn't say no.' She made to cross the road towards Edie and was nearly run over by a large black Bentley that was speeding down the hill. She jumped back, her ankle turning as the weight of the suitcase caused her to overbalance and she sprawled onto the ground.

'Are you all right?' Edie dashed over to help.

Now she was closer, she could see the woman was older than she'd first thought, with dyed blonde hair, dark at the roots, and deep wrinkles fanning out from her eyes.

Edie grabbed the woman's arm and helped her up. 'Bloody car! They didn't even see you!'

'Well, that's toffs for yer,' the woman said, leaning heavily on Evie's shoulder. 'Folk like us are invisible to the likes of them.'

'Let me take that suitcase,' Edie said once she was sure the woman could stand on her own. But when she bent to pick it up, she nearly fell over. 'Hell's bells, you got the kitchen sink in here?' she gasped.

The woman sniffed. 'That's my whole life right there,' she said glumly. 'Or what's left of it.'

Looking at her now, Edie realised the woman appeared shattered and her heart went out to her.

'Everything all right?' she asked.

'Not really, love. Been bombed out. All me worldly goods except me wireless and fur coat gone. Just got off the bus from Folkestone.'

'You poor thing. What are you going to do?' Edie asked sympathetically.

'Thought I'd go see my mate Nellie at the caff.'

'You know Nellie?' Edie asked.

'Don't everyone round these parts?' she answered. 'An' everyone knows if you need a hand, then Nellie Castle's the woman to talk to.'

'I suppose.' Edie smiled reluctantly. First Gladys and now this stranger; it seemed someone was trying to remind her that her mum wasn't all bad. 'I'm Edie Castle, by the way. Nellie's daughter. Don't think we've ever met?'

The woman stopped and stared at her, a wide smile on her face. 'Bless my soul. What are the chances?'

'Well, Dover's a small place – especially now most of the locals have left,' Edie said. 'I didn't know there'd been raids in Folkestone in the last few days, though. It's been quiet here.'

The woman paused for a moment, before saying, 'Shell landed on the house next door a week back. The roof collapsed so I been living downstairs – no water, no leccy. Merry Christmas to me, eh?' She gave a short bark of laughter. 'Then last night, I were on the sofa at the front of the house, when the kitchen wall collapsed. I were lucky to get out of there alive. That shell must have done more damage to my house than I realised and finally it couldn't take it anymore. An' I know exactly how it feels.'

'Blimey! Why didn't you leave sooner?'

19

'I would have if I had anywhere to go. But now I'm well and truly on me uppers and I got no choice but to throw myself on your mum's mercy.'

'You want to stay at the café?'

'Just till I get back on me feet. Last time I saw your mum she said to come to her if I needed anything. And if this ain't needing something, I don't know what is.'

'Sorry, I didn't get your name?' Edie was very curious now.

They had reached the corner of Castle Street and Market Square by now and Edie noticed the woman stop and gaze across the square to where the Bentley that had nearly run her over was idling outside the fishmonger's.

'Do you know that car?' she asked, distracted.

'As if,' the woman huffed. 'And as to who I am' – she nodded towards the old Market Hall where Lou Carter, who had been setting up her whelks' stall, was staring at them, a puzzled frown on her face – 'I'll tell you later. Cos I'd prefer to get settled before that one gets wind of me.'

'How do you know Lou?'

'Me and her was in the same class at school. Ain't seen her since I left – ooh, it's gotta be thirty years ago now. Anyway, let's just say my life ain't been entirely . . . *respectable*, and I'd rather she didn't see me till I can get meself dressed properly.'

Edie was very curious now, and she looked at the woman more closely. From the way she was dressed and her dyed hair, she certainly didn't look respectable. But how on earth would her mother know someone like this? she wondered with an inward smile. Well, this could be interesting, she thought, peering through the large plate-glass window of the café, noting the crowded tables and her mother, conspicuous in her ridiculous clothes, standing behind the counter, the parrot beside her. She had a feeling Nellie might prefer it if they went in the back door. But what fun would that be?

She pushed open the door and walked in.

'Back already?' her mother called. Then she caught sight of the woman walking in behind Edie and her mouth dropped open in surprise.

'Look who I found coming down the hill,' Edie said breezily, as she lugged the suitcase through the café. 'Apparently she's an old friend of yours?' Her mother's astonished expression was everything she'd hoped.

'But how—'

Grinning, she shrugged and went into the kitchen, dumping the woman's case at the bottom of the stairs. Much as she was desperate to stay, she knew she couldn't, so, ignoring Marianne's questioning look, she rushed out the back and started to jog up Castle Street, just as a bus rattled past, billowing thick black exhaust fumes. Sticking out her hand, she hurried towards the bus stop.

'Bus doesn't sound too clever today,' she remarked to the driver as she got on.

'Don't worry, love, she'll get you to the top of the hill at least.'

'She better. I'm late enough as it is. I'll find myself looking for a job at the bus garage if I'm not careful.'

The driver chuckled. 'I doubt old Clive'll let you go any time soon.'

Edie smiled with pleasure at his words, and went to sit down, laughing to herself as she remembered the disbelief on her mother's face when she'd caught sight of the woman. Whoever she was, she'd bet her last pound her mother wasn't too happy to see her. She couldn't wait to find out what it was all about.

As the bus neared the top of Castle Hill, it came to a juddering stop and Edie jolted forward, almost banging her head on the blue metal rail of the seat in front of her. Almost immediately there was a loud horn blast from behind them, and Edie realised the bus must have completely blocked the road in both directions.

She made her way down the aisle and jumped down on to the road. The driver had already got out and clambered up on to the wheel of the bus to open the bonnet.

21

'What's going on, Mr Benson?' she asked.

'Engine looks all right,' he muttered, shutting the bonnet and climbing down.

There was another loud beep and Edie followed the bus driver to the back of the bus, surprised to see the Bentley again. 'That car,' she murmured. 'Is it following me?'

The driver's window rolled down and a man poked his head out. 'Move the bus, wontcha!' he shouted.

Edie rolled her eyes. If they were in such a hurry, how come they'd been idling round the square earlier?

''Fraid I can't, mate!' Mr Benson retorted. 'Though you're welcome to move it for me.'

'For God's sake, you must be able to do *something*!' With a curse the man climbed out of the car and strode towards them, clapping his gloved hands against the cold. He was wearing a chauffeur's peaked cap and a scarf was wrapped around his face. His shoes, Edie noticed, were so shiny she could probably have seen her face in them.

'What's wrong with it?' he asked impatiently.

'It's stopped.'

'Well start it again, then, can't you?'

'If you're in such a hurry, mate, feel free to start it yerself.'

'It ain't my job to fix *your* bus! Seriously, *mate*, sort it out, or I promise you, my mistress'll be havin' words with your superior.'

Mr Benson turned his back on the man with a huff. 'I don't understand it,' he said to Edie. 'We were a bit short on diesel this morning so I filled her with me spare half gallon just before I got to Market Square. It should have been more than enough.'

'Let me take a look,' Edie suggested mildly, longing to give the arrogant chauffeur a piece of her mind. Just cos he was driving a posh car, it didn't give him the right to be rude.

The chauffeur looked at Edie fully now. He had small, dark-brown eyes set close together, and they made her shudder as his gaze moved from the long, dark plait emerging from beneath her tin hat, over

22

the scruffy donkey jacket that Mr Pearson had given her and finally resting on her sturdy work boots. Then he looked back at her face, his eyebrows raised in disbelief. '*You?*' he said scornfully. 'And what would *a girl* know about it?' He smiled nastily. 'Or are you, in fact, a boy? It's hard to tell.'

Edie suppressed the urge to wipe the patronising smirk off his face. 'Most people don't find it too difficult,' she said. 'Unless they're *really* stupid.'

She stomped to the side of the bus and removed the petrol cap, then pulled off her gloves and thrust her hand into the hole, her fingers closing over the filter. It took a moment before she was able to grasp the piece of cloth, which felt slimy to the touch. 'Looks like this might be the problem,' she said, holding the filter between her fingertips. 'The filter's blocked.'

'Now why didn't I think of that?' The bus driver smacked himself on the head. 'Mind you, my great big mitts won't fit through that hole, so just as well you were here, love.'

'Christ preserve us,' the chauffeur muttered as he stomped back to the car. 'The country is full of bloody idiots.'

Edie ignored him. 'See if you can start her up.'

The driver climbed back into the bus and started the engine. It spluttered and smoke once again poured from the exhaust.

The chauffeur was leaning against the bonnet of the Bentley, his arms folded. 'Well, there's a surprise,' he sneered.

'Try again,' Edie shouted.

This time, the engine caught. 'Thanks, girl,' Mr Benson called through the window. 'I weren't jokin' earlier, we could use a good mechanic down at the Russell Street garage, if you fancy it.'

She smiled. 'I'll be sure to remember.'

The car horn blasted again. 'If it's fixed, then move!'

'Keep yer hair on, *mate!*' Mr Benson shouted back. 'Anyone'd think he had the queen and the princesses in the back, way he's carryin' on,' he said to Edie.

23

'Maybe he has.' Edie grinned cheekily. 'Maybe they've popped down to Dover to give everyone a boost.'

Mr Benson laughed. 'That'll be the day, eh?' he said out of the window. 'See ya around, love.'

Edie stepped back as the bus moved off, followed immediately by the Bentley. As it passed her, she stuck her tongue out at the driver. But then her stomach swooped with shock as, just for a moment, she caught sight of a pale face with bright red lips staring out of the back window. Was that . . . ? No, of course it wasn't. Because why on earth would *she* be in Dover at this time in the morning?

24

# Chapter 5

'What the hell are *you* doing here?' Nellie's exclamation brought all conversation to a stop as everyone turned to look at the woman in the tatty fur coat who had just stumbled in behind Edie.

Feeling the weight of the collective gaze, the woman smiled, and putting one hand on her hip, sauntered up to the counter. 'All right, Nellie?' she said casually, reaching into her pocket and pulling out a dented cigarette case. She flipped it open, took one out then nudged a soldier sitting at the table nearest to her. 'Give us a light, duck,' she said, bending towards him.

Too shocked to comment, the man obediently picked up his lighter and flicked it on, holding the flame towards her. She reached out to hold his wrist steady, her eyes never leaving his face as she puffed on the cigarette, then she stood up and blew a plume of smoke towards the ceiling.

'What are you doing here?' Nellie said again, watching the performance with disapproval. The last time she'd seen this woman, she, Marianne and Donny had been sheltering in a cupboard under the stairs of her house and she'd looked completely different. Even respectable. But now ... She let out a deep breath. It looked like Hester Erskine – or rather Mrs Barker, Folkestone brothel madam – had come to collect on her promise.

She hastened around the counter and grabbed Hester's arm, dragging her towards the kitchen door.

'Ain't you pleased to see me?' Hester wheedled.

25

'Not when you look like *this*,' Nellie hissed. 'Castle's is a respectable establishment.'

Hester stopped. 'Too good for the likes of me, you mean?'

Nellie felt a twinge of conscience. She had no right to judge Hester, who had been forced to leave Dover after she fell pregnant when she was no more than sixteen. Younger even than Marianne had been when she'd had Donny. She sighed. 'No, love, that's not what I'm saying. Let's just get upstairs and you can tell me everything.'

'You remember me telling you about Hester Erskine, don't you, Glad?' Nellie said as she walked into the kitchen. 'Me and her are just going for a little chat, so could you take over out front for a bit?'

Gladys stared at Hester in astonishment, her mouth opening as if to say something but no words came out. Hester had left Dover before Gladys had moved there, and though she'd heard all about what had happened in Folkestone, she'd never expected to meet the woman in the flesh. And no matter that she'd helped Donny, Gladys just couldn't approve of the way the woman earned her living.

If Hester noticed Gladys's disapproval, she showed no sign of it as she called out, 'All right, Marianne, love. How's young Donny? I'm lookin' forward to gettin' reacquainted with the lad.'

'Mrs Barker?' Marianne smiled with pleasure; she owed this woman so much and she didn't care what she did for a living. As far as she was concerned, she'd always be welcome. 'Don's just gone out to see his friend, but I know he'll be happy to see you.'

'No need to stand on ceremony; call me Hester. You too, Gladys. Oh, and it's Erskine – Barker's me professional name.' She winked.

Marianne smiled. 'Would you like a cup of tea?'

'Love one,' she said as Nellie pulled on her arm to try to hurry her upstairs. 'You couldn't bring one upstairs, could ya? Seems your mum's keen to get me away from pryin' eyes.'

Once they'd gone, Gladys gasped indignantly. 'The cheek of it! As if we don't have enough to do without waiting on her hand and foot. And what's she doin' here? You can't trust a woman like that.'

26

Marianne raised her eyebrows. 'Wasn't Mary Magdalen a prostitute?'

'That's different. She's in the Bible.'

Marianne chuckled as she poured some tea for their unexpected guest. Sometimes there was just no reasoning with Gladys.

∽

In the sitting room Nellie plumped down on one of the flowered chairs by the fireplace and gestured to the seat opposite.

Hester sank into it gratefully, leaning down to undo the ankle straps on her shoes. 'Me bleedin' feet are killin' me,' she said, wiggling her toes on the purple and yellow carpet.

Her feet were filthy, Nellie noticed, then she took in the rest of the woman's appearance. She had unbuttoned her tatty coat to reveal a black rayon slip that reached down to her knees. Her legs were bare and mottled with cold, and her hair . . . she assumed it was meant to be blonde, but it had a greenish tinge that made Hester's face look sickly.

But this woman had watched out for Donny when he needed help and Nellie had made her a promise: *Anything you need, come to me.*

'What brings you here, Hester?' Nellie asked with a sigh.

Hester took a long pull on her cigarette, staring around the room. Finally, she said, 'I need a place to stay.'

Nellie nodded. 'I figured. Why?'

Hester stubbed the cigarette out in a glass ashtray on the low table in front of her. 'Bloody great shell landed smack on the roof next door to me house. I been managing all right, but last night, me wall caved in just as I were going to bed, so I picked up me suitcase and legged it.' She reached into her pocket for another cigarette.

Nellie picked up a box of matches from the table beside her chair and struck one, holding it out. Hester leant forwards and sucked deep on the cigarette, then sat back, eyes closed as she breathed out the smoke in a long huff. When she opened them again, Nellie could see that they were moist and she was ashamed. Hester had a good heart, and she needed help. The least she could do was give it.

'No one was hurt?' she asked.

'Nah. Since the shell, I'd shut up shop. I figured I'd get the place repaired and be back up and running soon. But now I've got nothing – no house, no business, no clothes . . .' She sniffed and took another long puff of the cigarette.

'What's in the case then?'

'A wireless. It's me most precious possession.'

Nellie sighed. 'So you've been left with nothing but your fur coat and slip?'

'It's not a slip, it's a *negleege*. And yeah, this is it. I'm all fur coat and no drawers.' She let out a short laugh, but it died away quickly. 'I'm finished, Nell. I'm too old and too tired to go back on the game. An' since so many of me girls had left to do war work, I'd been renting out rooms by the hour – if you get me drift. It had been workin' out lovely. Even had me a fella. But he upped and left and now the house has gone, and I don't know what to do. I've spent half me life on me back, so there's no way I could hack standin' on me feet all day in a factory, and there ain't much else open for old birds like us, is there?'

Nellie thought for a moment then nodded. 'All right. You can sleep in the boys' room. Marianne's in there at the moment but she can move back in with Lily. But there's to be *no* funny business and I'll expect you to earn your keep by helping out in the café.'

Hester spluttered with indignation. 'You think I'll be tryin' to set up a knockin' shop here?' she said. 'No chance! I mean, I like my rooms to be a bit more' – she stared around at the gaudy flowered wallpaper, the purple and yellow swirled carpet and the bright pink and blue flowered chairs – 'restful,' she said eventually. 'And this place looks like the bloody flower fairies have puked all over it.' She started to laugh, but seeing Nellie's stony expression, she stopped abruptly. 'No offence, Nell, obviously. Each to their own.'

Nellie bit back an angry retort. 'Don't you have any friends in Folkestone who could help?' she asked.

Hester raised one eyebrow – though it had been plucked so thin it was almost invisible. 'Considerin' most of the people I know are men and most of them have gawn to war, and those that are there live with their wives . . . You really think I'd be welcome in one of their houses?'

'There must be someone – maybe that fella you mentioned?'

Hester laughed bitterly. 'That bastard! No way. He turned out to be no good. As for the others, I tried, Nell. All those men as have been made welcome in my house . . . Not one was willing to help. A woman like me don't make too many friends on her journey through life.'

'What about your son? Can he help?'

Hester stared at Nellie wordlessly, her lips trembling as a single tear rolled down her cheek.

Nellie got up and put an arm around Hester's shoulders. 'Oh Hester, love. I'm so sorry.'

Hester shook her head. 'Not your fault, Nell. It's this bastard war and the people in charge – they're all murderers. Hitler, Churchill, the lot of them. They're the ones that killed my boy. Out somewhere in the Atlantic, trapped in a bloody tin can miles under the sea; I feel sick when I think about it.'

'When did this happen?'

'I got word not long after I saw you. My Tommy . . . he were the very best of me. The *only* good thing in me life.' Her shoulders shook as Nellie pressed her tightly to her, rocking her back and forth as she might a child.

'*You're* a good thing in your life, Hester. Me and Marianne won't ever forget what you did for Don and I'm not the sort to go back on my promises. You're welcome to stay as long as you need.'

Hester fished in her pocket, pulling out a grubby handkerchief and blowing her nose. 'Thanks, Nell. I'm not normally like this. I've had months to come to terms with it. But sometimes it just hits me like a bus and I turn into a blinking watering pot.'

'I understand, love.'

Hester regarded her through watery eyes. 'I don't think you do. And I pray to God that you never will.'

Nellie smiled sadly. 'As do I. Come on, let's find you something to wear.'

Hester sniffed and smiled bravely. 'Thanks, Nell. I always said you were a good 'un.'

Shame washed through Nellie; when she'd first caught sight of Hester, she'd been dismayed. But what gave her the right to judge? After all, she was hardly a saint. Six children from two fathers, and her poor husband dead after . . . Instinctively her eyes turned towards the wall beside the fireplace, before she quickly looked away and stood up, holding a hand down for Hester and heaving her to her feet.

'All I ask is that you don't tell anyone what you've been up to,' she said. 'And if you could make up some story about a dead husband, then it'll make all our lives easier.'

Hester raised her eyebrows. 'You really think people'll believe some cock and bull about me being a respectable widow?'

'Why wouldn't they?' Although maybe Hester had a point. Nellie had noticed Lou Carter with her nose pressed up against the café window as Hester had come in and given the Carter family's nefarious connections, she wouldn't be surprised if Lou was well aware of what her old friend had been doing. And Lou's mouth was as wide as the Channel, so she couldn't see her keeping quiet for long.

'Look at it this way, then,' Nellie replied. 'If any men know you they'll keep their mouths shut and the women won't have a clue – we're always the last to know,' she said bitterly, thinking about the sudden appearance of Donald's son in Dover earlier that year. Born on the same day as her son Jimmy, and she'd never suspected a thing.

'Maybe.' Hester didn't sound convinced.

'Why don't we say you were singing in a pub somewhere when your house got bombed, which is why you're wearing these clothes.'

Hester laughed. 'You ever heard my voice?'

'Don't matter. Long as you don't sing in front of anyone.'

'All right, you're the boss. But don't blame me if people start talking.' She nudged Nellie. 'Hey, can't wait to see that bastard Horace Smith's face when he clocks me in the café.'

'If only! But his house got wrecked and he's long gone. And good riddance, the disgusting hypocrite. Constantly going on at Marianne for being an unmarried mother – although she ain't unmarried anymore. She got wed to Alfie who's in my Jim and Bert's regiment up at Drop Redoubt. They brought him home on leave last Christmas, and what a gift he turned out to be.'

'Ah. I'm right pleased for her. Funny how people change, though, in't it? Horace were such a one for the girls back then. Wonder what happened to change him?'

Nellie snorted. 'I don't reckon he changed a bit. He just likes to pretend he's all about Christian charity now.'

'Yeah, you're probably right. You'd be surprised how many religious types ended up at my house. There's something about carnal sin that gets 'em all excited.'

Nellie frowned. 'Spare me the details, if you don't mind. Now, wait here, I'll get you some proper clothes. Might be a bit loose around the middle and a bit short in the leg, but they'll do for now.

'A bit?!' Hester said with a smirk.

Nellie pursed her lips in annoyance. 'Do you want some clothes or not?'

Hester held up her hands. 'Just jokin', Nell. No offence.'

Nellie marched into her bedroom and returned with a red and purple skirt and a blue and red checked jersey.

Hester baulked at the sight of them. 'You've got to be jokin'. Haven't you got something a little less . . . colourful?'

'I have, but I thought these might make you feel more cheerful,' Nellie huffed as she went back into the bedroom, returning shortly with a blue skirt and a grey jersey, bobbled with age.

Hester grimaced. 'What's with all the colours anyway?'

'I like 'em. And so did Jasper—' She stopped, realising Hester wouldn't know what had happened to Jasper.

'Jasper Cane? He ain't dead, is he?' Hester said. 'He's a true gent, that one. Did you know he gave me money to help me leave?'

Nellie shook her head, though she wasn't surprised. That was Jasper all over. 'He's not dead. Just . . . He's just . . .' But she couldn't say any more, she was trying very hard not to think about the awful truth of his condition. 'He's been sick and he's in hospital,' she said finally. 'But he'll be out soon. Now go and get changed.' She pushed Hester towards her room, then dropped on to the flowered sofa with a heavy sigh, wondering how much trouble a woman like Hester could cause. But how could she turn her away? To lose a son . . . She shuddered. There could be no worse grief than that. She made a promise to herself that she would do everything in her power to help Hester get back on her feet.

She'd been sitting there less than a minute when there was a loud crash. Seconds later, the air raid siren started to wail and she let out a hefty sigh. Chances were that this time it wasn't a false alarm, so they should probably get to shelter. She stood up just as her bedroom door burst open and Hester ran out holding the fur coat up in front of her, one strap of her negligee hanging down her arm. 'You got a shelter, Nell?'

'Downstairs in the basement. But don't you want to get some clothes on first?'

Hester shook her head. 'I ain't waitin' for nothing!' she shrieked. 'Not after me house nearly collapsed on top of me.' Shrugging on her coat, she ran towards the stairs, as another loud boom made the building shake.

Nellie followed her with a frown. It looked like Hester's introduction to the market square community was going to come sooner than she'd expected.

# Chapter 6

Lily walked quietly up to Jasper's bed. He was lying facing the wall, his white hair almost the same shade as the pillow.

'Are you awake?' she whispered, leaning down to smooth his hair back from his face.

Jasper turned his head and looked at her. 'Lily?'

Her heart jumped. 'Can you see me?'

He shook his head. 'I'd know your voice anywhere,' he said, reaching his hand up to stroke her cheek.

'Are you sure you can't see me?'

'I wish I could. I'd do anythin' to see your lovely face again.'

She grabbed the hand that still rested on her cheek. 'But you found my face immediately, almost as though you could see it.'

'Did I?' He looked confused.

'Can you see anything at all?'

'I don't think so.' He squeezed his eyes shut, then opened them again. 'Nope,' he sighed. 'Nothing. But hospitals are drab old places, maybe what I need's a bit of colour to perk me eyes up.'

'Good thing Mum's coming in later then,' she said.

Jasper puffed out his cheeks. 'Lily, love . . . Did your mum tell you about . . . ?'

Lily hesitated. On the one hand, she was relieved he remembered that he was her father. On the other, she hadn't intended to talk to him about this until he was stronger.

'About you being my dad?' she said softly. 'No, she didn't tell me. I found out from that awful Dick, Dad's – I mean, Donald's – abandoned son. You shouldn't have lied to me all these years. And neither should Mum.'

Jasper sighed. 'I'm so sorry, love. You'll never know how sorry. All them wasted years.'

'They weren't wasted. You were always there. And I always loved you.'

'And now? Can you ever forgive me?' he asked.

'I won't lie, I was angry with you. Both of you. But life's too short to waste in anger, so of course I forgive you. And I love you as much, if not more, as I always have.'

He smiled. 'Not as much as I love you. Oh, how I wish I could see your face.'

'Hopefully you will. If what Dr Toland suspects is right. That's why I'm here. She's asked Charlie to come and see you, because he specialised in brain injuries when he was training.'

'You reckon your doctor officer can make a blind man see?' Jasper snorted. 'He might be clever, but he's not flippin' Jesus! And anyway, there's nothing wrong with me brain!' Jasper said indignantly.

Lily chuckled and kissed his cheek. 'I know. But let him have a look, eh?'

'Don't see I have much choice, do I?'

There was a boom and for a moment the lights in the ward flickered. Lily sighed. 'Here we go again.'

As the muffled screech of the siren reached them, Jasper hit the bed in frustration. 'I should be out there helpin', dammit. Not lyin' here like a sack of rotten spuds.'

'Hey, stop it.' Lily grasped his hand. 'You've done your share of helping. And now it's our turn to help you. And hopefully one day soon you'll be back out there, ordering everyone around.' Lily looked towards the door. 'And looks like Charlie's arrived just in time to miss the raid.'

She beckoned Charlie over, her heart skipping a beat as she watched him lope towards her, his dark hair slicked back from his forehead and his brown eyes sparkling at the sight of her. *I should never have turned him down*, she thought for the millionth time. Just seeing him made her happy, and the fact that he was still willing to help her despite her rejection showed her more than words ever could what a wonderful man he was.

'Good morning, Mr Cane,' Charlie said when he reached the bed, his eyes sharp as he assessed Jasper's eye movements.

'Mornin', lad,' Jasper grumped. 'Lily seems to think you can work some sort of miracle on me.'

Lily tutted. 'No need to be rude, Dad. Just give him a chance.'

Jasper went still at her words. 'Say that again,' he said finally, reaching for her hand and holding it tightly.

'I said there's no need to be rude.'

'And the rest.'

Lily looked at Charlie who nodded at her encouragingly. 'Dad,' she whispered.

Jasper grinned. 'How can I refuse when my *daughter* asks me so nicely. Do your worst, Doc.'

Lily watched quietly while Charlie carried out a thorough examination, impressed at the gentle way he handled Jasper, building his trust and putting him at ease.

Finally, he sat back. 'Mr Cane, you were in the last war, weren't you?'

Jasper nodded.

'I imagine you saw a few of your comrades get injured or die.'

Jasper nodded again.

'And quite a few were blinded in the conflict, I understand.'

'Plenty,' Jasper croaked. 'Some were truly blind and others were— Hang on, are you suggestin' I'm faking? Listen, Doctor whatever-your-name-is, I'm not that sort of man! I keep going no matter what. Those lads . . . those lads who pretended, I never blamed 'em. Never. War does crazy things to all of us.'

'Most of those lads weren't faking, Mr Cane,' Charlie said gently. 'They were so shocked and in such distress that their minds played tricks on them.'

'And you think that's what's happened to me?' Jasper was astounded. 'Are you telling me my sight will come back?' He sat up straight, reaching towards Charlie and grabbing his lapels.

Charlie took hold of Jasper's wrists and pushed them back. 'I do think that's what's happened to you. You just grabbed me as though you could see me, and that tells me a lot. Dr Toland is thinking along the same lines. She just wanted to get a second opinion. I think – and please bear in mind this is almost impossible to confirm – but I *think* you might be suffering from what is known as "hysterical blindness".'

'What?!'

Jasper's shout made Lily jump. She'd expected him to be delighted at this news. She'd anticipated relief and excitement. But instead Jasper looked angrier than she'd ever seen him.

'I've never been hysterical in me life! Not during gas attacks in the trenches. Not when I picked up Donald from no-man's-land where he were lying screamin' an' shakin while the shells burst around him. Not when I was digging poor Daisy out of the rubble—' Jasper's chest was heaving.

Lily looked at Charlie in alarm. Jasper was always so calm and good-humoured; in fact, she didn't think she'd ever seen him lose his temper like this.

'Mr Cane . . .' Charlie began, putting his hand over Jasper's.

Jasper shook it off. 'Just go,' he hissed. 'And don't come back. And be thankful I can't see ya, or you'd not be stood there right now. You'd be flat on your back with a busted nose.'

'Dad!' Lily gasped. 'Charlie's only trying to explain what he thinks might be wrong—'

'No one tells me I'm hysterical and gets away with it,' Jasper gritted out. 'No one.'

36

Lily stood up. 'I'll deal with you later!' she said sternly to Jasper, then taking Charlie by the arm, she led him back through the ward and upstairs towards the entrance.

'I thought you said he was good-natured,' he said wryly.

'He is,' she replied. But at Charlie's raised eyebrow, she conceded, 'Usually. Maybe we should have waited. But with you leaving soon, I thought . . .' She shook her head. 'Do you really think he'll be able to see again?'

'I wish I could be certain. All I can go on are the few patients I've seen and the cases I've studied. This feels like a classic case of hysterical blindness.'

Lily huffed out a laugh. 'Please don't call it that.' She thought about what Jasper had said. 'I never knew that, though.'

'What?'

'That he saved Donald's life. He's never talked about the war before. He always said it was best forgotten.'

'Sometimes these things are best faced. Jasper's been through so many traumas in his life, maybe what happened a few months ago was the straw that broke the camel's back. He'll need some time to digest what I've said.'

'But how can we help him recover?'

'Mostly encourage and reassure him. His eyes seem to be working normally, but for some reason his brain isn't picking up the images. Look at the way he grabbed my lapel. He could see it, but he wasn't aware of it. He needs to be convinced that his eyes work.'

'So what can we do?'

'I'll speak to Dr Toland about bandaging his eyes for a couple of weeks. Retinal rest sometimes helps. But mostly it's a case of Jasper needing to believe it. It's his decision in some ways, though it's not one he can make consciously. I just wish I was able to stick around and keep an eye on his progress.'

They were standing at the entrance now and the all-clear was ringing out across the town. Charlie shrugged on his coat and

37

opened the door, shivering as a blast of icy air nearly blew his cap off.

'I'm sorry,' Lily said quietly, pulling her navy-blue cardigan more tightly around her.

Charlie paused and looked down at her, confused. 'What for?'

'Saying no.'

He shrugged slightly.

'Don't you care?' she asked, suddenly aggrieved that he seemed to be taking her rejection so calmly. 'Sometimes I wonder whether you were expecting me to turn you down. Perhaps you *wanted* me to.'

'Of course I care. I love you, Lily. I want you to be my wife, but you said no, and I can either walk away and never see you again, or I can spend as much time as I can with you and hope I can convince you to change your mind.'

Lily searched his face. Would he really wait for her? Or would his head be turned the minute he was away? 'Do you mean that?'

He pulled her into his arms. 'Yes, I mean that. You've broken my heart, but I still want to be with you. So I'll cling on till the very last minute, and maybe . . . maybe you'll relent.' He patted his pocket. 'The ring's still here, you know. So if you'd like to reconsider, I'll happily slip it on your finger right now.' He kissed her forehead.

Lily went still. It would be so easy to say yes and forget about all her other plans.

When she didn't respond he gave a short laugh. 'Seeing as you're not swooning with gratitude, I'm going to take that as a no. But you can't get rid of me that easily. Once I'm gone, you'll be buried under the number of letters I'll write. I'm not giving up on us, Lily. Not ever. And I want you to know that if we did marry, I'd never stop you doing anything you wanted to do.'

Lily leant her head against his shoulder. 'Maybe you wouldn't. But once the war is over and all the men come back, what then?'

Charlie tutted. 'You do know that Dr Toland is married, don't you? Yet here she is, working as a doctor.'

'She's an exception.'

'And the more exceptions there are, the more it'll become the rule.' He kissed her deeply. 'Is there any chance that you and I could spend some time alone before I leave?' he asked breathlessly.

Lily hesitated. Was it wrong, she wondered, to keep behaving as if she'd not rejected his proposal? She stared into his eyes, so full of love and desire for her that she couldn't say no. 'Yes,' she whispered. 'Tomorrow night? Usual place?'

Charlie grinned. 'I'll be counting the hours.'

'Don't do that,' she said earnestly. 'Every hour that passes brings us closer to the day you leave. And I don't want to think about that.'

He stroked her cheek. 'Nor me. Are you sure . . . ?'

She smiled, though her lips trembled. 'Stop it, I've made my decision.'

He sighed. 'See you tomorrow then.'

'Tomorrow,' she repeated, her heart sinking and her mind once again full of doubt as she watched him get into one of the military trucks parked on the drive. Because if she was honest, she wasn't sure why she was clinging so tightly to her independence when it seemed that being engaged to Charlie could only add to her happiness, whereas refusing him was making her miserable.

# Chapter 7

Edie's heart lifted as she walked towards Pearson's Garage. Situated in the shadow of the castle, opposite Constables Road, it was a small, neat white building, with a large forecourt that was currently crowded with a combination of military and private vehicles. Now that the sun had risen, Mr Pearson had opened the large corrugated iron doors to the garage, and she could see his figure bent over the bonnet of a Morris Minor.

'Morning,' she called cheerfully.

Mr Pearson's head popped up. He was a tall, thin man, with sparse grey hair. As always he had a pipe clamped between his lips, although it was unlit, and a flat cap on his head. His blue overalls were smeared with oil and she made a mental note to scrub them out for him tonight.

'Edie, love!' he exclaimed, his pipe bobbing up and down. 'By heck I've missed you.'

'Then you should have come and spent Christmas with us. The Perkins and Turners were there, as always.'

He shook his head. 'Never had much truck with all that since my Ruth was taken on Christmas Eve. I prefer to spend the day in remembrance.'

Edie gave him an awkward one-armed hug around the shoulders. It seemed they both had sad memories to deal with at this time of year.

'Don't suppose you could get me a cuppa, could you? It's perishin' out here.' Mr Pearson gently pushed her away from him.

She smiled, knowing this was his way of telling her not to make a fuss; he wasn't one to wear his heart on his sleeve. But then, he didn't need to, his kind nature was clear in everything he said and did.

As she hung up her jacket in the office, she sighed at the state of the place. It didn't take long for her boss to mess up her careful filing system, she reflected as she went to get changed into her overalls in the small bathroom.

'Looks like a bomb's gone off in the office,' she said mildly when she returned with two steaming mugs of tea.

Mr Pearson slammed down the bonnet of the car and took the pipe from between his teeth. 'Sorry, love. I was looking for the handbook for that Bedford over there.' He pointed with his pipe towards a large khaki truck with a canvas roof.

'Why did you need that? You've repaired tons of those.'

'And I repaired this one. But it's a new type. So they left the book with me just in case. Something about "not compromising the radio's battery pack".' He rolled his eyes. 'I mean, I were mendin' trucks on the battlefields of France before half the army were even born!' He sounded outraged and Edie grinned at him.

'Which is why they trust you with their stuff. So what's the problem?'

'Can't find the bugger. Swear I put it on the desk. But it's gawn.'

'I'll have a look for it, shall I?'

'Before you do, you couldn't slide under the Singer and help me with the drive shaft, could you? Me back's playing up so it's hell to get under there.' He took a slurp of tea.

Edie nodded. 'Course. Hey, did you notice a Bentley speeding along earlier. Bloody driver nearly ran someone over on Castle Street, and then gave Pete Benson a hard time when the bus broke down.'

'Bentley, you say? I noticed one coming down Dover Road earlier. I love me a Bentley. Fine cars.'

41

'Yeah well, the chauffeur had the cheek to suggest I couldn't mend the bus cos I'm a girl.'

Mr P spluttered out a laugh. 'And I bet you were happy to prove him wrong.'

'Too right. Anyway, if he comes round this way looking for his car to be mended, tell him to sling his hook.' She put her mug down and pulled a torch from her overall pocket. Putting it between her teeth, she lay down on the cold concrete floor and wiggled beneath the chassis of the Singer.

'I would, Edie, love. But business is business. And what I wouldn't give to get my hands on one of those.'

'Well, just so long as I'm allowed to get my hands on the driver, then I'll be happy,' she called from beneath the car, wondering again at the face she'd seen in the back. She hoped it had just been a trick of the light. Because the last thing she needed was for that woman to come back into her life.

Mr Pearson chuckled. 'Oh, it's good to have you back, love. You always cheer me up. Now, can you see where the shaft's snapped . . .'

Edie was just squinting up at the underside of the car when the siren went off. She stopped momentarily, waiting to see if it was another false alarm, but then she heard an explosion rumble up the hill towards them, followed by the boom of the anti-aircraft guns situated beneath the castle. Sighing, she wriggled out.

'I don't have time for this,' Mr Pearson complained as he helped Edie to stand. 'How am I meant to get everything done with the bloody siren going off two to three times a day.'

'We'll manage, don't worry. But by the sounds of it, we better get to the shelter.'

An explosion from somewhere close by made them both jump. 'That sounded like it were just down the hill,' Mr P said as they hurried through the office and out of the back door where he'd erected an Anderson shelter against the fence that bordered the field beyond. The corrugated roof had been covered with soil and planted with grass so that it blended in with the surroundings.

She pulled open the door of the shelter and ducked low, wrinkling her nose at the scent of damp mingled with the strong smell of stale cigarette smoke. 'Ugh. You taken up smoking fags? The place stinks!'

Sitting down on the bench, she grabbed a box of matches from a small table and lit the oil lamp.

Mr Pearson followed her in and shut the door. 'You know I never touch the things.' He sniffed as he sat down beside her. 'Anyway, I ain't been in since before Christmas. Didn't bother coming in this mornin'.

Against the opposite wall, Mr P had built narrow bunk beds and in the lamplight, Edie saw that the bottom bunk's blankets were rumpled.

'You been sleeping in here?' she asked.

'Course not. Looks like someone has though. That'd explain the smell.' He looked worried. 'But if they needed a place to stay, all they had to do was knock on the door. Everyone knows I'm happy to help.'

'Maybe it was someone who doesn't know you. Hey, do you think they could have taken the handbook?'

'Nah. Who'd want something like that?'

Edie nodded. It was true. She found the handbooks difficult to follow at the best of times, the instructions printed in tiny letters and incomprehensible to anyone who didn't work with engines.

'But I don't like it,' Mr Pearson continued. 'The thought that someone's been snooping around, staying in my shelter . . .' He shook his head. 'Doesn't feel right to me. Especially with all them army vehicles out front.'

'Well, looks like they've gone now.'

'Hmm.' Mr Pearson chewed on his pipe, his brow furrowed.

Anxious to stop him worrying, Edie changed the subject. 'You hear anything from Bill over Christmas?' Mr Pearson's nephew used to stay at the garage when he was growing up and Mr P had taught them both all he knew about engines. For the last few months he'd been in Scotland, training to be a pilot, and though they'd not always seen eye to eye, Edie had never forgotten how he'd saved her and Lily's lives when a Spitfire had crashed into the field behind the garage.

'Got a Christmas card,' he said as he drew a pouch of tobacco from his pocket and started to fill his pipe. 'Says he'll be taking his final exams before the new year. I wish he'd just stayed an erk, servicing the planes. Why does he have to be a pilot? You seen how many have been lost these past months? He's all the family I got now and if I lose him . . .' The worry was back on his face and Edie wished she'd not mentioned him.

'But then, it's almost as risky working at an airfield as it is flying. Greg told me they'd lost ground crew in bomb attacks at Hawkinge.'

'Ah, Greg. I'd forgotten about him. How is your Canadian pilot?'

Edie looked away, not really wanting to talk about him. Especially now she'd decided she didn't want to see him again. Not after what had happened on Christmas Eve. She swallowed back the feeling of anger – at herself and him. She should have been more forceful when she'd said no! What was wrong with her that she'd let him pester her into sleeping with him in the basement? 'All right, I suppose. He was at the Market Square Christmas party at the Oak.' Pushing thoughts of Greg out of her mind, she grinned at her boss. 'Hey, did you hear that Vera Lynn turned up? Bert couldn't take his eyes off her!'

'The whole of Dover's been talking of nothing else. How are your brothers? Bet your mum's happy to have all her boys stationed in Dover.'

'Rodney's the same as always – ever so serious. Too serious to notice that poor Marge Atkinson is madly in love with him.' She put her hand over her mouth. 'But don't say a word to Marge if you see her, will you? She likes to pretend we don't know. As for Jim, did you know that he's started walking out with Reenie Turner from the grocery shop!'

Mr Pearson's eyes widened. 'Is that a fact? I'd not have seen that comin' in a month of Sundays. I'd a thought she'd be a bit old for him. Sayin' that, she's a little love. Brings me fresh veg from the allotment whenever she's got some spare.'

'I know, you coulda knocked us all down with a feather. Still, I think she's helped him a lot. You know, after Colin went missing in Dunkirk.'

Mr Pearson sighed sadly. 'Whenever I think of your brother, I think of Colin Guthrie. Joined at the hip they were. This damn war! When will people learn that fightin' ain't the answer! That Churchill were always a warmonger.'

Edie was shocked. Her mother was a staunch supporter of the prime minister, and she'd just assumed everyone was. They sat in silence for a moment, until Mr Pearson lightened the mood. 'And what about young Bert? Has he got a girl?'

Relieved at the change in subject, Edie grinned. 'If he had his way, he'd be with Vera Lynn. And he tried, but she barely gave him the time of day.' She giggled. 'Which is just as well, cos his head's big enough.'

Mr Pearson chuckled. 'He takes after your dad, that one. In looks and the sheer brass neck of him when it comes to girls.'

Mention of her father sobered Edie for a moment. 'It's the anniversary of Dad's death today,' she said. 'I visited his grave first thing. By myself as usual.' She couldn't keep the bitterness from her voice.

'Ah, Edie, love. I'm sorry. An' don't blame the others. He weren't an easy man in his last years. Not his fault, mind, but still . . . it don't make it any less painful for people.'

Edie sighed. 'Yeah, maybe.' She paused, then asked, 'I don't suppose you remember what happened when he died, do you?'

'No, love. I heard about it same way most of us did – from someone else.' He thought about it for a moment. 'It were Brian Turner. Came in with his old delivery van. He were right upset. They'd not been close for years, but there was a time before the war they'd been

45

thick as thieves. But after . . . well, it were only Jasper he could stomach, though he even turned against him in the end. Terrible business.' He shook his head sadly.

'Poor Dad. No one seemed to like him by the time he died, even his own wife.'

'That's not fair, love. Your mum did right by your dad, despite everything. If that ain't love, then I don't know what is.'

'Maybe you're right.' Edie sat back and closed her eyes as another distant boom shook the shelter, making the oil lamp sway, throwing sinister shadows over the wall. 'But if that's love, then I want no part of it.'

# Chapter 8

Marge Atkinson shivered as she emerged from the tunnels beneath Dover Castle. Having just completed a twelve-hour shift, she needed some air. The plotting room had been blessedly quiet over Christmas, but today it seemed hostilities had resumed full force and one of the battleships that she'd been tracking had been blown up by a U-boat. It wasn't the first time this had happened, and though it hurt everyone, there were other ships out there that needed them, so their grief and shock had to wait.

But today it felt personal because on board had been a man she'd been at school with. Jackie Mason. They hadn't been particularly close – in fact, he'd spent most of their schooldays chasing after her friend Daisy. So much so that Marge had pushed him into the Dour one day in Pencester Gardens. The memory had made her smile briefly. But only briefly. Because in her mind's eye an image of Daisy had appeared, the sunlight shining on her bright blonde hair, as she'd collapsed onto the grass, tears of laughter streaming down her cheeks at the sight of Jackie floundering in the water, a clump of moss on his head. And the horrible truth had hit her again, as hard and as fast as the missiles that had sunk Jackie's ship. Daisy was gone.

The grief for her friend hadn't abated in the months since the Grand Hotel had collapsed, killing Daisy and several others. Sometimes it was bearable, a background hum of sorrow that she could cover with a joke and a smile. But then there were the times when it rose up like a monster, jaws gaping, threatening to swallow her down into a deep black hole. And after a long night's work, Marge simply didn't have the energy to fight it.

Taking out a cigarette she lit it with a trembling hand, then without thinking she started to walk up the steep path towards St Mary-in-Castro Church. She'd gone briefly on Christmas Day to listen to the carols, but found she couldn't stand the hypocrisy and had left, vowing never to return.

There was no God. Because if there was, Daisy wouldn't have died. Neither would the countless others she'd known – so many now, dead, lost or wounded. She needed to be alone right now, and she didn't know where else she could go. The castle was so full of people rushing around, and there was no peace to be had in the room she shared with nine other Wrens.

Puffing slightly, she neared the ruined Roman lighthouse, its battered stone walls outlined against the gloomy sky and leaning slightly, so that from this angle it looked as though the church was holding it up. *But it's still standing*, she thought. *Thousands of years of storms and wars, yet here it is.* She stepped through the open doorway, slipping a little on the frozen mud that had collected in the middle of the octagonal floor, and gazed up at the makeshift wooden ceiling.

Yes, this was exactly what she needed. A peaceful place that proved survival was possible, no matter how difficult the times.

Marge had been so intent on her thoughts that she hadn't noticed the faint droning of the aeroplanes. But then the ground shook as a stick of bombs landed close by, and she shrieked and dived into one of the recesses. Another boom followed and she heard the rat-a-tat-tat of machine-gun fire followed by a high-pitched screeching.

After all these months she knew immediately the noise came from a Stuka; a nasty mosquito-like plane that dived down, guns blazing, peppering anyone below them with bullets and dropping their bombs indiscriminately. Suddenly all the tension and grief rose up in her and she pulled herself to her feet and ran out of the tower.

'You bastards!' she shouted. 'Leave us alone, you buggers!' She waved her fists at the sky. 'I bloody *hate* you!'

As though the pilot heard her, the plane circled round and she watched as it dived towards her. 'Come on then! Do your—' Suddenly her feet were pulled out from under her and she crashed to the ground, moaning as another body fell on top of her and bullets flung up gouts of earth around them.

When it stopped, the man on top of her glanced up, and seeing the plane circling away, dodging the ack-ack shells that were trying to bring it down, he grabbed her under the arms and dragged her back to the tower, grunting with the effort.

'You stupid idiot,' he growled, dropping her onto the icy mud. 'Are you *trying* to get killed?'

Marge barely heard him as she beat her fists into the ground, screaming out her grief and fury. Finally, her voice gave out and she collapsed, breathless, onto the cold earth.

'Come on, up you get.' The voice was more gentle now and she once again felt herself being grasped under the arms. This time, though, he lifted her to her feet and pushed her through the door of the church, where he led her down the aisle and thrust her under a table covered with a heavily embroidered cloth, then crawled in after her.

'It's all right. You're safe now,' the man said, rubbing circles into her back.

Marge drew her knees to her chest and wrapped her arms around them, burying her face in the rough wool of her skirt, and sobbed.

Finally, her tears dried and she became aware that whoever had dragged her into the church was sitting beside her silently, a torch lighting the small space. She looked up and through tear-drenched eyes she noticed that the man was an army chaplain. He looked familiar, she thought. Then realised that he'd been at the church on Christmas Day and had called after her when she'd left, but she'd ignored him.

'Oh God, I'm sorry,' she said, wiping at her eyes.

The man raised his eyebrows and she looked away.

'I suppose I'm not meant to blaspheme in church, am I?'

'You can say what you like. God won't judge, and I'm sure he understands you needed to let off a bit of steam.'

She choked out a laugh. 'That's one way of putting it.'

'But perhaps next time you could do it somewhere a little safer? Or at least when a dirty great Stuka isn't bearing down on you.'

'I know. Not my finest hour.' She smoothed her bright red hair, looking around for her cap, but it had obviously come off when this mild-looking chaplain had pulled her to the ground. 'That was an impressive rugby tackle you did just then.' She attempted to smile.

'My sports master would have died of shock if he'd seen it. I was useless at rugby. Never could see the point of pushing my friends over just to get a ball.'

As they were sitting down, it was hard to tell how tall he was, but she could see he was slim. 'Yes, you don't seem built for rugby somehow.'

'Don't I know it; I'm more of a football man. Now, do you want to tell me about it, or would you rather sit quietly. I seem to remember last time I saw you you were running out of the church as if the hounds of hell were chasing you.'

'I suppose they were in a manner of speaking. And no, I don't want to talk about it.'

He nodded and settled back against the wall. 'I'm Philip, by the way. Padre Philip Sterling, and if you don't want to talk, I hope you don't mind if I have forty winks. Never seems to be time for sleep these days.'

'I don't mind at all, Philip. In fact, I think I might join you. And I'm Marge Atkinson.' She wriggled around so her back was against the wall and leant her head against the bricks. Despite the noise outside, it was strangely peaceful sitting under the table with a man she barely knew, someone who didn't demand she talk and just let her be, and soon her eyes closed and she drifted into sleep.

# Chapter 9

A sudden deathly silence descended on the occupants of the café basement as soon as Hester rushed in holding her coat together at her chest. The large space was crowded with people who had run in from Castle Street and Market Square and they were now either sitting on the cushions by the wall or gathered around the table, where Marianne was pouring tea while Gladys handed round the cups and saucers.

'You couldn't pour me some, could you, Marianne, love, I still ain't had a cup,' Hester said breathlessly.

Gladys picked up a cup and saucer and handed it to her and she grabbed it with a shaking hand, gulping half the contents in one. Then she stopped, suddenly aware of the silence.

'Everyone all right?' she said casually as she looked around for somewhere to sit. Spotting a gap on some cushions by the wall, she went over and squeezed in. The woman beside her wrinkled her nose at the smell of cigarettes and shuffled as far away as she could.

'Hester bloody Erskine!' It was Lou Carter, who'd been staring at the woman with a look of fierce concentration. 'I *knew* I recognised ya!'

Nellie scuttled in at that moment. ''Ere, Nellie, where'd you dig this one up from?' Lou screwed up her face. 'Hang on ... Didn't you end up runnin' a—'

'All right, Lou? Another cup of tea? Or a bun, perhaps?' Nellie said hastily, grabbing one from a plate on the table and handing it to her.

Lou grabbed it and stuffed half into her mouth, her narrowed gaze fixed on Nellie. 'Oh, I see how it is,' she said eventually, spraying crumbs over her ample chest. She looked over at Hester, who had gathered her coat more tightly about her. 'You remember good old Hester, dontcha?' she said to Mr Gallagher who ran the newsstand next to Perkins' Fish.

The man looked at Hester briefly then glanced away, his cheeks red. 'Can't say as I do,' he mumbled.

Hester raised an eyebrow at him, then turned to Lou. 'Haven't been back in years, Lou. Not many as'll remember me. Unless they have a memory like an elephant.' Her eyes swept over the woman. 'And not just a memory,' she muttered.

'Bloomin' cheek! You better hope I'm not the only one who knows what you been doin' or you won't last long round here.'

'That's enough, Lou!' Nellie slammed her hand on the table. 'Poor Hester was bombed out while she was performing her songs at the Junction pub in Folkestone, weren't you, love?'

Hester shook her head vigorously at her, but it was too late.

'Like hell you were!' Lou said, stuffing the rest of the bun into her mouth. 'I remember you getting' thrown out of the school choir cos your voice were like a pair of foxes goin' at it . . . Tell you what, how's about you give us a song to cheer us all up?' Lou gave her a malevolent grin and Hester glared back at her.

'Are you really a singer?' a little girl asked.

'One of the best, love,' Nellie said to the girl.

'Can you sing the song about the bunnies . . . It's my favourite.'

'Not sure I know that one,' Hester said evasively.

The girl's mother intervened. 'She means "Run Rabbit".'

'Yes please!' The little girl clapped her hands. 'I don't know all the words, I just knows "Run, rabbit, run, rabbit run, run, run",' she warbled.

Lou started to laugh. 'If that coat's anythin' to go by, the rabbit didn't get very far.'

The little girl stared at Hester's coat in horror. 'Is that bunny fur?' she squealed.

'Course it's not. It's fake. Just like the woman is. She can't sing a note,' Lou said.

'As it happens, Lou, I can't sing today cos I've got a bad throat.' Hester dug in her coat pocket and brought out a cigarette. 'Too many of these.' She looked around to see if anyone would offer her a light, but when they didn't she stuffed it back and folded her arms across her chest.

Marianne intervened. 'Like Mum said, Hester's been bombed out. So she's come back to the one place she knew she could find a help-ing hand. Because we look after our own here, don't we? Mostly,' she added as she looked around the room.

A few people looked slightly shamefaced, knowing she was referring to an incident in the summer when some people, led by Lou Carter, had turned against the Castles after Lily had been wrongly arrested on suspicion of helping a German pilot escape from the hospital.

'Quite right, Marianne. Didn't the Bible say, "If anyone has the world's goods and sees his brother in need, yet closes his heart against him, how does God's love abide in him?"' Gladys said. Privately she had her doubts about the woman, but it looked like Nellie had decided to help, so there wasn't much she could do about it.

'Give it a rest, Glad,' Nellie said. 'We don't need God dragged into this.'

A high, disapproving voice chimed in, 'The Bible also says, "He who loves wisdom makes his father glad, but a companion of prosti-tutes squanders his wealth."'

'I beg your pardon!' Hester stood up and went to tower over the small, thin woman with steel-grey hair pulled tight into a bun who was sitting primly on a wooden chair, knitting.

'I'm no fool,' she said. 'I know *exactly* what you are.'

'I'm a singer, like Nellie said. But I ain't no prostitute. Bleedin' cheek.'

'So much for Christian charity, eh, Adelaide Frost? Poor Hester needs a place to stay and we're all happy to make her welcome, aren't we?' Nellie looked around the crowded room.

53

'No skin off my nose,' Tom Burton said. 'I never had any argument with you, Hester. But I wouldn't have recognised you in a month of Sundays. Pretty little thing you were, back in the day.'

Hester choked on a mouthful of tea and glared at the man.

'But, Mum,' the little girl said, 'why can't she sing the song?'

'Because she's got a nasty cough is why,' Marianne said briskly. 'So, I'll start it off, shall I? Then you can join in.' Marianne was no singer, but Alfie had been teaching her to hold a tune, so she took a deep breath and started to sing.

The little girl joined in and soon everyone was singing stoically ignoring the sounds of the explosions that rumbled through the walls.

Nellie breathed a sigh of relief and exchanged a glance with Hester, whose cheeks were still burning with anger at Tom Burton's comment. This wasn't going to be easy, Nellie reflected. But then, when was her life ever easy? And compared to poor Hester, she had nothing to complain about.

# Chapter 10

'Marge?! Are you there?'

Marge jumped, staring around her, wondering where the hell she was. But then it came back to her: the Stuka, the padre, the church.

'Marge? Goddammit, where the hell are you?'

The light in the church went on, and she could hear footsteps on the stone slabs as they walked down the aisle.

'I think it's over,' she whispered to her companion.

The man sat quietly beside her listening for a moment. 'I think you're right.'

Together they crawled stiffly out from underneath the table, blinking in the light and watching as a tall, upright figure in an immaculate navy-blue uniform walked towards them.

'He doesn't look too happy with us, does he? Do you know him?' Philip whispered.

'It's Rodney,' Marge said, feeling absurdly pleased to see him. 'Lieutenant Rodney Castle.' Since the Christmas party she'd only seen him at a distance and she had the distinct impression that he was avoiding her. And it hurt – though, of course, she would never admit that to anyone – not even to Marianne or Reenie, her closest friends.

'Hello, Rodney,' she said, staggering to her feet. She felt strangely rested after crying and falling asleep on a stranger's shoulder. Almost back to her old self.

Rodney ran forward and grasped her by the shoulders. 'Where the hell have you been?' His fingers dug into her and she could tell he was resisting the urge to shake her.

'Uh, here,' she said drily.

Rodney's gaze shifted to the man beside her, who saluted smartly and said, 'Marge—' He stopped and gave Marge a questioning look.

'After saving my life, I think you've earned the right to call me Marge,' she said with a warm smile.

He blinked and cleared his throat before continuing. 'We, er, we had a bit of a close shave,' he said with understatement.

'Who are you?'

'This is—' Marge realised she had forgotten his name.

He stepped forward, hand outstretched. 'Padre Sterling,' he said. 'Philip. Marge and I had a rather unconventional meeting after I manhandled her into the church.' He grinned. 'But I think we're friends now.'

Now Marge could see the padre properly, she realised that he was young and rather handsome, with short brown hair and a sharp jawline.

'Oh yes, we're most definitely friends,' she said with a seductive smile at the padre, who blushed. It was bad of her, she knew. But after ignoring her for days, Rodney needed to know that she was most definitely *not* pining for him. 'Anyway, what are you doing here?'

'I was worried,' Rodney said shortly, looking between the two. 'The siren went off and I knew you'd just finished your shift so when you weren't in the tunnels I went looking for you.'

'In the middle of a raid?' she said, surprised. 'I didn't know you cared, Rodders.' Oh, it was good to feel her swagger coming back. Rodney always managed to bring out the best in her.

'Yes, in the middle of an air raid!' he ground out.

'But you could have been killed!'

'And so could you,' he retorted. 'How could you have been so stupid!'

'Hey, there's no harm done. At least I hope not? Any casualties?' Philip asked Rodney.

'Not that I know of. But maybe you better check,' he said pointedly.

The man could obviously take a hint and he turned to Marge with a slight, knowing smile. 'Any time you need to talk you know where I am. But maybe next time, don't make me wrestle you to the ground and drag you in here.' Then saluting Rodney, he hurried down the aisle.

'What did he mean by that?' Rodney asked after a short silence.

'He saved my life,' she replied. 'Rugby tackled me to the ground, then pulled me into the church kicking and screaming. Literally.' She laughed.

'He's quite the strong-jawed hero,' Rodney said sarcastically. 'I don't know why I was so worried; one way or another you always fall on your feet, don't you?'

He spun on his heel and marched out of the church, leaving Marge gaping after him in fury. She was sick and tired of him treating her like a sister one minute and something more the next. Was it really only a few days ago that they'd shared a passionate kiss under the mistletoe at the Christmas party? She'd thought then that maybe at long last, their friendship was deepening. Clearly she'd been wrong. She tossed her hair. Well, she knew better now, and next time Rodney Castle came running to her for a shoulder to cry on, as he tended to whenever his family were in trouble, she knew what advice she'd give him.

❧

It was a couple of hours before the all-clear sounded, and those in the basement at Castle's Café rose stiffly, anxious to get out to see if their homes were still standing. The sing-song had petered out after a while and people had sat in tense silence, lost in their own thoughts as they considered all they might have lost.

'All right if I go get changed now, Nell?' Hester asked, clutching the coat to her.

'Go on, love. And if you need a kip, go to the top of the house and it's the door on the left.'

'No, I said I'd pull my weight and I meant it. I've grafted all me life and I don't like to sit idle.'

Gladys watched her go with narrowed eyes. 'You sure about this, Nell?' she hissed once everyone had left the room.

'It's not like you to begrudge someone a bit of help. Just a moment ago you were quoting the Bible.'

'But don't you think it's strange, her turning up out of the blue like this? We ain't had a raid over Christmas, so how come she's suddenly homeless.'

'Oh, shut up, Glad. The woman's fallen on hard times, and the least we can do is help her out.'

'Well, I say there's something shifty about her, so you better keep your eye on her or we'll wake up to see the till broke open and the cash gone.' Gladys gave a disapproving sniff and followed the others out of the door.

Nellie was surprised. It wasn't like Gladys to take such an instant dislike to someone. Could she be right? she wondered.

Her doubts were dispelled, though, when Hester came downstairs half an hour later looking slightly comical in Nellie's too-short skirt and shabby grey jumper, but nevertheless her dyed blonde hair was neatly pinned back and she had a smile on her face. 'Right, what can I do for you?' she asked as she tied one of Nellie's colourful aprons around herself.

'Cheese and pickle for Mr Whittaker over there,' Nellie said, handing her a plate and nodding towards a man wearing a blue jacket and trousers, a grey grease-top hat sitting on the table beside him.

Hester obediently took the plate over and put it on the table. 'Here you go, love.'

The man squinted up at her. 'Hester Erskine?' he said.

'That's me name, don't wear it out.'

'You must remember me – Bunny Whittaker. We lived next door to each other as kids, up River.'

Hester's face broke into a smile. 'By heck, Bunny! I ain't seen you for years. How you doin'?' She indicated his uniform. 'You on the railway these days?'

'I am. You got time to join me?'

Hester glanced at Nellie, who nodded. 'Go on. A cup of tea and a chinwag'll do you good.'

Nellie's gaze shifted to the table behind them where a man wearing a dishevelled brown suit and a duffel coat had just sat down, placing a notebook in front of him. 'Anythin' to report, Ron Hames?' she called over. 'I hear the shops've run out of onions but Reenie's been growing 'em in the allotment, so's they'll have them in Turners' soon. As for the Perkins, they're only managin' to keep the fish shop open thanks to the fact that fish and chips ain't rationed. Mavis and Derek down the Oak are doin' a roarin' trade. And Donny had a cold over Christmas. That should keep your readers entertained, eh?'

Ron Hames was a reporter with the *Dover Express* and for the last few months, he'd taken to sitting in the café, listening in to conversations, ready to pounce on anything that might interest his readers. He claimed he got his best stories there but as far as Nellie could tell, all he got was tittle-tattle – mostly from Lou Carter's giant gob.

The man smiled at her. 'Don't worry about me, Mrs C, I've got plenty to keep the editor happy. Though if you could update me on Jasper's condition, that'd be much appreciated. My sources at the hospital have given me some interesting news and I was hoping you'd be able to confirm it.'

'Like I was telling everyone earlier, he's on the road to recovery,' Nellie said airily. Then she walked over to him, bending low to whisper, 'An' if I see one word printed about Jasper in the paper, then I'll make sure Terence Carter knows *exactly* who leaked the address of his operation to the police.' Nellie wasn't stupid, she knew it wouldn't be long before everyone knew about Jasper's blindness, but she'd hoped she could keep it quiet for a bit longer – or at least until Jasper was stronger.

The man gaped at her. 'How did you—'

Nellie tapped the side of her nose. 'You ain't the only one with sources, love. Do we understand each other?' In actual fact it had been a guess, but it looked like she'd been on the money.

'Terence Carter is a criminal black marketeer who should be in prison,' Ron hissed at her. 'But if your secret supplier were banged up, then where would you be?'

Nellie narrowed her eyes at him. 'Those supplies help feed people in this town. You think the tea stand in the caves is run on thin air? And how many times have you sheltered in my basement, enjoyin' a bun or a sarnie. Free of bloody charge!'

Ron Hames looked away guiltily.

'I thought as much. So, do we have an agreement?'

The man nodded. 'But in return, I want you to pass on anything you think might be of interest to me.'

Nellie snorted. 'You're not in a position to be making demands,' she said, then she straightened. 'Cup of tea, Mr Hames?'

He nodded, his expression surly.

Nellie walked back into the kitchen. 'Everything all right?' she asked Marianne, who was stirring the vegetable hotpot that she'd thankfully managed to prepare before the raid.

'Back on track, Mum. Though I won't have time to make the scones. Biscuits only for the stand tonight. But . . . like I said earlier, we're running short,' she whispered. 'On everything.'

Nellie sighed. 'I'll see what I can do.'

As she turned away she jumped as she realised that Hester was standing right behind her. 'What you doing?' Nellie gasped.

'Nothin',' Hester said innocently. 'But I couldn't help overhearing. An' you know I can help you with that.' She raised her eyebrows knowingly.

Nellie bristled. 'I don't know what you're talkin' about, love. Now, if you don't mind, take these plates out.'

Gladys poked her head around the door of the pantry. 'Or you could take over from me and do a bit of washin' up!' she said truculently.

Hester grinned. 'Love to, Glad. But it's mayhem out here. Soon as it quietens I'll be right in there with you.'

Gladys glowered as Hester hastened out of the kitchen.

'Never mind, Glad. Everyone knows you're the best washer-upper in Dover.' Nellie winked at her friend, before leaving hastily. When Gladys was in one of her moods, it was best to stay out of the way.

# Chapter 11

Lunch service was just winding down when the bell above the door tinkled and Nellie sighed inwardly as Roger Humphries walked in, his police helmet under his arm, and paced towards her, glaring disapprovingly at the parrot sitting on the counter.

'What can I do you for, Roger?' Nellie asked with a tight smile.

'Some disturbing events have come to light,' he said.

'Well, blow me down. Have you considered the possibility that it's cos there's a war on?' Nellie said, noting that Ron Hames was watching the proceedings with interest.

The policeman's lips twitched in annoyance. She was well aware that Roger still bore a powerful grudge against the family, not only because now Marianne was married to Alfie, he had no hope of winning her over, but also because Nellie had made him look a fool once too often. Sometimes, when she saw him loitering around, looking for anything to pull her up on, she wondered whether she should try to be nicer to him. But one look at his weasely face and his thin brown moustache convinced her that she just didn't have it in her.

He reached into his jacket pocket and slapped some screwed-up pieces of card onto the counter. Nellie looked at them, then back at the policeman, her eyebrows raised. 'My, that does look disturbing.'

He smoothed one of them out. 'Someone has been sticking these up around Dover.'

Nellie picked one of them up and holding it at arm's length, she read, '*Uncensored News. Hear the truth! NBBS 51m.*'

Ron Hames jumped up from his seat and rushed over. 'Let me see that!' He grabbed the card and stared at it. 'Where did you find these?' he asked.

'I have just scraped them off the wall of this very café on Church Street. And it's not the first we've found. *Someone*' – he gave Nellie a hard look – 'has been goin' around Dover, posting sedition and mayhem.'

Nellie started to laugh. 'What? A few silly stickers! I mean, you're not the sharpest knife in the drawer, but this is making me fear for His Majesty's Constabulary if you're the best they can do.'

'Mrs Castle!' Roger exclaimed. 'This is a *very* serious matter! These papers are advertising an *illegal* radio station!'

Nellie gaped at him. 'Wha—? What are you talking about? Do you know about this, Ron?' she asked.

He nodded gravely. 'I've heard of these sticky-backs before, but I've never seen them. And this is bad. Who could have been putting them up? I mean, Dover's a protected area – they don't let just anyone in.'

Nellie snorted. 'That's what they'd like you to believe. But they can hardly guard the whole town, can they? Anyway, those sentries are a waste of time. All they do is lounge about smoking and drinking tea. You can sneak past 'em no trouble, if you've a mind.'

'Speaking from experience, are you, Mrs Castle?' Roger said snidely. 'After one of your late-night *walks*.'

'I don't know what you're talking about. As for this' – she jabbed a finger at the sticky-back – 'it's nothing to do with me. Never heard of it in me life.'

She walked over to the kitchen door. 'Marianne, Glad, Hester, come look at this.'

Marianne and Gladys came out and stared curiously at the card. 'What?' Marianne asked.

'You seen this before?'

Both women shook their heads.

'Where's Hester?' Nellie asked.

'She just popped upstairs to the lav,' Gladys said.

'There you are then, Officer. No one knows what the hell this is all about, so why don't you take your enquiries elsewhere.'

'I intend to. But this café is a hotbed of gossip and chat, and you need to watch out. Walls have ears, Mrs Castle, and as this is your caff, it's *your* responsibility.' He slammed his helmet onto his head, then turned on his heel and marched out.

'*Café!*' Nellie shouted after him, but the policeman ignored her. As the door closed behind him, Nellie let out a huff. 'I've never heard such stuff and nonsense. As if that little piece of card could harm anyone.'

Ron Hames shook his head. 'Don't you believe it. If someone's sticking those things around the town, that means Dover could be harbouring dissenters. And in a place like this, they could do a lot of damage.'

'He's right, Mrs C,' a soldier said. 'My mate happened to mention that we was testing out a new type of gun in a letter, and he got pulled up and court-martialled. You can't be too careful.'

'What's that Roger Humphries want, Nell?' Lou Carter couldn't resist coming in to see what was happening.

'He were complaining that your whelks gave him the trots. Asked me to have a word.'

Lou grinned. 'Is that right? Nothin' to do with all them stickers that have been posted round town, then?'

'What do you know about those, Mrs Carter?' Ron asked.

'Nothing. Just I seen 'em around, and I seen 'em being ripped down. And if they're coming from here, Nellie, then I promise you, I won't keep quiet about it.'

Nellie let out a roar of laughter. 'The day you keep quiet is the day they measure you for your coffin.'

'That's where you're wrong, Nell. I keep my fair share of secrets. But not for something like this.' She left in a huff, ignoring the laughter that followed her out.

'By the way, Mum,' Marianne called through the hatch, 'I almost forgot, I can't come to the caves with you tonight.'

'Why not?' Nellie asked.

'I'm fire-watching with Reenie in the Market Hall.'

'Oh, for pity's sake! I can't manage on my own. Glad?'

'Sorry, Nell. I got a prayer meeting.'

Nellie rolled her eyes. 'Since when have you gone to prayer meetings?'

'Some days I need it more than others,' she said with a meaningful glare.

'What's so special about today?'

Gladys disappeared back into the kitchen, then returned and slammed the glass with the hyacinth stem onto the counter.

Nellie paled. 'I hadn't forgotten,' she whispered. 'Now get that away from me! I won't have grave flowers in the café.'

Gladys stared at her, unblinking. 'When you goin' to face it?' she hissed quietly in her ear.

Nellie turned away, ignoring the comment. 'Anyone else care to volunteer?' she asked loudly, cursing the slight tremble in her voice.

'I'll come, Nell.' It was Hester, who'd crept down the stairs without her noticing.

'Where you been?' Nellie asked, grateful that Hester's appearance had forced Gladys to move away from her. 'You disappeared quick when Roger came in.'

'Me and the police ain't been the best of friends over the years, so I thought it best to make myself scarce.'

'Now why don't that surprise me?' Gladys sneered.

'That's enough, Glad,' Nellie said sharply, her anxiety turning to anger at her friend. How dare she make her feel so guilty? 'Not all of us have had the luxury of living blameless lives full of prayer meetings.'

'And you've got to ask yourself why that is,' Gladys muttered.

'Let he who is without sin cast the first stone,' Hester retorted.

Gladys regarded her with surprise, then nodded. 'It's comforting to know you're not a complete heathen,' she said, picking up the glass and storming back into the kitchen.

'Why does she hate me?' Hester asked plaintively.

Nellie sighed. 'Ignore her, love. You've just put her nose out of joint. Although, I can't imagine why. She's always moaning about being overworked and her bloody bunions, you'd have thought she'd be kissing your feet with gratitude.'

'It's all right, Hester,' Marianne said comfortingly. It was clear that Gladys's bad mood today was not entirely to do with Hester's sudden appearance. And the way she'd brought out the flower from Dad's grave ... She didn't understand what had got into the woman. 'She'll come round. She just takes a while to warm up.'

'Hmm.' Hester didn't look convinced. 'Anyway, Nell, the caves. Count me in. I'll do whatever I can for the poor blighters, cos if it weren't for you, that's where I'd be right now.'

Nellie patted her arm. 'I don't care what Gladys thinks, you're a good sort, Hester. But you wouldn't mind taking over the washing-up, would you?' She walked through to the kitchen and took off her apron. 'Glad, love, take over out front. I'm off up the hospital. You got them mince pies ready, Marianne?'

Marianne nodded towards a tin with a picture of the king on the top that sat on the table. Nellie picked it up and put it in her voluminous black bag and shrugged into her purple coat. 'Right then, ladies, I'm off. Try not to fight while I'm gone.' She winked at them all, pretending not to notice that Gladys hadn't even looked at her.

# Chapter 12

Nellie walked swiftly up London Road, pulling her coat more tightly around her as the sharp wind blew directly in her face. Where once this road had been a thriving thoroughfare, now many of the buildings were either boarded up or partially demolished. It broke her heart to see her hometown being systematically destroyed like this and she was starting to realise that Dover might never be the same again. Despite this, though, the road was busy with traffic and the pavements crowded with people, many queueing outside the remaining shops.

Turning into the hospital driveway, she felt a quiver of anxiety. She wouldn't admit it to anyone else, but she couldn't help wondering whether Jasper had been pretending to be too tired to speak to her in the last few days. When he'd woken on Christmas Eve, they'd wept together, but since then, he'd kept his eyes closed every time she was there. Taking a deep breath, she strode forward. She just needed to be patient with him. No one could recover overnight from the sort of injuries he'd had. Problem was, patience had never been her strong point.

As usual, the hospital was a hive of activity and somewhere she could hear someone singing 'Stormy Weather' and she hummed along as she went downstairs to the ward. One way or another, everything would be fine, she reassured herself. Because she and Jasper shared a bond that went far beyond sharing a daughter. And hopefully he'd forgotten the cruel words she'd spoken to him.

She cringed at the memory of how she'd sent him away, telling him he didn't belong with their family. What had she been thinking?

He'd seen the family through thick and thin ever since he'd returned from the Front in 1918, leading a bewildered and shattered Donald into the café as gently as he would a lost child.

She'd thought everything would be fine then too. That after a bit of rest and recuperation she'd get her husband back – the one she had loved unreservedly for so many years. But nothing had ever been fine again.

'Stop it, Nellie,' she whispered to herself. Then, as she always did when thoughts of Donald's death threatened to engulf her, she straightened her shoulders, stuck her chin in the air and marched purposefully into the men's ward, walking to the end of the long room where the curtains were still drawn around Jasper's bed.

'Afternoon, Jasper,' she said cheerily. 'Hope you're more with it today. I've brought you some of Marianne's mince pies and your Christmas present.'

Jasper was lying propped up on pillows with his eyes closed, but at the sound of Nellie's voice, they flew open and he stared at her in confusion.

'Nellie?' He groped for her hand.

She leant down and kissed his cheek, noting the bristles were back on his chin. Briefly she inhaled his scent. Where once he'd smelt of his forge – open fires and molten metal – now he smelt of antiseptic. It would be a while before he was her Jasper again. If he ever was.

'Well, it's good to see you awake for once. How you feelin', love?'

'How d'you think I'm feelin'?' he said truculently. 'Lying here, day in, day out, unable to see.'

Nellie sighed. This brusqueness was new too. 'You want to open your Christmas present?' She took a package out of her bag and laid it on his lap.

He pushed it away. 'What's the point? Not as if I can see it.'

'Open it.'

He fumbled with the paper, finally managing to tear it off. It was a sleeveless pullover in bright cherry red that Nellie had spent the last

68

few months knitting for him, even though she wasn't sure he'd ever get to wear it.

Jasper brought it up to his nose and sniffed, smiling briefly. 'Smells like the café,' he murmured. 'Fried food and cigarettes.' He held it close up to his face and squinted. 'What is it? Is it red?'

'You can see that?' Nellie exclaimed, delighted. 'I unravelled my favourite jumper – the red one. No sleeves, mind, there weren't enough wool.'

He gave a short, bitter laugh. 'Least people'll see me coming when I wear this.'

Nellie sat down on the wooden chair beside the bed. 'Have you eaten today?' she asked.

He grimaced. 'Managed a bit of porridge. Disgusting, it was. If that's what they've been sticking down my throat all these months, it's no wonder I can feel me ribs.' He patted his middle. 'Don't think I've ever been so bony.'

'Well, you needed to lose a couple of pounds.'

'Pots and kettles, Nellie,' he retorted.

Nellie tutted. 'You're not the only one who's lost a bit of flesh. All the worry you've given me over the last months. Anyway' – she fished out the tin of mince pies – 'Marianne made you these.' She opened the tin and put one in his hand. He sniffed it, then put it on the bed beside him.

'I'm not hungry. An' the doc says I can't eat too much while my stomach adjusts, or something like that. As for this' – he threw the jumper on the floor – 'I don't want it. And now I think you should leave.'

Nellie was speechless. She'd not expected Jasper to be full of the joys when he finally woke properly, but of all the reactions, she hadn't anticipated this bitterness. Biting back an angry retort, she picked up the jumper and put it on the bed again.

'Cat got your tongue, Nell? That makes a change. Well, since I woke, I've been lying here with nothin' to do but think. And my

69

head's aching with all the rememberin' I've done. And I have a question for you.' He looked directly at her, almost as if he could see her. 'Why are you here?'

'Why wouldn't I be here? You're part of me life. Just like me and the kids are part of yours.'

Jasper shook his head. 'Just before I got injured, I told you, Nellie – I *told* you that we was finished. I meant it. All I want is Lily.'

'We'll never be finished,' Nellie said, trying to stop her voice from trembling. 'After all these years living in each other's pockets, how can we be? And when you get out of here, you're going to need help. You can't live at the forge on your own, so I've been thinking you'll have to come and stay with us. You can have my room and I'll—'

'Stop it!' Jasper interrupted her. 'Just stop and listen to me for once in your life, woman. You *told* me that I weren't part of your family. And you're right. I'm not. Lily's my family but you ain't. I don't want to end up like Donald.'

She gasped. 'What do you mean?'

'I mean that when we got back from war, he were bad, but he were still human. He could still come out of himself every now and then. But the longer he was home, the worse he got.'

'What are you implying?' she said sharply.

'I'm not implying anything. But I don't want your *tender* care, and I don't want to sit in your sitting room day in and day out like he did. So I'll be going back to the forge and I'll manage just fine.'

Nellie sat back, stunned. His words felt like a dagger, and the memories they evoked could still leave her on the verge of tears. Did he really believe that she was responsible for Donald's decline after he returned from the Front? *And weren't you?* a small voice murmured in her ear. She shook her head, refusing to let those thoughts in. Today of all days, though, it was harder than usual.

But she'd never been a woman to beg and she wasn't about to start now so she allowed the anger to wash through her, pushing away the unwelcome memories and hurt. She'd been to see him almost every

70

day over the last months, sitting by his bed, willing him to wake up. And when he'd finally opened his eyes, they'd embraced and cried in each other's arms. And this is how he thanked her! She stood up, the chair scraping against the linoleum floor. 'If that's what you want, Jasper. But don't come running to me the minute you want a good meal and a friendly chat.'

He squinted at her. 'Not like I'll be able to, is it?' He patted the bed, his fingers finding the jumper. He held it out. 'And take this with you,' he said.

'Keep it. It's no use to me now. And neither are you.'

She stomped away, holding back her angry tears and almost immediately regretting her words. But dammit, she'd always counted on him. He'd helped her for years, and now he wouldn't allow her to help him.

She was halfway down the drive when she stopped, her breath coming in short bursts, her last words running through her mind. The man had just woken from a coma unable to see, so of course he wasn't going to suddenly transform into the Jasper she knew and loved. He must be so scared, and he needed to take his anger and fear out on someone. And who better than her, one of his oldest friends?

And as usual she'd thought only of herself, of her own hurt. She smiled grimly. Maybe Jasper had finally softened her; it had taken years of trying, and if she had to pinpoint the moment that his war of attrition had finally been won, it was when he had given her his helmet, just before the wall of the Grand Hotel had come crashing down on him and poor Daisy. Putting her first, as he always had. Well, now it was her turn to put him first. To show him she had changed. To show him that she cared.

Gathering her courage, she turned round and walked back into the hospital.

When she crept up to his bed, Jasper was lying with his face turned to the wall, and she was dismayed to see tears trickling down his cheeks.

'I'm so sorry, Jasper,' she whispered. 'I didn't mean it.' She pulled the curtains round the bed.

His head whipped round and he held out his hand. She took it.

'I'm sorry too,' he said gruffly, wiping his bristly cheeks with his other hand. His hair was standing out in a stark-white bush around his head, and she smoothed it back before sitting down again.

They sat in silence for some moments. Finally, he said, 'If I could see the red of the jumper, how comes I can't see your colours, Nell?'

'I don't know, love. Cos I'm wearing the brightest I could find today, just for you. First time I've worn 'em since you got hurt and someone told me to dress me age.'

He snorted. 'Bein' old's never stopped you before.'

'I didn't say I was old!' she said indignantly, feeling a little swell of pleasure when he smiled. 'But it were something Lily said—' She cut off, not wanting to talk about those dark days after he'd been hurt. And she certainly didn't want to tell him that she wasn't sure if Lily had properly forgiven her for the lies yet.

'She were here this morning with that Dr Charlie. Bloody man told me that it were all in me head. That I'm hysterical!' His voice rose in anger.

'He never did!' Nellie gasped.

Jasper nodded. 'Reckons I'm like the lads I knew back in the first war who faked their blindness so's they could go home. It's just as well Lily turned him down, else I'd have been chasin' him off with me shotgun!'

'Don't be ridiculous. Charlie Alexander is a good man,' she said. 'And I'll be more than happy to welcome him into the family. You must have misunderstood.'

Jasper folded his arms across his chest and scowled, but didn't respond.

Just then the curtain was swept aside. 'I heard that, Dad! You're being a stubborn old fool. If Charlie says you might get your sight back, then you should be pleased.' Lily shot a frustrated glance at her mother. 'Sorry, Mum, but you're gonna have to go. The doctors want to bandage his eyes now. Then when the bandages come off, you'll be able to see again.'

Jasper's lips pursed, but he still didn't say anything.

Lily sighed and gestured to Nellie. 'Come on, Mum, I'll walk out with you.'

Nellie kissed Jasper on the cheek and followed her daughter back out into the corridor.

'You shouldn't give him false hope,' Nellie admonished. 'It's not fair.'

'It's not fair that he's blind, either,' Lily retorted. 'And anyway, isn't some hope better than none?'

Nellie patted her arm. 'Not always. Sometimes a bit of hope just makes the final disappointment even worse.' She smiled sadly at her daughter, then walked away.

Lily felt a flicker of worry as she watched her mother climb wearily up the stairs. Maybe she was right – she shouldn't have given him false hope. But what else did she have to offer at the moment?

# Chapter 13

Much later that night, Marianne hurried across the square, hefting a large wicker basket containing two blankets, a flask of tea and a package of meat paste sandwiches. She was exhausted after a long day's work in the café and wasn't sure how she'd manage to stay awake tonight, but at least she had Reenie to talk to – that is if her friend was still talking to her. The last time they'd spoken properly they'd argued about Reenie's relationship with Jimmy.

Marianne could wring her brother's neck for getting involved with one of her best friends. She loved them both and didn't want to see either of them get hurt, but she knew very well that Jim didn't love Reenie in the way she deserved and that knowledge had meant that she'd kept her distance from her friend.

She looked down towards the seafront where the searchlights from Granville Gardens criss-crossed the sky, reflecting on the water. At the moment, all was quiet, although the sky was clear and the gibbous moon bright – perfect bombing conditions, she thought grimly, hoping her services wouldn't be needed tonight. The wind gusted around her and she shivered, pulling her coat more tightly around her as she hurried on.

Pushing open the door of the Market Hall, she felt a pang of sorrow as she recalled the days when the place had been full of stalls and people. Now, it was deserted, the concrete floor strewn with rubbish and debris. Upstairs was no better. Once upon a time, the first floor had housed the town's museum, and the walls had been lined with glass display cabinets full of stuffed animals and birds, and ancient artefacts. But now, like the ground floor, the place was eerie and deserted. She swung her torch beam around, letting out a yelp of shock when the light glinted off the glass eyes of a stuffed bird. 'Hello?' she called uncertainly, taking a few tentative steps into the room, broken glass crunching beneath her shoes. Her foot nudged against something soft, and she shuddered as she realised it was the body of a fox, limbs sticking out stiffly, its tail lying next to it on the dirty parquet floor.

'Hello?' she called again, skirting round the creature. 'Reenie?' But there was no answer, so, muttering under her breath, she gathered the buckets of sand and water, and the stirrup pump together and crouched down beside the open door.

Finally, she heard someone coming in. 'Sorry I'm late!' Reenie called up the stairs. 'But I've brought some of Aunt Ethel's special fruitcake, so I hope that makes up for it. Not as good as yours, but it'll do.'

She dashed in, a basket over her arm. 'God, it's spooky in here,' she said. 'Let's just hope these creatures are really dead.'

Marianne giggled. 'Don't say that. Anyway, I've got everything together and it looks like we've got ten buckets of water.'

'Oh good. So if a hundred fire bombs fall on the Market Hall, we'll be fine,' Reenie responded sarcastically.

Marianne didn't want to think about that, instead she grabbed the blanket Reenie had brought and laid it out on the floor by the wall. 'Get your cake out and tell me what's been happening over at the shop. I feel like we haven't spoken properly for months.'

'Whose fault is that?' Reenie said bitterly.

Marianne sighed. 'I'm sorry. I've been distracted.'

Reenie snorted. 'Is that what you call it? Or is it that you just don't like to see me happy with Jim?'

'I want you to be happy more than anything. How's it going with him?' It was time, she decided, to accept the situation and try not to

75

worry. Jim was a good man and although he was in the wrong here, she knew he genuinely cared for her friend and hopefully that would be enough. But she doubted it. Jimmy's heart belonged to his best friend Colin, who hadn't made it back from Dunkirk. Only she and Alfie understood what this loss meant to Jimmy, who had confessed to her that he thought it was God's punishment on them both for their 'unnatural' behaviour.

And so he had decided to hide his true nature, to try to be like everyone else. But Marianne knew that pretending to be someone he wasn't could only ever bring him unhappiness. And not just him – Reenie too.

'Yeah, fine,' Reenie said. 'I mean, I think he's amazing. And I know you don't approve, but can't you just be happy for me? Please?'

'Oh, Reens, of course I'm happy for you! You deserve the best.'

'And I think I've finally got him,' she said. 'Who'd have thunk it, eh? Me with a man as handsome as Jim! And not only handsome, but kind, sweet and considerate.' She gave a short laugh. 'It's put Wilf's nose right out of joint . . . He's been on at me about the age difference and how it couldn't work out, but we're showing him.'

'What's Wilf got to do with anything?' Marianne asked curiously.

Wilf Perkins lived above Perkins' Fish Shop with his parents and his son Freddie – Donny's very best friend. When they'd been at school, Reenie and Wilf had always been close, until suddenly one day Wilf had upped and married Reenie's older sister June. Though she'd never said a word about it to Marianne, it had been clear to all that Reenie had been devastated. June had died of cancer not long after Freddie was born, but Reenie and Wilf's friendship had never rekindled.

'He's got nothing to do with anything!' Reenie said airily. 'He barely speaks to me for years, then soon as Jim comes on the scene, suddenly he thinks he has a right to give his opinion.' She plumped down beside Marianne and took one of the sandwiches, stuffing it into her mouth.

76

'Hmm,' Marianne said.

'What do you mean by that?' Reenie asked, her mouth full.

'Nothing.' Marianne hesitated a moment before adding, 'But don't you think it's curious that Wilf cares so much about who you're seeing?'

Reenie huffed out a laugh. 'He don't care; he just likes to sound off. But enough about him, I'm glad we got this chance to chat. I miss you, Marianne. With Daisy gone and Marge busy up at the castle, I feel so lonely. I thought Jim was enough, but he's not.'

Marianne put her head on her friend's shoulder, guilt washing over her. Reenie had been a tower of strength to her when Donny had been born and so many people had turned away from her, and now she was letting her friend down. But she was stuck between a rock and a hard place. If Reenie ever found out about Jimmy and Colin's relationship, she'd blame Marianne for not warning her to stay away, but Marianne couldn't say anything without betraying her brother. They were two of the people she loved most in the world, and if the truth ever came out, she could end up losing both of them.

'We'll always be friends,' she said softly. 'And I promise I will do my best to never upset you again.' She kissed Reenie's cheek.

'And I promise the same to you. Now come on, it's bloody freezing in here, so pass the blanket and let's get some tea down us.'

# Chapter 14

'Dinner's ready!' Edie called as she sat down at the small table in Mr Pearson's sitting room, surveying the plate of food in front of her with dissatisfaction. It was the one thing she missed about living at home – her sister's food. Today she'd cobbled together a meal of Spam, fried with potatoes and cabbage in the smallest sliver of margarine. With onions impossible to come by, she'd managed to get hold of a leek, which she'd sliced thinly and added to the mixture to try to give it a bit of flavour. In Marianne's hands, this meal would have looked and tasted as though it came from the Ritz, but Edie's skills were limited when it came to the kitchen. Still, her sister had given her a loaf of freshly baked bread that morning, so at least that would make up for it.

Mr Pearson looked distracted as he sat down. 'What's up?' Edie asked. 'I thought we did a good job of clearing some of the backlog today.'

He shook his head. 'It's not that, love. I'm just thinking about the shelter and who might have been in it. You know what them lot up at the castle are like about security. If they heard someone's been sniffing around and the handbook's gone missing, they'd take their business away like that.' He clicked his fingers.

'Course they won't. They trust you. Everyone trusts you, and with good reason. I'd trust you with me life.'

Mr Pearson smiled at her. 'As I would you, love. Who'd have thought all them years ago when you turned up at the garage like a little waif, that you'd become like a daughter to me. Me and Ruth

78

weren't blessed with kids, but we got the next best thing in you and Bill. I always hoped . . .' He trailed away, looking sheepish.

'Hoped what?' asked Edie, moved by his speech.

'Well . . . Bill's the only family I got left, and when I'm gone, this garage will be his. I couldn't think of anything better than if the two of you . . .'

Edie laughed. She and Bill had spent much of their childhood squabbling, and now they were older she wasn't sure he even liked her, so the thought of them getting together was as likely as Hitler walking in and sharing their Spam hash. 'I'm not sure Bill would be too thrilled by that idea.'

'Oh, I dunno. The boy plays his cards close to his chest, but I saw the way he looked at you. Why d'you think he was so upset when he found out that you was havin' an affair with that Henry Fanshawe?'

Edie squirmed with mortification at the reminder of the man who'd not only lied to her about being married, but had also, years before, seduced Marianne, leaving her pregnant with Donny. She was a terrible judge of men, she thought. Because she was beginning to realise that Greg was no better after the way he'd coerced her into bed with him – not once, but twice. Would she never learn? 'How did he look at me?' she said, her cheeks hot.

'Like his heart was waking up.' Mr Pearson looked at her steadily. 'I know you and he don't always see eye to eye, but he's a good lad. He didn't have the easiest time of it growing up, an' it's made him . . . cautious, I suppose. His dad ran off when my sister were sick and left poor Bill to cope, then he sweeps back in and drags him away from his home before poor Iris were cold in her grave.' He sighed heavily. 'But despite the fact Walter Penfold led her a merry dance, she loved the bones of that man. Never understood what she saw in him.'

Edie was fascinated. She knew little about Bill's parents, other than that his mother had died when he was young, and Mr Pearson rarely talked about personal stuff. 'And do you still hear from Bill's dad?' she asked.

'Well, you see, that's why he's come to mind. I ain't heard from him for years, then suddenly I get a letter.'

'And?

Mr Pearson shook his head, though he looked troubled.

'What did it say?'

'Nothing of interest.' He took a mouthful of food and hummed appreciatively.

Edie laughed. 'You don't need to pretend. It's awful.'

Mr Pearson grinned. 'Well, your talents lie elsewhere. An' my cookin's not much better.'

'Never mind, between us, we'll get by.' She cut a couple more slices of bread. 'So long as Marianne gives us bread, we won't starve.'

They ate the rest of the meal in silence, and when Edie began to stack the plates, Mr Pearson waved her away. 'I'll do it, love. You get off to bed. You never know, we might get a full night's sleep tonight if we're lucky.'

Edie was relieved to be let off. After so many nights disturbed by nightmares, she really was exhausted. She could cope with the raids as long as the nightmares stayed away.

After a quick wash, Edie fell asleep almost as soon as her head hit the pillow, so she had no idea what time it was when she was woken by the sound of footsteps moving past her door. She lay with her eyes closed, wondering where Mr P was going because the bathroom was in the other direction. She was considering whether to get up and check he was all right, when the tinkling of glass made her eyes fly open.

Scrambling out of bed, she walked across to the window and peeped round the blackout curtain. Outside, a flickering light illuminated the Anderson shelter and for a moment she stood frozen in shock. Then in the distance she heard the sound of a car starting up and driving away and it jolted her into action.

Throwing on her dressing gown, she stumbled into the hall, just as a loud boom made the building shake and the air raid siren began to wail.

'Mr P!' she called. 'I think there's a—!' Something caught at the back of her throat and she coughed. Her heart started to thump as she suddenly understood what the flickering was: his bedroom was on fire. She was about to throw open his door, when she paused; opening the door too quickly could fan the flames.

Cautiously, she pushed the door open an inch and peeped in, her eyes widening at the sight of flames licking up the blackout curtains, fanned by the draught coming in through the broken window.

'Mr P!' she shouted from the doorway. But the man didn't move.

Running to the bed, she saw that the rug on the floor beneath the window was on fire and the flames were spreading up the curtains.

Holding her breath to avoid inhaling the smoke, she reached over the bed and rolled Mr Pearson to the floor, then, with her hands under his arms, she pulled him out of the room, slamming the door shut behind them. Grunting with effort, she dragged him along the corridor. Mr Pearson was thin, but he was also tall and she was breathing heavily by the time she managed to get him to the front door of the flat, where she put him down gently and grabbed a scarf from a hook, wrapping it around her face. It was only then she realised that her face was wet with tears – whether because of the smoke or her fears for the man who meant so much to her, she wasn't sure.

Opening the door, she wailed in despair as she realised that somehow she had to get him down the stairs and out of the building before the whole place went up.

Kneeling down, she shook his shoulders again. 'Wake up. Please, wake up!' Her breath was coming in sobs now.

But the man's eyes remained closed. She put her hand on his chest, relieved to feel his heart beating strongly.

'Come on, Mr P! You have to be all right! I need your help to get you down the stairs.'

But still there was no response and she realised she had no option but to try to carry him down by herself. With an effort, she turned him and started to back carefully down towards the office. It was a slow process, and she winced each time his bare feet thumped on the wooden stairs, but at least his head was protected.

Once at the bottom, she dragged him outside where she lay him gently on the cold concrete, before collapsing, panting, on his chest, her arms clasped around him as she sobbed into his neck. 'Please be all right,' she whispered. 'Please. I can't bear to lose you. I'll do anything! Even marry Bill, if that will help?' She let out a strangled laugh, but when there was no movement, she sat up and looked around her, the sound of explosions nearby and the awful droning of the planes overhead ringing in her ears.

And rising above her, the castle stood out against a sky glowing red with fire.

'Bloody hell!' she whispered, suddenly aware that the fire at the garage was just one of many and she needed to get herself together, because help might be a very long time coming.

Wiping her nose on her sleeve, she took a deep breath of cold air, then, wrapping the scarf more tightly round her face, ran back into the garage.

# Chapter 15

'I need to get out of here,' Hester exclaimed as she packed up the basket with the empty tins in which she and Nellie had brought Marianne's biscuits and sandwiches. 'It's bloody freezing and it smells.'

'Won't be a tick. While I finish up here, go give these to poor old Mr Evans.' Nellie nodded over to one of the tunnels running off the large cavernous space where the tea stand had been set up, and handed Hester a paper-wrapped package of sandwiches and a Thermos of tea. 'Last bunk on the left-hand side, bottom bed, with grey curtains round it.'

Mr Evans was the longest-standing resident of Barwick Caves. He'd suffered badly with shell shock after the last war, and as soon as the shelling had started he'd moved in, too scared to go back outside. But everyone in town knew he was there, which meant he was probably better fed than most. Sometimes Nellie wondered if he was playing them all. She grinned to herself. Well, if he was, good luck to him. That sort of cleverness deserved reward.

Hester walked down the wide tunnel, the walls lined with triple-decker bunks, between which the chalk gleamed a dirty white under the dim electric bulbs that had been strung along the ceiling.

Stopping beside the bed Nellie had described, she crouched down. 'Mr Evans?' she said. 'Are you there?'

An old man wearing a flat cap poked his head out. His eyes were rheumy and his lips were sunken. 'Hello there, love,' he lisped. 'Just a mo.' His head popped back and when he reappeared, she could see he'd put his teeth in.

'These are for you.' She held up the Thermos and the sandwiches. 'From Nellie Castle.'

The man smiled. 'Thanks, love.' He squinted at her. 'Who are you?'

'Hester Erskine. I grew up here. Didn't you used to run the ice-cream stand on the seafront way back when before the last war?'

The man cackled. 'That I did. It were me dad's business, and his dad's before him. All gone now. Still, not much call for ice cream in wartime, so it don't matter no more.'

Hester took hold of his wrist and placed the Thermos in his hand. 'Are you warm enough?' she asked. 'Your hands are like ice.'

He cocked his head and cupped his hand over his ear. 'Are you warm enough?' she repeated, much louder this time.

'All right, love, no need to shout, I ain't an idiot,' he grumbled. 'An' I got everythin' I need, thank yer. That Mrs Palmer from the WVS is an angel an' Mavis from the Oak comes in regular with a bottle of stout for me. Gawd bless you all.'

Hester tutted. 'It ain't right, you livin' here in the cold and damp. You should be housed somewhere proper.'

'I'm all right. Truth is, this is better than the room I used to live in. An' there's always someone to chat to.'

'Even so, after all you suffered for this country in the last war, least they could do is give you somewhere to live. Funny how they find the money for war but not to look after those in need.'

Mr Evans gave her a quizzical look. 'You one o' them commies?' he asked.

Hester laughed and stood up. 'No fear. I just tell it how I see it. An' it's an injustice and a scandal.'

Mr Evans shrugged and looked behind her. 'All right, Mrs C. Thanks for the grub.' He tapped the parcel of sandwiches.

'Pleasure, love. Just be sure to let us know if you need anything else. Hester,' she said in a sterner voice. 'Time to go.' Nellie stomped towards the entrance.

Hester smiled at Mr Evans and struggled to her feet.

'Why's that lady cross?' a small girl huddled under a pile of blankets on the bunk opposite asked.

'Oh, ignore her. She's always angry. Anyway, look at you, snug as a bug in a rug,' Hester replied.

The girl giggled, then said, 'Our house got knocked down.'

'That's a shame, lovey.' Hester went and knelt beside her. 'Is this your new house?'

'No, silly. This is a cave.' She started to cough, a rattling chesty cough that Hester didn't like the sound of.

'Do you like it here?' she asked.

The girl nodded. 'It's all right. An' tomorrow Miss Andrews is bringin' her violin to play some songs.'

'Well, aren't you the lucky one.' Hester patted the little girl's hand.

In an alcove next to the bunk, a woman was warming milk on a small oil stove. Hester watched as the smoke from the stove drifted towards the ceiling and with nowhere to go, dispersed around the small space. She could feel fumes tickling the back of her throat; no wonder the poor child had a cough. 'Are you sure that's safe?' she asked.

The woman scowled at her. 'You got a better idea? My Martha likes a cup of warm milk before she goes to sleep, so that's what I'll give her.'

Hester shrugged. 'Sorry, didn't mean anything by it, just her cough sounds nasty.'

The woman put her hands on her hips. 'Of course it's bloody nasty! She's livin' in a bloomin' cave like a bat, barely leaves the place. But the house has gone an' there's no one to take us in, so here we'll stay till it's safe to come out.' The woman sniffed and wiped her sleeve over her eyes.

'You should talk to Nellie Castle. She can help you out with food and that.'

'She already does, bless her. She's a good woman. An' sorry for shouting, but I'm at my wits' end.'

'I bet you are. Like I was sayin' to Mr Evans here, don't you think it's strange that the government has millions to splash about when it comes to war, but when it comes to ordinary folk who've lost the lot, there's not enough to give you a hand.'

'They ain't got a choice, though, have they? Anyway, I could go get us evacuated, if I chose – what with the little 'un and all. But I don't wanna live with strangers in a strange place; this is my home. I can't abandon it. Once we get shot of them Nazis, that'll be the time for the bigwigs to sort the rest of us out.'

Hester raised an eyebrow. 'Like they've always done, you mean?'

The woman frowned at her. 'That's different,' she said weakly.

'I'll tell you what I think, love. The money's always been there. It just don't suit 'em to have the people comfortable. Far better that we're all scrabblin' around tryin' to survive – it means we got no time to pay attention to what's really goin' on.'

'Hester!' It was Nellie again. 'We need to leave now. And don't worry, Mrs Williams, I'll get some linctus for young Martha here and bring it next time I'm in.'

'Thanks, Mrs C,' the woman replied, and with a last uncertain glance at Hester, she lifted the pot of milk from the stove and poured it into a mug.

Nellie grabbed Hester's fur-clad arm. 'What sort of talk was that?' she whispered as they walked to the entrance.

'Just the truth.'

'Where d'you get that poppycock, anyway?'

Hester shrugged. 'I got eyes to see, just like everyone else. But you're all too blinkered by that bastard Churchill and the rest of 'em to question anythin'.'

Nellie was shocked at Hester's vehemence. 'Listen, I understand you've had it rough, but I don't want to hear any more of this talk,' she said severely. 'We're all under the cosh, and we've got to pull together. You got good reason to be upset, what with poor Tommy and losin' your house, but I don't want no trouble at the café.'

Hester snorted. 'Sounds like you've swallowed the schtick hook, line and sinker. Time you opened your eyes.'

'All I'm saying is if that Ron Hames heard you talking like that, he'd be naming and shaming you in the *Dover Express*, and seeing as you live with me, it'd be my business that took the flak.'

They'd reached the entrance now and a stiff sea breeze blew straight into their faces, making Nellie shiver. She stared out into the blackness, looking out for the telltale flash of red from across the Channel that would warn of a shell being fired, but aside from the stars and moon and the inevitable searchlights all was dark.

'Anyway, enough of that. How about we drop in on the Market Hall on the way back?' she said.

'Do you mind if I get back?' Hester yawned. 'It's been a helluva day. Not sure I've had more than a couple hours' kip.'

Nellie patted her arm. 'Course not, love. You go and stick the kettle on. I'll only be a mo, then maybe a nightcap before bed, eh? We've earned it, and I bet you could use it.'

'Thanks, Nell. You've been a true friend. An' I swear I'll not let you down.' Hester reached for Nellie's hand and gave it a squeeze.

'Oh, pisht,' Nellie said. 'You've already proved a godsend today. I reckon I'll be thanking *you* before too long.'

As they turned on to King Street, they became aware of the drone of aircraft. Suddenly, the ack-acks boomed and the siren started to wail.

'Looks like we'll have to get straight home now,' Nellie groaned. But as they hurried up the road, a loud bang made the air shiver and the women gasped as the reverberation knocked the breath from their lungs. All of a sudden, the night sky brightened and across the market square, she saw flames leap up on Cannon Street.

'Bloody firebombs!' Hester cried.

Nellie's shocked gaze turned to the Market Hall, and through the first-floor window, she could see a flickering yellow light. Without thinking, she dropped her basket and ran towards it.

# Chapter 16

'Get that, Reenie!' Marianne shouted urgently as she poured sand on the flames that had sprung up on one of the wooden display cases. Sparks had burnt through the tarpaulin on the roof and around the large hall, small fires had broken out.

Reenie had long given up on the pump, but luckily they had more than enough water to deal with the flames. As soon as they were out, the girls glanced out of the window.

'Hell's bells,' Reenie muttered at the sight of buildings illuminated by fire. 'We better get down there.' She picked up the pump and a bucket of water and staggered towards the stairs, leaving Marianne to heft a couple of buckets of sand.

They were so intent on keeping their balance as they made their way down the stairs that they didn't notice Nellie coming up until she bumped into Reenie, who nearly lost her balance as she dropped the pump, water sloshing out of the bucket and up her legs.

'Watch where you're going!' she shouted.

'What are you doing here, Mum?' Marianne puffed.

'I saw flames . . .'

Before she could say more, Hester pushed past her and grabbed the bucket of water from Reenie, then turned and headed back down the stairs. Reenie followed close behind, scooping up the pump as she went.

Out on the street, a fire engine rushed past, heading towards Cannon Street where it seemed the worst of the fires had broken out and they watched as the firemen pointed their hoses at the flames leaping from the roof of the hat shop.

'Over there!' Reenie exclaimed, heaving the pump to the middle of the square where some rubbish had started to burn.

With Hester's help, she set up the pump in the bucket of water, but before she'd managed to use it, Marianne emptied some sand over the small fire.

'Hey!' Reenie called. 'That was *my* fire.'

'If we'd waited for you to get that thing set up, the whole square would have gone up,' Marianne called back, laughing.

'What's the point of those things anyway?' Nellie said.

Hester kicked the bucket, sending the water splashing out over the cobbles. 'Stupid ruddy thing. That's what I been saying. They got money to spend on useless pieces of equipment that they figure will make them at least *look* as if they care. But it's all a bunch of tosh, and as always, it's the workers who suffer!'

The three women stared at Hester in bewilderment. 'I been thinkin' exactly that,' Nellie said. 'Soon as I saw them contraptions, I thought to meself, they'll try anything to win us over.'

'Exactly, Nellie. That's exactly right,' Hester agreed enthusiastically.

'What are you talking about?' Marianne asked.

'You can just picture it, can't you: a bunch of toffs sitting around, smoking their cigars and sayin', "Give 'em a pump, that should keep 'em quiet."' Nellie cackled. 'And then they thought, "If we really want to make them proles happy, give 'em some sand to play with as well. That'll distract them from the fact there's not enough food cos there's a bloody great war on!"' She shouted the last few words, then started to laugh. Her laughter was infectious and as the stress of the fire bombs abated slightly, Marianne and Reenie joined in, slumping to the floor, their backs against the wall of the Market Hall.

Hester stood in front of them, arms folded, then her shoulders relaxed and she chuckled. 'All right, all right. Mebbe you've got a point,' she said, sitting down next to Nellie. 'But you gotta admit, you'd have more hope puttin' out a fire with a pair of me old knickers than you would with one of them things.'

This made them whoop all the louder.

'If you lot are drunk, I'll take you straight to the nick!' An icy voice interrupted them.

They looked up to see Roger Humphries silhouetted against the flames.

'Sorry.' Reenie tried to stop laughing. 'It was just ... we were just ... letting off steam. After the shock of the fires and all.'

The man's torch shone into Marianne's face. 'Is that you, Marianne? This isn't the sort of behaviour I expect from you. And anyway, you should all be in the shelter. Where the hell is Mr Bulger? He should be enforcing the rules and instead he's nowhere to be seen. Sooner Jasper gets back to his regular duties, the happier I'll be,' he muttered. 'He might even be able to catch the buggers sticking up those notices.'

Marianne put her hand over her mouth to try to stop her giggles and Roger scowled at her. 'Does your husband know about this?' he asked.

'Looks like you had a lucky escape, Roger,' Nellie remarked. 'Imagine having to arrest your own wife!'

The women started to laugh again.

'Get to the shelter now before I arrest the lot of you,' Roger huffed. 'And next time I might not be so forgivin'.' He looked over at Hester. 'Who are you?' he asked.

'That's Hester. She's staying with us for a bit. A regular commie, she is,' Nellie said.

'Is that right? Didn't see her when I was at the café earlier,' he said suspiciously. 'An' if you're a commie, perhaps you know something about the seditious material that's been popping up around the town?'

Hester jabbed Nellie in the ribs in annoyance. 'She were jokin', Constable,' Hester said. 'I'm a fine upstanding citizen just like the rest of you.'

90

'Prove it by doing what I say.'

The women clambered to their feet and while Marianne and Reenie went back into the Market Hall to continue their long, tedious night, Nellie and Hester walked back towards the café.

'Cor, that were close,' Hester hissed.

'What?'

'That policeman.'

'But we weren't doin' anything.'

'Don't matter. Coppers'll nab you, guilty or not.'

Nellie sighed. 'Give it a rest, will ya.'

'Take it from me, the police're evil bastards, every last one of 'em.'

'Whatever you say, love,' Nellie said distractedly as she looked up towards the red glow behind the castle. Anxiously her eyes moved to the left, hoping to spot the garage. Just for a moment, she could have sworn she saw the flicker of flames through the trees, but it could have been anywhere, she reasoned. Edie would be all right. That girl was a survivor.

91

# Chapter 17

'Fire!'

Marge's head shot up from her pillow as the cry reverberated through the room.

'Shut up!' someone groaned. 'I've only just gone to sleep.'

Marge pushed back her covers and swung her legs over the side of the bed.

'Oy!' the girl in the bottom bunk moaned as Marge thumped to the ground by her head. 'Be quiet, can't you?'

'Get up!' she hissed. 'All of you. There are fires to put out!'

'Christ's sake! Can't they give us a moment's peace.' It was her friend Jeanie, who hopped down from the bunk opposite and began to get dressed.

Marge did the same and soon they were running out into the tunnel and winding their way to the top. As they neared the exit, they could smell smoke. Marge grabbed a couple of buckets of sand that stood by the entrance, while Jeanie made for a tap in the parade ground where a chain of people – many in various states of undress – were handing buckets along a line that stretched up to the top of the castle grounds. They'd all been drilled on what to do in the event of an incendiary attack.

Marge ran up the path to the top of the hill, the shadow of the Roman lighthouse eerie against the red sky. The planes, having dropped their initial load, seemed to be circling away and the ack-acks opened fire. For once, they had some success, as from her vantage point by the top wall, Marge saw a plane burst into flames and dive down out of sight towards the water.

'Serves you right, bastard!'

'Language, Margaret,' a voice said beside her.

She looked up to see Rodney Castle. In the flickering light, she could see that, unusually for him, he had a smudge of soot on his cheek and his hair was messy. Suppressing the urge to smooth it, she scowled at him, the memory of his words earlier that afternoon still ringing in her mind. 'You can sod off as well,' she said grumpily.

'What, and leave you to fend for yourself?' There was a smile in his voice.

'Shouldn't you be firefighting?' Marge responded, still not ready to forgive him.

Rodney nodded towards a couple of fire engines that were racing up the road towards them, bells clanging. 'I thought I'd leave it to the professionals,' he said drily, as the firemen hopped out. 'Their hose trumps your sand any day.' He grinned and Marge smiled back reluctantly.

'In which case, I'm going back to bed.'

'I'll walk down with you.'

'Why?'

'Because I want to apologise.'

She stopped and fished in her pocket, pulling out a notebook and pencil. 'What's the date?' she asked urgently.

'Well, it's past midnight, so it's the twenty-eighth. Why?'

She licked her pencil and started to write. 'Twenty-eighth of December, 1940, Rodney Castle apologised.'

'Ha ha, very funny.'

She looked up at him with a smile. 'Go on then.'

He sighed. 'I'm sorry. I was wrong to make assumptions about you and the strong-jawed padre.'

'And what assumptions were they? That he and I had been having it off under the altar table?'

93

He looked shamefaced. 'No. Well, maybe . . .'

Marge huffed. 'I have *never* had it off under the altar table!'

Rodney started to laugh. 'Oh God. I really am sorry, Marge. I don't know what came over me. Forgive me?'

'I suppose.' She smiled inwardly, her heart feeling lighter than it had for a while at the realisation that he'd been jealous.

'How is he anyway?'

'Who?'

'You know who.'

'No idea. I've not seen him since you told him to bugger off.'

'I never said that!'

'You did! Or as good as.'

They were walking near the entrance of the tunnels now and a shout went up over by Constables Road. 'We need help down here!'

They started to run towards the voice.

'It's the garage,' someone panted. 'It's on fire!'

'Oh Christ! Edie!' Rodney started to run full tilt, Marge not far behind.

As they neared the garage, they could see that the vehicles on the forecourt appeared untouched, although there was a flicker of flame from the back of the building. But what drew their attention as they approached was the figure lying in front of the building.

'Edie!' Rodney yelled, his heart rate going up a notch. But as he drew closer, he saw with relief that it wasn't his sister. He knelt down beside the figure. 'Mr Pearson!' He shook the man's shoulders.

Mr Pearson started to cough and opened his eyes, looking up at Rodney in bemusement. 'Wha'?' he choked.

'Where's Edie?'

Mr Pearson could only shake his head as another coughing fit overtook him.

'Look after him,' Rodney ordered Marge. 'I'm going in to find her.'

∽

Edie poured a bucket of water over the mattress, holding her breath against the smoke, then backed out of the room, slamming the door behind her as she returned to the kitchen, where she filled the bucket once again, wiping her brow as she willed it to pour more quickly. She was a curious combination of cold and sweating, and she was anxious about Mr Pearson, lying out there freezing on the ground.

Once the bucket was filled, she heaved it out of the old Belfast sink and turned to go back to the bedroom. But her way was blocked by a tall broad figure, and she stumbled back.

'Edie?'

Edie felt a rush of relief and putting down the bucket, she threw herself against her eldest brother. 'Rod! Thank God you're here!' she gasped, squeezing him tightly around the waist. He could be pompous and stuck-up but there was no one in the world she'd rather have by her side in a crisis.

Rodney took hold of her arms and held her away from him. 'Are you all right?' he asked anxiously.

Edie nodded, but realised he probably couldn't see her in the dark. 'Yes. I'm trying to put out the fire in Mr P's bedroom.'

Rodney bent and picked up the bucket. 'I'll do it. Get outside, Marge'll look after you.'

'It's almost out now anyway.'

'What about the rest of the flat?' Rodney sniffed the air. 'It stinks of smoke.'

'It's fine. Just the bedroom.'

'Go on, now. I'll see you outside.'

More than happy to let her brother take charge, Edie made her way outside, where she found Marge sitting with Mr Pearson propped up against her, his head resting on her shoulder. She'd wrapped her coat around him, but even so, Edie could tell he was shivering even as he continued to cough.

'Where's the ambulance?' Edie called to a soldier who was running towards them.

'On its way!'

Marge held tight to Mr Pearson. 'Not long now, and we'll have you tucked up nice and cosy in bed,' she said gently.

'Edie,' the man croaked.

Edie knelt down beside him. 'All right, Mr P,' she said soothingly, rubbing his arms. 'Everything's fine. There's hardly any damage, so all you need to worry about is getting yourself better.'

But she wasn't sure he heard a word as he started to cough again. She got up and started to pace restlessly, her eyes straining for any sign of an ambulance. Finally, she heard the familiar clanging of bells and breathed a sigh of relief as one drew up beside them, its headlights dim and pointed towards the ground.

'Let's be having him, then,' one of the ambulance men said as he pulled a stretcher out of the back of the van. 'Any burns, or is it just smoke?'

'Just smoke, I think,' Edie said. 'He's been coughing fit to burst.'

The men knelt beside Mr Pearson, lifted him onto the stretcher then stood up. 'Anyone else?'

Marge shook her head.

'We'll be off then. We're taking him to the Casualty.'

As the ambulance sped away, Edie and Marge went upstairs and found Rodney emerging from Mr Pearson's room.

'I think it's out now,' he said. 'Although it's a bit of a mess. I doubt Mr P'll be sleeping in there for a while.'

'Just as well they've carted him off then,' Edie said wearily, shivering as the shock caught up with her.

Marge tutted. 'You should probably have gone too. Just to check you're all right.'

'I'm fine,' Edie said impatiently. 'Do you know what happened?'

'Incendiaries,' Rodney said grimly. 'Edie, you look freezing; get a blanket round you, while I make some tea. Marge, why don't you get back and try to get some sleep. I'll stay here tonight.'

Edie felt a flash of relief. The thought of being in this smoky place by herself after everything that had happened didn't appeal to her. 'You sure, Rod? You won't get in trouble?'

'Course he won't,' Marge said drily. 'Lieutenant Perfect never gets in trouble.'

Rodney grinned at her. 'Perfect, am I?'

Marge tutted in annoyance and went over to give Edie a hug. 'Let me know if you need any help, all right?'

Edie hugged her back tightly. Before the war, she and Marge hadn't had a lot to do with each other, but over the past year, they'd all grown closer, particularly since Daisy's death. 'Thank you,' she whispered.

'Come on, I'll walk you out,' Rodney said, taking Marge's arm.

In the office, downstairs, Rodney switched on the light and turned to look at Marge. Her face was pale and her bright red hair straggled around her shoulders. A far cry from the confident, stylish woman he was used to.

'Shall I walk you back?' he asked.

'No. Stay here and look after Edie, I can manage.'

'I know you can. That's what I like about you; nothing seems to faze you.'

'Not true,' she said, feeling a little aggrieved. It would be nice, she thought, if Rodney recognised that she needed support as well sometimes. But then, that was Rodney for you. Loyal and caring he might be, but he was not a man known for his insight.

Then he surprised her by smoothing a strand of hair away from her face. 'Be sure to take care of yourself, won't you, Marge.' His eyes dropped to her shoulder. 'What's this?' He wiped his fingers on her jacket. 'Are you hurt?'

She looked down, confused. 'No.'

He held his hand up, the tips of his fingers coated with blood.

'That's where Mr P's head was resting . . .' She frowned. 'But how did he get a cut to the back of his head?'

'Must have been when Edie dragged him down the stairs.' He bent to kiss her cheek. 'I'll see you soon.'

Rodney watched as Marge walked away, admiring how, even after the events of the evening, her head was upright, her shoulders straight. She was so different from his family who seemed to lurch from one crisis to another; sometimes it felt that he was the only one keeping them all on the straight and narrow.

Upstairs, he found Edie huddled on the sofa under a blanket.

'You do know you're gonna lose her if you're not careful, don't you?' she said.

Rodney frowned abstractedly. 'Lose who?'

'Marge!'

'How could I lose her? I always know exactly where she is.'

Edie sighed with frustration. 'I'm too tired to argue about this tonight. And too grateful that you're here.' She smiled slightly at him. 'You're stubborn and opinionated, but you're all right really.'

'Wow! High praise indeed from my temperamental, easily offended sister. Now, drink your tea, then you need to get to bed.'

Edie did as she was told and soon he led her into her bedroom, which, despite the smell of smoke, was completely untouched, and tucked her into bed.

Bending down he kissed her on the forehead. 'I'm glad you're all right, sis. When they said the garage was on fire, I thought . . .' He smiled. 'Well, let's just say I suddenly realised that even though you can be more aggravating than the other four and Mum put together, I wouldn't be without you.'

'Gee, thanks, Rod!' Edie said sleepily. Then she yawned widely, closed her eyes and was asleep before her brother had tiptoed out of the room.

# Chapter 18

'Mummy!'

The cry brought Rodney's eyes flying open, although he hadn't been asleep – the sofa was horribly uncomfortable. There was another scream and he leapt up and ran to Edie's bedroom.

His sister's head was tossing on the pillow and there were tears on her cheeks as he reached down and gently shook her awake.

'Edes,' he whispered. When she didn't respond, he shook her harder. 'Edie, wake up!'

Edie opened her eyes and stared up into Rodney's face in bemusement.

'You were having a nightmare.' He sat down on the bed beside her.

Edie clapped her hand over her mouth and jumped up. 'I'm gonna be sick!' she muttered as she stumbled out of bed and ran out of the door. Rodney followed, rubbing her back as she retched into the toilet.

Finally, she sat back. 'I'm sorry,' she hiccuped. 'I don't know what came over me.'

'You've had a pretty rough night. I'm not surprised you had a nightmare.'

Edie shook her head, her face pale and blotchy. 'I wasn't dreaming about today,' she said, getting up to rinse her mouth.

'What then?'

'I think you know what,' she whispered. 'Unless you've forgotten what day it was yesterday.'

'Ah. Right.' Rodney took her arm and led her back to bed.

'Haven't you got anything to say?' she asked.

'No.'

'Don't you care?'

'No.' He pulled back the blankets and gestured for her to get in.

'God, you can be a cold bastard, Rodney,' Edie said, immediately regretting it when she saw his stricken expression.

'I must take after our father then,' he said shortly. 'Except I hope I'm not as violent.'

'It wasn't his fault,' Edie said.

He shook his head. 'And was it ours? Was it Mum's? Did she deserve to be nearly strangled?'

'What? What are you talking about?'

'He . . . he thought she was a German soldier come to kill him. So he tried to get in first. I heard her screaming.' He swallowed. 'It was me that got him off her. We had to lock him in his room. Gladys went to get the doctor, while I helped Mum over to Jasper's. I think that must have been the night that Lily . . .' He waved his hand expressively.

Edie stared at him with wide eyes, her hand over her mouth, feeling nauseous again. 'Please tell me that's not true,' she gasped.

Rodney shrugged. 'I can't. He was frightening, Edie. He scared us all half to death . . . Except you, of course.' He smiled sadly. 'He *loved* you.'

'I know,' she whispered. 'And I loved him too. And I really *need* to know what happened when he died, Rod. Why won't anyone tell me?'

'He shot himself; what more do you need to know? Anyway, it's been thirteen years, why this sudden urge to know more?'

'Because . . . because ever since we found out about his other son, the nightmares have been back and I *know* it's something to do with when he died. And . . . I think Mum was there.' Her voice dropped as she said this.

'Well, she probably was. She was always home back then.'

Edie's brow furrowed as she tried to remember images from her dream, but they drifted away like morning mist, leaving her with a

100

bang, a scream, blood on the walls . . . 'I mean, I can't help wondering whether Mum . . .' She trailed off.

'What? Mum, what?' When Edie didn't answer, Rodney stood up and began to pace, his hands thrust into his pockets. 'No! Mum . . . . Mum looked after him. She refused to have him put away and she nursed him day and night. Bloody hell, Edie! I know you two don't get on, but how could you even think that?'

Edie looked down, her fingers fiddling with the counterpane. 'I didn't mean she killed him,' she said weakly.

'Didn't you?' He glared at her angrily. When she didn't respond, he sighed. 'Go back to sleep, and let's not say another word about it.' He strode out of the room, his shoulders stiff.

'Rodney!' Edie called as he was shutting the door. 'I'm sorry!'

'So am I. Let's talk in the morning.'

Edie lay down, but sleep was impossible now. She turned over and punched her pillow. Could it be true? she thought. Could their father really have tried to kill their mother? And if so, what would that have done to her? For all her faults, Edie couldn't deny that her mother was fiercely protective. Was it possible that she would commit the ultimate crime to keep her children safe?

Edie shook her head. No, of course she wouldn't. No matter how much her mother aggravated her, she couldn't imagine she would do something so dreadful. Would she?

# Chapter 19

'What a night,' Lou Carter exclaimed as she walked into the café and slumped into her usual seat by the window. 'Cup of tea and some toast when you're ready, Glad,' she called.

Nellie frowned at her. 'Wait your turn.'

'I said when you're ready, didn't I? Bloody uppity cow,' she muttered. 'You seen my stall? It's ruined. Second time in a few months it's been burnt down. Might have to move me pitch.'

'We can but hope,' Nellie said drily and was rewarded with guffaws from around her and a furious glare from Lou.

'Here you go, Lou, love.' Hester came over with a cup and saucer and put it on the table. 'Sorry about your stall.'

'Thanks, Hester. Sorry I was rude yesterday. I'm glad to see yer, really.'

Nellie rolled her eyes. 'Now isn't that touching. But, Hester, there are others who was here first.' She glanced round at the packed tables.

Phyllis Perkins from the fish shop across the square popped in then. 'Couple of sausage sarnies to go, if you got any, Nell. Me and Reg could do with it after last night's kerfuffle.' She peered into the kitchen. 'You all right, Marianne, love? Bugger of a night to be fire-watching. My Reg was out there with the firemen doing his bit.'

Marianne came over to the hatch, which was set in the wall behind the counter. After a night without sleep, she was pale and there were dark shadows under her eyes. 'I'm surviving. Just,' she said. 'How is Mr Perkins?'

'He's all right, bless him. He's no stranger to fires and danger after the last war. None of us are.'

'It was the same at the castle. Chaos it was with everyone rushing around trying to put out the flames. Noticed an ambulance at the garage as well,' one of the soldiers remarked.

Nellie gasped. 'What? Was Edie hurt?'

The man shrugged. 'Dunno. Coulda been anyone.'

'I need to get to the hospital,' Nellie said, untying her pink apron.

'It's all right, Mrs C,' Ron Hames called. 'According to my sources, Clive Pearson's in for smoke inhalation and a nasty bump on the head, but Edie's fine, or at least, she's not in hospital, which is probably the same thing.'

'Don't go, Nellie,' Gladys said. 'We've got enough to do without you gallivanting off again.'

Nellie sighed and retied her apron. 'Fair enough. Seems you do have your uses after all, Ron.'

'Was anyone else hurt?' Hester asked, as she placed a plate of scrambled eggs and toast in front of the journalist.

'Who else would there be?' he asked.

Hester shrugged. 'I dunno, I were just askin'.' She flounced back to the kitchen.

The door opened and a middle-aged woman wearing a smart blue wool coat, which looked incongruous when paired with the helmet on her head, came in and hurried over to the counter.

'Only me!' she trilled. 'I can't stop, but I saw our Mr Hames was in here and wanted a quick a word.' She smiled ingratiatingly at the journalist.

Nellie bit back the expletive that jumped to her lips. Muriel Palmer ran the Dover WVS, and though they'd become cordial over the months as they both worked to run the tea stand in the caves, she still found her annoying. It went against the grain to take orders from anyone. 'For the good of the town,' she murmured to herself,

103

remembering Muriel's own words after she'd covered for the fact that Nellie was storing black market goods in the basement.

'Muriel,' she said brightly, 'what's so urgent?'

'Well, three things! First, I heard there was a new helper in the caves last night. She made quite the impression on dear Mr Evans.'

Hester came over and held out her hand. 'That'll be me. Hester Erskine. Nellie's putting me up till I find somewhere to live after me own place got shelled.'

'Very nice to meet you, Mrs Erskine.' Muriel shook her hand, looking the woman up and down, noting the ill-fitting clothes she was wearing. 'I see you may be a bit short in the clothing department. Come along to WVS HQ whenever you like and we'll sort you out with something a bit more your size, shall we say?' She shot a glance at Nellie, who chose to ignore the insult.

'You said there was more than one thing, Muriel?' she said.

'Yes! I have news!'

'Must be good news. You look like the cat that's got the cream,' Nellie remarked.

'Not the cream, Nellie,' she tittered. 'But I've had word that come the New Year, Dover WVS will be taking delivery of a rather splendid mobile kitchen donated by our twin town in Massachusetts.'

Nellie's eyebrows rose. 'Massywhatsit?'

'Massachusetts in America. Our friends across the Atlantic have been reading about our plight and have raised the funds to send us a fully equipped mobile kitchen. Isn't that wonderful? And I thought I'd offer you, Mr Hames, an exclusive opportunity to photograph it for the *Dover Express*.' She beamed at him.

The journalist looked unimpressed. 'I'll send my junior. Not the sort of thing I cover. Now, if you'd come in to tell me they were sending their troops over, that'd be different,' he grumped. 'Cos let's face it, a cup of tea ain't gonna help us win the war, is it?'

'Does this mean you won't be needing me at the caves no more now you've got your shiny new kitchen?' Nellie asked, feeling slightly disgruntled. She didn't enjoy going to the caves – nasty, damp, smelly place – but she didn't like the thought of being replaced.

'Oh no, Nellie, we'll need you more than ever. And not just you. One of our other vans has given up the ghost, so I was wondering if your Edie could take a look sometime – free of charge of course.'

'You'd best go to the garage and ask her yourself. Though why she'd rather live up there than in her own home with her mum is a mystery.'

'Is it, though?' Ron Hames interjected. 'You're not the most relaxing person to be around, are you?'

Nellie flushed. 'Well, excuse me for finding our current situation a little tense! Our town's being destroyed brick by brick and I've spent more time in the basement in the last few months than I have tending to my business. And you don't make things easier, neither. Sitting there with your notebook and your big flappy ears.'

The journalist held his hands up. 'Keep your hair on, I was just joking.'

'You find it funny, do you? The shortage of food, the destroyed lives – the sheer bloody grind of trying to keep our heads above water while dodging bombs and shells?'

His smile faded and he bowed his head. 'Mrs Castle, you're right as usual. Didn't mean to offend you.'

'Goodness, I seem to have caused a touch of consternation,' Mrs Palmer said, staring between the two. 'So I shall take my leave. Perhaps you could ask Donny to take a message to Edie for me? There'll be a penny in it for him.'

Nellie sighed. 'Fine. An' I'd thank you not to mention constipation when people are trying to eat!'

There was a short silence as everyone gaped at Nellie for a moment, before Mrs Palmer giggled. 'Oh, Nellie, you are funny.' She waved gaily, then click-clacked out of the café.

Nellie stared around in bewilderment, but Marianne had withdrawn her head from the hatch, while Gladys had disappeared back into the kitchen, from where she could hear muffled giggles. Ron Hames cleared his throat and turned to stare out of the window.

Hester grinned. 'Good one, Nell.'

Nellie smiled tightly, still unsure what the joke was.

'Now you've finished chit-chatting, Mrs C, any chance of some food?' one of the customers called.

Nellie huffed, relieved to have a distraction and went to the hatch. 'Marianne, get a move on dishing up those eggs.'

'Get a move on!' Polly squawked, turning full circle on her perch.

Nellie sighed. 'And can you tell your son to stop teaching the bloody bird more words,' she called.

'Bloody bird!' Polly repeated.

'Oh, shut up!' Nellie exclaimed, throwing a tea towel over the birdcage as the customers erupted into laughter.

# Chapter 20

The next time Edie woke, Rodney was putting a cup of tea on the bedside table.

'Morning, sleepyhead. How are you feeling?'

Edie sat up, pushing the hair out of her face. 'What time is it?'

'Nine. You've slept through.'

Edie let out a little shriek and jumped out of bed. 'Why didn't you wake me?'

'Because you were exhausted and needed a lie-in.'

'I've got so much to do! You've seen all the bloody vehicles out there.'

'It's all right. A Mr Cooper already called in and said not to worry, he'll come back tomorrow. And a Captain Tarrant was here earlier and said he'd arrange to take the some of the trucks elsewhere.'

'What? He can't take the business elsewhere! What'll Mr P say?' She put her head in her hands. 'Why didn't you wake me, for God's sake.'

Rodney folded his arms across his chest. 'That's a nice way to thank me for nearly crippling myself by sleeping on the most uncomfortable sofa in the world.' He rubbed his neck. 'And if you spend your evenings sitting on that thing it's no wonder you're always so bad-tempered.'

'I am not bad-tempered!' she railed. 'But with Mr P in hospital, *I'm* in charge here. What'll he say when he comes back and finds I've lost all his customers?'

'Calm down, will you? One day isn't going to hurt. Before I go, though, I need you to tell me what happened last night.'

Edie pulled a thick jersey over her head. 'Firebombs happened,' she said, her voice muffled by the wool.

'But how come Mr P's room was the only one to catch fire. If sparks had landed on the roof, it would have taken hold of the entire building.'

Edie shrugged and undid her plait before picking up her hairbrush and pulling it through her long dark hair, then replaiting it.

'Come with me.' He walked out of the room and she followed obediently.

Opening the door to Mr Pearson's bedroom, he stood back to let her enter.

'Christ, it's freezing in here.' She wrinkled her nose and looked around. Opposite the door, the window was smashed, the cold wind whistling into the room, the ragged remains of the curtains flapping against the wall. 'What am I meant to be looking at?'

Rodney pointed upwards. 'The roof is undamaged.'

She looked up and smiled. 'Well, thank God for that.'

'If the roof is undamaged, then where did the fire come from?'

Edie shook her head, still not sure what Rodney was getting at.

'Tell me what happened last night.'

Edie thought for a moment. 'I heard footsteps in the hall. I assumed it was Mr P, but I did think it odd, cos his room is right by the bathroom, so he wouldn't pass my door. Then a little bit later I heard a window smash. I looked out of my bedroom window and the Anderson shelter was all lit up and then I heard a car start up . . . ' She trailed off and put her hand to her mouth and stared at her brother wide-eyed. 'But Mr P was in his room unconscious when I found him and I didn't hear him walk back . . . Which means someone else was here.'

'And the siren? When did that go off? Before or after the glass?'

'After. Definitely.'

Rodney gestured to the charred floorboards. Usually they were covered by a rag rug, but it had been destroyed by the flames. As for the bed, it lay in a mass of twisted metal, the mattress half burnt and the bedclothes destroyed. 'Look at that. It looks like something was thrown in through the window and landed on the floor here. If it had landed on the bed, Mr Pearson would be dead now.'

Edie gasped. 'Are you saying someone tried to *kill* him? But why would anyone want to do that?'

'I don't know. But all the evidence points to it. First by smashing him on the head, then by setting his room on fire.'

Edie paled. 'Yesterday in the shelter it looked like someone had been in there. Mr P was worrying about it, but we decided it was probably a vagrant who needed a place to sleep. But maybe someone's just been waiting for their chance.'

Rodney regarded her sharply. 'I don't like it. I'm going to talk to the military police at the castle.'

'Why does it have to be the military police and not the normal police?'

'Because of where we are, what's here. You know, I've heard stories of people setting fire to houses to show the planes where to bomb,' he said distractedly.

'Who'd do that?' Edie asked in disbelief.

Rodney shrugged. 'The world is full of people who think they know best.'

Edie folded her arms. 'Don't I know it? I'm talking to one of them.'

Her brother rolled his eyes, but chose not to comment as he continued, 'And if they want directions to the castle, then this is as good a place as any to set their fire.'

'I don't know, Rod. I mean, the castle's not exactly hidden from view, is it? Even in the dark it can't be hard to find.'

'Hmm.' He rubbed his chin. 'Maybe you're right. But clearly *something* has been going on.'

Edie remembered what Mr Pearson had said about the missing handbook, and she was just about to tell Rodney, then decided against it. She'd already lost Mr P some business today, if she mentioned that as well, he could get in real trouble.

'Right, well, I need to get back and talk to some people. In the meantime, you should pack your things and get back home; you can't stay here tonight,' Rodney said briskly.

'No. I'm going to do some work first. Then I need to go to the hospital and see how Mr P is. After that, I'll make a decision about where I sleep tonight.'

'Look, Edie, I know you don't like living with Mum, but after everything you've told me, this place feels unsafe.'

Edie sighed and nodded. Her brother was right, she conceded. And if she was honest, she would be scared to stay at the garage on her own tonight.

Footsteps thumping up the stairs from the office distracted them and Rodney strode out of the room. 'Who the hell are you?' he said sharply.

Edie peered round Rod's tall frame and was startled to see the arrogant chauffeur from the day before.

'What are *you* doing here?' she asked.

'You know this man?'

Edie folded her arms. 'No. But I saw him yesterday.'

'It's the lady mechanic.' The man smiled, but his small brown eyes were cold as he examined her and Edie shuddered inwardly. Yesterday she'd thought him arrogant and rude, but today there was something about him that felt menacing.

'Or just "mechanic" would do,' Edie said irritably, refusing to be intimidated. 'Lady or not makes no difference.'

'Of course not. Although I hope you're a better mechanic than you are a housekeeper. What the hell have you done to the place?'

'What have *I* done?' Edie was outraged.

'Incendiaries,' Rod intervened. 'Mr Pearson's been taken to hospital.'

'Blimey,' the man said, wrinkling his nose against the smell and looking around. 'I'm surprised there's not more damage.'

'You haven't told us who you are,' Rod said.

The man stepped forward, hand outstretched. 'Walter Penfold. Clive's brother-in-law.'

Edie stared at him in surprise. She'd barely heard anything about this man in all the years she'd known her boss, and yet now he'd turned up twice in as many days. 'What are you doing here?' she asked suspiciously. After everything she'd learnt the night before, she didn't think Mr P would be too happy to have his brother-in-law turning up out of the blue. 'And why didn't you pop in yesterday when you were driving past in your fancy car?'

'Cos I was working. And we were late thanks to that stupid bus. Luckily you were there to save the day. Anyway, seein' as I'm here, how about I help you clean up this mess?'

'I have to get off,' Rodney interrupted, glancing at his watch. 'I'm on duty in an hour and I need to wash and change. I'm going to send some MPs down to take a look at the place.'

'MPs?' Walter exclaimed. 'Why the hell do you need to get the military police involved?'

Rodney regarded him calmly. 'That's not really your business,' he said.

The man's cheeks flushed angrily. 'Clive's me late wife's brother. Me and him were mates, and seein' as the only other family he has is my son Bill, who's up in the wilds of Scotland, it's only right I step in to help, seeing as he can't.'

'We don't need your help,' Edie said coldly. 'And Mr P'll be out of hospital soon.'

'Well, that is good news.'

From his tone, Edie wasn't sure whether he meant it or not.

111

'Good, now that's settled, I need to get on.' Rodney nodded at Walter Penfold as he left.

After he'd gone, Walter took off his coat and suit jacket and started to roll up his sleeves. 'Right then, let's clean this place up, eh? Wouldn't do for poor old Clive to come back to this mess.'

'Like I said, I don't need your help – and how do I know you are who you say you are?' Edie asked, arms folded defensively across her chest. 'There's been odd goings-on here, and for all I know, you could be the one responsible.'

'Odd goings-on, eh? Sounds interesting. Although I can't imagine Clive bein' involved in anything odd. He's salt of the earth, but he's not exactly the life and soul.'

Edie felt her dislike of the man increase. 'We think someone's been sleeping in the Anderson shelter.'

'Probably some poor sod that's lost his home.'

'Maybe it was you.'

Walter started to laugh. 'Do I look like a man what's been sleepin' rough? I got a good job, as it happens. Chauffeur for rich folk up near Hawkinge. Why would I need to kip in the Anderson? Only reason I'm here is cos I dropped the mistress at a friend's and thought I'd come and see how Clive were getting on. Look, this should convince you.' The man fished in the inside pocket of his coat and drew out a letter, which he held out to her.

Edie looked at the front. It was addressed to Walter Penfold at an address in Folkestone. She looked back up at him. 'I thought you said you lived in Hawkinge.'

'I only started recently. Go on, take a look.'

She pulled out a piece of paper. The top had the address of an RAF base in Scotland, and the letter was dated a couple of months previous and started, 'Dear Dad'. Looking swiftly down the sheet, she saw that it was from Bill. She handed it back, feeling slightly ashamed. 'Sorry,' she said. 'Just, you can't be too careful these days.'

'That's all right, love. You're right to be cautious. So, now I've set your mind at rest, why don't you let me help you? I could even see to some of them cars out there. Then I can drop you back home before I go pick up the boss.'

She shook her head. He might be Bill's dad, but she didn't trust him an inch. 'Without Mr P's say-so, I'm not letting you anywhere near the cars.' With a toss of her head, she stalked down the stairs.

Behind her, Walter let out a guffaw and followed after her. 'Quite the wildcat, aren't yer?' he said. 'Always loved my women with a bit of spirit.'

Edie ignored him as she walked into the garage, mentally ticking off the jobs she needed to do before she left. But then her attention was caught by a beautiful sky-blue car that sat gleaming on the forecourt.

'Oh . . .' she whispered reverently. 'An Alvis.' She walked over to it and ran her hand along its sides. 'I've never worked on one of these before. Does it belong to the family you work for?'

Walter grinned. 'Yup. And a little beauty she is too.' He patted the bonnet fondly. 'The number of cars that family's got is criminal. Still, I'm not complainin' if it means I get to drive cars like this.'

'Who do you work for?' she asked.

Walter tapped his nose. 'Ah, now, that'd be telling. But if you let me help you with your work, then I might drive you back home in her.'

Edie was torn. On the one hand, she wanted this man gone. But on the other . . . when would she get the opportunity to ride in a car like this again? She opened the bonnet and peered inside, admiring the clean lines and gleaming cylinders of the engine.

'Well?' Walter asked.

She shut the bonnet decisively. 'No. Thanks for the offer, but I need to get on.'

Walter shrugged and got into the car. 'Suit yourself,' he said, starting the engine. 'Though I wonder what Clive'll say when he hears you turned down help.' Then tipping his hat, he shut the door and drove away.

Edie watched him go with a frown. She'd seen that car before, she realised, trying to remember where. Suddenly it came back to her and her stomach started to churn. It had been sitting outside Henry's house – the one he'd said he lived in by himself, but which in fact had belonged to his wife. Which meant that the woman she'd seen in the back of the Bentley yesterday had not been a figment of her imagination – it really had been her.

Clapping a hand over her mouth, she dashed back into the office, making it to the small bathroom just in time.

# Chapter 21

It was nearing lunchtime when a small figure wearing a black coat and a helmet crept into the café and sat at a table by the window. Her face was wrinkled and careworn, and she looked as though she hadn't slept in a week. At the sight of her, Nellie's eyes widened with surprise and she immediately left her place behind the counter and went to talk to her.

'Mary, love. I'm so happy to see you. What can I get you?'

Mary Guthrie smiled tiredly at her. 'Just a cup of tea, Nellie, ta.'

'I don't usually see you out at this time. In fact, I haven't seen you in here since . . .' Nellie paused, looking uncomfortable.

'Since Colin went missing.'

Nellie blushed. 'Yes, since Colin.'

'Why do people think they can't mention his name?'

'It's not that . . .' Nellie couldn't add what she really thought. That Mary's stubborn refusal to acknowledge that her son was probably dead and her habit of snapping at anyone who failed to agree with her was the reason everyone was walking on eggshells around her. She sighed. 'Cup of tea coming right up. And one of Marianne's special rock cakes made fresh this morning. On the house.' She bustled back to the counter.

'Who's that?' Hester asked curiously – it wasn't often that Nellie put herself out to serve a customer personally.

'That's Mary – she married Paul Guthrie from the bakery after you left, so you probably never met her.' Nellie cast a glance behind her, then whispered, 'Poor love lost her son at Dunkirk. Jimmy's best friend Colin. Lovely young lad, he was. Him and Jim was thick as thieves. He were like another son to me.' She shook her head sadly. 'She still believes he's alive, though, cos there's been no official confirmation. But Jim insists he's dead.'

Hester looked over at Mary sympathetically, recognising the grief in her slumped shoulders and reddened eyes. When Nellie had poured the tea, Hester took a rock cake from under the glass dome on the counter. 'I'll take it over. Me an' her have a lot in common, and I've learnt that talkin' to people in the same boat can help.'

Nellie nodded her agreement and Hester threaded her way through the tables.

'Mind if I join you, love?' she asked as she placed the tea and cake on the table in front of the other woman.

Mary looked up in surprise. 'N-no. I suppose not.'

Hester sat down and smiled kindly at her. 'I hear you an' me have something in common,' she said quietly.

Mary raised her eyebrows. 'Do we?'

'Our boys.' Hester sighed deeply. 'We are united in grief.'

Mary's eyes suddenly filled with tears. She fished in her pocket for a handkerchief, then dabbed at her eyes. 'I'm so sorry,' she whispered. 'I cry at the drop of a hat these days.'

Hester put her hand over the other woman's. 'It's the same for me.'

'Is it?'

Hester nodded solemnly. 'An' the worst part is, I don't know whether my Tommy's alive or dead. All I have is a bloomin' telegram to say he's missing.'

Mary nodded. 'Yes. Oh yes, that's exactly the same for me.'

Hester suddenly slapped her hand on the table and leant forward, her face screwed up with emotion. 'And what the hell do *they* know about missing? Missing is when your heart aches so bad that every beat sends pain shooting from your head to your toes. Missing is when your pillow is wet every morning from the tears you cry in your

116

sleep. Missing is . . .' She took a deep breath, then continued, 'Is when your anger burns so hot and so high that you feel you might explode with the pressure.' She swallowed, her gaze never leaving Mary's face.

'Who are you?' Mary asked, staring at Hester with wide eyes.

'I'm Hester. Was bombed out a few days back, so Nellie's taken me in, and my son Tommy . . . well, he were on the subs' – she shrugged – 'but who knows where he is now.'

'Oh, you poor dear.' Mary sat back, her hand on her chest. 'There are so many of us heartbroken mothers up and down the country. I lost my brother in the last war. My mother died soon after of a broken heart.' Her eyes filled again. 'And now it's my turn,' she whispered.

Hester leant over and grasped Mary's hands. 'No, it's not. You are strong and you will survive.' She continued to talk for some minutes, still holding on to the other woman's hands, while Mary listened intently, her eyes never leaving Hester's face.

When Hester had finished, Mary squeezed the hands that were now hot and sweaty in hers. 'You and me might never have met, but we are sisters. You *know* me,' she said. 'And I know you. I'm so dreadfully sorry for your loss, Hester.'

'And I yours. People like us need to stick together. After last time, it ain't right that they're sending the young men to their deaths again. Didn't they learn anything?'

Mary nodded, but she was no longer looking at Hester, because through the window she'd spotted a tall, dark-haired man wearing khaki pushing open the door of the Turners' grocery shop across the square.

Hester followed her gaze. 'Who's that?' she asked.

'That's Jimmy Castle. My Colin's best friend.' She snorted. 'But look at him. He doesn't have a care in the world.'

'So that's one of Nellie's boys, is it? I shoulda known; he has the look of his dad.' Her gaze returned to Mary, noting the bitterness on her face. 'Mary, love, it's not his fault,' she said gently. 'Don't take your anger out on him.'

'Why shouldn't I? He left Colin to die in that place and now look at him! Romancing that Turner girl while my boy—' Her voice broke and she continued in a whisper, 'My boy might never come back to me.' Mary fished in her sleeve for her handkerchief and wiped her eyes again.

'You're blaming the wrong person,' Hester said urgently. 'That lad over there, he's as much a victim as your son.'

'How can you say that!' Mary snapped. 'Look at him!'

'Some wounds you can't see, Mary. You an' me know that better than most.'

Mary blinked at Hester, her lips a thin line, her chin stuck out at a stubborn angle, then, shaking her head, she picked up her bag and put on her helmet. 'There are things you don't know, Hester, and I'm not gonna share. But take it from me, that boy has no right to be happy!'

She stood up, her chair scraping on the floorboards, then paused and leant towards the other woman. 'But if you do hear anything . . .'

Hester sighed and nodded, realising there was little she could say to change Mary's mind. 'I'll be sure to let you know. Take care of yourself, love.'

'God bless you. Come visit me any time you need to talk. We mothers in arms need to stick together.' Then she hurried out of the café.

At the table behind them, Ron Hames watched Hester speculatively as she walked back to the counter.

# Chapter 22

Despite the fact that she was feeling decidedly shaky, Edie pushed all thoughts of Walter and who his employer might be to the back of her mind as she set to work, keen to get as much done as she could before she went to the hospital. She wasn't sure yet whether she'd mention that Walter had turned up at the garage; she'd wait to see how Mr P was before adding to his problems.

She was kneeling on the ground tightening the nuts on some new tyres when she heard loud footsteps marching into the garage. Startled, she looked up to see two men wearing khaki uniform with white belts and peaked, red-topped caps – it was a uniform she recognised as belonging to the military police. Beside them was Rodney, who had reverted to his usual neat, uptight appearance.

She stood up slowly. 'Can I help you?' she asked, casting an anxious glance at her brother.

'We need you to vacate the garage while we conduct our investigation into the events of last night,' one of the policemen commanded.

'What do you mean?' Edie asked, alarmed.

The other policeman sighed officiously. 'You need to leave so we can look around to see if there is anything suspicious.'

'Suspicious?! Like what?'

Rodney stepped forward. 'Edie, if you could just tell these men what you told me.'

Edie nodded and explained what had happened.

'And didn't you mention something about the shelter?' Rodney prompted.

'We think someone's been sleeping in there,' she said. 'Maybe they're the ones who started the fire.'

'Right. Corporal, start your search in the shelter, I'll do the office. As for you, Miss Castle, I must repeat my command. Please leave. This garage is now under investigation and you are not permitted to remain here.'

'Rodney?' Edie threw a desperate glance at her brother.

Rodney took her arm and led her outside. It was cold and drizzly out of the shelter of the garage, and the sea breeze blew rain into her face. 'What the hell have you done?' she hissed.

'I haven't *done* anything, Edie. I told you I was going to talk to the police. This garage is in a very sensitive area and we can't be too careful.'

'Too careful? Too careful about what? You can't seriously be suggesting that Mr Pearson is up to something dodgy!'

'Of course not. But . . .'

'But what?'

'Look, I was serious. There are people who'd start a fire to show the planes where to bomb.'

'But not Mr P!'

Rodney shrugged. 'But they need to make sure, Edie. You must understand.'

'Oh, for God's sake! You can't seriously believe—'

'No! Of course I don't believe,' he interrupted impatiently. 'But it has to be investigated. So get your stuff and go home.'

Edie narrowed her eyes at her brother. 'You know, you really are a jumped-up little Hitler, aren't you?'

Rodney took a deep breath, reining in his anger. 'Listen, this isn't about me or you, or Mr Pearson. This is about the country. This is about what we're all working towards, sacrificing so much for. Can't you see that? The only way we can win this war is if *everyone* is pulling together. And whoever was here last night is not working for this country. They're working for the Nazis. Do you understand?'

Edie paled, then shook her head. 'You know very well that Mr Pearson would *never* do anything to jeopardise the war effort. You *know* that, Rodney!'

Rodney let out a long breath. 'Maybe I do. But someone has been round here. Someone set the fire and someone was walking around the flat. You're the one who heard the footsteps! Mr Pearson had a wound on the back of his head, for God's sake! Are you sure it couldn't have happened when you dragged him down the stairs?'

'No, I protected his head ... Oh God.' She put a hand to her mouth. Somehow she'd managed to put the idea that someone might have been in the flat and tried to do Mr Pearson harm to the back of her mind. 'If someone was trying to kill him, why didn't they try to kill me too?'

'I have no idea. But that's why you need to go home. I want you safe, Edie.'

Edie nodded, her anger fading in the face of his concern. 'What about the brother-in-law?'

'I'll mention him to the police. Do you know much about him?'

Edie shook her head. 'Only that I didn't like him.'

Rodney laughed softly. 'If they arrested everyone you didn't like, then I'd not be here long.'

Edie stared at him regretfully. 'I'm sorry about what I said.'

'I know. And I also know that Mr P is a good man. I'll do what I can for him. I've already vouched for you. Hopefully, this will all blow over.' Rodney put his hand on her shoulder. 'But for now you really need to leave.'

Edie nodded. 'I just need to get my coat.'

She hurried back to the office, where the policeman was busily emptying the filing cabinets. Going over to a hook on the wall, she grabbed a set of keys, then shrugged into her donkey jacket. She turned to the man. 'You should know that Mr Pearson has always been honest and upstanding. He's never done anything wrong in his life.'

The man looked up at her. 'As far as you know.'

Edie bit back an angry retort, realising that if she got his back up, she'd only make matters worse for Mr Pearson and herself, so without another word, she left the office and went round to the back where Mr Pearson kept his old Ford, which he rarely used other than as a taxi when it was required. She felt guilty about using the petrol, but she knew her boss would understand; this was an emergency, and she intended to do everything in her power to clear his name and bring him home safely, because life without him in it was unimaginable.

# Chapter 23

'Hello there, young Jimmy,' Ethel Turner said brightly. 'What brings you here today?'

'Just a flying visit.' Jimmy Castle smiled at his mother's friend.

Ethel raised her eyebrows knowingly. 'Ahh, you've come to see our Reenie, have you?'

He grinned. 'You know me too well, Mrs T. Is she here?'

In the small stockroom at the back of the shop Reenie had been unpacking a box of tinned fish, but when she heard Jimmy's voice, she straightened the red scarf on her head, and hastily checked her nails. She'd allowed herself a few days away from the allotment over Christmas and for once there was no trace of dirt. Pinching her cheeks to bring some colour into them, she popped her head round the curtain and drank in the sight of the tall, dark-haired soldier. She still couldn't believe he was interested in her. He might be five years younger than her, but when she was with him, she felt like a schoolgirl again. He was her first proper boyfriend and every time they walked out, she felt a swell of pride.

'Fancy a walk, Reens?' Jimmy asked when he saw her. 'I've got a couple of hours off and I couldn't think of anyone I'd rather spend them with.'

'Well ... I'm meant to be unpacking boxes right now.' Reenie looked at her aunt hopefully.

'Oh, get on with you, love. As if I'd make you stay in the back room like Cinderella when you've got a handsome man asking you to walk out. Though it don't look like the weather for it. But then, I remember when me and your Uncle Brian were courtin', we'd have gone out in a blizzard if it meant we could be alone.' She winked at her niece, then shooed her off to get her coat.

'You been over to the café, Jim?' she asked once Reenie had gone. 'Seems your mum's taken in another waif and stray. A woman who used to live round here.' She checked around her, then whispered, 'Left under a bit of a cloud, if you know what I mean.' She winked at him meaningfully, and Jimmy looked at her blankly. He had no idea what she was talking about, but though he was curious, if he went over to investigate, his mother would insist he stayed for lunch and he'd end up spending his precious hours off with his mother bending his ear about local gossip.

Reenie returned wearing a thick duffel coat with a green woollen hat pulled over her blonde curls, and putting her arm through Jimmy's, she pulled him out of the door.

'So, what would you like to do?' she asked as they turned in to King Street.

'I thought we could grab a bite to eat at the Oak.'

'Ooh, lovely. What's brought this on?'

Jimmy shrugged. 'I haven't seen you since Christmas Eve, and I've missed you.'

Reenie squeezed his arm. 'That's good, cos I've missed you something rotten too. Christmas Day was a bit of a damp squib round yours, to be honest, and Wilf was playing silly buggers . . .' She caught sight of a dark-haired man wearing bright yellow waterproofs making his way up New Bridge. 'Speak of the devil,' she murmured. Impulsively, she stopped and, pulling Jimmy's head down, she kissed him on the mouth.

Jimmy stepped back in surprise and glanced around. The pavements were crowded with people, but no one was paying any attention. But then his gaze fell on a woman wearing a black coat who was standing stock-still on the other side of the road staring at them. He started as he realised who it was. Colin's mother. And the look of sheer anger she was giving him made him recoil. He'd not spoken to her for months, and he felt ashamed of himself. Even from this distance he could see the accusation in her eyes, and he didn't blame her.

Noticing Jim's distraction, Reenie felt embarrassed at kissing him so openly in the street. Especially as she'd only done it to get at Wilf, who hadn't seemed to notice anyway. Glancing up at Jimmy's face, she saw he was staring across the street at Mrs Guthrie. Reenie waved at the woman, then grabbed Jimmy's hand and pulled him across the road, narrowly missing a soldier on a motorbike and an army jeep.

'Hello, Mrs Guthrie,' Reenie said warmly. 'I haven't seen you in ages. We missed you at the Christmas party, didn't we, Jimmy?' She nudged Jim, who was standing stiffly beside her, his expression inscrutable.

'Yes, well, I don't feel much like celebrating these days,' Mary said. 'Nice to see you looking so well, Jimmy. It's been a while.' Her tone was accusatory.

Reenie looked between them. The tension was palpable, so in an attempt to dispel it, she put her mittened hand on Mrs Guthrie's arm. 'I'm so sorry. That was insensitive of me. Of course you don't.' She sighed. 'We all miss Colin dreadfully. I don't suppose . . . ?'

Mrs Guthrie shook her head. 'The whole of Dover would know if we heard anything. But he's still alive. I just *know* it in here.' She thumped her chest. 'But I seem to be the only one who thinks that.' She looked at Jimmy, who cleared his throat.

'I'm sorry, Mrs Guthrie. I'm so sorry,' he whispered.

'Are you, Jim?' she asked. 'It don't seem it to me.' Then with a tight smile, she turned and walked back towards the market square.

Reenie let out a breath. 'Gordon Bennett,' she whispered. 'I've never known Mrs Guthrie to be so . . . so . . . *nasty*. It's almost as if she blames *you* for Colin's death.' She grasped his arm again and tried to urge him on, but Jimmy didn't move.

125

He was standing frozen to the spot, staring after the small, upright figure who was pushing her way through the crowds of shoppers.

'Jim?'

He looked down at her briefly, his eyes glittery with tears. 'She does blame me,' he said softly. 'And she's right to. I should have saved him. But she's wrong about the other thing.'

'What other thing?'

'He's dead. Colin's dead, but I just can't bring myself to tell her what I saw.' He took a deep breath and looked up at the sky, wishing that Mrs Guthrie hadn't seen him kissing Reenie. But then, was it any of her business? He wasn't doing anything wrong. Unless she knew . . . ?

He blew out a breath, trying to calm his anxiety. As far as he was aware, only Marianne understood that Colin hadn't just been his friend – he'd been his lover, his soul mate. And in the weeks after his return from Dunkirk, the pain of his loss was so acute it was as if someone had cut open his chest and wrenched out his heart.

Then Reenie had written to him to tell him how sorry she was. No one else had even thought to. And why would they? Colin was just one of many men their unit had lost – Alfie had lost his friend John as well – and they all carried on as if nothing had happened. Only he, it seemed, was mired in self-hatred, guilt and grief.

Reenie's letter had been so warm and gentle, so full of sympathy, it was as though she understood what it was like to have the one you loved ripped from you so suddenly. So he'd replied. And now here they were, a couple. And though his heart never beat with excitement when she was near, for the first time he was living without shame and the fear of discovery. He glanced down at Reenie: her cheeks were flushed with cold, her upturned nose covered with freckles and her blue eyes wary and questioning and he felt . . . affection, warmth. It might not be the burning passion he'd felt for Colin, but it was enough. It had to be. Because what he'd shared with Colin had been dangerous for both of them, and he could never risk it again.

'Jim, we've talked about this. None of it is your fault. I understand Mrs Guthrie's devastated but she has no right to make you feel guilty. Come on, let's get to the Oak; you'll feel better after something to eat.' She pulled at his arm again and Jimmy allowed her to lead him towards the pub on the corner of Cambridge Road, but his thoughts had returned to those hellish moments in Dunkirk when he'd watched helplessly as Colin disappeared in a ball of flames. He closed his eyes and swallowed. Those images came back to haunt him every night in his dreams, but he *wouldn't* think of it in daylight. He'd go mad with the horror. Impulsively, he pulled Reenie to a stop and whirled her round to face him.

'Or maybe we should find somewhere more private?' he whispered.

'Where did that come from?' Reenie asked in astonishment. Jimmy had always been a perfect gentleman with her. In fact, sometimes she thought he was too much of a gentleman, that maybe he didn't find her as attractive as he claimed. But even so, she wasn't sure she was ready to take a step like that with him. And in the middle of the day too! It seemed indecent, somehow. What if she got pregnant? Would he want to marry her? She knew she wanted to marry him, but she wasn't so sure his feelings ran as deep as hers.

'I need you, Reens,' he said, tears in his eyes.

Reenie lifted a hand to his cheek. 'I know, love,' she said softly. 'But that's not good enough for me . . .' She hesitated. 'I want to know if you love me.'

Jimmy's blue eyes stared deep into her own and she could see herself reflected in the tears that were hovering on his lashes. Then he looked away.

'It's all right,' Reenie said softly, although her heart was breaking. 'I think I understand. You're still coming to terms with what happened. I still miss Daisy every day, so I know how you feel.'

Jimmy shook her hand off his arm. 'No. I really don't think you do. Sorry, Reenie, let's do lunch another day.' Then he walked away down Snargate Street.

Reenie stood for a moment, barely noticing as the crowds jostled by her. She was used to Jimmy's sudden mood swings – one moment kind and loving, the next distant and taciturn – and if she was honest she wasn't sure how much more she could take. Because sometimes the way he talked to her felt very much like rejection. Surely love shouldn't be so complicated?

# Chapter 24

Edie pulled the car to a jerky stop outside the hospital; Mr Pearson had taught her how to drive in this car a couple of years before, but she hadn't driven much since, so her skills were rusty. She threw open the door, ran up the drive and crashed into the main entrance. She knew the hospital well from her visits to Jasper, so she made straight for the stairs down to the basement where most of the wards were now situated.

'I've come to see Mr Pearson,' she gasped to the nurse at the desk by the door of the men's ward.

The woman flicked a glance over her. 'I'm afraid that won't be possible,' she said sternly.

'Why?'

'Mr Pearson is not allowed visitors.'

Edie paled. 'Is he that ill?'

'Excuse me.' The nurse got up from her chair and walked briskly down the aisle between the beds and Edie got the distinct impression that she'd only done that to avoid answering her question.

Edie looked along the row of beds, hoping to spot Mr Pearson's familiar face, but the only person she recognised was Jasper, who was sitting up in his bed, his eyes bandaged. She dithered for a moment, wondering whether he might know anything, but then decided the best person to ask was Lily.

Whirling round, she raced to the end of the corridor where she knew the canteen was situated. Pushing through the double doors, she searched each table, praying that Lily was on her break.

She was in luck. Over against the far wall, she spotted her sister sitting with her friends Dot and Vi.

'Lily!' Edie raced over.

Her sister looked up in surprise. 'What are you doing here?'

'It's Mr Pearson. He was hurt in the attack last night, but they won't let me see him.'

Lily frowned. 'But why not? I saw him first thing this morning and he seemed all right. A little fuzzy from the bump on the head, but his breathing had stabilised.'

'He's not there. You have to help me find him. There's a problem at the garage . . .' She glanced at the other two nurses, not willing to go into details in front of them.

'Hello to you too, Edie,' one of them said sarcastically.

Edie looked at her briefly. 'I don't have time for this, Vi,' she said.

Vi looked at the watch pinned to her chest. 'Then that makes two of us.' She smiled sweetly at Edie. 'I just don't have a second to spare to tell you what you need to know.'

'You know where he is?' Edie grabbed her arm. 'Have they let him out?'

Vi shook her hand off and tapped the watch. 'Like I said, no time.'

'Vi!' Lily said sharply. 'If you know something, tell her.'

'All right,' she huffed. 'Some old bloke got moved out of the men's ward just before I came on my break. They took him to one of the small rooms and no one's allowed to see him. In fact, there's a very dishy MP standing guard outside.' She smirked. 'Might go see if he wants anything.'

'What do you mean, he's being guarded?' Edie wailed. Was it possible that the policemen had found something suspicious at the garage?

'I dunno. I'm just a trainee. No one tells us anything. Unless, of course, it's Lily doing the asking.' She pouted.

Edie ground her teeth. She'd never much liked Vi. She was pretty with her slanted green eyes and blonde hair, but she was always scowling. She had no idea why Lily was friends with her.

Dot, the other nurse, rolled her eyes. 'You ever going to get rid of that plank of wood on your shoulder, Vi?' she asked. Then she stood up, smoothing down her frizzy brown hair. 'I know where he is. Come on.'

'I didn't say I wouldn't take you,' Vi said. 'But go ahead, Dot. Don't mind me.'

Dot grinned at her. 'I don't.'

Lily and Edie followed Dot down a long corridor, through some doors and down yet another corridor. Edie hadn't realised quite how enormous the hospital basement was and by the time they stopped, she realised that she was completely lost.

'There.' Dot pointed to where a man in khaki uniform, white belt and red beret stood out like a sore thumb against the drab grey walls.

Edie hurried up to him. 'The man in there, Mr Pearson, can I see him?'

The policeman looked Edie up and down, then his gaze moved over her shoulder to Lily and Dot. 'Depends,' he said with a smirk.

Edie sighed with annoyance. 'On what?'

'On whether you'll go for a drink with me.' He flicked a glance at Lily. 'But I'll take the blonde if you can't, I'm not fussy.'

'I'll go for a drink with you,' Dot called.

'No offence, love, but I'll pass.' His eyes ran over her frizzy brown hair and stout figure.

Lily stepped forward, her eyes sparking with anger. 'Listen, creep, will you let her see him or won't you? And you do know my friend was only joking, don't you?' She looked him over scathingly.

'I weren't,' Dot said. She walked up to the man and poked him in the chest. 'I reckon me and him would get on like a house on fire. He reminds me of my youngest brother. He thinks he's God's gift as well. And none of us have had the heart to tell him that he looks like a troll.'

The man grunted in annoyance. 'Troll, is it? Well, I hate to be the one to break it to yer, love . . .'

131

While he was distracted, Edie slipped past him and went into the room where she found Mr Pearson lying in bed looking pale and exhausted.

'Mr P!' She ran over to him. 'Are you all right? There's police at the garage, and now this. What's happening?'

He grasped her hand. 'I don't know, Edie. But whatever it is, you must know I ain't got nothing to do with it.'

'Of course you haven't!'

'You need to get hold of Bill,' he said urgently. 'And when you do, tell him—'

'Oy! Get out now before I arrest you an' all!' the man shouted, coming into the room and grabbing Edie's arm.

'I'll get help! Don't worry about a thing,' Edie said as she was dragged out. 'You're not alone!'

Outside the policeman growled, 'You better leave. And if you're not careful, I'll report you two to the Matron.'

The girls scurried away and when they got back to the main corridor, Edie turned to Lily. 'Can you ask Matron if I can see him?'

Lily shook her head. 'Even Matron's got no power over the military.'

Edie slumped against the wall. 'What am I going to do? It's all bloody Rodney's fault. I swear I could strangle him! He's the one who got the police involved!'

Lily glanced at her watch. 'I've still got half an hour of my break left, why don't we go see Jasper. Then you can tell us both exactly what's happened and he might be able to help. Thanks, Dot,' she said to her friend.

Dot nodded. 'Good luck,' she called after them as Edie and Lily hurried away. 'And let me know if I can do anything.'

When they arrived at the men's ward, Edie sprinted down the aisle. 'Jasper!' she cried urgently as she neared his bed. 'Jasper, I need your help!'

Jasper turned his head in her direction. 'Edie? What're you doin' here? You do know I'm neither use nor ornament in my current state, dontcha?' He gestured towards the bandages covering his eyes.

132

Edie sat down on the chair by his bed. 'It's Mr P,' she said. 'He's been arrested.'

Jasper gasped. 'What the bleedin' heck for?'

'I don't know! But he needs help.' Edie proceeded to tell him everything and by the time she'd finished, Jasper was shaking his head. 'No, no, no! Clive Pearson can't tell a lie to save his life. He'd die before betrayin' his country.'

'That's what I said, but no one's listening. I blame Rodney and his inflated sense of importance for setting the police on Mr P in the first place! I will *never* forgive him for this.'

'Hush, now,' Jasper admonished. 'Rodney can't do nothing but his duty, so there's no point blaming him.'

'But he *knows* Mr Pearson. He knows—'

'Edie!' Jasper held up his hand. 'All he knows is to do what's right according to the law of Rodney Castle. And that is to protect his family and to protect his country. He does everything by the book, so there's no point getting upset with him.'

'He's right. Rod was probably concerned for you. You know he hasn't done this maliciously,' Lilly added.

'Maybe not, but the result is he's ruining the life of one of the best men I know. I *have* to help him. Before I left, he told me to get hold of Bill. Which reminds me, did you know Walter Penfold, Jasper?'

'Not really, love. And what I did know, I didn't much like, so I steered clear.' He thought for a moment. 'Hey, how 'bout you go see that lawyer Mr Wainwright what's helped both Lily and Marianne. The man's sharp as a tack and if anyone can get to the bottom of this fiasco, then he's the one. He's got an office in Victoria Crescent.'

'Yes! That's a brilliant idea.' Edie leant forward and pulled him into a hug.

Jasper laughed, pleased. 'I only wish I could do more. These bloody bandages, though. When can I take them off, Lily?'

'You've only had them on five minutes. Be patient.'

'Hmph. I tell you, girls, I'm not sure I can wait much longer. I'm sick and tired of sittin' here like a lame duck.' He reached up to the bandages and started to pick at them.

'Stop it!' Lily grasped his wrists and pulled them away.

Jasper sat back sulkily, his arms folded and Lily gave him a quick kiss. 'Right, I've got to get back to work and, Edie, you have to go see Mr Wainwright.'

Edie stood. 'See you soon. And thank you.' Impulsively, she threw her hands round Jasper's shoulders and squeezed. 'Oh, it's so good to have you back,' she whispered.

Jasper patted her back. 'And it's good to be back, love. And if you run into any more problems, come and see me, all right?'

As the girls' footsteps moved away, Jasper sat back with a smile. Even when he was sitting here blind and useless it seemed the family still needed him. The thought warmed him, and he began to realise that even if his sight didn't return, he could still be useful. And if that Dr Charlie was right, maybe his life could go back to exactly the way it had been. He sighed. Well, maybe not *exactly*. Because after everything that had happened, he wasn't sure things between him and Nellie could ever be the same. Deep in his heart, he knew he couldn't hold on to his anger. But that didn't change the fact that there was no way he'd burden her with another invalid to care for. He'd seen what looking after Donald had done to her, and he'd rather die alone than see her suffer like that again.

# Chapter 25

Edie careened wildly down London Road, looking out for Victoria Crescent. It was close to the post office, so if she could park up there she could talk to the lawyer before sending a telegram to Bill.

Without checking to see if anyone was coming towards her, she turned the car violently to the right, narrowly missing a pedestrian, and pulled up outside the address that Jasper had given her. She sat for a moment to catch her breath, her head on the steering wheel. Her hands were shaking, she realised, and the nausea was back. But considering the last few stressful hours, she shouldn't be surprised. Taking a deep breath, she gathered her courage and opened the door.

When she rang the bell on the neat door set in the Georgian terrace, however, it was to be told by a terrifying woman wearing a long, old-fashioned black dress, her grey hair styled in an elaborate bun, that Mr Wainwright was away visiting his sister for the next few days. Her stomach sank. 'I really need to speak to him,' she said urgently. 'Clive Pearson from the garage has been arrested, and he needs his help.'

'Mr Pearson, you say?' the woman said, her manner softening slightly. 'Dear, dear, he's always seemed such a kind man.'

'He is! Will you get a message to Mr Wainwright?' Edie asked.

'I'll do my best,' she said, 'but I can't promise anything.' Then she shut the door in Edie's face.

Suppressing a scream of frustration, Edie hurried away towards the post office. Hopefully she'd get more joy from Bill. Mr P had said he'd be finishing his training before New Year, so perhaps he could come to Dover to help her.

Standing at the post office counter, Edie chewed on the end of a pencil as she contemplated what to write.

Finally, as she didn't have enough money on her to say too much, she decided to keep it as short as possible. Because what she really needed was to talk to him. Bending over the paper, she wrote:

Bill,
Fire at the garage. Your uncle in hospital. Your dad also here. We need to talk.
Edie

After she'd handed the paper to the telegraphist with the details of Bill's RAF station, she turned to go and nearly bumped into a girl with shiny black hair who was just entering. They both apologised before looking at each other.

'Susan Blake?' Edie said wonderingly.

'Edie Castle?' the girl answered, a grin spreading over her face.

Then they both started to laugh as they fell into each other's arms.

'I can't believe it's you,' Edie said finally. 'I haven't seen you for ten years!' Susan had been one of her very best friends until her parents had moved away from the area and they'd lost touch.

'Blimey, girl, it's good to see you. I'm staying at my aunt and uncle's and Aunt Mary told me you was at the garage. I was gonna come see you, but I've not had a chance yet – I only arrived yesterday.'

The smile left Edie's face. She'd forgotten that Susan was Colin Guthrie's cousin. She must be mourning him too. 'I'm sorry about Colin. We all loved him so much. How are your aunt and uncle?'

Susan sighed. 'Heartbroken. We all are. He was such a lovely bloke. Aunt Mary's built a little shrine to him in his room and spends all her spare time in there. It's so sad.'

'Have you got time to talk?' Edie asked.

'Not right now. I've got to post this parcel then get back to the bakery.'

'How about we meet for a drink at the Oak tonight? Say seven?'

'Love to. I've got so much to tell you.' Susan smiled and waggled her left hand where a small emerald glittered on her ring finger.

'Oh!' Edie laughed. 'I want you to tell me *everything*.'

'Don't worry, I will.' She winked at Edie then hurried towards the counter.

Bumping into Susan had momentarily driven Edie's problems from her mind, but she felt the worry and panic return as she left the post office and she had to lean against the wall as nausea swirled in her stomach and the world spun uncomfortably around her.

'You all right, love?' a woman walking past asked.

'Y-yes . . . Yes. I'm fine, thank you. I just felt faint for a moment.'

The woman peered closely at her pale face, then smiled sympathetically. 'Not to worry, it'll soon pass.'

Edie smiled. 'If only I could be sure.'

The woman patted her arm. 'I've had five of me own, so take it from me.'

The flaming cheek, Edie thought indignantly as she watched the woman walk away, did she look that fat? She looked down at herself, acknowledging that the donkey jacket wasn't the most flattering garment. Still, it could be worse, she supposed – she could actually be pregnant. The thought brought Edie up short as she counted back over the weeks. Oh God . . . surely life couldn't be that cruel!

# Chapter 26

With shaking hands, Edie started the ignition, then steered carefully back on to London Road, her mind full of the possibility that, on top of everything else, she could be pregnant with Greg's child. Her stomach roiled at the thought and she swerved into the kerb, oblivious to the beeps of the truck behind her. She turned off the engine and sat still, eyes squeezed shut as she breathed deeply, trying to overcome her panic. She'd missed two monthlies, she realised, but that wasn't unusual for her.

She took a deep breath. 'One thing at a time, Edie,' she murmured, repeating Mr Pearson's favourite mantra. Her boss needed her more right now, so that is what she would concentrate on. She'd deal with the rest once she knew he was safe. For now, though, she needed to get the car back to the garage before the petrol ran out – which would also give her a chance to talk to the MPs and hopefully discover what it was they'd found.

❧

When she steered the car on to the forecourt, she noticed with alarm that there seemed to be several people scurrying around. Rod, however, was nowhere to be seen, which was probably just as well. No matter what Jasper had said, she was still furious with her brother.

She got out of the car and walked towards the office, but she'd gone no more than a few steps when her way was barred.

'No unauthorised entry,' a policeman said pompously.

'But I need to get my things,' she said.

'Sorry, orders are orders. You'll have to leave.'

Edie sighed but did as she was told, then, taking a quick peek over her shoulder to make sure no one was watching, she ran round to the back of the building. She knew she wouldn't get far, but she was desperate to see what was happening inside. Staying close to the wall, she bent low to avoid the windows and made her way to the back door. The Anderson shelter seemed to have been dismantled and the bunks, benches and tables now lay discarded outside.

Reaching the back door, she turned the handle, then slowly pushed it open.

'What do you think you're doing, miss?' It was one of the policemen she had met earlier.

Edie jumped. 'I, er ... I need to get my things,' she said again, glancing around at the mess in the office. Every drawer in the filing cabinet had been pulled out and emptied onto the floor. 'You could have been a bit tidier!' she exclaimed. 'This is going to take me ages to sort out.'

'I don't think you need worry about that,' the man said snidely. 'I doubt the place will open again. But what you do need to worry about, Miss Castle, is that you are now trespassing on military property. And your brother can't protect you forever.'

'What do you mean?' she asked.

'I mean, if your brother hadn't vouched for you, and got the backing of the admiral himself, you, miss, would be sitting under guard, just like your boss is.'

Edie gasped. 'You can't be serious?'

'Deadly. Now go.'

Without another word, Edie whirled round and ran out. If Rodney could protect *her*, she thought angrily, why couldn't he extend that to Mr Pearson! Barely noticing the rain that had started to fall, she crossed the road and ran towards Harold Passage, a steep path that led directly down to Castle Street. She was running so fast she nearly didn't notice that the end of the passage was blocked by debris. Skidding to a halt, she glanced up to her left; St James's Church had taken another hit, and bricks and timber lay across the path. Yet, on the other side of the passage, the White Horse pub remained untouched.

The church must be cursed, she reflected. It had been damaged in the last war as well. On one of his very infrequent outings, her dad had brought her up here to watch the workmen restoring it.

'Doesn't matter what they do, it'll never be the same,' he'd said mournfully. 'Nothing lasts forever, Edie; not churches, not life, not love. Remember that.'

Goose pimples broke out all over her body and she shivered; it had felt as though the words had been whispered directly into her ear, and yet the passage was empty. Was she going mad? she wondered. First the nightmares, and now this. She shook her head. She didn't have time for this. Mr Pearson was languishing in captivity, and it seemed that she was the only person he could rely on to get him out. And she was determined not to let him down.

As Edie approached the café's back gate, there was the sudden telltale whistle of a shell as it flew over her head. She ducked instinctively, putting her hands over her head. Then cursing, she stood straight again and began to run as the familiar flash of panic made her heart flutter. No matter how many shells landed on the town, she never felt prepared. As a loud crash reverberated through the air, the siren let out two sharp bursts. The shell warning.

'Shelter's this way!' she shouted, pushing open the back gate and standing aside to allow people to pass. Once everyone was in, she followed them into the kitchen and down the steps to the basement.

'Edie? What the devil are you doin' here?' Her mother's voice greeted her the minute she walked in.

Edie opened her mouth to reply, but she found she didn't know what to say. Everything was such a terrible mess – Mr P arrested, her job seemingly gone, Jasper sitting in hospital, his eyes covered with bandages and unable to help her, and . . . She squeezed her eyes shut as she resisted the temptation to put her hand on her stomach. She would *not* think about that right now.

'Edie?' her mother said in a softer tone. 'What's happened, love?'

She shook her head. 'Oh, Mum . . . I-I don't know.' Then she burst into tears.

Marianne rushed over and put an arm around her shoulders. 'Come and sit down.'

Edie sat down at the table and accepted the cup of tea her sister pushed across to her.

Her mother took the chair opposite and reached for her hand. 'Do you want to tell me about it?'

'I don't know where to start.' She glanced around, then lowered her voice. 'Last night—'

'Is Clive all right?' her mother interrupted. 'Ron Hames told us he'd been taken to hospital.'

'He's . . . he's . . . Oh, Mum, he's been arrested.' She whispered the last, not wanting the whole basement to hear.

'Arrested?!' Nellie squeaked. 'Why?'

'Shhh,' she hissed. But it was too late. Everyone had heard and Ron Hames stood up and came towards her.

'What's that about Clive Pearson?' he asked, reaching into his jacket for his notebook and pencil.

'None of your business!' Nellie exclaimed. She threw an apologetic look at her daughter. 'Edie just said that he's being rested, didn't you, love?'

If the situation weren't so dire, Edie would have laughed.

Ron sat down next to her. 'Edie, I understand that you don't want everyone to hear, but if you have some news, I'd be grateful if you could share it with me.'

'Please go away,' Edie said. 'I don't want to talk to you.'

'You heard her, Ron. Get lost.'

'With all due respect, Mrs C, I can't exactly leave, can I?'

141

As if on cue, the walls shook just as the basement door opened and a man wearing a smart overcoat and peaked cap came in.

'Afternoon,' he said politely. 'Hope you don't mind me joinin' you, but didn't fancy me chances out there.' He caught sight of Edie and smiled. 'We meet again, Miss Castle.'

Edie scowled at him. 'I thought you'd be gone by now.'

'Still waiting for the boss. And this little lot'll hold her up even more.'

'Who are you?' Nellie asked.

'Walter Penfold at your service,' he said, glancing around, looking for a place to sit.

Edie was watching him carefully and she could have sworn that when he caught sight of Hester, he gave her the ghost of a wink. She switched her attention to the woman and was surprised to see a flash of fear cross her face. But as quickly as it had arrived, it was gone.

When Edie looked back at Walter, he had taken a seat on some cushions on the opposite side of the room where Lou Carter had shuffled along to make room for him.

'Walter Penfold?' Nellie asked.

'Mr Pearson's brother-in-law,' Edie clarified.

'Of course! Knew I'd seen him before. He were never around much, then soon as his wife died he upped and left, taking poor Bill with him.'

'I need to speak to him,' Edie said. 'I'll explain everything later.' She stood up and walked over to Walter. 'You wouldn't mind swapping seats, would you, Mrs Carter?' she asked politely.

Lou glanced between them then gave her a knowing smile. 'Bit old for you, ain't he? But be my guest. Bit too polished for my taste.' She got up and went to join Nellie at the table.

'What are you doing here?' Edie whispered to the man, swallowing back nausea as the strong musky scent of his cologne made her stomach rebel.

'Like I said, I got all day to kill, so I was just takin' a little walk around. Poor old town's lookin' a bit ropy these days.'

'War does that to a place,' Edie said sarcastically. 'But listen, the army's searching the garage and won't let me back in – they say it's been seized. And Mr Pearson's been arrested. Why would they do that?' she asked.

For a moment, Walter looked startled, but then his smirk returned. 'Well, it were bound to catch up with him sooner or later.'

'What do you mean? He's never done anything wrong in his life.'

Walter stared at her steadily. 'Everyone's got a past, love. Even good old Clive.'

Edie snorted. 'The only past Mr P has is one of hard work, honesty and kindness. He's done *nothing* wrong, and I'm going to prove it. Will you help me?'

'Me? I'm just your common or garden driver with a fancy uniform. No one listens to someone like me. An' they won't listen to a little grease monkey like you, neither.'

Edie's eyes narrowed. 'Then I'll make them.'

Walter sighed. 'I'd leave it, if I were you, love. Look, I know how much you like the bloke, but he's no saint. A few years ago Clive got hisself involved with that Moseley's lot. Went up to London in a black shirt and everythin'. Nasty they are. They don't like Jews an' they don't believe in this war, and they'll do anything to end it.'

'What are you talking about?' Edie was astonished.

'You never knew? Well, that's Clive for you. Not a big talker, but still waters run deep. I'll bet you any money he's been up to his old tricks and it's caught up with him.'

Edie felt as if she'd been punched in the stomach and she sat back against the wall, her mind whirling as she tried to make sense of what Walter had said. She'd worked closely with Mr Pearson for nearly four years, and lived with him for the last few months; if he was involved in that sort of thing, she'd know about it. Then again, he had made those remarks about Churchill just the day before. But so what? Just cos he didn't like the prime minister didn't mean he'd done anything wrong.

'You're lying,' she hissed. 'I think someone tried to kill him last night, and now suddenly he's been arrested at exactly the time you come back into his life. Is this your doing?'

Walter laughed. 'You've got a good imagination, love. But I got no interest in anything Clive does, nor do I have a reason to kill him. For a start, why would I risk it?'

He had a point, she supposed. But it didn't matter what he said, she just didn't trust him. She glanced around the room, noticing that Hester was watching them, but as soon as Edie caught her eye, she looked away. Edie frowned. Everything had been fine until she'd turned up yesterday. But then Hester had no reason to harm Mr Pearson, either. Unless ... there'd been that tiny acknowledgement between her and Walter earlier. Were they in this together?

She shook her head. She was being ridiculous. Mr Pearson ran a small garage in a war-torn town; he wasn't rich, he wasn't influential – he just got on with his job and did it well. She shut her eyes and leant her head back.

'The question I'm asking meself, though,' Walter whispered to her, 'is how come you're still here?'

'What do you mean?'

'Well, with you an' Clive bein' thick as thieves, why are you sittin' here, while he's banged up.'

'Neither of us have done anything wrong,' Edie replied fiercely. But it was unsettling to realise that if they had any suspicions about her, it was very unlikely they'd listen to a word she said.

144

# Chapter 27

Edie sat in silence for the rest of the raid, breathing through her mouth as she tried to avoid the smell of the man next to her, and aware all the time of her mother's concerned gaze and the curious stare of Ron Hames.

When the all-clear finally sounded, Nellie stood up and clapped her hands. 'Sorry, folks, café's shut now.'

'But I didn't finish me stew,' an old man said.

'Then we'll put it in a bowl and you can take it home.'

'It'll be cold. I hate me food cold, an' me leccy ain't been workin' for weeks.'

'Oh, stop moaning. Food's food, and you're lucky to get anything. Now get on with you.'

Walter chuckled. 'Your ma's a right one, ain't she? She should watch out, though. A gob like that can get you in trouble.' He stood up and tipped his hat at Edie. 'Maybe I'll see you around. And don't worry about Clive. The man's a survivor.'

Edie watched as Walter made for the door, keeping an eye out to see if he acknowledged Hester in any way, but the two didn't even glance at each other. Perhaps she'd imagined it before. She remembered the letter he'd shown her that had had a Folkestone postmark – maybe Walter had been a client at some point, which would explain why they'd kept away from each other.

Once everyone had left, she stood up and wearily made her way out of the basement, wishing she'd not arranged to meet Susan tonight.

Because what she really needed was a plate of her sister's delicious food and then a long sleep – undisturbed by nightmares, sirens and fires.

As she walked into the kitchen, though, her arm was caught by Ron Hames. 'Can we talk?' he asked.

Edie shook her arm free. 'What about?'

'Clive Pearson and what's happened at the garage.'

'If you're so curious, why don't you go up there yourself.'

'All right, then, perhaps you could tell me about that Walter Penfold.'

'I don't know him,' she said dismissively.

'Really? Coulda fooled me, the way you two were whispering to each other.'

'Look, it's none of your business, all right?' she snapped as she brushed past him.

'If Clive Pearson's been doing stuff he shouldn't then it's very much my business,' he responded persistently.

'He's done *nothing* wrong! He's got more honesty in his little finger than you have in your entire body. Leave him alone!'

She turned away, desperate to escape upstairs, but her mother was standing in her way. 'Are you going to tell me what's going on?'

'I'll tell you later,' she said, very aware of the journalist close behind her. 'Once everyone's gone.' She inclined her head towards the man.

Nellie nodded. 'All right, love, you get upstairs. You look all in. As for you, Ron, leave Clive Pearson alone. The man wouldn't say boo to a goose, so before you go printing any of your lies, get your facts straight.'

'That's exactly what I was trying to do, but Edie isn't inclined to talk to me.'

'Wise girl, my daughter. Takes after her mum. Now, I take it you're busy and need to get on?' She indicated the door. 'And maybe you'll be too busy to come in tomorrow as well?'

Ron laughed. 'All right, all right. Even a thick-skinned old hack like me can take a hint. I promise, I'll be as silent as the grave.'

Nellie snorted. 'The grave's the only thing that will shut you up.'

Chuckling, the man left by the back door.

Hester appeared just then wearing her coat and looking pale and anxious. 'I gotta go out, Nell. Won't be long.'

She left before Nellie could reply.

'Where's she off to in such a hurry?' Gladys poked her head out of the pantry. 'There's something about that woman I don't trust,' she said darkly.

'Yes, Glad, you've mentioned that fact once or twice.' Nellie rolled her eyes.

'And I might have known she'd disappear just as there's cleaning up to be done,' Gladys grumbled.

Nellie sighed and shook her head. 'Never known Glad to take such a powerful dislike to anyone,' she said to Edie. 'Now, go rest and I'll be up soon as I can.'

Edie walked up the stairs, wondering whether Gladys had a point. Because why was Hester so anxious to go out all of a sudden, and did it have anything to do with Walter?

She'd got only halfway up the stairs when her mother called to her. 'Edie! Telegram!'

She rushed back down and snatched the paper from her mother's hand.

'Who's it from?'

'I don't know, do I?' she snapped as she tore the envelope open. Inside was a message from Bill.

WILL CALL OAK. 6.30 TONIGHT.

BILL

From the swiftness of the reply and the fact he wanted to speak to her as soon as possible, Edie guessed that he was as worried as she was. It made her feel a bit better to realise she wasn't completely alone in this. Hopefully he could help her work out what on earth was going on.

# Chapter 28

Lily gazed up at the small circle of yellow light on the ceiling of Jasper's bedroom. She'd taken to using her father's small flat above the forge in Castle Street to study in and now the collection of *Grey's Anatomy* that Charlie had given her – her most prized possession – was lined up neatly on a shelf in the sitting room. But in truth it wasn't the only reason she came here. She felt a small twinge of guilt as she turned her head on the pillow. Charlie was fast asleep beside her, his long lashes lying against his tanned cheeks, and in repose, the dimples at the side of his mouth had softened. She rolled on to her stomach and stroked his dark hair back from his face, her heart aching at the realisation that this was possibly the last time they'd be together like this. She felt tears rise at the thought.

God, she was a fool. This man had shown her nothing but care and concern and love. Even when she had rejected him, he hadn't held it against her. So what was holding her back?

Charlie's eyes opened and he smiled sleepily at her as she leant down and kissed him softly on the mouth.

'I've been thinking,' she whispered softly.

Charlie didn't say anything, just stared steadily into her eyes.

'I made a mistake.'

Charlie turned on to his side and propped himself up on one elbow. 'What are you saying?'

'I think I'm saying . . . No, I know I'm saying that if the offer's still open, then I'd like to accept.'

An enormous smile broke out on Charlie's face and he swept her into his arms, kissing her deeply. Finally, he pulled back. 'Please tell me you mean it! You won't get cold feet and send me a Dear John letter?'

Lily shook her head and nestled against his chest. 'Never. I could never find another man like you. Just because I found you so early in my life, doesn't mean it's the wrong thing. It just means I'm very, very lucky.'

Charlie leapt out of bed and hurried to the corner of the room where his uniform jacket had been hastily discarded. After rummaging in the pocket, he pulled out the box that he'd carried with him since Christmas Eve in the hope that Lily would change her mind. She'd never even seen the ring, he realised, suddenly nervous.

He opened the box and took it out. 'Close your eyes and hold out your hand,' he said as he walked naked back to the bed.

Lily did as she was told, holding her left hand out towards him.

Gently, he slid the ring on to her finger, pleased to see it fitted perfectly. He kissed her hand. 'You can open them now,' he whispered.

Instead of looking down, Lily stared straight into Charlie's warm brown eyes, mesmerised by the love that was shining from them.

'Don't keep me in suspense,' he urged. 'Tell me if you like it.'

'It doesn't matter. You chose it for me, so I know I'll love it.' She grinned. 'Are you scared?'

Charlie looked sheepish. 'Not half as scared as I was the first time I asked you.'

Lily reached up her left hand to stroke his cheek. 'I'm sorry I hurt you,' she whispered. But then her attention was caught by the ring on her finger and she gasped.

'Oh, it's beautiful, Charlie!' She stared transfixed at the tiny diamonds arranged in the shape of a flower on a slim gold band.

He blushed. 'I'd have liked to get you something a little more fancy, but . . .' He shrugged.

Lily twisted her hand, the tiny diamonds throwing multicoloured rainbows around the room. Suddenly, tears came to her eyes and she started to sob.

'Hey.' Charlie pulled her into his arms. 'If you hate it, I can take it back and you can choose your own.'

Lily shook her head. 'It's perfect,' she wailed. 'I love it so much!' She fell against him, the tears falling faster now, wetting the dark hair on his chest.

'Are you sure?' He kissed the top of her head. 'I never want to make you unhappy, my Lily.' He grasped her shoulders and moved her away. 'Look at me, darling,' he whispered.

Obediently, she opened her eyes, blinking away the tears.

'I love you. I could spend the rest of my life searching and I would *never* find a girl as perfect for me as you are. And when this war is over, you will study to be a doctor and I will help you. And I promise I will never ever hold you back. Do you understand?'

She smiled tremulously. 'Thank you,' she whispered. 'Thank you, thank you, thank you!' She threw herself back into his arms, feeling happier than she had in months. She knew she was doing the right thing. Because with Charlie by her side, she could achieve anything. Soon, their kisses became more urgent and they fell back on the bed.

Sometime later, Charlie sighed. 'I have to go.'

Lily nodded. 'So do I. I can't bear that this is the last time we'll be together like this.'

'It's not the last time, my love. It's the first time. The first of many times. If I wasn't leaving tomorrow, we could get married straight-away. Maybe get a train up to Gretna Green.' He grinned wickedly. 'In fact, I rather like that idea.'

Lily laughed. 'That sounds romantic. Let's do it next time you're home.'

'Whatever you want, love. I'd be happy doing it at the bus stop if that's what it took.'

Lily pursed her lips. 'I'm not sure your idea of romance quite matches mine, Charlie Alexander.'

'Every moment with you is romantic to me.'

Lily kissed him again then reluctantly untangled herself from him. After dressing hastily, they left the flat and went outside, standing in the doorway of the forge for a few moments, holding tight to each other, secure in the knowledge that no one could see them in the pitch-black.

'Thank you for saying yes,' Charlie whispered.

'Thank you for being so patient,' Lily replied. 'I promise I will do everything I can to be the best wife in the world.'

'You don't have to do anything special. I just want you as you are. Don't change a thing.'

With Charlie's arm wrapped around her shoulders, they walked down towards Market Square, stopping on the corner of Church Street.

'When will I see you again?' Lily whispered.

He sighed. 'I wish I knew. But even though we're not together, you'll always be right here with me. In my heart, in my mind.'

In response, Lily reached up and kissed him on the lips, then he turned quickly and walked away.

Lily stood for a long while staring into the dark, her emotions mixed. She was deliriously happy at the thought of being Charlie's wife. But tomorrow he would be gone, and she didn't know when, or even if, she would see him again.

# Chapter 29

The smoky fug of the pub enveloped Edie as she walked into the Royal Oak later that evening. Mavis was standing at her usual spot behind the bar, her brown hair in curlers under a blue scarf.

'Hello, Edie, my love,' she greeted her warmly. 'You meeting your handsome pilot tonight?'

'Not tonight, Mrs Woodbridge, but I am waiting on a phone call from Bill Penfold. I hope it's all right for him to call here.'

Mavis raised her eyebrows. '*Two* pilots? Some might say that's being greedy,' she chuckled.

'It's not like that,' Edie giggled as Mavis pulled a pint of bitter for a grizzled old man in a fisherman's jumper that smelt as though it hadn't been washed in a while.

'What's it like, then?' Mavis slid the pint across the polished oak, taking the coins the man held out, then turned her attention back to Edie.

Edie waited for the man to leave, then leant over the bar. 'I sent him a telegram about the fire at the garage. And now he wants to talk to me. What do you know about Walter Penfold?' she asked.

Mavis tutted. 'Walter? He used to come in here when Iris were alive. Finger in every pie and a right one for the ladies. Not many that'd welcome him after the way he treated that poor woman. Don't tell me he's back?'

Edie nodded. 'I saw him yesterday and today. All dressed up in a chauffeur's uniform and driving a fancy car. An' he said some stuff about Mr Pearson . . .'

'Did he now? Well, I can tell you that him and Clive never saw eye to eye. Mostly cos he were such a bad husband. An' there were some kerfuffle over poor Iris's will, but for the life of me I can't remember what. Last time I saw him, he sat over there' – she nodded towards the end of the bar – 'muttering darkly about being cheated.'

Edie frowned. 'When was this?'

'Ooh, it must have been not long after Iris died . . . About ten years ago, maybe. Then he upped and left, taking poor Bill with him.'

'What do you mean by a finger in every pie?'

'Oh, you know . . . wheeling and dealing, this and that.'

'Sort of like Lou Carter's Terence, then?'

Mavis nodded. 'Exactly that. Which reminds me, I heard through one of my regulars – a copper – that the police have got their eye on him.'

'Surely that wasn't Roger?'

'As if Roger would know what was goin' on. No, another bloke. So if you could just let your mum know . . .'

Edie was surprised. 'Why does Mum need to know about that?'

Mavis smiled slightly and shook her head. 'Nothin', love. Ignore me. Anyway, come on through if you want to wait for the call.' She lifted the flap in the bar and Edie ducked through to the back where there was a small office with a wooden desk, piled with neat stacks of paper. On one corner, in pride of place, was a large black Bakelite telephone. It started to ring almost as soon as she sat down and she snatched up the receiver.

'Bill?' she said urgently.

'Edie!' The line was crackly. 'What the hell's going on? How's Uncle Clive?'

'He's . . .' Edie hesitated, not sure how she could break this gently. 'He's been arrested, Bill,' she whispered, glancing over her shoulder to ensure no one was listening.

'What?! But why?'

Edie explained what she knew, but really it wasn't a lot. 'And they've seized the garage. I don't know what to do! When he gets out, there'll be no business to come back to.'

153

There was a long silence, then Bill said, 'You said my dad was there.'

'Yes. And he's—' She stopped, suddenly aware that Bill might love his dad.

'It's all right, Edie, whatever you've got to say, I won't be shocked.'

'I don't trust him. He's working as a chauffeur and first time I saw him was yesterday. Then this morning he turns up again . . . I'm sorry, Bill, I know he's your dad, but there's something fishy going on.'

Bill didn't respond to her statement, instead asking, 'Where's he working? Last time I heard from him he was in Folkestone.'

'He wouldn't say. But I think I might know.' Edie closed her eyes as she said that, the sick feeling returning to her stomach.

'Tell me about the fire.'

'I thought the firebombs caused it, but it doesn't seem like it was them. And your uncle had a nasty bang on the back of his head.'

'Listen, see what you can find out. I've got my final exam tomorrow, then I have some leave and I'll come straight down.'

'How am I meant to find out anything?'

'I don't know. Use your imagination!'

Before Edie could reply, a voice came on the line. 'Time's up, caller.'

'I'll be back New Year's Eve,' Bill managed, before the line went dead.

Edie stared at the phone for a long time, wondering what on earth he expected her to do. She replaced the handset and glanced up at the clock, pleased to realise that Susan would be there soon; she'd never needed to see her old friend more than she did now. Even if it was only for the distraction she'd provide.

'Everything all right, love?' Mavis asked as Edie walked back into the saloon.

'Not really. He didn't know his dad was here either. He doesn't seem too pleased about it.'

Mavis grunted. 'I'm not surprised. He led poor Iris a merry dance, and no son likes to see their mother upset. Just like no mother likes to see their child's heart broken.'

Edie felt guilty as she realised she'd not even asked Mavis about her son. 'How is Stan? And little Maggie?'

Mavis's smile slipped. 'Like I said: his heart's broken. But they're as well as can be expected, love. I don't think he'll ever get over Daisy, though. And nor will I.' She blinked back the tears that had sprung into her eyes, before looking over Edie's head. 'Yes, love, what can I get you?'

Edie glanced round. The pub had filled up since she'd arrived and a group of men in navy uniform now stood behind her. She spotted Susan sitting in one of the snugs by the door, her eyes fixed on it as she studiously avoided the stares of a couple of soldiers who were hovering nearby; Edie could tell it wouldn't be long before they made their move.

'I'll see you later, Mrs W,' she said.

Mavis winked at her, then looked back at the man she was serving. Edie was full of admiration for her; she knew she hadn't imagined the woman's tears, but looking at her now, no one would ever guess at the tragedy she was hiding.

Hurrying over to Susan, Edie dropped into the seat opposite her. 'Sorry I'm late,' she said. Then she glared at the men who'd been leering at her friend. 'And you two can sling your hook. As you can see, she has company tonight.'

The men nudged each other. 'We don't mind watching,' one of them said with a smirk.

'I bet you wouldn't, cos watching's about as close as you'll ever get. Now go on, hop it.'

The men scowled and turned their backs. 'Creeps,' she muttered.

Susan giggled. 'I forgot what a temper you had. Even when we was little you used to fly off the handle at the smallest thing.'

'Did I? I just remember being sad. And after you left I was even sadder.' She reached over the table and took Susan's hands in hers. 'It's so good to see you, Sue. Tell me everything that's happened since you left. And why you've come back. I mean, it's not the first place people would choose to come.'

155

'Yeah, well . . . I have my reasons.' Susan blushed prettily as she held her left hand up, showing the gold ring set with a tiny emerald she'd shown Edie earlier.

Edie took her hand and examined it. 'Lovely,' she said. 'I hope he's worth coming into a war zone for.'

Susan's shiny black hair gleamed under the electric lights and her brown eyes sparkled as she leant forward, a huge smile on her face. 'Oh, he's just perfect. Clever, handsome and everything I ever dreamt of. But . . .' Susan's smile faded.

'But?'

'I haven't heard from him in months. He came back from Dunkirk and then got sent here. He promised he'd write, but there's not been a word. I asked his mum and dad and he's been writing to them, so I know he's alive. I love him so much, Edie. I don't understand why he's stopped writing. I'm starting to think he might have met someone else.'

Edie squeezed her hand in sympathy. 'How did you meet him?'

'My mum and dad have a grocery shop in Cambridge. His parents run the butcher's next door. I've known him for years . . . I've been asking around, but so far no one knows him. That's mostly why I'm here – to track down Charlie.'

Edie looked up at that. 'Charlie?' she said, startled. But then there were an awful lot of men called Charlie, so it could be anyone.

'He's so dreamy, Edie. And he's a doctor!'

Edie's stomach started to swirl. Surely she couldn't mean Lily's Charlie?

'What's his name?' she asked faintly.

'Dr Charlie Alexander. You ever come across him?' she asked eagerly.

# Chapter 30

For a moment, Edie thought she must have misheard. 'Charlie Alexander?' she repeated slowly.

'That's right,' Susan said. 'Do you know him?'

Edie shook her head, as anger started to rise within her. Charlie had fooled them all, the pig! Thank God Lily had turned him down! And when she saw him next, she'd be giving him a piece of her mind!

'Have you tried the hospitals?' she asked faintly.

'Yeah. They say there is a doctor of that name, but he don't work there. But they won't tell me where he is. All this secrecy is stupid! I mean, what harm could I do?'

'There are lots of secrets in this town, it seems,' Edie said distractedly while inside her thoughts raged. If this was true, what was she going to do about Lily? Should she tell her? Or should she just let things run their natural course? After all, the man was leaving tomorrow so maybe he'd stop communicating with Lily, just as he seemed to have done with Susan.

Then she pictured her sister's face when she was with Charlie – her eyes shining, her cheeks flushed. No matter that Lily had turned down his proposal, it didn't change the fact that her sister was head over heels in love with the man, and finding out that Charlie was already engaged to someone else would devastate her. But how could she prevent her finding out? she wondered. Because at some point Lily and Susan's paths would cross, and with Lily working at the hospital, she couldn't imagine her friend wouldn't ask her if she knew Dr Charlie Alexander.

There was a loud shout from the bar area and Edie looked over to see her brother Bert standing in the middle of a group of men, pint in hand, as he regaled them with some story. No doubt it was made up, she thought, but he'd be the perfect distraction right now.

'Remember my brother Bert, Sue?' she asked, pointing over at him.

Susan looked over. 'Course I do . . . But I don't remember him looking like that! He's almost as handsome as my Charlie.'

Edie stood up. 'Oy, Bert!'

Her brother looked over and grinned, then his gaze shifted to Susan and his smile became more seductive.

God, he's a smarmy bastard, Edie thought, glancing apologetically at her friend. But Susan was smiling back at him, her cheeks bright red. And suddenly Edie could see the solution to the problem: if Bert could make Susan fall in love with him and get her to break her engagement, then maybe Lily would never have to find out that the man she'd fallen for had been lying to her all the time. And hopefully over time the two would drift apart, and Lily could find someone more worthy of her love. She smiled grimly. Yes, it was perfect.

She beckoned him over, and after a brief word with his mates, he strolled up to the table.

'Hello, little sis. And who do we have here?'

'You must remember Susan?'

Bert looked blank and Edie waved her hand. 'Never mind, we were friends when we were little. But you'll never guess what, she's Colin's cousin! Staying with the Guthries while she looks for her fiancé . . .'

Bert held his hand to his chest. 'I should have known a beautiful girl like you would be taken,' he said with mock sorrow.

Susan fluttered her eyelashes. 'Afraid so, Bert. I'm hurt you don't remember me.'

'Don't worry, I won't be forgetting you again.'

'Her fiancé is called Charlie Alexander,' Edie said meaningfully. Bert's smile dropped and he turned to look at his sister. 'Do you know anyone with that name?' she asked, holding his gaze and shaking her head ever so slightly.

Bert caught on quickly. 'Never heard of him. But I can promise you one thing, if I do find him, I'll beat him to a pulp.'

'That wouldn't be very nice, would it?' Susan giggled.

'Well, the man should know better than to steal *my* girl. Hold on while I get me drink. Because you an' me, Susan, need to get better acquainted.'

Edie smiled at her brother and he gave her the smallest nod back as he walked away.

When he returned, Bert focused his bright blue eyes on Susan, and for the next fifteen minutes, Edie watched in admiration as her brother worked his magic. Blimey, he's good at this, she thought. For a moment she felt a pang of pity for her friend, who didn't seem to stand a chance against her brother. But surely it was better to manipulate her into breaking off her engagement than to tell her the truth. And the same went for Lily. Once Charlie had gone, Lily might forget all about him. And if she didn't, Edie would find another way to help take her mind off him.

Were all men liars? she wondered. Apart from Jasper and Mr Pearson, and maybe Rodney and Jimmy, the answer was probably yes. As for Bert – she watched as he took Susan's hand and kissed it gallantly, staring deep into her eyes as he did so – he was most definitely a liar. But at least on this occasion he was lying for a good cause.

Her stomach grumbled and she realised she was starving. After the raid, she'd only just had time to get changed and run over to the pub. 'Well, much as I've loved sitting here watching you flirt with my old friend, Bert, I'm starving, so I need to get home.'

Bert looked up. 'Sorry, Edie, but how could I resist such a beautiful woman.' He smiled at Susan.

Edie rolled her eyes as her friend giggled again. She wasn't sure whether it was the fact that Susan was engaged to her sister's boy-friend, or the way she had succumbed so quickly to her brother's charms, but she had a feeling that she and her old friend had much less in common than they used to.

'Bert was just telling me about the free concert for the troops on New Year's Eve at the Hippodrome. Sounds like fun.'

Edie smiled. 'Yeah. Marianne's husband Alfie will be playing his trumpet, so we're all going. Hey, how about you come too?'

'Oh . . . I'm not sure I can. I feel I should stay in with my aunt and uncle.' Edie could tell that Susan was desperate to go, but perhaps it was for the best. Lily would be there, and she really didn't want those two bumping into each other.

'Well, seeing as you're engaged, maybe you're right,' she said.

Susan blushed and glanced at her ring. 'Oh, er, yes. Promise to let me know if you come across Charlie, won't you?' she breathed. 'I know most people in Dover end up at the café sooner or later.'

'Like I said, if I ever find the man, he'll be hearing from me,' Bert interjected. 'But now, let's get you both home. I'll drop you off on the way, Edie.'

As they left, he waved briefly at his friends. 'See you back at barracks, lads.'

They looked over and wolf-whistled when they saw him with a pretty girl on each arm.

'Want me to take one of them off your hands, Bert,' one of the men shouted. 'Seems greedy for you to have both.'

Edie made a rude gesture back at him, and his friends jeered and clapped him on the shoulder.

'Flaming cheek of them,' Edie fumed. 'Can't they see that you and me are related?'

Bert chuckled. 'Ignore them. They're just having a laugh.'

'Yeah, well, it's not funny,' Edie muttered. Today had been disas-trous enough, and now this . . . Mr Pearson and Lily were two of her favourite people in the world. And though she wasn't sure what she could do for her old boss, she wasn't quite as powerless when it came to protecting her sister.

Outside in the freezing dark, the girls took hold of one of Bert's arms each, Susan chattering happily about how good it was to be back in Dover.

'Really?' Edie said. 'You seen the ruins?'

'I know. It breaks my heart. But still, there's no place like home, is there? And Dover still feels like home, even though I left it so many years ago. I mean, Cambridge is all right, but I never made any proper friends there.'

'Apart from this Charlie Alexander,' Edie said snidely.

'But he's a bloke, so it's not the same. I've missed having a good girlfriend.'

Edie suddenly felt bad about her uncharitable thoughts towards her. None of this was Susan's fault. And she'd end up just as hurt as Lily in the end. But it couldn't be helped – her loyalty had to be to Lily, because the Castles always stuck together, no matter what.

When they reached the café, Bert bent to kiss his sister's cheek. 'I'll be back,' he whispered hurriedly, before walking towards Biggin Street where the Guthries lived above their bakery.

Edie let herself in to the café and went upstairs.

'Where've you been?' Nellie asked without looking up from her knitting. 'We ate hours ago.'

'I went to the Oak,' Edie said. 'Bumped into Bert.'

Nellie raised her eyebrows. 'What you doin' going to the pub on your own? You'll get yourself a reputation.'

'At least it couldn't be worse than *your* reputation,' Edie retorted.

Hester laughed. 'You're a proper livewire, just like your mum.'

'No, she's just rude,' her mother responded sharply. 'But we're used to it. There's steak and kidney pud and boiled spuds in the oven. And I'm still waiting to hear what happened with poor Clive. There's some awful rumours flying about. Has he really been arrested?'

Edie sighed and briefly explained what she knew. 'I blame bloody Rodney!' she said fiercely. 'If he hadn't opened his big gob, this would never have happened.'

'Why's Rodney poking his nose in? Surely they can't just arrest someone on his say-so?'

Hester snorted. 'Don't you believe it, Nellie.'

'Oh, shut up, Hester. I could do without your conspiracies right now. Does this mean you'll be moving back for good?' she asked Edie.

Edie sighed heavily. 'Looks like I'll have to for now.'

Nellie grunted and returned to her knitting. 'From the look of you, anyone would think *you're* the one what's been arrested!'

'You know, Mum, it might have been easier if I had. But don't worry, I'll be moving out soon as I can.' Ignoring her mother's angry exclamation, Edie went to collect her food from the kitchen. This surely had been the longest day of her life, and she didn't have the energy to argue any more.

'Where's Lily?' she asked as she returned with her plate, hoping to stop her mother questioning her further.

'Came in half an hour ago and went straight upstairs. That girl works too hard; if she's not at the hospital, she's over at Jasper's studying those books Charlie gave her. She'll go far that one. Once this bloody mess is over, she can be whatever she wants.'

Edie rolled her eyes at the pride in their mother's voice, wondering if she ever talked about her like that; somehow she doubted it. But maybe she wouldn't be quite so gloating if she knew what Lily really got up to over at Jasper's. Especially if she found out what sort of a man Charlie Alexander was.

She looked down at the plate of food and suddenly couldn't stomach it. While she'd been in the pub, Lily had been at Jasper's with a man who had clearly been lying to her for months. *God help Charlie if I ever get my hands on him*, she thought fiercely.

There was a loud bang and the windows shuddered. Polly, who had been asleep on her perch, flapped her wings. 'Oh no! Not again!'

she squawked as Donny came out of his room and Marianne came down the stairs, closely followed by Lily, who was shrugging into her dressing gown. Her cheeks were flushed and her blue eyes were sparkling. She looked even more beautiful than usual, Edie thought, swallowing down a sick feeling of dread.

Nellie heaved herself to her feet with a sigh. 'Jesus, don't the bastards ever sleep? This is the sixth since yesterday morning!'

The shell warning sounded out as they trooped down to the basement, Edie carrying her plate with her.

As they entered the kitchen, Bert burst through the door, panting. He stopped short at the sight of Lily, then went over and put his arm around her. 'How's my favourite sister?' He kissed her on the cheek.

'What do you want?' Lily asked suspiciously.

Bert looked hurt. 'I just wanted you to know how much I love and appreciate you.' He looked over to Edie and raised his eyebrows.

She shook her head.

'Well, this is a nice surprise,' Nellie said. 'To what do we owe the pleasure?'

'I was taking a pretty girl home and thought I'd drop in to see the woman who I measure all others against.'

Nellie rolled her eyes and continued down to the basement. 'Come on then, if you're comin'. And who's this pretty girl? Anyone I know?'

Bert didn't follow and motioned with his head that Edie should stay there.

Once the others had disappeared, she whispered, 'What shall we do?' Then she jumped as a crash nearby made her heart start to race.

Bert barely seemed to notice as he replied, 'Not a lot we can do. But when I see that man, he'll be sorry.'

As the noise from the exploding shell dissipated, a loud shout drifted up through the open door of the basement. 'Lily Castle, what's that on your finger?'

Edie felt a pit open up in her stomach and she looked at Bert to see if he'd drawn the same conclusion.

'That bastard!' he muttered. 'I can't believe she finally accepted his proposal today of all days!'

Edie gritted her teeth. 'What are we going to do?' she repeated.

'We're going to make sure he ends up with no one, that's what we're going to do. And *I'm* going to make sure he knows exactly what happens to people who mess with the Castles.' He punched a clenched fist into his palm.

'Don't do anything stupid,' Edie cautioned. 'We don't want you up on a charge.'

'Don't worry about me. He says a word about it, I'll make sure Lily knows everything.'

'And what about Susan? If we tell her, she'll be bound to mention it to Lily.'

Bert let out a humourless laugh. 'Leave Susan to me. For an engaged woman, she's *very* easily distracted, if you know what I mean.'

Edie shook her head at him. 'Try not to break her heart. She doesn't deserve that.'

Bert held up three fingers. 'I'll be gentle with her. Scout's honour.'

# Chapter 31

Edie woke during the night with a start, the sweat standing out on her forehead and the familiar sick feeling in her stomach. She sat up and put her head between her knees, taking a deep breath as she tried to calm her heartbeat. She'd been dreaming again, and the sound of her cries reverberated in her ears.

'You all right?' Lily asked sleepily.

'I'm fine. Go back to sleep,' Edie whispered.

Lily turned over with a slight groan and Edie sat for some time listening to her sisters' soft breaths on either side of her. 'Oh God,' she groaned quietly. It wasn't just the dream that was making her feel nauseous; it was Mr P's arrest and the discovery of Charlie's betrayal on the very day Lily accepted his proposal – at least she hoped that was all it was.

Sitting in the basement the night before had been torture as everyone had chatted excitedly about the ring and how wonderful Charlie was, while she had sat in silence, trying to eat the cold steak and kidney pie. But she had at least gleaned one useful piece of information: Charlie would be on the seven o'clock train to London this morning and Edie had decided she would make sure he had a send-off he wouldn't forget.

Turning over, she allowed the rhythmic sound of her sisters' breathing to soothe her; she might not have wanted to come home, but sometimes it was nice not to be alone at night. Her brothers and sisters had always been her main source of comfort, and even

165

though her mother drove her round the bend, she knew she'd always be there to back her up, no matter what. It was time she started to count her blessings.

When Edie woke again, Lily was already getting dressed and Marianne's bed was empty. She scrambled up, realising that if she didn't hurry, Charlie would be gone before she had a chance to speak to him.

'How you feeling?' Lily asked with concern. In the lamplight, the ring on Lily's finger glittered, making Edie's stomach lurch uncomfortably.

'Never better,' she lied, raising her arms in a stretch. 'But more importantly, how are *you* feeling now you're an engaged woman?'

Lily smiled widely. 'I don't know why I was so scared. There's no one more perfect for me than Charlie.'

'Are you sure? I once thought Henry Fanshawe was the only man in the world for me and look how that turned out.'

'Yeah, but you never had a proper relationship with him, did you? It was all hole-in-the-corner stuff. Charlie's stood by me through thick and thin over the last months. Even when everyone thought I'd helped that prisoner escape, he didn't believe it. I think I might be the luckiest girl alive.'

'Really? The absolute luckiest?'

Lily's eyes narrowed. 'I thought you liked Charlie.'

Edie looked away. 'It's just ... You've only known him a few months. How do you know you can trust him?'

'Marianne only knew Alfie for a few months before she accepted his proposal. In fact, less than that if you take into account him being away for so long.'

'That's different.'

'How?'

Edie shrugged and undid her long plait of hair, brushing the dark strands over her face to hide her expression. She was useless at lying, and Lily knew her too well to be fooled for long.

'You're jealous!' Lily said sharply.

'I am not!' Edie tossed her hair away from her face. 'Why would I be jealous of you and Charlie?'

'Well, despite that little episode I interrupted in the basement on Christmas morning, Greg's not exactly a regular visitor, is he? And you've always hated it when I've got something and you haven't.'

Edie's face flushed with temper. 'That is not true! And believe me, I don't want Charlie Alexander, no matter how good-looking he is. As for Greg, he's busy fighting the war. He can't just pop down for an hour when he fancies it like Charlie can.'

'I don't believe you,' Lily said. 'And I don't have time for an argument. I want to tell Jasper the good news before my shift starts.' She threw her cape around her and stalked towards the door, stopping to look back over her shoulder. 'And by the way,' she said icily. 'you do realise that nightmares and stress aren't the only things to make you feel sick in the mornings.'

'You can be a right bitch sometimes, Lily Castle!' Edie gasped. 'And do *you* realise that just cos a man says he loves you, it doesn't mean he does?'

'Maybe that's your experience,' Lily said furiously, 'but it's not mine.' Her eyes dropped to Edie's stomach for a moment, before she looked back at her face. 'And when you're ready to acknowledge the truth, come talk to me.'

With a toss of her head, she left the room and Edie slumped back onto the bed, her hand on her stomach. *It's not true*, she thought. *It can't be true.* Lily was just lashing out at her because she was angry. And she understood why. Her sister had been so happy about her engagement last night, and Edie hadn't even managed to congratulate her. But one day, she'd understand, and once she'd got over her heartbreak, maybe she'd thank her.

She jumped up from the bed. One thing at a time, she thought. And right now, she needed to get to the station.

167

Once dressed, she dashed down the stairs and after hastily collecting her helmet and coat, she ran out of the door before Marianne could try to engage her in conversation.

Hurrying along Marine Parade, Edie turned her collar up against the fierce wind that was blowing in from the sea, thankful that the dark hid the ruined Georgian terrace on the other side of the road. Dover used to be so beautiful, but the war was barely a year old and already she could tell that the place would never be the same.

Despite the early hour, the station was full of khaki-clad men and she stopped in the large entrance, remembering the previous summer when the town had come together to help the soldiers returning from Dunkirk – it had been the first time the war had seemed real to them. Back then, Daisy had been alive, Jasper could see, the town had been unblemished and no one had been forced to live in the caves. It felt like a lifetime ago.

She pushed through the throng, hoping to spot Charlie's tall figure. But with everyone in uniform, it was hard to distinguish one person from another. She stopped in the middle of the large concourse and turned slowly, keeping her eyes peeled. Perhaps he was in the waiting room or having a cup of tea. A quick glance into the waiting room proved fruitless, but then she spotted him in the café, sitting at a dirty Formica table, his head bowed over a cup of tea, his cap pulled low over his face. If she hadn't known better, she'd have thought he was hiding from her.

Storming over, she dropped into the empty seat opposite him. Across the table, Charlie didn't move, if anything he hunched further down into his coat.

'I think you've got some explaining to do,' she said finally.

He looked up quickly, then lowered his head again.

Edie gasped at the sight of him. His right eye was swollen almost completely shut and the bruising had spread around his eye and across his nose.

'Go away,' he said and he looked so miserable that Edie almost felt sorry for him.

'What the hell happened to you?'

He sighed. 'What do you think?'

She grinned. 'Good old Bert. That'll teach you for messing with a Castle.'

He looked up at that, his one good eye shooting sparks of fury. '*Good old Bert* could have blinded me,' he ground out.

Edie sat back and folded her arms. 'Oh dear. I'm so sorry. I'll be sure to have a word with him.' She smiled sweetly. 'Seeing as Bert seems to have said everything far more effectively than I ever could, I'll be on my way.' She stood up and stared down at Charlie's hunched figure, then she bent down and whispered in his ear. 'And if you ever try to contact Lily again, a black eye will be the least of your troubles.'

She whirled round, but her progress was abruptly halted as Charlie grabbed her jacket. She looked round. 'Let go,' she said icily.

He did as she asked and stood to loom over her. 'Listen to me. Whatever that girl said is a lie. You have to believe me. I love Lily. I would *never* hurt her. That girl – *Susan*' – he spat the name out – 'is a liar. She used to follow me round all over the place, but I swear on my mother's life that the most I ever did was be friendly to her. She's a bloody fantasist, just like her weird parents.'

Edie narrowed her eyes. '*A fantasist?*' she repeated, ignoring the comment about Susan's parents – her memory of them was faint. 'So that emerald ring on her finger is a figment of her imagination?'

He shook his head. 'Anyone can wear a ring – it doesn't mean anything. Edie, I swear, the girl is crazy. Don't let her worm her way into your life, because you'll regret it.'

When Edie just scowled at him disbelievingly, he persisted, 'I mean it. There's something wrong in her head and I honestly think she could be dangerous.'

Edie let out a snort of derision. '*Susan*, dangerous?! God, I really misjudged you! How you've managed to fool us all so convincingly is beyond me. But listen to me,' she hissed, '*no one* hurts my sister, so you better not show your face in this town again.'

Ignoring Charlie's devastated expression, she stormed away and fought her way back through the crowds and out into the bitterly cold morning where she stopped and took a deep breath, replaying their conversation in her head. What did he mean about Susan being crazy and dangerous? She'd never heard anything so ridiculous in her life. She'd love to know if he'd said something similar to Bert. That is if he managed to get a word in before her brother floored him. She smiled briefly at the thought. Her brother had his faults, but if you needed a bit of muscle, then there was no one better.

But as she walked back along the seafront, the castle emerging through the early morning mist, looking as though it were floating on a cloud, she felt a glimmer of doubt. He'd proved himself to Lily again and again, and if anyone had asked, she'd have sworn on her own life that Charlie would never do the dirty on her sister – after all, she was beautiful, clever and kind. Any man would be a fool to give that up, and Charlie had never seemed like a fool to her. Even if he had once been engaged to Susan, the man she'd come to know would have ended it before proposing to someone else.

She stopped and stared out over the sea. The coast of France was hidden by mist, but she could make out the ghostly outline of a small convoy of ships making its way across the Channel. She shook her head. No, Charlie was lying. Because in her experience, if you thought a man was being dishonest, then the chances were that he was. Now all she had to do was keep the truth from Lily. And if Bert could persuade Susan that she didn't want to marry Charlie, then he'd lose them both. And serve him right.

# Chapter 32

'Nellie!' Muriel Palmer bustled in through the door, her coat tightly buttoned and her tin hat slightly askew on top of her woolly hat.

Nellie smiled through gritted teeth. 'Muriel. Cup of tea, is it? And perhaps a spot of breakfast.'

'What I wouldn't give,' she exclaimed. 'But there's simply no time to stop, what with one thing and another.' She came and leant up against the counter. 'I was wondering if your Edie was around.'

'Why, what's she done?'

Muriel smiled. 'Nothing at all. Just I wanted to remind her about the van. And I hear that the garage has been closed up.' She shook her head, and leant closer to Nellie. 'And what's this about Mr Pearson being arrested?'

'Who told you that?' Nellie said sharply.

'Dr Palmer. He heard it from someone at the hospital. But why have they arrested him? He's such a nice man.'

'He is. It's obviously a mistake. And not for the first time. After what happened to my Lily, I don't trust the police – military or not.'

'Quite right too, Nellie. Like I've always said.' Hester bustled out of the kitchen carrying a couple of plates of food.

'This is different, surely,' Muriel said, eyebrows raised.

'Course it's not. When men are arrested for no good reason it breeds fear. People start lookin' around at their neighbours, reportin' the slightest thing. You mark my words, we're one step away from a police state.'

Muriel gaped at Hester. 'Are you suggesting the British government is no better than the Nazis? I'm willing to believe that Clive Pearson's arrest was a mistake, but a police state? Poppycock.'

'Hester's just upset about Clive. The man was a great favourite with her,' Nellie interjected.

Hester rolled her eyes at her and continued on her way.

'You can't let people talk like that in here, Nellie,' Muriel hissed.

Nellie raised her eyebrows. 'So you're sayin' she can't say what she likes?'

Muriel's lips tightened. 'Of course not, but . . .'

'But she can only say stuff you agree with, is that what you mean?'

Muriel didn't have an answer for that and Nellie nodded. 'Exactly. The Nazis haven't invaded yet, and we need to hang on to our freedom – Hester's right about that, at least. Now, if you hold on a tick, I'll see if I can find Edie.' She went over to the hatch. 'Any sign of Edie, Marianne?' she called.

'No!' Marianne shouted. 'She disappeared early. No idea where she went.'

Gladys came out of the pantry, drying her hands on a tea towel. 'Anything I can help with, Mrs Palmer?' she asked.

'Well, if you could fix my engine troubles, I'd be eternally grateful, Gladys,' Mrs Palmer tittered. 'But somehow I'm not sure that's one of your talents. Now, if I needed some flowers arranging, you'd be the first person I'd call on. Or one of your *most* delicious herbal teas.'

Nellie shot a sharp glance at her friend. 'What herbal tea?' she asked.

'When I was suffering from a touch of nervous exhaustion a few years ago, Gladys made me the most wonderful infusion that not only calmed me right down, it also perked me right up. Truly a magical potion.'

'Can't imagine Dr Palmer were too happy about that,' Nellie remarked.

Mrs Palmer put her gloved hand beside her mouth to shield what she was saying. 'I never told him,' she whispered. 'You know what he's like. I love him dearly, but he has no imagination. Says home remedies are the legacy of witchcraft.'

'Maybe he's got a point. A cup of tea's all very well, but it's not likely to cure any illnesses. Believe me, I know all about that.' She threw Gladys another look, but her friend refused to meet her eyes.

'My Terence could take a look,' Lou Carter called over.

Muriel's face froze. Terence Carter was not the sort of man she wanted associated with the WVS. 'So kind, Mrs Carter,' she said primly. 'But I think I need a *professional* to look at it.'

'Suit yerself,' she muttered. 'Snotty old cow.'

Muriel's lips thinned, but she didn't reply. 'Don't forget to ask Edie to pay me a visit when she's got a moment. I do so admire a woman trying to make her way in a man's world. If there's one good thing that might come out of this whole ghastly business it's that we women might finally be able to prove we are capable of almost any job.'

'Huh. Fat chance. It'll be like last time. Soon as the men come back, it'll be "Ta, very much, ladies, we'll take it from here." And then we'll be right back where we started – in the bloody kitchen and the bedroom,' Nellie said sourly.

Marianne was putting some plates of food on the hatch. 'Hey, there's nothing wrong with being in the kitchen,' she said.

'Nor the bedroom,' Hester said with a wink.

Mrs Palmer ignored the comment and laid her hand on Nellie's arm. 'Present company excepted, though, Nellie. What with your Donald being the way he was, you still carried on regardless. *Such* an inspiration.'

'Isn't she just,' Gladys interjected drily.

Nellie narrowed her eyes. 'What do you mean by that?'

Gladys shrugged. 'What I said. You carry on, Nell. That's what you do. That's what we all do. But some of us are better at it than others.' Gladys walked back into the kitchen and Nellie frowned. She couldn't help feeling that there was a barb hidden somewhere in her words.

173

She shifted her gaze back to Mrs Palmer. 'If that's all, then, Muriel, you're not the only one who's got things to do.' She gestured around the busy café.

'Right you are, Nellie. And I look forward to seeing you down the caves, Mrs Carter. Perhaps a stint serving tea to those worse off than you might teach you some manners.'

Lou scowled at her. 'I do my part. Just cos it's not in your precious caves it don't mean I don't help. Just yesterday, I was busy up the Lord Warden serving whelks to those brave navy boys. Which reminds me, you'll never guess who I spotted.' When no one seemed interested, she continued anyway. 'That Walter Penfold! I didn't say anythin', cos your Edie was very keen to talk to him. He likes them young, it seems, cos when I saw him, he were having a chinwag with a *very* pretty young girl – all black hair and white skin, like Snow White. Right up close and personal they was too.'

'It's not really our business,' Nellie said.

'It is your business if he's set his sights on your daughter, though, in't it?' She stood up and swung an old-fashioned khaki great coat around herself, then stuck her tin hat on her head. 'Be seein' you.' She waved her hand vaguely towards Nellie, clapped Hester on the shoulder, then went out into the square to get her stall ready for the day's business.

Ron Hames stared after her looking thoughtful. Finally, he made a note in his notebook, then stood up as well. 'Thanks for breakfast, Mrs C.'

Nellie watched as he chased after Lou.

'That man's making me nervous. Recently his nose's been twitching like a greyhound after a rabbit. What do you think it's all about?'

'Oh, ignore him,' Mrs Palmer said as she turned to leave. 'Those reporters make mountains out of molehills.'

'He's always asking questions about what we do as well,' a Wren sitting near the counter offered. 'Obviously we can't say anything, but every time he speaks I feel like he's testing us.'

'He's just doin' his job,' Gladys countered.

Nellie went to stand by the window and looked out through the criss-cross of tape at the busy square. Shoppers were already out, eager to get their supplies before the morning siren went off, and the traffic was building up along King Street, crawling round the square and up Cannon Street. You'd never guess that petrol was scarce the way the military got through it, she thought. Seemed to her that they loaded soldiers into trucks, drove them round Dover all day, then dropped them back. Despite the crowds, though, she could clearly see Lou and Ron conversing intently.

But then her attention was caught by a slim figure wearing a donkey jacket coming up King Street. And where had Edie been so early this morning? she wondered. By the looks of her, wherever it was hadn't brightened her mood any. In fact, she looked even more miserable than she had the night before when they'd been celebrating Lily's engagement. But then she'd had a terrible day, and this business with Clive Pearson was very worrying. And, of course, this time of year was always difficult for the poor love. Just as it was for Nellie herself; the memory of Donald's death hanging heavy over her heart.

But even so, she could have made a bit of an effort. Instead, she'd sat, arms folded across her chest and her face like a slapped arse. She'd been tempted to give her a piece of her mind – but that wouldn't have been fair on Lily, who deserved some happiness after the tumultuous few months she'd had. Perhaps she was jealous, Nellie considered. Because she would bet the café that whatever was going on between her and the flashy Canadian pilot, it wouldn't go much further. Which was just as well. He seemed nice enough, but he was foreign and she'd rather all her children were within reach. She and Edie might fight like cat and dog, but if she left Dover, how would they ever manage to mend the rift that had lain between them for well over a decade now?

'Nellie, come quick!' A cry from the kitchen brought Nellie's attention back to the present. Gladys was standing at the hatch waving frantically at her.

'What now?' Nellie said irritably as she threaded her way through the tables, ignoring the curious stares of the customers. When she got to the kitchen, Marianne was sitting on the floor, Hester kneeling beside her holding a glass of water to her lips.

'Marianne, love! What happened?'

Marianne's face was deathly pale, dark circles standing out beneath her hazel eyes. 'I . . . I don't know,' she said weakly.

'Poor girl fainted, Nell. You've been workin' her half to death,' Gladys fumed. 'Look at her, she's no more than skin and bone! Come on, love, let's get you upstairs, eh?' Gladys gently helped Marianne to her feet.

Nellie budged her out of the way. '*I'll* look after her, thanks very much,' she said indignantly.

Marianne sighed and leant against the table. 'I'm fine,' she said. 'But could you *please* stop arguing!'

Both Gladys and Nellie looked shamefaced at that. 'Sorry.' Nellie rubbed her arm. 'Tell you what, you get yourself upstairs and I'll take over the cookin'.'

'Blinking heck! Get that Ron Hames back in here quick!' Hester exclaimed with a laugh. 'He'll want to report this.'

Nellie threw a furious glance at her. 'She *said* no more fighting,' she ground out.

'Sorry, love,' Hester said. 'Look, I'll get in the pantry, shall I? Give Gladys a break from the washing-up?'

'That'd be a help, thanks, Hester.' Marianne smiled at her tiredly.

Donny came into the kitchen then, looking for his breakfast. 'Mum?' he said. 'What's wrong? You look funny.'

'Just a bit under the weather, Don,' she said. 'You couldn't help me upstairs, then bring me a cup of tea, could you?'

Donny took her arm with alacrity. 'Gran, could you bring the tea. I don't want her to be on her own.'

Nellie smiled at him. Bless the boy; he was growing up fast.

'I'll do it, Nellie,' Gladys said quickly. 'Maybe one of my calming teas would help. Didn't Mrs Palmer just say how much it helped

176

her ... Now, let's see, a pinch of camomile, a spot of mint and ginger—' She counted the ingredients off on her fingers.

'You will *not*!' Nellie interrupted.

Gladys looked at her startled. 'Why not?'

'You know very well why not. So pour her out a *normal* cup of tea, please.'

Gladys's cheeks flushed. 'One cup won't do no harm,' she said truculently.

'I said *no*!' Nellie's voice rose.

'But it'll help her.'

'What's going on?' Edie asked, coming in the back door.

'Your sister's been taken a bit faint and I were just suggesting one of my calming teas,' Gladys said.

'Oh, like you used to make for Dad?'

'I said *NO*!' Nellie repeated, louder this time.

Edie looked at her mother in surprise. 'But why not?'

'For pity's sake!' Marianne slumped against the wall by the stairs. 'Is there anything you won't argue about? A cup of tea! That's all I want.' She straightened and, with Donny's arm tight around her waist, she went upstairs.

There was a brief silence in the kitchen as the four women looked at each other guiltily, then Edie moved to the pantry and brought out a cup and saucer. 'Any spare sugar, Mum?' she asked as she poured the tea.

'White tin in the pantry,' she said, rolling up her sleeves and picking up the discarded spatula from the table, before hurriedly removing the eggs that had been frying on the range. 'Plates, Glad! Quick, before this lot burns.'

After adding a couple of lumps of sugar to the tea, Edie took it upstairs to the bedroom where Donny was sitting beside his mother.

'You all right, love?' she asked.

Marianne sighed. 'I'm just a bit rundown is all. A morning in bed will sort me out.'

Edie gestured to Donny, and after kissing his mother on the cheek, he left the room.

'You gonna tell me what that was all about downstairs?' she asked.

'Nothing. Just . . . everyone's so bad-tempered at the moment. It's upsetting. And you're no better.' She narrowed her eyes at Edie. 'Last night, you barely said a word. What was all that about?'

Edie was desperate to confide what she'd discovered about Charlie, but one look at Marianne's pale face convinced her to keep quiet. 'Nothing. I was just upset about Mr P. But here, drink this and get some sleep. I'll see you later.'

She hurried out of the room, her mind on the argument between her mother and Gladys. Now that she'd been reminded of it, she remembered how Gladys's home remedies had always calmed her father. So why was her mother so set against them?

# Chapter 33

In the bedroom, Marianne took the letter she'd just received out of her apron pocket and reread it.

*26 December 1940*

*Dear Miss Castle,*

*We regret to inform you that Mr Ernest Fanshawe passed away last week. You and your son, Donald, will be required to attend The Gables, Hawkinge for the reading of the will on 4 January 1941. The family has asked me to inform you that Henry Fanshawe will also be present.*

*Yours sincerely,*

*Edwin Billing, Solicitor*

Marianne shuddered. It was the shock of those final words and the terror that Henry might once again try to take Donny away from her that had made her feel faint. And even if he wasn't going to be there, the last thing she wanted to do was visit that house again. To her shame, she'd taken Donny to visit his grandfather only twice since the summer, although she'd made sure Donny wrote to him every week. He always received a letter back, but she knew that her son viewed the letters more as a chore. And who could blame him? His father had treated him abominably, and Henry's wife had done nothing but insult them all. No, she wouldn't go, she decided. She wanted nothing to do with that family, no matter how much money they had. But then, was that fair to Donny?

She needed to talk to Alfie, she realised. Because this wasn't just about Donny, it was about her and Alfie, too.

Throwing back the covers, she put her shoes back on and sneaked down the two flights of stairs to the ground floor. Poking her head around the kitchen door, she waited until her mother's back was turned and Gladys and Hester were occupied, before slipping unnoticed out of the back door.

As she puffed up Cowgate Hill, the cold wind blowing straight into her face, Marianne thought about the strange argument between Gladys and her mother that morning. She remembered a time when her mother used to welcome Gladys's remedies, and they had all benefitted from them at one time or another, so she couldn't understand her reaction today. Still, who knew what went on between those two? Even though Gladys was devoted to her mother after she'd taken her in when she'd become homeless during the last war, sometimes they argued like cat and dog. But she couldn't deny the mood between them had soured since Hester had arrived.

As the sentry box at the entrance to Drop Redoubt came into view, she put it from her mind and quickened her pace.

'All right, Marianne.' The soldier on duty recognised her instantly. 'If you're lookin' for Alf, you might be in luck. He drove through a short while ago. Come in out of the cold and I'll ring through.'

Gratefully accepting a cup of tea from the sentry's colleague, Marianne kept her eyes fixed on the entrance. She'd seen Alfie less than a week ago, but it felt like a lifetime.

A short while later, her heart leapt with joy as Alfie strode towards her, a broad smile on his beautiful face. She ran into his arms, clinging to him as if he were her last hope of survival.

'Hey,' Alfie said, kissing the top of her head. 'What's all this?'

'I just needed to see you,' she said into his shoulder. 'I miss you so much.'

Alfie pushed her away gently and tipped her chin up so he could look into her eyes. 'Marianne, love, what's wrong?'

'Nothing, I just . . . I . . . Can we walk?'

Alfie took her arm and together they made their way down to the little cave on the side of the steep hill overlooking the harbour where Alfie had first proposed to her. Sitting down just inside the mouth so they were sheltered from the worst of the wind, Alfie put his arm around her shoulders and pulled her close. 'Now will you tell me what's up?'

In answer, Marianne pulled the letter from her pocket. 'I got this,' she said, holding it out to him.

Alfie frowned. 'If you want my opinion, then you're gonna have to read it to me.'

*How could I have forgotten he can't read?* she thought, feeling guilty. It was another reminder of how, even though they were married, their lives were still so far apart.

When she'd finished reading, Alfie let out a low whistle. 'Well, that's a turn-up. How do you feel about it?'

'I don't want to go. I don't want to see Henry and his nasty wife again. I'm scared he'll try to take Donny from me again.'

'Nah, I think that ship has sailed. And what's the problem with his wife?'

'She's a cow: snooty, superior and so full of bitterness. I'm not sure which of us she hates most – me, Edie or Donny.'

'I suspect it'll be Donny. Cos from this letter and everything you've told me, Mr F will be leavin' him a share of the business. And as she doesn't have a child of her own and her husband was banged up for draft-dodging, she might end up with nothing. I wonder how much Donny'll get?'

'Whatever he's been left, I'm not accepting!' Marianne exclaimed fiercely. 'Don't you see that if Donny inherits a share of the brewery, then we'll be linked to that family forever?'

'Is that so bad? He's already linked by blood, after all. And think what you could do with the money. Donny could go to a brilliant

181

school, we could buy a house and set up home. You'd never have to work another day in your life . . . Not that you will anyway,' he said hastily. 'Once the war's over, I'll get back on the band circuit and be able to support us all.'

'For God's sake, Alfie!' Marianne cried, aware she was being unreasonable but unable to stop herself. She'd wanted Alfie to agree with her, she realised. And the fact that he didn't seem to made her more annoyed than it should have. 'I don't want their stinking money! We're fine as we are. And who's to say I *want* to stop working! Anyway, it won't be *our* money, it'll be Don's.'

Alfie was taken aback by her vehemence. 'All right,' he said slowly, unsure what he should say now. 'In which case, you could invest some of Don's money and open your own little café. Get out from under your mother's thumb and build a nice inheritance for him.'

'What do you mean by that?' she said sharply. 'Are you saying I can't stand up for myself?'

Alfie sighed; it seemed no matter what he said, it wouldn't be right. 'I just mean that if you had your own place, then you could get someone in to help and you wouldn't have to work so hard.' He stroked her face, worried at the pallor and the huge dark circles under her eyes. 'And then maybe you could start taking more care of yourself,' he said.

'I'm fine! But I am *not* about to accept anything from them.'

'All right, then. If you don't want to, you don't have to,' Alfie soothed. 'You, me and Don will do just fine without their money. I mean, things won't be easy, but we're both grafters, so we'll get by.'

'Yes, we will,' she said. 'And now old Mr Fanshawe has died, we don't need to have any more to do with them.'

'Seems to me you'd already made up your mind,' he said mildly. 'So why did you want my opinion?'

'I had.' She put her head on his shoulder. 'Sorry for snapping. I just wanted you to reassure me that it was the right decision.'

He kissed her head. 'You do what you think's best, love. I will back you whatever you decide.'

'Do you mean that? Like you said, the money could make a huge difference to our lives. You won't resent me for turning it down?'

'For richer, for poorer, Marianne. I said it and I meant it. So as long as you're sure, then that's all I need to know.'

Marianne leant forward and kissed him tenderly on the lips. 'Thank you,' she said softly.

Alfie smiled into her eyes. 'You're thanking me for loving you?'

'Yes. And for being the best man in the world.'

'Yes, you are a very lucky woman.' He grinned, his green eyes sparkling. 'And once the concert on New Year's Eve is finished, you an' me are gonna dance the night away.'

She laughed slightly. 'All right. But wear your steel-capped boots.' She put her head on his shoulder again and they sat quietly for a moment. 'I love you, Alfie Lomax,' Marianne murmured, raising her head to kiss his cheek. 'And I'm sorry that I won't take the money.'

'Pah. What do I need money for? I'm already the richest man in the world.' He turned his head towards her and kissed her deeply.

'Alfie,' she said when they drew apart, 'can I ask you a favour?'

'Anything.'

'Rather than dancing, could we maybe do something else at New Year?' She tried to smile seductively, but realised she'd failed miserably when Alfie merely looked puzzled.

'Like what?' he asked.

She sighed. 'Well, Don'll be staying with Fred, Lily and Edie'll probably be out, Mum'll go and see her friends, so why don't you and me sneak back after you've played your bit and have our own little party? And I promise you won't need your steel-capped boots.'

'Now you're talking,' Alfie whispered, kissing her again.

'Yuck!'

Marianne and Alfie jumped apart and looked up. Donny was hovering over them, hands on hips. Beside him, Freddie's cheeks had gone bright red with embarrassment. And behind the boys, much to Marianne's surprise, was Hester.

'This isn't a place for kissing,' Donny said sternly. 'This is an observation post.' He pointed down towards the sea. 'We see everything from up here.'

'Looks like someone's feelin' better.' Hester smirked. 'Good to meet you, Alfie. At least, I hope you're Alfie!' She cackled.

'This is Hester Erskine, Alf. Remember, she was the one who looked after Don in Folkestone?'

Alfie's eyes widened in surprise, but he smiled and held out his hand. 'Nice to meet you too, Hester. I've heard all about you from these two.'

'Shouldn't you be working?' Marianne asked the woman.

'Your mum wanted me to take some supplies over to the caves for old Mr Evans and that little girl as has the cough,' Hester explained.

'Why are you up here then? The caves are down there.'

'She wanted to see our observation post,' Donny piped up. 'An' she brought a Thermos and some cake so's we could have tea while we keep an eye out.'

Marianne looked out over the sea, which was choppy and uninviting under the grey sky. 'Not a lot to see today.'

'Yes there is. Look.' He pointed towards Admiralty Pier, where tiny navy-blue-clad men and women hurried in and out of a large white building. 'The *Lord Warden*'s called HMS *Wasp* now,' he said importantly. 'An' we're keeping it under close watch.'

Alfie raised his eyebrows. 'They're lucky to have you,' he said. 'The navy have never been very good at taking care of themselves.'

'Yes they have. Uncle Rod says we have the greatest navy in the world.'

'Ah well, if Uncle Rod says it, it must be true,' Marianne said drily as she stood up.

'You should be in bed, Mum,' Donny said.

'Why? What's wrong with her?' Alfie asked.

'She fainted this morning. Then Gran and Gladys argued about what tea to give her, an' Mum shouted at everyone.'

'You didn't tell me you'd fainted,' Alfie said with concern. 'Don's right – you should be in bed.'

'I feel much better now,' she said defensively. 'And you should keep your mouth shut,' she said to her son.

'She's just exhausted,' Hester interjected. 'This bloody war's takin' it out of all of us.'

'Unless you faked it to get a day off cooking,' Donny said suspiciously.

'No, I did not!' Marianne grabbed him round the neck in mock anger.

'So, if you weren't faking, you should go back to bed. That's what you'd say if it was me.'

'All right, all right, I'm going. But I want you home before dark, young man. You've got schoolwork to do.'

Donny scowled and nodded, then he and Freddie crawled into the space she and Alfie had recently vacated. 'Come on, Hester, there's plenty of room.'

'God bless 'im,' she murmured to Marianne. 'So like my Tommy when he were this age. Treasure this time, cos he'll be grown in the blink of an eye, an' he won't be interested in his mum no more.'

Marianne put her hand on Hester's arm. 'I will, Hester,' she said sympathetically. 'I bet you were a brilliant mum.'

Hester sighed and stared out to sea. 'I did my best, love. But it weren't easy. An' Tommy weren't too happy with the way I earned my living. It drove him away in the end and we never got a chance to make our peace.'

'Hester, come on!' Donny said impatiently.

Hester blinked and smiled. 'Comin', Don. An' I reckon it's time to take out the rock cakes, what do you think?' She bent down and crawled into the space.

Marianne sighed as she and Alfie walked away. 'Poor Hester. She's right – I should enjoy Donny and not worry so much about his future.'

'Yes, you should. Anyway, it looks like he'll be heir to a beer fortune, so you don't need to worry about his future now.'

Marianne tutted. 'What did I just say? He won't be heir to anything that you and me haven't earned ourselves.'

'But it would solve a lot of problems, don't you think?' Alfie said carefully.

Marianne whirled round, her eyes flashing. 'You just told me you didn't mind! "For richer, for poorer," you said. If he has that money, his life will change and he will never be able to be the carefree boy he is now. Don't you see?'

'Of course it won't change,' Alfie said. 'He don't need to know about any of it until he's grown. Why are you creating problems that don't exist?'

'Don't exist?!' Marianne stormed. 'If Donny inherits Henry's share of the business and any money that comes with it, as Mr Fanshawe suggested he would, then his father will never be out of his life; he'll do anything he can to get his hands on what he considers is rightfully his. And if Henry doesn't, that wife of his will, because I can't see her letting this go.'

Alfie held his hands up. 'All right, all right. Like I said, you do what you think's best and I'll support your decision.'

'So you said earlier, but it sounds like you didn't mean it!'

'Of course I meant it,' Alfie said, exasperated. 'I just think that maybe—'

'If you meant it, then there is no "maybe"!' Marianne interrupted, furious with him.

Alfie sighed deeply. 'Fine. Do whatever you want.'

'Don't worry, I will!' Marianne snapped, veering off to the right towards Cowgate Steps without even turning to say goodbye.

'See you New Year's Eve,' Alfie called after her.

But she didn't reply, and he turned away feeling frustrated. His wife could be as stubborn as her mother, which was something he was only just discovering. They'd known each other for over a year, but they'd spent hardly any time in each other's company. Sometimes he wondered if they'd ever get the chance to lead a normal life. He'd made peace with the possibility that he might not survive the war, but what kept him awake at night was the thought that it could just as easily be Marianne, living right in the line of the shell fire, who might not make it.

# Chapter 34

Later that afternoon, Edie was in the pantry doing the washing-up – something she'd always hated, but she welcomed it now, because it meant she didn't have to talk to anyone. And after the stupid argument that morning about the tea, Gladys and her mother were bickering like schoolchildren. The two had always had their moments, but Edie had always known that they loved each other. This time, though, it felt different. There was real venom in the way they spoke to each other.

Perhaps it would be better if Hester was here, Edie considered. Despite feeling suspicious of the woman, she was brilliant with the customers, and she made her mother laugh. And right now, they could all do with some of her humour to lighten the atmosphere.

As though Edie's thoughts had conjured her up, Hester came in the back door and poked her head into the pantry. 'All right, love? How's Marianne?'

Edie looked round and shrugged. 'Sleeping, I think. She rushed in a while back and it looked like she'd been crying.'

'I saw her up Western Heights with that lovely man of hers. Think they might have had a bit of a barney.'

That'd explain Marianne's tears, Edie thought.

'Anyway, listen, love.' Hester looked over her shoulder, then came to stand right beside her. 'I heard what Lily said to yer this mornin',' she whispered.

Edie whirled round to face her. 'What!?'

'About . . . you know.' She gestured at her stomach.

'You were eavesdropping?' she said, outraged.

'No, I were just in my room and I could hear you two rowin'. Then Lily opened the door, didn't she? I didn't mean to hear but seein' as I did, I thought I should have a word with you.'

Edie swallowed. 'You're not going to tell Mum, are you?'

Hester snorted. 'I'm no snitch. So I take it you are?'

Edie shook her head. 'I don't know,' she whispered.

'Feeling sick? Missed a couple of monthlies? How about dizzy, tired?'

Edie looked away.

'I think you know, love. And do you want to marry the bloke?'

Edie shook her head vigorously.

Hester put a comforting hand on her shoulder. 'Look, this ain't exactly an unusual situation in my line of work. Maybe I can help.'

'How? Do you know someone who could . . . you know, get rid of it?' Edie asked hopefully.

'I do, as it happens. But no way I'd send you to one of 'em. Too risky. But there are other ways.'

'Like what?'

'Just a little infusion of herbs. A secret recipe passed on to me by someone who sorted me out on occasion.'

'Is it dangerous?'

'Everything comes with a risk. But put it this way, it's a lot less dangerous than goin' to one of them women, or even havin' it, come to that. So have a think about it and when you're ready, just say the word.'

Edie grasped her arm to stop her walking away. 'Can you do it now?'

Hester nodded. 'I'll see what I can do.'

'What are you two whispering about in there?' Nellie's shrill voice interrupted them. 'And where the hell have you been, Hester? Get in here, will you?'

'Duty calls.' Hester winked at her. 'And don't worry about a thing. Auntie Hester'll sort it out for you.'

Edie stood with her hands in the cold water, staring out of the window that looked into the backyard. For the first time in a while, she felt a flicker of hope. Maybe this was a sign, she thought. A sign that everything would be all right in the end and her life would go back to normal. And all thanks to Hester, a woman who she'd been previously regarding with suspicion.

Which reminded her. 'Hester,' she called.

Hester popped her head back in. 'Yes, love?'

'Yesterday . . . that man, Walter Penfold. Do you know him?'

Hester grinned and tapped her nose. 'I don't kiss and tell. I've learnt to be discreet over the years. Which is why you needn't worry about me mentioning your little problem to a single soul.'

So she'd been right about Walter – he'd been a customer of Hester's. She shuddered. He was a horrible, sleazy little man and she hoped she'd never see him again. Now if only Hester could help her sort out what had happened to Mr P as well, she'd be laughing.

# Chapter 35

By New Year's Eve, though, laughing was the very last thing Edie felt like doing as she stood behind the counter moodily contemplating her problems. The café was quiet this afternoon and she and Hester had been left to hold the fort while Marianne popped across the square to visit Reenie and her mother had gone to the hospital to see Jasper. As for Gladys, God knew where she'd disappeared to. She'd walked off after yet another row with Nellie; this time because Nellie had told her to wash up some of the pots again. If those two didn't sort themselves out soon, Edie wouldn't be surprised if Gladys walked out for good.

But what was worrying her even more was the fact that she'd still not managed to find out where Mr Pearson had been taken or why. Just the thought of him lying in a prison cell, scared and injured, thinking that his friends had deserted him was enough to make her want to sob. What would Bill think when she told him she'd not managed to do anything? 'Use your imagination,' he'd said. Well, she'd tried, and it had got her nowhere. Mr Wainwright still hadn't returned and no one else seemed willing or able to give her the answers she needed. Reluctantly, she had to admit that as a man and a pilot in the RAF, the police might be more willing to talk to Bill than they were to her. Which made her furious, but there wasn't much she could do about it.

The bell above the door tinkled and she looked up, hoping it was Bill at last, but it was just the messenger boy, who stomped over to the counter and slapped down a telegram.

'For Edie Castle,' he said. 'Any reply?'

Hoping it wasn't Bill saying he'd been delayed, she opened it and her spirits fell further.

MEET ME AT HIPPODROME. SIX THIRTY SHARP.
LET'S HAVE A NEW YEAR TO REMEMBER.
GREG

As if she didn't have enough to contend with, now she was going to have to face Greg and tell him she never wanted to see him again. She rubbed her stomach absently, wishing with all her heart she'd never met the man.

Just for a moment she thought of replying to say she couldn't make it. But then, he'd probably come to the café to find her, so she may as well face him sooner rather than later.

'No,' she said faintly. 'No reply.'

The boy turned sharply and left. Hester, who'd been in the kitchen scrubbing the table, poked her head through the hatch.

'Everything all right, love?' she asked.

'Not really,' Edie replied, handing the telegram to her.

'This the father?' Hester whispered.

Edie nodded.

Hester patted her hand. 'He gives you any trouble, let me know.'

Edie smiled at her gratefully. Hester and Donny seemed to be the only people unaffected by the poisonous atmosphere in the café. Donny was usually out with Freddie, while Hester was unfailingly good-humoured and helpful. She'd also become a great favourite with the customers – particularly Mary Guthrie, who now came in regularly to have whispered conversations with her, and the train driver, Bunny Whittaker.

Edie sighed and glanced at the clock. Only a couple of hours until she'd have to see Greg, she realised.

The bell tinkled, and once again, she looked up hopefully, and once again she was disappointed as Susan walked in, looking very

192

pretty with her red coat and hat complementing her pale skin and black hair.

Edie closed her eyes in despair. Christ, she thought, the only way this day could get any worse was if Lily walked in.

'Sorry I've not been in sooner, Edie,' Susan said cheerfully. 'Been busy at the bakery. Just thought I'd pop in to wish you a Happy New Year in case I don't see you later.'

Hester came out of the kitchen. 'Hello, Susan, love. How's your aunt?' she asked.

'Much the same, thanks, Hester. But she's always cheered after she's seen you. And thank you for . . . Well, you know.'

'You two know each other?' Edie asked in surprise.

'Course we do. Met her the other day when I went to visit Mary.'

'Of course,' Edie said distractedly, the small emerald on Susan's ring finger winking at her mockingly. 'You managed to track down your fiancé yet?' she asked.

Susan nodded sadly. 'Sort of. Bert told me he left the day after we were in the pub.'

'Oh, so you've seen Bert again?'

Susan blushed. 'Once or twice. The first time was when he came to tell me about Charlie. He was so lovely about it. Took me for pie and chips at the Oak. Said he wanted to break it to me gently.'

Edie smiled inwardly; good old Bert, aside from Vera Lynn, there were few women who could resist him. 'Ah,' she said. 'Maybe it's time to break it off with this Charlie then.' She stared at the ring pointedly.

Susan hid her hand behind her back. 'Maybe I would, if I could find him.'

Edie smiled sympathetically. 'Really? You'd give him up for Bert?' she asked.

'To be honest, Edie, I'm so confused. Bert looks like a film star and he makes me laugh so much. And the way he kisses . . .' She shivered dramatically.

Edie grimaced.

Susan giggled. 'Sorry, but he really is something special. All the girls fancy him, but he's chosen *me*. Whereas, Charlie . . . Well, he's an officer and a doctor. If I was with him my future would be secure, and he loved me, Edie, I *know* he did.'

'The man's been ignoring you for months! Surely you don't really believe that.'

Susan looked away, clearly upset. 'I don't think he's been ignoring me as such,' she said. 'He's just been busy. He'll come back to me. And when he does, I can decide what I want to do.'

Edie searched Susan's face, puzzled. Why would any woman insist on waiting for a man who clearly wasn't interested in her? Charlie's words came back to her. *She's a bloody fantasist!*

Had he been telling the truth? Lily had already received a couple of telegrams from Charlie telling her how much he loved her. Whereas Susan claimed not to have heard a word. Maybe Charlie's only crime was to change his mind and not tell her. It still made him a toerag, but perhaps she'd been too harsh on him.

'How are your parents?' she asked suddenly.

Susan shrugged. 'They're fine. Why?'

'Just wondered. They still in Cambridge?'

'Bleedin' heck, Edie, what is this? An interrogation? Poor girl's come in for a cuppa and a friendly chat, and instead she gets you firin' questions and upsettin' her. Go and sit down, love, and I'll join you in a tick.'

Susan smiled uncertainly at Edie, then did as she was told.

'What's got into you?' Hester hissed. 'I thought she were meant to be your friend. Poor girl's lost her fiancé and her cousin to this flamin' war and she don't need you going on at her.'

'She's not lost her fiancé, though, has she? He's run away.'

'All the more reason to be gentle.' Hester poured out a cup of tea and went to sit down with Susan where they proceeded to have a hushed conversation. Edie couldn't begin to imagine what the two women had to talk about, but she didn't have time to think about it for too long as Lily, still wearing her uniform, walked up behind her.

Edie sighed inwardly. Of *course* Lily had come back. What else had she expected?

'Who's that?' Her sister nodded at Susan.

'Oh, talking to me now, are you?' she sniped, desperate to turn Lily's attention away.

'I was never not talking to you,' her sister responded coolly.

'Coulda fooled me.'

Lily folded her arms across her chest. 'Tell me this, if you said you'd got engaged to Greg and all I could do was scowl, how would you feel?'

'I'd wonder why,' Edie said. 'Maybe you should too.'

'All right. Why?'

Edie looked away. 'Well, you know . . .' she stammered, searching for inspiration. 'You were always on about wanting to qualify as a nurse and stuff, be independent . . . But now you're just giving it all up for a man. I thought better of you.'

Lily stared at her sister, hurt by her words. 'I don't believe you,' she said finally. 'Like I said before, I think you're jealous. Because the best you've managed is a married man and some bloke who's probably only seeing you so he can get his leg over in the basement.'

Edie's temper rose. 'That's not fair—'

'It's true, though,' Lily interrupted. 'And what about that other thing?' Her eyes dropped to Edie's stomach. 'Are you finally able to face the truth?'

'Yes,' she hissed. 'I'm pretty sure I am. But don't worry, I'm not keeping it!'

Lily's manner softened. 'Oh, Edie, I'm sorry. But you might change your mind once you have it. You know we'd all stand by you.'

'That's not what I mean. You don't have to stand by me cos it will *never* be born!'

She whirled round and rushed upstairs, leaving Lily stunned.

'What's up with her?' Hester asked.

'It's nothing,' Lily said hastily. 'You couldn't close up, could you, Hester? Edie's a bit . . .'

'That's all right, love. Leave it all to me and go look after your sister.'

Lily gave her a grateful smile before heading upstairs.

'I'm sorry, Edie,' she said when she went into the bedroom. Edie was standing in front of the wardrobe, flicking through the clothes. Lily tried to give her a hug, but Edie pushed her away.

'No, you're not. You're delighted to get your revenge on me for not being happy about your engagement.'

Lily sighed. 'I'm sorry I was a bitch. But I was hurt.' She tried to hug her again and this time Edie let her.

'How sure are you?' Lily asked.

'About as sure as I can be,' she replied. 'Oh God, Mum'll kill me! What am I going to do?'

Lily stroked her hair. 'You're going to have to talk to Greg.'

Edie shook her head. 'I can't. I don't want it! And I don't want him! And now he wants to meet me tonight!'

'So tell him tonight,' Lily said. 'If he really likes you, he'll stand by you.'

'No! I don't want him to stand by me. Anyway, like you said, all he wants is to get his leg over; you really think a man like that would do the honourable thing?'

Lily didn't reply. In truth, she didn't know Greg well enough to judge.

'But it's all right. Hester heard us talking the other day and she thinks she can help me.'

'What?! No! She'll send you to some awful old woman who might kill you!'

Edie pushed away from her and sniffed, rubbing her sleeve over her nose. 'It's not up to you. This is *my* body, *my* decision. I will do what I like.'

Lily was silent for a moment. 'You should at least tell Greg. Give him a chance,' she said softly.

'No, I shouldn't. This has nothing to do with him. In fact, when I see him this evening, I'm going to end it with him.'

Lily stared at her sister's tearful face, knowing there was nothing she could do to change her mind. 'All right,' she said eventually. 'I can't stop you doing anything. But please, Edie, promise me one thing: whatever Hester suggests, talk to me about it. I've seen a girl die after trying to abort her baby, and I don't want that to happen to you.'

'Right now dying seems like a very good solution.'

Lily pulled Edie back into her arms. 'How about we forget all our troubles tonight and try to have a good time? We can pick it all up again tomorrow.'

'How can I have a good time when I'm meeting Greg? Will you go and tell him I'm not well?' she asked hopefully.

'No way! Anyway, I might be tempted to tell him *why* you're not feeling well.'

Edie scowled at her. 'Well, if Bill turns up before I go out I won't be going.'

'All about Bill now, is it?' Lily teased, hoping to lighten the atmosphere.

'For God sake!' Edie turned on her. 'It's all about Mr Pearson! I need Bill's help because *no one* will talk to me. As for Greg . . .' She sighed. 'I wish I'd never met him.'

'Well, we'll all be at the Hippodrome so if you need some moral support, just say the word,' Lily said sympathetically.

Edie clapped a hand over her mouth as a thought occurred to her. 'Where's Bill going to stay? The garage has been boarded up and I bet those flaming policemen made a right mess when they searched it.'

'In the basement?' Lily said, straight-faced.

In spite of everything, Edie let out a huff of laughter.

There was a knock on the door just then and Hester popped her head in. 'Everything all right, loves?' she asked.

Lily glared at her. 'Edie told me what you said, and if you do anything to put her in danger, then I will personally chuck you in jail and throw away the key.'

'Quite right too,' Hester said mildly. 'I don't deal with them backstreet butchers. There are other ways. Anyway, I thought this might cheer you up.' She held up a bottle of wine with one hand and a corkscrew with the other. 'Go on, have a coupla glasses while you're getting ready for your concert. You'll feel better in no time. Might not feel so great in the mornin', but then I imagine you don't anyway.'

'Thanks, Hester. This is exactly what I need.' Edie reached for the bottle eagerly.

'I'll leave you to it then. Have fun tonight and don't do anythin' I wouldn't do,' she said with a throaty laugh as she left the room.

Edie pulled the cork out with a pop and raised the bottle to her mouth, taking a hefty slug.

'Edie, whatever she's suggesting, it's a really bad idea,' Lily said urgently.

Edie took another gulp, then wiped her mouth, handing the bottle to Lily. 'I'll do what I have to. And nothing you can say will make me change my mind.'

# Chapter 36

Marianne hummed happily as she walked up the stairs to get changed for the New Year's Eve concert. She and Reenie had had a good chat that afternoon and for the first time in days she was feeling a little brighter. And the more she thought about her decision not to attend Mr Fanshawe's funeral, the better she felt about it. She'd done a lot of thinking over the past couple of days, and the words that kept going round and round in her mind were Hester's. *Treasure this time, cos he'll be grown in the blink of an eye, an' he won't be interested in his mum no more.* It had made her realise that if Donny inherited half the business, the family would try to take over. Maybe send him to one of those posh boarding schools rich people were so fond of. And then she'd lose him. He'd change, become one of them. He might even become ashamed of his humble roots. There was no amount of money in the word that would be enough for her to risk that. Especially now.

'Someone's looking better,' Hester remarked as she came out of her room. She was dressed in a bright yellow blouse that Marianne recognised as belonging to her mother and a blue skirt she'd got from the WVS; she'd smeared red lipstick over her mouth and her yellow hair was carefully curled and pinned, disguising the dark roots.

'I'm feeling much better, thank you.'

'I suppose it's the thought of seeing your handsome young man that has put the roses back in your cheeks. If only I were twenty years younger . . .' Hester grinned.

Marianne laughed. 'I'm glad you're not. I bet you were a looker back then.'

'I didn't get many complaints. Now, I've left a little present for you girls in the room, so you better hurry in and get your share before it's all gone.'

'Where are you going?'

'Things to do, people to see.' She winked and tapped her nose as she tripped past Marianne in her red high-heeled shoes. 'Oh, and Happy New Year, love,' she called, glancing round and blowing a kiss.

In the bedroom, Lily and Edie were already dressed. Edie in a green dress with a peplum skirt and Lily wearing her favourite red dress. 'You two look like Christmas,' she said.

'And you will be the sugarplum fairy.' Lily gestured at the lilac chiffon dress that she'd laid out on Marianne's bed.

Marianne smiled. It was the dress she'd worn to marry Alfie, and also the one she'd been wearing at the dance when he'd first kissed her.

'No complaints?' Lily asked.

'Nope. Alfie loves that dress and I want him to find me irresistible tonight.'

'I don't think you need the dress for that,' Edie remarked, taking a swig from the bottle of wine.

Lily took it from her and handed to Marianne. 'You better have some of this before Edie drinks it all.'

Marianne took the bottle and sniffed. 'Ugh, no thanks,' she said, wrinkling her nose.

Edie snatched it back. 'All the more for us then.' She took another healthy gulp.

Lily rolled her eyes. 'Rate you're going, you'll have passed out by midnight.'

'Here's hoping.'

Marianne looked questioningly at Lily, who just shook her head.

Edie put the bottle down and took a last look in the mirror, patting her hair, which Lily had pinned up for her, and pinching her cheeks. 'I suppose I better go meet Greg then,' she said with a heavy sigh.

'You don't sound too happy about it,' Marianne remarked as she pulled her sweater over her head.

'I'm not,' Edie said abruptly as she left the room.

'Poor old Edie,' Marianne said. 'She's really going through it at the moment.'

'Aren't we all?' Lily said, thinking of Charlie and the fact that she had no idea where he was or if she'd see him again. He'd only been gone a few days, but it felt more like a year. She knew she could manage without him, but oh, how she wished she didn't have to.

∞

'That you, Edie?' Nellie called as Edie walked past the sitting room door.

Edie gritted her teeth. 'How did you know?' she asked, leaning on the door jamb. Her mother was wearing her purple dress with red flowers and a half-full glass of sherry sat on the table beside her.

'Cos you come down the stairs like a baby elephant,' Nellie said. 'Marianne's footsteps are soft like a cat, while Lily's are like the pitter-patter of rain.'

'Thanks very much,' Edie said moodily.

'I happen to like baby elephants,' Nellie said. 'So get that look off your face and come and have a drink with me.' She held up a glass, but Edie shook her head.

'Can't,' she said shortly, before carrying on down the second flight of stairs.

Nellie sighed heavily. Every year, she made the resolution to somehow make it up to her daughter for everything that had happened, but Edie could be as prickly as a cactus and as distant as the moon, and she had no idea where to even start. When she'd mentioned it to Jasper that evening, he'd laughed. 'Only way to bridge a gap with Edie is to take her hand and coax her across as though she's a frightened dog. And you ain't got the patience. Talk to Glad, maybe she can help.'

But there was no way she'd be speaking to Gladys about this. Not ever.

∽

Outside, the streets were full of happy people; some were already drunk – a bit like her, Edie thought as her head swam. But frankly, she wasn't nearly drunk enough. And now she had to face Greg. She burped and winced as acid burnt her throat. The wine had tasted bitter and metallic to her, but she'd hoped it would at least bring her to a point where she no longer cared about anything. But no such luck.

She turned into Snargate Street and walked towards the large arched doorway of the Hippodrome Theatre, where she slipped through the blackout curtains. The foyer was dimly lit, and as it was still an hour before the concert was due to start, there weren't many people around. Through the door that led to the auditorium, she could hear the piano playing and someone was singing 'Auld Lang Syne'. Just then a trumpet joined in and she went and peered down through the empty seats.

Alfie stood in the middle of the stage in his usual pose – back arched, head back, feet tapping – and Edie felt a surge of affection for him. He was such a lovely man; Marianne really was lucky. If she could find someone half as nice as Alfie, then she'd be doing well.

'Hey, beautiful!'

Edie jumped as a hand snaked round her waist and someone kissed her on the neck.

'God! Don't scare me like that,' she snapped, turning into Greg's embrace.

He grinned down at her, his bright blue eyes sparkling as he bent and kissed her lips, and Edie felt a flash of annoyance.

'Did you miss me?' he murmured.

'No,' she answered truthfully.

But rather than taking offence, Greg just laughed. 'You're lucky I know you don't mean that,' he said.

'I do mean it,' Edie replied, emboldened by the wine.

A flash of anger passed over his face, then he grinned. 'Feisty as ever, I see. Maybe you can put some of that aggression to good use later.' He winked suggestively and Edie resisted the urge to smack him. 'Let's go and find a seat.' He went to take her hand, but Edie avoided him.

'Let's go downstairs to the bar. We might be able to get a cup of tea or something.'

Greg grimaced. 'You know I hate damn tea,' he grumbled. 'I thought maybe we could find a seat at the back.' He bent and whispered in her ear, 'You know you want to.'

'Is that all you're after?' she asked tartly.

'No, of course not.' Greg looked offended.

'Then let's have a drink. I'm sure they'll have beer.'

He sighed heavily as she led the way downstairs where they took a seat on a couple of barstools.

Edie turned to Greg. 'I think we need to talk,' she said.

Greg raised an eyebrow. 'Uh oh, that sounds serious.'

'The thing is . . .' Edie began, trying to pick her words carefully, unable to meet his eye. 'I think—' But before she could say any more there was a loud crash that made the room shake, the light swing and flakes of plaster drop on to the bar in front of them.

Edie let out a squeal of alarm and dropped to the floor. Greg followed her, putting his arm around her protectively as the lights went out.

'That felt as though it was upstairs,' Edie exclaimed, her voice shaking.

'I think it was,' Greg grunted.

'Oh God, Alfie's up there!' Edie stood up and began to feel her way towards the stairs.

Vaguely, she heard Greg shout out, 'Edie! Get back here. There could be another one at any moment.'

But Edie ignored him. As she reached the foyer, a frantic voice yelled, 'Everybody out!'

Where just moments before the place had been almost deserted, now it seemed full of people rushing around and no one noticed her as she made her way to the auditorium and started to stagger down the aisle, the dim beam of her torch wobbling in front of her. Briefly someone caught her arm, but she managed to shake it off as she continued on, dust tickling her nose and throat. The lights flickered back on, and blinking against the glare, Edie saw that the piano seemed to have fallen through the stage. Beside it, a man was sitting with his knees drawn up to his chest and his arms around his head, as though trying to shield himself from the falling rafters. She looked up and saw a jagged hole through which the stars were faintly visible.

'Turn the bloody lights off!' a man shouted. 'Or do you want to show 'em where to drop the next one!' Immediately they were plunged into darkness again.

# Chapter 37

'We're off, Mum!' Lily said, leaning on the sitting room door. 'Last chance to join us?' She didn't like the thought of her mother sitting in alone on New Year's Eve.

'No. Me, Ethel and Phyllis'll be popping into the Oak later to see Mavis. Not sure there'll be much celebrating though,' Nellie said grumpily. 'This next year'll be worse than the last. Mark my words.'

'Maybe we'll join you after the concert,' Lily said.

'You do that, love. And make sure Edie enjoys herself, won't you? The poor girl needs some cheering up, what with this business with Mr Pearson.'

'We'll do our best. Try not to worry about her.'

'I worry about all of you,' Nellie said. 'After the last war ended I thought that at least my children wouldn't have to go through all that. And now look . . . If anything it's worse.'

'Oh, Mum. We're fine. Honestly.'

Nellie smiled a little. 'For now, love. For now.'

'Bye then, Mum,' Marianne said, pulling on Lily's arm and shaking her head at her. They didn't have time to indulge their mother's maudlin mood right now.

As they hurried out of the café, they were aware of voices and shouting around them. For a moment, across the road in the rooms above Perkins' Fish, Marianne spotted a chink of light and a couple of heads outlined against it. 'Oy!' She ran over and gestured up towards them. 'Shut the bloody curtains!'

The light disappeared abruptly and she sighed. 'Honestly, you'd think those boys would've learnt by now,' she said.

'Give 'em a break. Don was desperate to come to the concert tonight to see Alfie play.'

'Yes, well, he can't always get what he wants. The Hippodrome's no place for a young boy. The amount of strippers they've had there recently . . . Bert tried to get Alfie to go to see some the other night. Flamin' cheek.'

Lily laughed and dragged Marianne back along the pavement. 'Even if he'd gone, you know you don't have anything to worry about with Alfie.'

'Even so, I don't like the thought of him ogling naked women.'

A droning overhead made them stop abruptly. 'Oh Jesus,' Lily whispered. 'Can't they give us just one night of fun?'

Within seconds the noise seemed to be right overhead, and as the air raid siren started to screech, there was a crash as the plane released its stick of bombs.

The explosion made their ears ring, and around them people started to shout and run for cover. Marianne and Lily looked at each other in alarm. 'Was that over Snargate?' Marianne whispered.

'I don't know, but it sounded bloody close.'

They began to run down King Street, while above, the solitary plane turned and flew back across the Channel towards France.

By the time they reached the theatre, the place was crawling with rescue workers and ARP wardens. The street seemed relatively unscathed, but the fact that so many people were focusing on the Hippodrome made Marianne's heart leap with fear.

She ran up to the man guarding the entrance. 'Where did it drop?' she screamed. 'Tell me! Did anyone see where?'

'Northampton Street. Other side.'

Marianne gasped. The back entrance to the theatre was on that street, and, she knew, that was the side where the stage was situated –

the stage and the dressing rooms where the performers changed and waited to make their appearance.

'Let me in! My husband's in there!' she screamed.

'Sorry, love. It's not safe. Get to a shelter and wait for the all-clear.'

Marianne tried to dodge around him, but he caught her arm and swung her out into the street.

'I said no!'

Lily pulled Marianne back. 'He's right,' she said. 'Come on, over here.' She led her sister to the other side of the road, where a crowd had gathered.

'That you, Marianne, love?' a voice said. It was Ethel Turner.

'Mrs Turner, could you look after her, I'm going to help – they'll need people to give first aid,' Lily said.

'No!' Marianne wrenched her arm away. 'I am *not* standing here doing nothing when Alfie might be lying dead under a pile of rubble!' Her voice broke and she ran back to the entrance, dodging past the warden, who was busy holding others back, and disappearing inside.

Lily followed after her. 'I'm a nurse,' she said breathlessly. 'I can help.'

He nodded and allowed her to pass and she ran into the dark foyer. With her torch beam waving in front of her, she could see Marianne standing in the doorway to the auditorium. 'Alfie!' Marianne screamed, her voice cracking.

Lily joined her; it was completely dark inside, the occasional flicker of a torch all that could be seen.

'Marianne, go back,' she said gently. 'I'll find him.'

But Marianne ignored her and disappeared into the darkness.

207

# Chapter 38

In the brief moments that the lights had been on, Edie had spotted Alfie kneeling beside a man lying in front of the stage. 'Alfie!' she called over to him, training her torch in his general direction.

'Edie? Get over here. I need some help.'

Edie picked her way carefully towards him, trying not to breathe in too much dust, and knelt down beside the man, who was groaning and grasping at his crotch.

Alfie thrust a wad of cloth at her. 'Press it against his groin,' he shouted. 'We've got to stop the blood. I'm gonna help over there.'

Edie took the cloth and trained her torch on the man on the floor. A dark stain was spreading over the front of his trousers, and quickly she unbuttoned his fly and, seeing that there was a long, deep cut at the top of his thigh, she pressed down on it as hard as she could.

'Aargh! Get your hands off me!' the man shouted, his voice high and shrill.

'Oh, shhh. I need to stop the bleeding,' she admonished.

'Christ!' he groaned, lying back on the floor. 'To think I need to be bleedin' to death before I can get a pretty girl to touch me.'

Despite the situation, Edie let out a short laugh. 'Must be your lucky night.'

'Ain't it just.' Despite his humour, though, the man was shaking with pain and shock.

'It's all right. Take a deep breath,' Edie soothed, forcing her voice to stay calm, even though her heart was hammering and her armpits were damp with sweat.

Someone touched her shoulder and she squinted up, just making out Greg's face in the torchlight. 'Jesus Christ, Edith. Don't leave me in the middle of an air raid! You coulda been killed!'

'I'm fine,' Edie said through gritted teeth. 'But I think help's needed over there.' She nodded in the direction Alfie had gone.

Greg kissed her quickly on the head. 'All right. But wait for me outside when you're done. Don't disappear again.'

Edie returned her attention to the soldier; her arms were trembling with the strain of pressing down on the wound and her throat was stinging from the dust. From somewhere, she could hear people groaning. A man shouted out, 'Rosie Lockwood, are you safe?'

A woman's voice called back. 'I'm safe. Meet me outside.'

'And they say . . . romance is . . . dead,' the soldier gasped, attempting to laugh, but then falling back with another groan.

'Lie still. You've lost a lot of blood so you need to conserve your energy.'

'You a bloomin' nurse or sumfing.'

'A mechanic,' she replied drily.

The man let out a snort. 'Christ preserve me. You'll be pouring petrol down me throat if I'm not careful.'

Suddenly another pair of hands appeared, knocking her own out of the way. 'What do you think you're doin', girl?'

'Hey!' Edie cried. 'I'm trying to stop the blood.'

'Young girl like you's got no business touching a bloke down there. Leave it to me and get out.'

She recognised Mr Bulger, the man who had been filling in for Jasper over the past few months. 'I don't think he's in a position to take advantage,' she said, choking back a hysterical laugh.

'I'm . . . really . . . not,' the soldier panted.

'Don't matter,' he tutted. 'Jasper'd never forgive me. Nor would your mum. Go on, get out of here.'

Edie sighed. 'All right.' She patted the injured man on the shoulder. 'Get well soon.'

'Name's Frank,' he whispered. 'Frank Murphy. Look me up some time.'

Edie stood up to see what else she could do to help. In truth, she was relieved to be leaving the poor man, but now she realised that her hands were sticky with blood and she could feel that her skirt was damp. Her best dress ruined, she thought ruefully, but so what? As long as no one had died, that was all that mattered.

'Anyone need help?' she called, shining her torch around.

'Over here!' It was a woman's voice.

She swung the beam around and saw a woman in a Wren uniform. 'Marge?' she said in astonishment as the light shone on the woman's bright red hair.

'I need some light,' she said. 'Phil's stuck.'

Edie could see that Marge was frantically trying to pull one of the heavy auditorium chairs off a man's legs.

'Who's Phil?' she asked when she'd managed to stumble over to Marge.

'That'll be me,' the man said.

She shone the light at him. 'Hello, Phil,' she said, then she put the torch down and, between them, the two women managed to heave the chair off him and throw it to the side.

The man gasped with relief. 'Who knew a chair could be so heavy,' he said.

'Can you move your legs?' Marge asked urgently.

Phil obligingly bent his knees. 'No permanent damage. A couple of days' rest and I reckon I'll be fine.'

'Let me help you up, and we'll see if we can get some sort of transport back to the castle.'

They managed to heave the man upright and he swayed for a moment, before standing up straighter. 'Good as new,' he said, taking a stumbling step forward and almost collapsing back on to the ground.

'Whoa there, mister,' Marge said, putting her arm around his waist. 'Lean on me and I'll help you out of here. Thanks, Edie. Seems we're always meeting over injured men these days.'

Edie watched as the couple made their way slowly up towards the exit, Phil's arm around Marge's shoulder, hers clamped tight around his waist. Where was Rodney? she wondered. As far as she'd been aware, Rodney had been going to come to the concert with Marge, but clearly she'd had other plans. Well, good for her, Edie thought. Maybe a bit of competition would bring her brother to his senses and he would finally admit that Marge was perfect for him.

A shout at the entrance to the auditorium brought Edie's attention back to the present.

'Alfie!' a voice screamed.

Edie made her way up the aisle, past Marge and Phil.

'It's all right, Marianne,' she called out, even though she was certain her sister couldn't hear her.

When she reached the door, Marianne was being held back by a fireman.

'Alfie's fine,' Edie gasped. 'He's just helping people, but there's not a scratch on him, I promise.'

Just then, Lily barrelled in. 'I'm a nurse. Let me through.'

The man stood aside without a murmur, and Marianne took her chance, rushing into the dark theatre and promptly tripping on a seat that had been thrown into the aisle, nearly knocking over Marge and Phil in the process.

'Steady on!' Marge exclaimed as the two of them struggled to stay upright.

'Sorry—' Marianne squinted at the dark figures in front of her. 'Marge?' she exclaimed.

'Marianne!' Marge said at the same time.

211

'Ladies, this ain't a social occasion. Now, I told you to get out.' The fireman grabbed Marianne's arm and pulled her back to the exit. 'And as for you, miss' – he turned a stern glance on Marge – 'get that man to the ambulance outside, then hop it.' He looked at Edie. 'And you too. You're hampering rescue operations.'

Seeing the sense of his words, they trooped outside where an ambulance was parked in the street. 'Bloody hell!' Edie said, wrapping her arms around herself and starting to shiver as the shock caught up with her.

One of the medics brought over a blanket and wrapped it around her, while Marge helped Phil into the back of the ambulance. 'Who's he?' Marianne shouted over the wail of the air raid siren.

Edie shrugged. 'I don't know,' she said, teeth chattering.

Marianne put her arm around her shoulders. 'Sit down, Edie. I'll go see if I can find some tea. Was it very bad?' she asked.

'There weren't that many people in there, so considering there's a bloody great hole in the roof, it wasn't nearly as bad as it could have been.'

She stared up at the building opposite. The windows were blown out, but otherwise it appeared untouched.

'Girls, get to shelter,' a warden called, waving his torch beam in their direction.

'I need to wait for my husband,' Marianne shouted back. 'I'm going nowhere.'

'It's your bloody funeral, then,' he said, moving down the street to urge others who'd come out to see the damage to get to the nearest shelter, which was probably Barwick Caves at the end of the road.

A horn beeped and there was a loud rattling as the WVS van made its way slowly down the road. Edie watched it, her ears ringing from the explosion and the air raid siren.

'Stay there!' Marianne shouted, then she walked into the middle of the road. 'This way!' she called, waving her arms, although Edie couldn't imagine the driver would hear her.

The van stopped and Mrs Palmer leant her head out of the window, her tin helmet askew on her perfectly coifed hair. 'Anyone for tea?' she called.

'Bloody fool woman,' the warden muttered beside her. 'Tea in the middle of a raid, I ask you!'

Edie felt her shoulders start to shake and suddenly she was laughing hysterically. But soon the laughter turned to sobs and she pulled the blanket tighter around her and gave in to the tears.

'No milk or sugar, but it's hot.' Marianne had returned. 'Edie?' she said softly, crouching down beside her. 'Hey, love, it's all right. Nobody died.'

'That's not why I'm crying,' Edie sobbed.

'Why then?'

'Everything's so awful.' She leant her head on her sister's shoulder.

'Did Greg say something to upset you?'

'Nooo! I don't care what Greg says.'

Just then Marge came and sat beside them, putting her head down between her knees. 'Hell's bells,' she gasped. 'That was a bit too close for comfort.' She sat up and leant her head against the wall for a moment. 'Is she all right?' she said when she noticed Edie held tight in Marianne's arms.

'I'm f-f-fine,' Edie stammered between her sobs. 'Just the sh-sh-shock.'

'Marge, look after her, will you. I'm going back in. No one'll stop me this time.'

Marge nodded and put her arm around Edie's shoulder, pulling her close, and soon Edie's sobs died down.

Finally, she asked, 'Wh-who's Ph-Phil?'

Marge chuckled. 'A bomb's just dropped right in front of you, the air raid siren's wailing, there's blood and mayhem everywhere you look and that's all you've got to say?'

Edie nodded against her shoulder. 'Y-y-yes. And where's R-R-Rodney?'

'Phil's an army chaplain I got to know recently. A very nice man, as it happens, and not afraid to tell a girl when he likes her. Unlike some I could mention. As for your brother, last I heard, he was planning on joining us later.'

'Has anyone seen my girls?' a familiar voice shouted.

'Over here, Mrs C,' Marge called.

Soon Nellie dropped down in front of them. 'Thank God!' She pulled Edie away from Marge and pressed her head tightly into her shoulder, muttering, 'Thank God, thank God!'

Edie sank into her mother's embrace, comforted for a moment by the familiar smell of her lavender soap . . . But then suddenly she felt suffocated as a memory came back to her: her mother squeezing her tight, pressing her head to her shoulder, not letting her look at something behind her.

'Let go,' Edie mumbled, trying to catch her breath. 'I need to see!'

'Shh, love. You're safe now,' Nellie said soothingly.

'No! I need to see.' Edie wrenched herself free.

'What's wrong?' her mother asked, bemused.

In the dark Edie couldn't see her mother's expression, but her voice had sounded strange to her. Her ears started to buzz, nausea swirling in her stomach and she turned her head and was sick on the pavement.

'It must be the shock,' Marge said sagely, getting up and crouching beside Edie. 'Here, love, take a sip of tea.'

Edie felt a cup pressed to her lips and she took a grateful gulp. 'Sorry,' she muttered. 'I don't know what happened . . .' But she did. Because that grip, that smell . . . it made her feel exactly as she did when she had those nightmares.

She stood up, throwing off the blanket, suddenly feeling too hot, despite the winter chill.

'Come on, I'll take you home.' Nellie stood up with her.

'No! Just leave me alone!' Edie shouted as she started to run down the road, shoving past anyone who got in her way.

In the theatre, Marianne stumbled down the central aisle, one hand stretched out to the side, brushing over the chairs. 'Alfie!' she called into the dark. When there was no answer, she started to move more quickly. 'Has anyone seen the trumpeter?'

'Marianne!' Her heart leapt at the sound of her husband's voice coming from somewhere near the stage.

'Alfie, I'm here!' She reached the front and turned right. 'Where are you?' Suddenly she felt strong arms come round her and she smelt Alfie's unique scent of Imperial Leather soap and the sandalwood of his hair oil. She buried her head in his shoulder, sobbing with relief.

'I thought you were dead,' she whispered.

His arms squeezed her tighter. 'It'll take more than a bomb to kill me off. You shouldn't have come in here. It could've been dangerous.'

'But you're in here. What else could I do?'

He caught hold of her hand and they sat down on the dusty seats. 'I don't think it's as bad as it looks,' he said. 'Far as I can make out, there's a few that need treatment, but no one's died. It's a bloody miracle. Concert's off though. Bang goes New Year! Literally!' He gave a wry laugh.

'Are we going to let those buggers ruin our New Year?'

For a moment, the noise ceased as people looked towards the stage.

A torch went on and Herbert Armstrong, the theatre manager, held the light to his face. 'Well, are we?'

'No!' A man's voice echoed down from the gods.

'Right, then. All those treating the injured, keep up the good work. Meantime, I need a group of strong lads over here. We're gonna dig the piano out and have the concert of our lives. Are you in?'

'You go, love,' Alfie said to her gently. 'I'm going to help old Armstrong, and I need to find my trumpet. It's around the stage somewhere.'

Marianne gave him a kiss. 'Don't be long. I have something to tell you.'

# Chapter 39

Head down, arms folded tightly across her chest, Edie walked blindly towards King Street. As she turned the corner, she walked straight into a man who was walking from the opposite direction.

'Look where you're bloody going,' she shouted, though she knew it wasn't his fault. It was pitch-black and she'd not been paying attention, which in the current circumstances was foolish.

'Sorry,' the man said. 'Are you all right?'

The voice was familiar, and she looked up at him. He was wearing what looked like a pilot's cap. For the first time that evening, Edie felt her heart lift.

'Bill?'

'Edie? Christ, were you there? I only got in an hour ago. Went to dump my bag at the garage to find it boarded up.'

'Oh God, Bill, it's all such a mess!' She threw herself against him and his arms closed round her.

'Did the theatre get bombed? Is anyone hurt?' he asked with concern.

'I don't know. I think we've all had a lucky escape,' she said vaguely. 'But I have to go.' She turned right and started to walk towards the seafront.

'Hold up!' he called. 'Where are you going? We're in the middle of a bloody raid.'

She stopped and looked up towards the sky, cocking her head to listen for planes, but the only noise was the sound of voices calling out to each other and the relentless screech of the siren. 'They've gone,' she said. 'Do you know if anywhere else has been hit?'

'I don't know. But from the sounds of it, it looks like they dropped one bomb, then hightailed it out of here. Look, let me take you back to the café. It's not safe out here right now. Then I want you to tell me everything.'

Edie didn't protest as he led her back up King Street; in fact, she was relieved. She'd wanted to get away from her mother and the sudden memory that her embrace had evoked; to try to work out what it could mean. But now she realised she wasn't sure she wanted to know. Her stomach fluttered with anxiety, and she clung to Bill's arm more tightly. 'I'm so glad you're back,' she said, leaning her head against his shoulder. 'I've felt so alone.'

'I'm flattered.' Bill's tone was dry. 'I wasn't aware that you'd missed me quite so much.'

'I haven't,' she said bluntly. 'But no one else seems to care about your uncle, and I don't know what to do! And then there's your dad . . .'

Bill was silent for a moment. Then he sighed. 'Yeah. Stuff tends to get strange when Dad's around.'

They had reached the back gate to the café by then, and Edie pushed it open. 'What do you mean?'

Bill didn't reply as he walked through the yard and opened the back door.

'Please tell me. What do you mean?' she repeated as they entered the kitchen.

He looked at her, his expression bleak, but it quickly turned to one of concern. 'You're covered in blood!'

Edie glanced down at her dress. The green fabric was stiff with dried blood while her hands were streaked with brown.

'Oh God.' The room started to spin around her, and noticing her pallor, Bill gently pulled her towards him.

'It's all right,' he said softly, holding her tight against his chest. 'You're all right.'

'That poor man. I tried to stop the bleeding . . . There was so much of it . . . I don't even know if he's still alive.'

'Come on.' Bill took her hand and led her to the stairs. 'Wash and change first, then we'll talk.'

She followed him, too exhausted to argue and while Bill sat in the sitting room, she walked slowly up the stairs and went into the bathroom. Staring at herself in the mirror, she could see why Bill had been so concerned. Her hair was matted with blood from where she had run her hand through it, and there was a dark-red smudge on her cheek, while her blue eyes were shadowed. She scrubbed her face with cold water until her cheeks were rosy, then tried to rinse her hair in the sink, but she soon gave up, snatching up a towel and rubbing at it instead, leaving dark-brown streaks on the white cloth. Her mother would not be happy with that, she thought wryly. Then she gathered up the wet strands of hair and pinned them into a bun.

Once she'd changed into some trousers and a warm jumper, she returned to the sitting room and for the first time since she'd bumped into him, she looked at Bill properly. The last time she'd seen him, he'd been wearing oily overalls, and had been nothing like the polished man in RAF uniform in front of her. He seemed larger somehow, his shoulders broad and strong beneath his jacket, his brown hair short and Brylcreemed away from his forehead.

He glanced up at her and smiled. 'That's better. Here.' He held a teacup out to her. 'I nicked some of your mum's sherry. Couldn't find the glasses, though.'

Edie grimaced. 'I hate that stuff.'

'Just a sip. For the shock.'

She reached out for the teacup, but as she did so, her vision blurred as the picture of another hand, holding a similar cup, came into her mind. Her ears started to buzz again as the familiar ball of anxiety returned to her stomach. She slumped onto the sofa beside

Bill and put her head in her hands. What was happening to her? First her mother's smell, then this . . . Was she going mad?

'Edie?' Bill said. 'Are you all right?'

She looked up at him and managed to smile. 'Yes. Sorry. I think the evening's catching up with me, that's all.'

He pressed the cup into her hand. 'I'm not surprised. You've had a horrible shock. Come on, just a small sip.'

She took the cup and drank, relishing the sting of the alcohol as it worked its way down her throat. 'Tell me what you meant about your dad,' she said, determinedly shaking off the strange vision.

Bill took a sip of his own drink. 'You weren't the only one whose dad was changed by the war. Though of course I didn't realise it when I was young. I'd never known him any other way.'

'What do you mean?'

'My dad . . . he's the life and soul, always got a laugh and a joke. Everyone loves Walter.'

'I don't think they do,' she responded. 'I certainly don't, and nor does Mavis at the Oak, or Jasper. As for your uncle . . . Well, I don't think there's much love lost there either.'

'No, there isn't. But my mum adored him, even though he wasn't around much. He'd come home for a few weeks, then go off again. We never knew what he did or where he went. He always said he needed to clear his head and it was better if he wasn't near us when the moods came.'

'He was probably right,' Edie said. 'Though it must have been hard on you.'

Bill shrugged. 'More so for Mum, but she never said a word against him. As for me, I had Uncle Clive and Auntie Ruth. But I can't forgive Dad for not being around when Mum got so sick.'

'Why didn't you stay with your uncle after your mother died?'

'Dad and Uncle Clive fell out – something about Mum's will. See, Grandad left the garage to both his children, so when Mum died, Dad assumed he'd inherit her share. I'm not sure what happened about that. Anyway, he got a job as a chauffeur for some retired general in Cambridge that came with a nice little flat and I think he took me to spite Uncle Clive. It was only once I was living with Dad all the time that I started to understand what he was really like . . .' Bill paused, as though trying to find the right words.

Finally, he said, 'He's a bitter, angry man, Edie. He was in the navy in the last war and was horribly injured in the Dardanelles. He has scars all over his body from the burns. But he was one of the lucky ones. A lot of his shipmates were burnt alive in front of him.'

'Oh, that's awful,' Edie gasped. 'He must have suffered dreadfully.'

'He was in hospital for over a year. Churchill was in charge of the navy at the time, and Dad hates that man. Even before he became prime minister, Dad never shut up about him. But since Churchill took charge, it's made him even more angry. And he *hates* this war.'

'We all hate this war, Bill,' Edie said. 'It's not exactly a controversial view.'

'I phrased that wrong. He doesn't just hate this war; he doesn't *believe* in it.'

Edie stared at him in confusion. 'That's hardly a criminal offence though, is it?'

Bill sighed. 'That depends on whether you decide to actively do something about it. The family he worked for . . . they ran this group called The Link. And my dad became interested. He started to go to their meetings. He and the general became great friends.'

Edie's brow furrowed in confusion. 'What sort of meetings?'

'Meetings with people who believe that Hitler is some sort of genius and that only he can bring peace to the world.' Bill couldn't meet her gaze as he said this. 'Fascists,' he whispered finally.

'But that's what your dad said about Mr P. He said that was probably why he'd been arrested.'

'That's a bloody lie!' Bill exclaimed, standing up and beginning to pace in agitation. 'It was Dad who did those things! Hang on . . .' He paused for a moment, collecting his thoughts. 'You don't think he could have, I don't know, implicated Uncle Clive in some way?'

'It's possible, I suppose,' she said uncertainly. She explained what had happened the night the garage had caught fire. 'Rodney thinks that someone threw a Molotov cocktail through the window. And there was someone in the flat before the window broke. And your dad was in Dover the day it happened and the day after . . .'

'Oh God.' Bill collapsed back onto the chair and put his head in his hands. 'I need to talk to him. Do you know where he is?'

Edie nodded.

'Where?'

'In Hawkinge. I think he's working for the Fanshawes.'

'The beer family? Hang on, wasn't that man you were going out with last year one of them?'

Edie flushed, lowering her eyes to stare down at the purple and yellow swirls on the carpet.

Bill started to laugh but there was no humour in it.

'It's not funny,' Edie said sullenly.

'Well, it is a bit.' He picked up his cup and downed the sherry in one. 'I was going to ask you to come with me when I confront him, but I'm guessing you won't be too keen.'

Edie's stomach roiled at the thought of going to Henry's home, but she'd promised she'd do anything to help her boss, so how could she refuse? 'I'll come if you want me to,' she said reluctantly. 'I've been trying to speak to a lawyer – Mr Wainwright – we should go see him too.'

Bill nodded. 'Maybe. God! I hate feeling so helpless!'

'I know. But at least we can work on this together now.'

'You really love Uncle Clive, don't you?'

'He's one of the best men I know,' Edie said simply.

Bill smiled and nodded. 'He is. Thank you for believing in him.'

Despite everything, Edie found herself smiling back at Bill. 'I'm just glad you're here.' She reached across for his hand and he took it in a firm grasp.

'Me too,' he said. 'Me too.'

# Chapter 40

By the time the all-clear sounded, quite a crowd had gathered outside the theatre, and despite the situation, the news that there had been no serious injuries meant people were almost cheerful as they drank tea from the WVS van. In the dim light of its shielded headlights, Marianne could see Mrs Turner and Reenie, along with several others, starting to clear some of the debris from the road.

'Good evening, Marianne. I'm relieved to find you unharmed.' It was Roger Humphries.

'Roger,' she said, sighing silently.

'Officer Humphries,' someone called out, coming towards him. 'You got any news about this latest attack? Seemed a bit odd, don't you think? One plane, one bomb. And directly on the theatre where there was a free concert for the troops tonight.'

'I have no idea what you're talking about, Mr Hames,' Roger said. 'And if you will excuse me, I'm rather busy discharging my duties.'

'As you wish, Officer. But I thought you might be interested to know what I saw not long before the bomb dropped.'

'And what was that?'

'Well, I was on my way to the stage door on Northampton Street, when I saw someone with a torch. Not your ordinary torch, mind, this threw out a lot more light. But get this, I heard a plane and then I swear that torch flashed up towards the sky. Three long flashes. Then not two minutes later – *Boom!*'

'And did you see who was holding the torch?' Roger asked.

'No.'

'Any impression at all? Sex, size, height?'

'You been nosing about again, Ron?' Nellie joined them.

'Just saying what I saw. And no, sorry, I couldn't make out anything about them.'

'This is very concerning,' Roger said, unsure what he should do about it.

'Perhaps you'd like me to come and make a statement at the station tomorrow,' Ron suggested helpfully.

'Yes! Yes, that's what you must do. I shall inform Inspector Forrest.'

Nellie laughed. 'Oh yes, the great detective, who tried to get my Lily done for treason. That'll be a help.'

'This is serious, Mrs C,' Ron said. 'Things have been strange in Dover recently. I mean, look at the fire at the garage, Mr Pearson's arrest on some unknown charge, the sticky-backs that appeared in the town . . . And now this.'

More people gathered around them, as news of what Ron Hames had seen spread.

'Are you suggesting someone's out to cause mischief?' Brian Turner asked.

'It's possible.'

'Give me strength,' Nellie snapped. 'You seen the town recently? Are you seriously suggesting that all this destruction is cos someone shone a torch?'

'Of course not,' Ron said. 'But this seems different.'

'Seems exactly like always to me. You're just looking for a sensational story for your rag.'

Somebody burst out of the theatre at that moment, shouting, 'Make way! Make way!'

Everyone stopped as a trumpet started to play 'In the Mood'.

'What the . . .' Roger muttered. 'This can't be allowed.'

224

But nobody listened to him as Mr Armstrong, still dressed in his tails – now slightly dusty and with a rip in one sleeve – called out, 'Who's in the mood for a party!'

A cheer went up. 'Right then, please follow Private Lomax to the market square. The theatre might be down, but the players are most definitely NOT OUT!'

He stepped to the side, and a group of men staggered out carrying the piano between them. Marianne noticed that Greg was among them, his cap sitting askew on his fair hair, a broad grin on his face as he looked around, presumably searching for Edie. Marianne wondered briefly where her sister had got to, but then the piano was set down on its wheels and pushed up the street.

Nellie clapped her hands and slipped her arm through Ethel Turner's. 'I've had enough of people who see conspiracies wherever they look. You should be reporting on this, Ron. Because this is Dover! Nothing keeps us down, and we stick together. There ain't a soul in this town that I wouldn't trust with me life. So put away your damn notebook just for one night and come and see what Dover's really all about. Come on, Ethel, you ready to dance the night away?'

Ethel laughed. 'Not half. Hey, where're Phyllis and Mavis? Let's get the old gang back together for a bit of sing-song.'

The two women marched away to follow the procession to the square, while Muriel Palmer watched from her van in astonishment, before hastily pulling down the hatch, then, beeping her horn, she drove carefully away in the opposite direction.

Lily emerged from the theatre, her hair was straggling around her face and her dress had a dark smudge on it, but she laughed as behind her, from the direction of Barwick Caves, a group of soldiers suddenly appeared.

'Is the concert off?' one of them asked.

'Not on your life! Make your way to the square, lads,' Mr Armstrong called. 'Jerries have put a bit of a dent in our celebrations, but it don't mean we can't have a damn good time!'

Marianne squealed as someone caught her round the waist. 'Come on then, sis! Get moving!' It was Jimmy, and before she could protest, he picked her up and threw her over his shoulder while Bert did the same to Lily.

Marianne thumped her hands on Jimmy's broad back. 'Let me down, you great lump!' she screeched. But Jim ignored her and Marianne was laughing too much to protest any more. As they got nearer the square though, she started to feel sick.

'Seriously, Jim, I'm gonna be sick,' she shouted.

Jimmy stopped abruptly and set her on her feet while Marianne leant against the wall of the Westminster Bank and tried to catch her breath.

'Sorry,' he said. 'I didn't mean to make you ill. Bert, get Lily over here,' he called to his brother who had been following just behind them.

'Marianne? Are you all right?' Lily put her hand up to feel her sister's forehead. It was cool and clammy.

'I'm fine.' Marianne flapped her hands at her siblings. 'Go and join the fun, I'll be with you soon as I get my breath back.'

'You sure there's nothing wrong?'

Marianne looked at her sister and smiled. 'I'm very sure. In fact, it's the opposite.'

Lily frowned for a moment, but then her expression cleared and she grinned. 'You mean . . . ?'

'Shh. Just between you and me for now. Alfie doesn't know yet.'

Lily stepped forward and hugged her. 'Oh, love. That is the very *best* news.' Inside, though, she couldn't help worrying what this would do to Edie. The contrast between her sisters' situations couldn't be more stark, but it seemed likely that come the summer – no matter what Edie said – there might be two babies at the café, and the prospect filled her with misgiving. This would set her mother in a spin and no mistake.

'If you're feeling better,' Bert said, 'let's go join the fun.'

226

Lily linked one arm through Marianne's and they followed after their brothers.

'Jim!' Reenie called. 'I've been looking everywhere for you. Come on, let's dance!'

'Sure you're all right, Marianne?' Jimmy said over his shoulder as Reenie dragged him into the centre of the square.

'Yes! Go, enjoy yourself,' she called after him. She looked around expecting Lily to still be beside her, but she too had disappeared, as had Bert.

As the piano began to play 'Roll Up the Carpet', Alfie started to sing and people began to emerge from the nearby buildings. Soon Market Square was filled with dancing shadows. The piano had been set up by the war memorial, and in the light of the moon, Marianne could see Alfie's silhouette. She pushed towards him, standing as close as she could. He spotted her as he took a break between songs, and pulled her to stand with him.

'My wife, Marianne Lomax, everyone!' he cried. 'The most beautiful woman in the world.'

There was a cheer and Marianne buried her face in Alfie's shoulder, her heart almost bursting with love, as he began to play 'You Are My Sunshine'. She touched her stomach and smiled; she couldn't wait to tell him her news. This baby would have the best life, she thought fiercely. War or no war, it would never be ostracised because its mother was unmarried like poor Donny had been. And though there was so much hardship and danger around, with new life came hope, and this coming year suddenly felt like a new beginning.

'Come and join us, Marianne!' It was her mother, who was in the middle of a circle of people, dancing with three of her best friends – Mavis, Phyllis and Ethel – no Gladys, though, she realised with a pang of pity for the other woman. Just for a moment, her happy bubble dissipated as she thought of her own three best friends – now only two: Marge and Reenie. She should share this moment with them.

After giving Alfie a quick kiss on the cheek, she shoved through the crowd, searching for her friends. For a moment her attention was caught by a couple of small figures darting out of Perkins' Fish. She smiled indulgently. Little monkeys, she thought. But who could blame them? What child would be happy to stay inside while all this excitement was going on outside their window. Let them have their fun while they could. Soon enough reality would be crashing back down on them, but for this one night, she'd let them off.

She went to stand by the café window, listening to the music and tapping her feet. Somebody caught her arm and dragged her into the square. It was Marge. Soon, Reenie joined them and the three girls danced together into the crowd.

# Chapter 41

Edie and Bill sat in silence, the warmth of Bill's hand in hers comforting after the roller coaster of emotions she'd gone through. If only he really did have the power to solve all her problems, she thought, as she pressed her other hand into her stomach, wondering whether, if she hit it hard enough, she could somehow force this little alien creature out.

Suddenly her eyes widened. 'Oh God! I forgot Greg!'

'Who's Greg?'

'He's ... he's ... just some man I was going to the concert with.' She got up hastily and started across the room. 'I left him at the Hippodrome.'

Bill raised his eyebrows. 'A boyfriend?'

'No!' Edie said defensively. 'At least, not anymore.'

'You don't sound very sure.'

'Of course I'm sure,' she snapped more harshly than she intended, but thoughts of the baby and Greg were making her tense again.

He held up his hands in apology. 'Edie, it's none of my business. You don't have to explain to me.'

'No. Sorry. I'm just—' She was interrupted by loud cheering outside and the sound of a trumpet playing 'In the Mood'. 'What's happening?' She went to the window. 'Turn out the light, Bill. I want to have a look.'

He did as she asked and came to join her at the window. It was a clear, frosty night and the sky was awash with stars, the nearly full moon throwing its silvery light on a large crowd jostling into the square, all of them apparently following a group of men who were half pushing, half carrying a piano, which they put down beside the war memorial.

'What are they doing?' Bill muttered.

'Oh my gosh,' Edie said wonderingly, the tension she'd felt just a moment earlier suddenly dissipating. 'They've brought the concert to the square.'

'I always said the people in this town were crazy.' Bill started to laugh. 'Come on, let's go and join in.'

Edie shook her head. 'I don't really feel like a party. You go.'

'Oh come on, don't be a spoilsport. God knows we both deserve a bit of fun. Didn't you say you needed to find this Greg?'

'No, really. I'm not feeling all that well. My ears are still ringing from the blast and I have a terrible headache.'

'Oh, Edie, I'd almost forgotten. Of course you're not up to it. Do you want me to stay with you?'

'No. You go and have fun. The others will be there somewhere. And if you need a place to stay tonight, I'm sure Mum won't mind you kipping on the sofa. Hester's in the boys' room, so maybe tomorrow we can jig things round a bit so you can have a bed.'

'Who's Hester?'

Edie smiled slightly. 'It's a very long story. Come on, I'll let you out of the front door.'

They went down the stairs where Edie unbolted the door. Bill gave her one last searching look. 'Are you absolutely sure you don't mind?'

She shook her head and he smiled. 'I won't be long,' he said as he pulled the door open, only to be confronted by a tall man who was lurking outside.

'Who the hell are you and where's Edith?'

Edie closed her eyes. Greg. She wasn't sure she had the energy to deal with him right now, but she supposed she owed him an explanation.

Bill backed into the café and Greg followed.

'Uh, I'm guessing you're Greg?'

Edie sighed, then making sure the blackout curtain was shut, she turned on the lights.

'Jesus H. Christ, Edith! I've been looking for you everywhere and it turns out you're cosied up here with another man!'

'It's not like that. You go, Bill.'

'I think I should stay,' he said, throwing a challenging glare at Greg, whose face had flushed unattractively.

'No! Please. I need to talk to him on my own.'

Bill nodded. 'All right.' He turned to Greg. 'Listen, mate, she's had a rough night, so take care of her.'

Greg didn't answer. His eyes were fixed on Edie, and she quailed slightly at the anger in them. She'd never seen him like this. But then, every time they'd met over the past few months, they'd been having fun – or at least, he had.

After the door had closed behind him, Greg walked forward and grabbed Edie by the upper arms. 'Are you going to tell me what all that was about? I've been worried sick that you were lying dead or injured and all the while you've been with some other guy. How could you be so selfish!'

Edie pulled herself away from his grip, rubbing at her arms. 'I'm sorry. I just … Well, I just needed to come home. And I bumped into Bill. He's Mr Pearson's nephew, so we had a lot to talk about.' She realised as she said this that Greg had no idea what had been happening at the garage, and frankly right now she couldn't be bothered to tell him.

'He seemed mighty concerned with your welfare! Have you been playing me for a fool? Or is it just you've got a taste for pilots?'

'That's enough!' Edie exclaimed, her patience gone. 'If you don't want to talk rationally, then you need to leave!'

'Oh, that's just great. You arrange to meet me, then run off with another guy, and *I'm* the one in the wrong?'

231

'For God's sake, Greg! *You* arranged to meet *me*! I didn't even want to see you. Now, I'm tired, my head aches and I don't have the energy for this! Please, just go. And don't come back.'

'You little tart!' Greg raised his hand and Edie backed away from him, her heart starting to thump.

'Oy! Get away from her, or I swear I'll knock your teeth so far down your throat, you'll be spitting them out for weeks!'

Edie whirled around, her eyes widening at the sight of Jasper standing in the kitchen doorway. So much thinner than he used to be, his white hair standing out around his head, and, most miraculously of all, his blue eyes focused on Greg.

Greg let out a laugh. 'You could try, old man, but it'd be the last thing you ever did.'

Ignoring Greg, Edie let out a squeal and ran forwards, throwing her arms around Jasper's neck. 'Jasper! Oh my God, Jasper, you can see!'

Jasper gathered her close, but his gaze never left Greg. 'I can see, all right. And what I see is a big strong man raising his hand to a woman. You better get out now, sonny Jim, before I call the coppers.'

Greg stood for a moment clearly unsure what to do. Finally, he spat on the floor. 'She's just a common whore anyway!' Then he spun on his heel and slammed out of the front door.

Edie started to sob and Jasper kissed the top of her head. 'It's all right, love. He's gone now. You didn't think old Jasper would ever let anything happen to you, did you?'

Edie shook her head against his chest, but found she couldn't stop crying.

After a while, Jasper spoke again. 'Edie, love. Can I sit down? We managed to cadge a lift from the hospital, but they couldn't get down Cannon Street what with all them crowds, and the walk's done me in. Poor old Dot had to half carry me the rest of the way.'

Edie pulled away and wiped her sleeve across her nose. She'd not even noticed Dot was there. 'I'm sorry. I just can't believe you're here. And you can see!' She led him to his usual table at the side of the counter near the kitchen door, then gestured to Dot to sit down as well. 'Thank you for bringing him back, Dot. I think you could both do with a cuppa.'

She bustled into the kitchen and put the kettle on, annoyed to notice that her hands were shaking. Greg's threatening behaviour had shocked her. He might have pestered her in to bed, but he'd not *forced* her; she'd never suspected he could be like that. She braced her arms on the range and bent over, taking deep breaths to try to calm herself. At least one good thing had come out of this awful, endless evening. He might look older and thinner, but what did that matter? Because now Jasper was back, things didn't seem quite as bad as they had.

Once the kettle had boiled, she took the tray of tea back into the café and set it down on the table.

'So, when did you find out you could see again? Mum didn't mention it when she got back earlier.'

'Your mum don't know. It were after she'd left. I were sittin' there and I heard the explosion and I thought to meself, J*asper, if you don't get off your arse soon, you'll never see the town again.* And anyway, after the other day when you came in, I been worryin' myself sick about you and poor old Clive. You need me, love. So here I am.'

Edie smiled, her eyes swimming with tears, and she put her hand over his large veiny one. 'We do need you. Nothing is right when you're not here.'

Jasper squeezed her hand, looking pleased.

Dot took up the story. 'I was just doing a last quick check before I went off duty and found him tugging at the bandages. He wouldn't listen to a word I said, so in the end, what could I do but help him? If Matron ever finds out, she'll have me out on my ear!'

Jasper laughed. 'No chance. Apart from my Lily, you're the best of the bunch up at that hospital.'

Dot gave him a light punch on the arm. 'Anyway, I started to unwind the bandages. Oh my, Edie, my heart was in my mouth. If he couldn't see, then it would've bin awful. But then Jasper says—'

'Hey, can someone turn off the lights?' Jasper interrupted with a guffaw. 'I couldn't believe it. I had these pads on me eyes, so they've been shut, but then the bandages came off and the pads were loose and I couldn't wait any longer and I blinks them open and pull the pads off and the first thing I see is this one starin' down at me like I'm some sort of circus freak.'

Dot giggled. 'You coulda knocked me down with a feather. An' then he says, "I mean it, turn the ruddy lights out!"'

Jasper laughed again. 'Speakin' of, you couldn't dim these a bit, could ya?'

Edie got up and turned off the café lights, allowing just the light from the kitchen to shine through the door.

'Cor, that's better,' he said. Then he reached out a hand and stroked Edie's cheek. 'It's so bloody good to see you again, love.'

Edie felt the tears gather again, but she held them back. 'You will never know how happy I am, Jasper. We all love you so much. Mum's gonna be speechless when she sees you.'

Jasper grinned. 'Now, ain't that a thought. I known your mum for most of me life, and I can count on one hand the number of times she's been speechless.'

Outside, they heard the trumpet start to play 'Auld Lang Syne' and they stopped and listened. Then Edie held up her cup. 'Happy New Year, everyone. Now you're back, Jasper, I think this year might be better than any of us could have hoped.'

234

# Chapter 42

By the time the last notes of 'Auld Lang Syne' had faded away, Roger Humphries had returned with reinforcements from the police station to disperse the crowd.

One of the policemen raised a megaphone to his lips. 'You have fifteen minutes to leave the square. Anyone caught out after that will be arrested.'

There were loud boos, but gradually the square started to empty. When only the residents were left, Nellie said goodbye to her friends and made her way to the front door of the café. It was only as she was entering that she realised that since Edie had run away from her, she'd not seen her at all. She sighed. The music and dancing had taken her mind off what had happened earlier, but now it was all coming back. Surely it had just been the shock that had caused her to react so violently to the hug? But she couldn't deny it had hurt.

She walked through the blackout curtain and stopped short at the sight that greeted her. Was it possible to wish for something so badly that your mind conjured it up? she wondered. She blinked and looked again. He was still there. She opened her mouth to say something, but she was shaking so much, she couldn't get a word out.

'Well, what d'you know? The sight of me really has shut her up.' Jasper laughed and suddenly Nellie launched herself across the floor and threw her arms around his neck.

'You can see!' she gasped. 'You old fraud! You was faking all along. You just wanted a bit more time in bed.'

'Fooled you, though, didn't I?' He patted her back. 'But seriously, fair play to Lily's Dr Charlie cos that rectal rest did me the power of good.'

Dot spat out her tea. 'How many times do I have to tell you, it's *retinal*!' She giggled.

'Let me look at you,' Nellie said, cupping her hands around his face, studying him intently through the tears that had gathered in her eyes.

Jasper stared back and they were silent for a moment. 'By God, it's good to see you, Nellie,' he whispered finally. 'Few more wrinkles than last time, mind.'

Nellie laughed. 'That'll be all the sleepless nights you've given me. And anyway, have you seen your hair? It looks like the snowy peak of a mountain.' She stroked it fondly and Jasper caught her hand.

'I have seen it, as it happens. Makes me look distinguished, dontcha think?'

'No, it makes you look old,' Nellie responded quickly. 'But I don't care. Oh my goodness, this is the very best New Year. This calls for a celebration!'

She ran back to the door and soon they heard her voice, high and shrill as she called out across the square.

'Marianne, Lily, Bert, Jim, Rodney! Get your arses in here now!'

Then she rushed back. 'Edie! There's a coupl'a bottles of champagne left over from Marianne's weddin' in the basement. And there's some beer somewhere.'

Smiling, Edie stood up and went to find the drink. She was still exhausted, but the worst of it had passed as soon as she'd spotted Jasper, and seeing her mother so animated made her feel almost happy. Lily was right, her problems could wait until tomorrow. Tonight, she would celebrate with her family.

∽

In the doorway of the Westminster Bank across the square, Bert was kissing a petite dark-haired girl. At the sound of his mother's voice, he looked up. 'Sounds like I'm being summoned,' he murmured. 'But I'd rather stay here with you. I missed you tonight. Where were you?'

Susan giggled. 'That'd be telling.'

'Well, I don't care where you were. You're with me now and that's all that counts.'

'I really shouldn't be doing this.'

'No, you shouldn't. You are a very, very naughty girl.' He kissed the side of her neck.

'Oh, you have no idea, Bert. But I could show you sometime, if you like?'

'What about your fiancé?' he whispered.

'I won't tell if you don't,' she panted as Bert's hands fumbled beneath her sweater.

Bert pushed back. 'No. That's not good enough for me,' he said seriously. 'Either you want him or you want me. But until you break it off with him, then I think we shouldn't see each other anymore.' He turned abruptly and started to walk away.

Behind him, Susan cried out desperately. 'Bert, come back! It's you, Bert. It's you I want!'

'I need proof that it's over,' he called over his shoulder. 'Until then, I'll be seein' ya.' He walked on, grinning to himself. God, he was good. It had taken only a few days to win her round. Edie would be very pleased with him.

'Who's that?' It was Lily, who had been on her way home, but had stopped to have a quick chat with a friend.

Bert cursed under his breath. 'Don't be nosy.'

'She sounds upset. And what does she mean, "It's you I want." Please don't tell me you've taken up with a married woman?'

Bert laughed. 'Married people are more in Edie's line than mine.'

'Don't be horrid. You know that wasn't her fault.'

Bert grunted. 'Maybe, but still . . . And as for that one, she's nothin' for you to concern yourself about, I promise you that.'

Lily shrugged and allowed her brother to lead her across the square. Whoever it was, she felt sorry for her. Bert was a great brother, but he liked to play the field and the unfortunate woman he'd left in the doorway would no doubt be history by next week.

∽

By the door of Turners' grocery, Reenie pulled her lips away from Jimmy's. 'You better go.'

Jimmy shook his head. 'I don't think I can face one of my mother's dramas right now. You go. There's someone I want to see.'

Reenie stared after his dark figure as it loped away up Cannon Street. Jimmy had been distracted all evening, and though he'd laughed and danced and kissed her, she could tell that his thoughts were elsewhere. If it had been anyone else, she'd have worried he had another woman somewhere, but it was Jimmy, and she could guess where he was going: to see Colin's parents. Although surely they'd be in bed at this time – she couldn't imagine they'd have wanted to celebrate the new year.

Sighing, she turned blindly to cross the square, curious about what had caused the excitement in Nellie's voice.

'Hold up, Reenie,' someone called, grabbing her arm and swinging her round so she knocked into him.

'Oof!' Wilf staggered back. 'If I were any smaller, I'd be halfway across the square. You're not exactly a feather.' He chuckled.

'Shut up, Wilf,' Reenie said resignedly.

He nudged her. 'I were only joking.'

'Yeah, I always find it funny when people call me fat.'

'When did I call you fat?' Wilf sounded puzzled

'"You're not exactly a feather",' Reenie replied in a mocking voice. It was bad enough that Jimmy had just walked off and left her in the middle of the street – again – the last thing she needed was bloody Wilf Perkins making jokes at her expense.

'I didn't mean to imply . . . Look, I was just having a laugh. You know, like we used to. And I don't think you're fat. You're sturdy and strong and just right.'

'*Sturdy!* Wilf, I swear to God, you better stop now before I clump you one.'

'Come on, Reens, it's New Year; let's make a resolution that you an' me'll be nicer to each other.'

'Fine, I'll be nicer to you. Now I'm going over to the café to see what's going on. You coming?'

'Isn't lover boy goin'?'

'He'll be coming later.'

'He ran off the last time I saw you two as well.'

'So you did see me that day?'

'Of course I saw you.'

'Why didn't you say hello?'

'Because to begin with you looked a bit busy, and after . . . well, you looked so upset after he walked off that I didn't think you'd want to talk to me. Look, Reenie, I've got nothing against Jimmy Castle – in fact, I like the bloke – but I don't think he's the man for you.'

Reenie snorted. 'Luckily, it's what *I* think that counts.'

'And you're happy with him doing that?'

Reenie sighed. She didn't want to have this conversation with Wilf of all people. 'No, of course not. But he's going over to the Guthries . . . Colin's death hit him hard.'

'He's going visitin' at this time? Won't they be asleep?'

'Mrs Guthrie's always up. She hardly sleeps these days.'

'Still, it's a bit strange, don't you think? This excessive grief.'

'What do you mean?'

'I mean that lots of us have lost people. But Jimmy's grief seems a bit extreme.'

'Colin was more like a brother to him, really.'

'Brother, is it?' There was a sarcastic edge to his tone that Reenie didn't like.

'Oh, just go away, Wilf. It's none of your business who I see. And by the way, you can make as many New Year resolutions as you like, but as far as I'm concerned, nothing's changed between us.'

'Suit yourself,' Wilf called after her as she stomped across the square, but Reenie ignored him.

Time was, she'd have been thrilled to have him pay her this much attention, but those days were long gone. And it was all thanks to Jimmy Castle. And if Jim needed time to get over the death of his friend, then that is what she would give him.

✺

Marge was walking past Church Street with Jeanie and a few of the other Wrens she worked with when she heard Nellie's shout. She stopped for a moment, curious to know what the woman was so excited about. Some way ahead of them, Rodney was making his solitary way back to the castle. They'd barely spoken all evening. In fact, she wondered why he'd come at all, because she hadn't seen him dancing. She shrugged. She didn't care, but it sounded like his mother needed him.

Putting her fingers to her lips, she let out a loud wolf whistle. 'Rodney! Get back here!' she called.

There was no reply, so she tried again. 'Rodney Castle! Your mother needs you!'

A muffled voice came back. 'Tell her I'm busy.'

'Tell her yourself!' she called back.

Jeanie giggled. 'Honestly, you two. Can you just get it together so we can all stop this will-they, won't-they game. It's blooming exhausting. And anyway, I've got a couple of bob says you two will finally sort it out by summer, so you need to get on with it.'

'You've wasted your money, Jeanie. I'm seeing Phil now.'

'Pah. Padre Philip's good-looking and nice and everything, but you with a man of the cloth! I don't think so. Whereas if you and

Rodney ever get it together. Phewee! The sparks that come off you two would put them firebombs to shame.'

Marge tutted, her eyes fixed on the figure she could just make out coming down the road towards them.

'What's up now?' Rodney asked when he reached them.

'No idea. Your mum's just been shouting her head off out of the front door.'

He sighed. 'Right. I suppose I better go make sure no one's dying then. Or arrested. Or conspiring with traitors . . .' He walked towards the back gate then stopped.

'Well, are you coming?'

Marge had half a mind to say no, but she was desperately curious to know what was going on.

Jeanie gave her a small push. 'Go on, for God's sake. You know you want to.'

Marge bent and kissed her friend's cheek quickly, then hurried after Rodney.

❧

'Alfie,' Marianne whispered to her husband as he bent to put his trumpet back into its case.

'What is it, love?' Alfie asked distractedly.

'Do you remember I said I had something to tell you?'

'I remember everything you've ever said to me,' he replied.

She laughed. 'Liar. But I do want to tell you something.'

Alfie stood up and put his arms around her, pulling her in for a deep kiss. Finally, he pulled back. 'Go on then. Tell me.'

Before she could speak, her mother's voice rang across the square and they both sighed.

'Another drama at Castle's Café,' Alfie said with a chuckle. 'Let's go see what's happening.'

241

'No, wait,' she said. 'This is more important than anything Mum has to say.'

'What could ever be more important than your mother?' he said drily.

'We're going to have a baby,' Marianne whispered.

'What?' Alfie went still. 'Are you sure?'

Marianne giggled. 'Sure as I can be! Feeling sick, bad moods, missed monthlies, exhausted. Oh, it's the best feeling in the world!'

Alfie whooped and swung her off her feet, whirling her round until she had to beg him to stop or she'd be sick all over him. He lowered her gently to the ground. 'I love you so much, Mrs Lomax,' he said. 'I'm going to have a baby!' He shouted this last and Marianne shushed him.

'I don't want the whole square to know.'

'Why not? They will soon enough. When you start getting fat.' He patted her flat stomach. 'When?'

'Around July or August, I think.'

Alfie was silent for a moment. Finally, he said, 'I might not be here.'

'I know.' Marianne put her arms around him. 'But she'll be waiting for you when you get back.'

'She?'

'I fancy a little girl. A little girl called Daisy.'

Alfie stroked her cheek. 'Daisy Lomax,' he murmured. 'I love her already. Almost as much as I love her mother.' He bent his head to kiss her again.

After a while, Marianne pulled away. 'We better go in or she'll come out and drag us back,' she said, turning to look round the square. In the moonlight she could see Reenie and Wilf having a heated conversation, but there seemed to be no sign of Jimmy.

'Coming, sis?' Bert and Lily brushed past her.

'Doesn't seem like we have a choice. Any idea what's going on?' she asked as she and Alfie fell into step with them.

'None at all. But it better be good.'

'Bert was just having some *loving* in the bank doorway,' Lily said.

'Ugh. I'd rather not know,' Marianne said.

'Was it that bird you hit Ch—'

Bert elbowed his brother-in-law hard in the stomach.

'You hit a man over a girl?' Lily gasped. 'Sometimes I don't think I know you at all.'

'Maybe you don't. And Alfie, I prefer not to talk about it.'

'Course.' Alfie's voice sounded muted and Marianne squeezed his arm.

'That was uncalled for Bert,' she admonished.

'Sorry,' Bert said, though he sounded far from sorry.

Luckily the discussion was brought to an end as they reached the door where Reenie was waiting for them.

'No Jimmy?' Marianne asked.

'He, er . . . he said he had to see someone. Is it all right if I come in?'

'Of course. You're family, aren't you?' Marianne said, pushing the door open and slipping through the blackout curtain. Then she stopped abruptly and let out a gasp.

# Chapter 43

Jimmy walked up to the Guthries' door, his heart in his mouth. It was stupid, he knew, to be calling round at this time of night, but he'd had a sudden urge to talk to Colin's family. He'd been avoiding them for too long.

He stood on the doorstep for a few minutes, trying to gather his courage to knock. Before he did, though, a dark-haired young woman approached.

'Who are you?' she asked sharply.

He looked over his shoulder, and in the moonlight he recognised the woman he'd seen with Bert. He smiled. 'It's Susan, isn't it?' he asked.

She squinted up at him for a moment then her face relaxed. 'Jimmy Castle?'

He nodded.

'Blimey, you look like your brother. What are you doing here?'

Jimmy shrugged. 'I thought . . . Well, I just wanted to talk to your aunt and uncle.'

Susan dug a key from her pocket and unlocked the door. 'I'm not sure Aunt Mary will want to see you,' she said frankly. 'You're not exactly her favourite person.'

Jimmy sighed. 'I know. And I suppose that's why I've come. Your aunt was like a second mother to me when I was growing up and I . . . I . . .' He took a deep breath. 'I don't want her to hate me anymore.'

'Hmm. Well, not sure that'll ever happen, but come in if you must.'

Jimmy followed the girl upstairs. Once upon a time he'd been in and out of here all the time. The two of them used to help out in the bakery during the summer, Jimmy staying in Colin's room, getting up at four a.m. to turn the ovens on ... That had been the start, he remembered with a pang of longing for those far-off days. There'd been shame, it was true, but also pure joy.

In the sitting room, the air was thick with pipe smoke, and seated on two drab blue armchairs were Colin's parents.

'Mr and Mrs Guthrie,' Jimmy said humbly, taking off his hat.

Mary Guthrie looked at him through narrowed eyes. 'Shouldn't you be with Reenie?' she said bitterly.

Jimmy gazed down at the floor, not sure how to answer.

'Can you give us a moment, Jack,' Mary said to her husband. 'You too, Susan. Me and Jim's got things to talk about.'

Jack Guthrie stood up and put his arm on Jim's shoulder. 'It's good to see you, lad. Me and Mary have missed you.'

Jim felt a fresh wave of guilt. What would Colin say if he knew Jimmy had abandoned his parents when they'd needed him most?

Once the sitting room door shut, Mary gestured to the chair opposite her.

Jimmy sat down, fiddling with his cap on his knee.

'Well?' Mary said eventually. 'What have you got to say for yourself?'

Jimmy cleared his throat. 'I'm just so sorry, Mrs Guthrie. There was nothing I could do to save him ...'

'He is *not* dead!' Mary shouted. 'And the fact that you've given up on him so easily ...' She lowered her voice to a hiss. 'Did you think I didn't know? About you two?'

He looked up at her in alarm, his cheeks flushed red. 'You've never—?'

'Told anyone? Of course I haven't. Colin's my son. My heart, my life. You think I care who he loves – man, woman, dog ...? Whatever makes him happy. But I don't feel like that anymore. And do you know why?' She leant forward. 'Because you're not worthy of him. How could you go running off with some girl the minute you thought he was gone? How *could* you?' She shook her head. 'If there's one thing I know for sure, it's that Colin would *never* have done that if you'd been the one left in that stinking hole. Never! He'd have moved heaven and earth to find you. And I'd have helped him!' She stood up. 'Now, I want you to leave.'

Jimmy stood up, his head bent, his stomach swirling with shame and grief. 'I'm so sorry . . .'

'I don't care how you feel! And listen, as soon as Colin comes back to me, I'm going to tell him exactly how you've behaved. Because he deserves better than a snivelling coward like you.'

Blindly, Jimmy rushed out of the door, not noticing Susan standing in the dark kitchen doorway, a curious look on her face.

Out in the street, Jimmy leant against the wall, taking deep breaths. Everything Mary Guthrie had said had been justified. The pain of losing Colin hadn't lessened with the passing of time. He'd thought that maybe if he created a new life for himself, it would ease. But six months on, he was finding it harder and harder to face the day. Colin was gone, but Marianne had been right. He shouldn't pretend to be someone he wasn't – it would only make him more unhappy in the end.

Crouching down against the wall, Jimmy put his head in his hands and wept.

# Chapter 44

'Evenin' all,' Jasper said as everyone jostled into the café behind Marianne. 'And a Happy New Year to you.'

Lily was the first to react. 'Dad! What the hell are you doing here?'

'Thought I'd come to celebrate new year with my favourite people.'

'Dot, how could you? You know what Charlie said!'

Dot grinned and shrugged. 'Your dad can be very persuasive.'

The others started to laugh as they crowded round the table, just as Marge and Rodney entered through the back door.

'Bloody hell, he's back!' Rodney exclaimed, dashing forward to shake Jasper's hand.

Nellie bustled to the basement door. 'Edie, where's that champagne?'

In the basement, Edie was staring at the cushions where just a week ago she and Greg had slept. What had she been thinking, getting involved with another man? After Henry Fanshawe, she should have learnt her lesson: men were not to be trusted. Well, she'd learnt that well now. If she and Greg had continued, who knew where it could have ended. With him blacking her eyes when she said the wrong thing, no doubt.

Her mother's voice brought her back to the present, and she went to the back of the basement where she knew the bottles had been stored. The roof sloped low here and she bent to retrieve them, flicking back the cloth that covered a set of shelves. There was nothing on them and she wondered why they'd been hidden so carefully.

Crawling back out of the space she took a deep breath, steeling herself to go back upstairs and act cheerful. Of course she was over the moon that Jasper had regained his sight and was back where he belonged, but she was so desperately tired. All she wanted now was to crawl into bed and forget the last week had ever happened.

When she got upstairs, it was to find that Hester had arrived back and was dancing around getting glasses from the pantry.

'Isn't this the best New Year ever?' she trilled.

Edie shrugged. 'I suppose,' she said unenthusiastically.

Hester gave her a sympathetic look. 'Come on, love, try to forget about your little problem for tonight, eh? Don't forget, your Auntie Hester's got a plan, and soon all your troubles will be over.'

Edie smiled wanly. If only, she thought. But even if she did manage to get rid of her pregnancy, her problems were far from over. 'Thanks, Hester. I owe you.'

'Don't thank me yet. It ain't an easy route to take.'

'Easier than the alternative, though.'

Hester's eyes went misty. 'Depends who you're talkin' to. I doubt Donny would agree. Or Marianne, for that matter.'

Edie shrugged. 'I bet she would have if you'd asked her before he was born.'

'That's the thing with kids, love. Wanted or not, they usually manage to wrap themselves round your heart in the end. Take it from one who knows. Are you sure this is what you want?'

'I've never been more sure of anything.'

She nodded. 'Say no more, then. Now, help me with the glasses and let's get this party started!'

Edie obediently followed Hester and soon Nellie had popped the cork and the glasses were filled. She took a sip, noticing that Marianne didn't touch hers.

As the clamour in the café continued, Edie sat quietly by herself, so she was the first to notice when the front door opened and Bill walked in, a kitbag over his shoulder.

'Sorry to intrude, Mrs Castle,' he said with a charming smile.

'Bill Penfold. Come in, lad, and join the celebrations!' Nellie said expansively.

'Oh, I forgot!' Edie slapped her head. 'Mum, Bill's just got back on leave and he's got nowhere to stay now the garage's been seized.'

'Oh. Well, now Jasper's back . . . We're bursting at the seams as it is.'

'Hang on there, Nellie, we've discussed this. I'm goin' back to me own place, and Bill's welcome to the spare room. It'll be a sight quieter than it is here.'

Nellie's lips tightened with annoyance but she held her tongue. It was a good solution, even if she wasn't happy with it. She'd set her heart on Jasper continuing his recuperation under her roof.

'If you're sure, Mr Cane, I'd be grateful.'

'Course I'm sure. An' if there's anything I can do to help poor Clive, just ask. It's a scandal what's happened. Carted away without a word and no one any the wiser as to where he is.'

'Don't surprise me,' Hester interjected. 'This country's turned into a totalitarian state. Worse than anythin' Hitler could do.'

For a moment everyone was silent, then Jasper leant across the table. 'You don't know what you're talkin' about. We're at war! Things happen. Sometimes they're unjust, but don't you *dare* speak like that about this country.'

Rodney, who had been sitting back watching the argument with a slight smile, suddenly sat up straighter and focused a stern look on Hester. 'Where did you hear that rubbish?' he asked icily.

Hester coloured. 'I didn't hear it anywhere. It's just what I think. An' if you're sayin' I'm not allowed to have me own private thoughts, then you've just proved my point!'

'Oh, shut up, the lot of you!' Nellie exclaimed. 'This is a celebration! Hester, you can think what you like, but keep it to yourself. As for you two' – she cast stern looks at Jasper and Rodney – 'pipe down. Now, Reenie, love, where's that beau of yours got to? He won't want to miss this.'

'I saw him walking up to the Guthries just after I'd left,' Hester said sullenly. 'An' I've half a mind to join him.'

Nellie sighed. 'Poor love. Not sure Mary will welcome him. She seems to have a powerful grievance against him. If she weren't so broken-hearted, I'd have it out with her. But how can I, when my son is walking around fit and well and hers is—' She stopped and put her hand on Hester's arm. 'Sorry, love.'

Hester shook her head. 'It's the truth, ain't it. Now pour me some more some champagne and we'll say no more about it tonight.'

'Actually, Mum, Alfie and I have something to tell you,' Marianne said.

'Oh, yes?' Nellie said distractedly as she poured more drinks. Then she stopped and put the bottle down. 'Oh, yes?' she said again with a smile.

Lily felt her stomach sink and got up swiftly to go and sit beside Edie. She'd hoped she'd at least be able to prepare her for the news before Marianne announced it.

Edie looked at her questioningly as Lily took her hand, but Lily's gaze was fixed on Marianne.

'Sometime in the summer,' Marianne said proudly, her arm through Alfie's, 'there's gonna be another addition to the café!'

In the midst of the general outcry, Edie pulled her hand away from Lily's and rushed for the stairs.

# Chapter 45

'Why, the little madam!' Nellie exclaimed. 'Every time one of her sisters has good news, she behaves like it's the end of the world. Well, I won't have it!' She started to stand, but Jasper put his hand on her arm.

'Leave it, Nell. She's had a hell of a night. When I came in that no-good Canadian pilot were raising his hand to her.'

'What?' The cry came from Bill. 'That bugger. I knew I shouldn't have left her.' He stood up and went to go for the stairs, but Lily stopped him.

'I'll go,' she said.

As she made her way upstairs, Lily thought about the evening. It had been memorable, that was for sure. And now this. Poor Edie. It was no wonder she'd run out after the evening she'd had. She just wished she could find a solution that wouldn't involve her sister taking some concoction that a brothel madam was offering her. She knew, though, that no matter what she said, her strong-minded sister would go her own way. She sighed, wishing Charlie was here so she could talk to him. But she knew that even he wouldn't be able to solve this problem.

Slowly, she opened the door. Edie was lying motionless face down on the bed and Lily went to sit beside her, stroking the hair away from her face.

'Go away.'

'No.'

'You knew, didn't you?'

'Marianne told me when we were out in the square. I didn't expect she'd tell us all tonight. I was going to warn you.'

Edie didn't reply.

'Edie, look at me.' Lily pushed on her sister's shoulder, trying to make her turn over. Finally, Edie complied. She looked terrible; her eyes deeply shadowed.

'Oh, Edes.' Lily gathered her up and hugged her, rocking her back and forth.

'What am I going to do?' Edie wailed into her sister's shoulder.

'You are going to stay calm and I'll help you. But you'll have to tell Mum at some point. This isn't a secret you can keep for long.'

'Just as well I won't have to then.'

'Whatever Hester's suggesting, it's dangerous. You could die.'

'I could die in childbirth.'

'You could, but what if you manage to end this pregnancy but it leaves you so damaged you can never have another child?'

'I don't care. I just want rid of this one. And don't start with the tell Greg thing. He frightened me tonight. If it hadn't been for Jasper turning up, I don't know what could have happened. God, I'm a *terrible* judge of men.'

'No, you're not. You've just been unlucky.'

'I'm *always* the unlucky one!' She started to sob.

'Oh, give it a rest! Marianne's been far more unlucky. Ten years of misery, Edie. Ten years, she suffered people slinging insults at her because she was an unmarried mother. But look at her now.'

'And you think that's going to make me feel better?' Edie started to laugh hysterically and Lily held on to her more tightly. That had been a stupid thing to say, she acknowledged to herself.

Finally, Edie calmed down and pulled away. 'There's nothing you can do or say. If there's any chance of getting rid of this *thing* then I'm going to take it.'

Lily nodded, resigned. 'Just let me know when you do, so I can be on standby.'

'I don't need you to be. Hester told me it's just herbs. I'll be fine.' Edie threw herself back on the pillow. 'I can't believe how fast everything's gone wrong. My life has been ruined in the space of just one week. How can everything have been destroyed so quickly?'

'I don't know, love. The same happened to me.'

'That was different. At least you weren't pregnant. And you had Charlie. Although . . .'

'Although what?'

Edie could have slapped herself. She'd been about to say, 'Although maybe that wasn't such a good thing.' But she just couldn't. 'Although I know that was really hard for you,' she said instead.

'Yeah, it was. But I got through it. And you will get through this.'

'I'm not sure I have the strength.'

'Of course you do. And we'll all help.'

'No! I don't want anyone else to know! Promise, Lily!' She grasped her arm.

'Of course I won't tell anyone.'

Edie nodded. She trusted her sister implicitly and she hadn't needed to ask; they'd been keeping each other's secrets all their lives. She yawned. 'I need to sleep now.'

'You do that.' Lily bent to kiss her forehead. 'Things will look brighter in the morning.'

Edie doubted it. But whatever the next day brought, surely it couldn't be worse than what had already happened.

There was a timid tap on the door then and Marianne came in looking pale and upset. 'Are you all right, Edie?' she asked.

At the look on her older sister's face, Edie felt immediately guilty. 'I'm sorry, Marianne. I didn't mean to upset you. I'm so happy for you and Alfie. Really I am. And I can't wait to meet my new little niece or nephew.'

'Why did you run out like that?'

'I suddenly felt really ill. The night's catching up with me. But I promise it had nothing to do with you. Will you apologise to Alfie for me?'

Marianne nodded but she seemed unconvinced. She looked at Lily for reassurance.

'It's true. She's really not that well, so let's leave her to sleep,' Lily confirmed.

Marianne didn't believe a word of it. She knew her sisters, and she knew that, whatever her faults, Edie would never have ruined her moment without a very good reason. But there was no point pursuing it now. No doubt she'd find out sooner or later anyway.

After her sisters had left, Edie fell asleep almost instantly. But once again she was disturbed by nightmares, although this time, along with the usual images, the smell of lavender soap wafted through her dreams, and Greg was there, his arm raised and pointing a gun at her heart.

# Chapter 46

Early the following morning, Edie got up and dressed quietly in the dark. Sometime during the night, she'd remembered something that Mr Pearson had said to her on the day of the fire – he'd mentioned a letter he'd received from Walter, and he'd seemed troubled by it.

Maybe if she found the letter, they might get some answers about what Walter was doing hanging around Dover. Because after everything Bill had told her about his father, she was becoming more and more convinced that he was behind everything that had happened – perhaps he'd even been the one creeping through the flat. But he hadn't reckoned on Edie being back that night. Maybe he hadn't been aware that she lived there at all.

She made her way up Castle Street towards Harold Passage. Overnight the clouds had moved in and the bright moon that had lit up the dancing figures in the square was nowhere to be seen. A thin drizzle was falling, turning to ice as it landed on the freezing ground and making her progress up the hill precarious in the dark.

At the top, she turned left, but instead of heading to the forecourt as usual, she skirted round the back on to Upper Road, walking to the field behind the garage. The wire fence was easily climbed over, then crouching low, she made for the back door, praying it hadn't been secured. To her surprise, it hadn't and she slipped inside. After a week of being unoccupied the smell of motor oil and diesel fumes that usually pervaded the room had gone, and it smelt damp and neglected.

Taking out her torch, she sat down on the floor and began systematically sorting through the mess of papers that the police had pulled from the filing cabinets and carelessly discarded on the floor. It took longer than she would have liked, and by the end, she'd found nothing more than invoices, bills and letters from customers.

She sat and thought for a moment, trying to remember where Mr Pearson had kept his personal correspondence. If a letter came, he'd always put it into his overall pocket to look at later . . . She jumped up and ran upstairs, remembering how she'd insisted her boss put his filthy overalls in the laundry so she could scrub them later. She'd not got round to it that night, so they should still be in the old wooden chest in the bathroom where they put all their dirty washing.

Hurrying into the bathroom, she saw that the chest had been upended and the dirty clothes, including her dirty knickers, she noticed with a blush, covered the floor. Crouching down, she sifted through the pile. Finding the oil-smeared overalls, she reached into the pockets. Almost immediately, her fingers found an envelope and she let out a small cry of triumph. This had to be it!

Taking out the single sheet of paper, she read the contents with growing disbelief. No wonder he'd looked so worried when he'd mentioned he'd received a letter from him.

Clive,
    I've been patient long enough and now it's time you gave me what I'm due. Either we can come to a civilised agreement or I'll have to find another way. Up to you.
    Walter

What on earth was he talking about? She remembered Bill saying something about an argument over his mother's will. Is that what Walter was referring to? She needed to show the letter to Bill. Maybe he'd have a better idea.

Jumping to her feet, she stuffed the letter in the pocket of her jacket then ran back down the stairs, scrambling over the fence and back along the road.

By the time she reached Jasper's forge on Castle Street, the stitch in her side almost made her double over with pain, but she refused to slow down. She banged on the door, realising how good it felt knowing Jasper was inside. She'd missed his reassuring presence.

The first-floor window above the door opened and Jasper stuck his head out. 'Do you know what time it is?' he shouted. She stepped back so he could see her, shocked again by the whiteness of his hair.

'Is Bill there? I need to speak to him urgently.'

Jasper sighed and withdrew his head. Soon, wearing pyjamas and a brown and beige striped dressing gown, he opened the door. 'I don't know, I been gone three months and nothin's changed. How did you all manage without me?'

Edie kissed his cheek. 'We didn't. We just ran around like headless chickens.'

Jasper rolled his eyes. 'Come on up. Bill's just making tea.'

Leaving Jasper to come up more slowly, she ran up the stairs and into the dark and slightly dingy flat. The brown wallpaper was peeling, and the green velvet armchairs seemed to absorb any light that came in through the windows, giving the place a gloomy air. But Lily had kept it clean while Jasper had been ill, and there was the smell of toast coming from the kitchen.

Bill came out of the tiny galley kitchen with two cups of tea. 'Hope you've recovered after your little performance last night,' he said with a frown of disapproval.

Edie coloured. 'I've apologised to Marianne, if that's what you mean. But that's not why I'm here. I've been to the garage.' She reached into her pocket and pulled out the letter, throwing it onto the small dark-wood table by the window.

Bill's eyebrows rose. 'You went there alone?'

257

Edie folded her arms. 'I'm not a child. I am capable of getting from one place to another without an escort.'

Jasper laughed as he came into the room, puffing from the unaccustomed exertion of climbing the stairs. 'That told you, son. Now, what's this all about, Edie?'

'Read it, Bill. Your dad threatened Mr P just a few days before Christmas. He *has* to be behind everything!'

Bill snatched up the envelope and pulled out the sheet of paper, his brow furrowing. 'I don't understand,' he murmured. 'I mean, I knew there'd been something about Mum's will, but . . .' He sat down on one of the wooden chairs.

Jasper took the letter from his hand and scanned the contents. 'Well, I'll be . . . I didn't know your dad well, no one did – bit of a man of mystery. But why's he threatening Clive?'

Bill jumped up. 'We need to speak to him. Do you know how to get to the Fanshawes', Edie?'

She nodded, although she was vague about the directions and wasn't sure how they'd find the house, but presumably if they went to Hawkinge and asked around, most people would know where they lived.

'Fanshawe? But that's the bloke—' Jasper started.

Thankfully, Bill wasn't listening and talked over him. 'We'll take Uncle Clive's car.'

'Umm. I'm afraid I used all the petrol,' Edie said, shamefaced.

'No matter. He always kept a secret stash. I know where it is. Come on.' He snatched his coat from the hook and dashed out of the door, Edie close on his heels.

'Hey!' Jasper called after them. 'What'll I tell your mum if she asks?'

'Whatever you want,' Edie called back.

With Bill dragging her, the walk up to the garage didn't take long, and as soon as Bill had unearthed the secret can of petrol and filled up the old Morris Minor, they leapt in.

'Hold on to your hat,' Bill said as he sped out of the forecourt, screeching right on to Dover Road, 'it's going to be a bumpy ride!'

# Chapter 47

Bill hadn't been lying about that. Many of the roads had been damaged by bombs and they bounced and jolted over the holes, swinging round the larger ones, scraping the sides of the car against the spindly hedgerows that lined both sides of the country roads.

'Your uncle will never forgive you if you damage his car!' Edie shouted above the engine noise.

'If we get him out of prison, he won't care if he never sees it again,' Bill called back.

When they finally reached Hawkinge, after being forced to take several detours due to the roads being impassable, they stopped the first person they saw and were directed down a muddy country road. If Edie had hoped Bill might take things more carefully now they were so close, she was disappointed, and the little Morris Minor splashed through the potholes at such a speed she was sure he'd snap the suspension. But she wisely kept her mouth shut. Since they'd left Dover, apart from curses, Bill had hardly said a word as he drove, a look of fierce concentration on his face.

He pulled the car to a stop at the bottom of a curved driveway and they stared at the large red-brick Victorian house with mullioned windows that stood at the end.

'What do we do now?' Edie whispered, though why she felt the need to keep her voice down, she had no idea.

'We go and find my bloody dad,' he said grimly, getting out of the car and starting to walk up the drive. Edie hurried after him, noticing the hacksawed iron stumps where the railings would once have stood.

By the time she'd caught up with him, Bill had already rapped on the front door. Finally, it was answered by a bald man wearing a black three-piece suit.

'Can I help you?' he asked, his attitude thawing slightly when he noticed the RAF uniform.

'I'm looking for Walter Penfold,' Bill stated.

'Who is it, Jones?' a female voice asked.

Edie's stomach started to swirl. She'd know that snotty voice anywhere. She stepped behind Bill, hoping that if Elspeth Fanshawe came to the door, she wouldn't notice her.

'Young man enquiring after Mr Penfold,' Jones said.

'He's out on an errand.'

'Who shall I say called?' the butler asked politely.

'His son. I need to speak to him, so perhaps I could wait in his room? I'm sure he'll be glad to see me.'

A woman with platinum-blonde hair swept up in a neat chignon and wearing a black dress that clung to her slim curves appeared at the door.

'His son? How charming. I must say you're a lot more handsome than your father.' She let out a tinkling laugh. 'Such a shame he's not here. I'd invite you in, but my father-in-law died just before Christmas and we're not receiving.'

Edie cringed and tried to make herself as small as possible behind Bill.

'Perhaps I can wait for him in his rooms,' Bill insisted.

'Who's that behind you?' Elspeth asked, ignoring his request.

Edie squeezed her eyes shut and held her breath.

'Show yourself!' she said sharply.

With no other choice, Edie stepped out from behind Bill, raising her chin defiantly.

It was a moment before Elspeth recognised her, but when she did, her demeanour changed from flirtatious to pure fury. 'You!' she spat.

'How dare you come here at a time like this? Did your sister send you?' She raked her eyes over Edie contemptuously. 'As for you' – she pointed at Bill – 'if you think I'd ever allow that . . . that *whore* anywhere on this property, then you're sorely mistaken. Jones, make sure they leave the premises.' She whirled around and left them standing stunned on the doorstep.

'I think you better do as she asks,' Jones said. 'I'll tell your dad you were here.' Then he shut the door.

Too embarrassed to look at Bill, Edie rushed down the drive and got into the car, folding her arms across her body and staring sightlessly out of the window, her face hot with mortification.

After a moment, Bill got in. 'With hindsight, I should have suggested you stay away,' he said mildly. 'I take it that was Mrs Henry Fanshawe?'

Edie nodded miserably. 'I'm sorry. I don't know what I was thinking coming here. I suppose I just assumed I wouldn't see her.'

Bill sighed. 'Well, there's not much we can do about that now.' He sat for a moment in silence, then switched on the engine and turned the car around.

'Don't you want to wait for your dad?' Edie asked.

'I've had a better idea. Chauffeurs almost always live in a little flat above the garage. And the garage is almost always at the back of the house, usually hidden by trees and bushes because God forbid the toffs have their view ruined. So, we're going to find a back entrance and sneak in.'

'Are you mad?' Edie squeaked.

'You can wait in the car if you're too chicken.'

Edie huffed. 'I will not! I'm coming with you. That cow can go do one.'

'That's more like it.' Bill laughed as he put the car in gear and they bumped off down the track. 'Now, keep your eyes peeled for a turning.'

'There!' Edie shouted after they'd been driving for a few seconds.

Bill cursed and swung the car violently to the left. 'You could have told me sooner,' he grumbled as the twigs scraped the sides of the car.

'If you hadn't been driving so fast, I might have been able to,' Edie retorted.

He made no reply as they wobbled over the muddy ground, soon coming to a two-storey, whitewashed building with black-painted wooden double doors.

'What did I tell you?' Bill crowed triumphantly as he pulled the car to a stop and got out.

Edie followed a little more reluctantly. She wasn't at all sure this was a good idea.

Bill went to open the doors, cursing when he discovered they were locked. 'There's got to be a way in somehow,' he muttered, going round the side of the building. But the ground floor was windowless and there was no obvious route in. He stepped back, looking up at the first-floor windows. 'That must be the bathroom.' He pointed up at a frosted glass sash window that had been left open a crack. Beside it was an iron drainpipe.

'I hope you're not expecting me to climb up there!' Edie shrieked.

Bill took off his coat and handed it to her. 'Nope. You stay here and listen out for anyone coming.'

He grasped the pipe and climbed nimbly up. As he reached the window ledge, he leant over and with some effort managed to lift the window just enough for him to wriggle through. Once in, he opened the window properly and poked his head out. 'Come on. It's not high.'

'No fear! Come down and open the door.'

Rolling his eyes, Bill disappeared and soon Edie heard a key being turned in the lock. He opened the door and she slipped through into a large garage with room for five cars. Edie spotted the Bentley straightaway and noticed a beautiful green two-seater MG sports car along with a Rolls-Royce and a more serviceable black Ford Coupe.

'Look at these,' she whispered reverently, making a beeline for the sports car. 'What I wouldn't give to drive around in this. Your dad must have taken the Alvis.'

'An Alvis?' Bill whistled. 'Nice. Dad'll be in seventh heaven driving that. Come on. I'd love to sit and stare as much as you, but we don't have time.'

Edie obediently followed him to some narrow wooden stairs which opened up directly into a small, neat sitting room with a tiny kitchenette at the back. It was spotlessly clean, the wooden counter in the kitchen scrubbed and the taps in the sink sparkling.

'He has his faults, but my dad was always scrupulously tidy. He blamed the navy for that. But it'll make our job easier.'

Pulling open a drawer in a desk by the window, Bill started to sift through some papers, while Edie opened a door that led to the bedroom. As with the sitting room, it was very neat with no clutter. A clothes rail by the wall was hung with suits, the colours going from black to blue to grey, and a small selection of hats was lined up on the shelf above it. Beneath the rail were his shoes. She ignored these, making straight for the bedside table and pulling open a drawer. There were cufflinks and two slim books. She pulled them out.

'Hey, Bill, look at these.'

He came through. '*Fascism for the Million* and *The Great Britain*. What did I tell you? My dad is an out and out fascist.'

'But it's not illegal to own these, is it?'

'Maybe not, but they didn't put that Oswald Moseley in prison and ban his political party for nothing. And the fact that he has these proves who he is.'

'I never doubted that. But I'm not sure these books are enough to help us. Have you found anything?'

'A few letters. One from a man called Admiral Domvile. Never realised my dad was so well connected. But I suppose he might have come across him in the last war.'

'What does it say?'

'Nothing. Just thanks him for his help and wishes him luck in his latest endeavour. But I've no idea what that help might have been, or what his endeavour is. I've pocketed it anyway, just in case.'

'Nothing else?'

'No.'

Just then they heard a clatter of footsteps coming up the stairs and Edie went to stand beside Bill as they both watched the door with wide eyes.

'You must think I'm stupid.' It was Elspeth Fanshawe.

'Look, Mrs Fanshawe, I apologise. But like I said, I urgently need to speak to my father. He wouldn't mind me waiting for him here.'

Elspeth's eyes wandered round the bedroom, falling on the open drawer, the papers on the bed. 'And would he not mind you searching his private property? Jones!' she called.

The butler entered with a man wearing dirty overalls who was clearly a gardener. 'Escort these people out.'

'Wait!' Bill shouted. 'Did you know my dad's a fascist?'

Elspeth glanced over her shoulder with a look of disdain. 'Unlike our government, this family doesn't police the thoughts of its staff. In the short time he's been here your father has proved himself to be both competent and loyal. Now, gentlemen, do your job.' She nodded at the butler, who stepped forward to grasp Bill's arm.

Bill shook him off angrily. 'Fine, we'll go.' He threw the books on the bed. 'But we'll be back. We have some questions for him.'

He stalked from the room, followed closely by Edie. As she passed Elspeth, the other woman grabbed her arm. 'By the way, slut,' she hissed, 'tell your sister that if she thinks her filthy little brat will get one penny out of this family now that Ernest is dead, then she'll have a fight on her hands. And I don't think she'll enjoy it.' She smiled nastily.

The woman's touch made Edie's insides quake, but she refused to let it show. So, raising her chin, she lifted Elspeth's hand from her arm and dropped it, pointedly wiping her hand on her jacket. Then she looked her straight in the eye. 'Filthy brat? You mean your husband's son? A son *you* failed to provide him with.' She laughed slightly. 'Donny is a Fanshawe by blood, whereas you're nothing but a parasite with a deranged criminal for a husband. So I think you need to be very careful what you say, because we both know who's got a fight on their hands. And it's not my sister.'

She turned and clattered down the stairs after Bill, her legs shaking.

Bill didn't say a word as he started the car and they bounced back down the mud track, and Edie was grateful. Coming face to face with Elspeth had brought back all the old feelings of humiliation and betrayal and she was finding it hard to hold back the tears.

Finally, though, Bill said, 'You going to tell me what all that was about? Cos it sounded a bit more than you having an affair with her husband.'

Edie sighed, realising that Bill had no idea that Henry was Donald's father. Nor that Ernest Fanshawe had cut Henry out of his will, instead leaving Henry's share in the Fanshawe Brewery to any children he might have – i.e. Donny.

Taking a deep breath, she explained everything that had happened the previous summer, including how Henry had kidnapped Don, then abandoned him at Hester's house – she didn't mention it was a brothel, though; it was embarrassing enough talking about her and Marianne's tangled romantic history with Henry Fanshawe, without bringing a brothel into it as well.

When she'd finished, Bill blew out a long breath. 'Wow,' he said. 'Life's never dull round you, is it?'

Edie didn't reply.

'So let me get this straight: you had an affair with Fanshawe, which exposed your sister's deepest secret, turned the bloke into a criminal, got him cut out of his dad's will and made his wife your sworn enemy. Which in turn means she's never going to let us near the place again.'

'You can't blame me for the fact that your dad is a stinking fascist!' Edie snapped. His words hurt, though. Because he was right in one way. It was all her fault. It always had been. Yes, Henry had deceived her, but there had been plenty of warning signs.

Silence descended again and Edie stared out at the sheep dotted about on the hills, wondering vaguely whether the shells and bombs ever bothered them. Looking at them now, grazing peacefully, anyone would think life was normal, that Dover was safe, and the war to end all wars had brought eternal peace.

Finally, Bill sighed. 'Of course I don't blame you. But what now? Any suggestions how we might find Dad?'

Edie was still too angry to reply.

'What about that lawyer bloke you mentioned? You reckon he'll be back?' Bill continued.

Edie shrugged. 'He might be,' she managed, hanging on to her temper with an effort.

'Then let's go see him. Where does he live?'

She shrugged again.

'Oh, for God's sake, stop acting like a spoilt brat just cos I told a few home truths.'

Edie turned to him, her eyes sparkling with rage. 'You know what, Bill? If it wasn't for your uncle, I'd get out of this car right now and walk the rest of the way and sod you!'

He slammed his foot on the brakes and leant over to open her door. 'Be my guest! I'd rather do this on my own than have to go any further with a stupid little girl who can't admit to her own mistakes!'

'Fine!' Edie snapped, getting out of the car and slamming the door as hard as she could. Then she watched as Bill drove off at speed and disappeared over the hill.

Good, she thought mutinously. She'd never liked him anyway. Putting her hands in her pockets and hunching her shoulders, she began the long walk home.

# Chapter 48

Nellie woke suddenly and lay still for a moment, trying to work out why she had such a God-awful headache. Then as the events of the evening before came back her face broke into a grin. Jasper could see! It was a miracle. And not only that, but she had the prospect of another grandchild to look forward to. This time, though, she'd be able to celebrate its arrival in a way she never could with Donny. The only fly in the ointment was Edie. Just because she was going through a hard time didn't mean she could get away with sulking whenever something good happened to her sisters. She'd be having words with that madam later. But today, as the café was closed, she had better things to do than arguing with her recalcitrant daughter.

And the first item on her list was to go and talk to that stubborn old man. She needed to know whether he had forgiven her, or whether he was just tolerating her for the sake of the kids.

She took longer with her morning routine than usual, carefully taking out her curlers and brushing her hair until the curls bounced around her head. Then she dressed in one of her favourite bright red blouses and teamed it with a purple wool skirt. A fuchsia-pink cardigan completed the outfit, and for luck, she put on a slick of pink lipstick. She stared at herself in the mirror and nodded with satisfaction; she'd do.

Before she left she went to open the blackout curtains in the sitting room, whipping the cloth off the birdcage as she did so. 'Wakey, wakey, rise and shine,' she trilled.

The parrot blinked at her for a moment before squawking, 'Grub's up. Get a move on.'

Nellie laughed. 'Wish me luck, Polly. I'm gonna need it.'

The bird stared back at her blankly.

'Say "Good luck, Nellie".'

'Get a move on.' Polly flapped her wings.

'Oh, bugger you then, you stupid bird.'

'What more luck do you need? You got all your kids within a stone's throw, a smasher of a grandson and another on the way, and a thrivin' business.'

Nellie whirled round to see Hester standing in the doorway wearing a too-large green dressing gown that belonged to one of the boys, her bleached blonde hair hanging around her face.

'Bleedin' heck, you nearly gave me a heart attack.'

Hester smiled slyly. 'I'm guessin' you need luck with old Jasper. Don't think you need worry on that score.'

'Really?' Nellie's heart lifted as she straightened her cardigan. 'How do I look?'

Hester regarded her for a moment before saying carefully, 'Put it this way, I don't think he'll have trouble spotting you, blind or not.'

'I'll settle for that.' Nellie paused a moment, remembering the conversation last night. 'Hester, all that stuff you've been spouting – about the government and that – you don't mean it, do you?'

Hester's smile dropped. 'Why? You gonna throw me out cos I've not been taken in by all them news reports on the BBC?'

'No, but listen, I know I've said it before, but I'm serious; keep your thoughts to yourself, eh? Especially when Ron Hames is about.'

'I'll say what I like and damn the consequences. No one's gonna stop me speaking my mind.'

'Even if the consequence is jail?'

'What are you talkin' about? I ain't done anything except tell people what I think.'

Nellie hesitated. 'I just . . . I mean, look at poor Clive Pearson. The man wouldn't say boo to a goose, and yet they've banged him up on some trumped-up charge. You can't be too careful.'

Hester laughed. 'Listen to yerself! Imagine livin' in a country where you worry about that sort of thing. Now get on with you. Go see your man and stop worryin' about me. I can take care of myself.'

'What are you doing today?' Nellie smoothed her hair.

'Might drop in to the caves – I promised I'd take Mr Evans his baccy. An' I got some pencils and paper for the kids in there. Then maybe a nice walk along the cliffs. Blow away some of the cobwebs after all that champers last night.'

'You know you're not allowed up there? They tolerate the boys, but not sure they will you.'

'I'll go where I please, thank you very much. Anyway, maybe I'll take 'em with me. We had a fine old time last time we was up there.'

Nellie shrugged. 'Then I'll see you later.' But she couldn't help feeling worried. She wasn't a fool – she knew the news wasn't always completely truthful. But it seemed that after losing her son and her house, Hester was now treading a very fine line. One that could lead straight to prison. Nellie hadn't been keen on having the woman here when she'd first arrived, but she'd grown fond of her and she didn't like the thought of her in trouble. But then Hester had lived on the wrong side of the law for most of her life, so she probably didn't care much about that. Which worried Nellie even more.

Still, there wasn't a lot she could do about it, so she pushed the problem to the back of her mind and after packing a bag with fresh bread, cheese and a Thermos of Marianne's leek and potato soup, Nellie made her way up Castle Street.

As she neared Jasper's forge, she stared up towards the first-floor windows, memories of what he'd said to her the last time she was here coming back to her: *You've finally shaken me off, Nell.*

Huh! She'd see about that. She straightened her shoulders and rapped on the door, then stood back. Soon Jasper's head appeared at the window.

'Christ alive,' he exclaimed. 'It ain't even midday, and this place 'as been like Piccadilly Circus all mornin'.'

'You gonna let me in?' she called.

He shook his head. 'I been out of a coma a week and them stairs are steeper than I remember. You got your key?'

Nellie smiled. He must have forgiven her if he was happy for her to use the key. She fished in her big black bag then held up a large iron key. 'On me way.'

When she entered Jasper's flat, she found him sitting in his usual chair by the fireplace, his dressing gown pulled around him, and his white hair standing up around his pale face. 'You won't mind if I don't get up?' he asked with a tired smile.

'You stay right there. I'll make tea.' She bustled into the kitchen, noting the toast crumbs littering the counter. 'Where's bloody Bill? He should be helping you, not creating more mess.'

'Raced off with Edie first thing.'

Nellie peered out of the small galley kitchen. 'With Edie? Why?'

Jasper looked evasive. 'Not my place to say.'

'If this concerns my daughter, then I've got a right to know.'

Jasper smiled faintly. 'No, you don't. She's an adult now.'

'She lives in my house!' Nellie said.

Jasper's eyebrows rose. 'You here for any particular reason? Or did you just want to moan about Edie?'

'I wanted to see you, is all,' Nellie muttered, disappearing back into the kitchen.

'All right. And now you have, you can leave if you want.'

Nellie's hands stilled as they lifted the electric kettle, unsure how to respond. Then deciding the best way was to ignore his comment, she poured the water into the teapot and carried it into the sitting room.

'I also came to bring you some food so you don't have to cook for yourself. Though you could always come to ours if you prefer.'

'I weren't jokin' when I said them stairs were steep. Bill had to half carry me home last night. Didn't realise how weak I was.'

'Then why don't you come stay at the café? Just till you feel a bit stronger,' she said hopefully.

Jasper sighed. 'No. An' you don't have to keep comin' over. Lily said she'd be round later and I got Bill here for a bit. I don't need you fussin' over me.'

'You call bringing over a bit of soup and making a cup of tea fussing? Clearly you've never met Muriel Parker.'

Jasper chuckled and Nellie relaxed slightly as she poured the tea then placed his cup and saucer on the low table beside his chair, before taking a seat opposite and watching him over her teacup. When he didn't meet her eyes or seem inclined to speak, she put her cup down with a clatter. 'Are you ever going to forgive me?'

'I don't know,' he said. 'You forget, Nell, that what happened months ago to you seems like yesterday to me. All them months of thinkin' have been lost. And for the last week, my every waking moment has been spent wonderin' whether I'll ever be able to see again.'

Nellie sat back with a huff. 'Have it your way then. But let me know when you have. You owe me that at least.'

'I owe you nothin'. I love your kids, I even love you . . .'

Her heart leapt at that.

'. . . but that don't mean things will ever be the same between us.'

Nellie smiled brightly. 'Good. Cos that's not what I want either.'

Jasper looked startled. 'So why are you here? And all dolled up as well?'

'Like I said, just wanted to make sure you're all right. And there's nothin' wrong with takin' pride in my appearance.' She slapped her hands down on the arms of the chair and heaved herself up. 'And now I see you're fine, I'll be off. Give me a shout if you need anything else.'

271

She swung her coat back on, patted him on the arm, and walked away, leaving Jasper staring after her in bafflement. He shook his head, trying to ignore the ache that had suddenly started somewhere close to his heart.

Walking back to the café, Nellie smiled to herself. It was only his stubbornness that was holding Jasper back. But he'd come round, even if she had to force him.

∽

'Marge!' The call bounced off the curved walls of the tunnel and Marge turned to see Philip walking towards her with a slight limp, although his uniform was neat and his brown hair Brylcreemed and shining under the lights.

'Back already?' She was relieved to see he seemed to have recovered from the night before.

'Just wanted to thank you for helping last night.'

'If you know anyone that'd just have left you trapped, show them to me and I'll give 'em a beating. Of course I helped you!'

'Still.' He shuffled his feet slightly. 'Anyway, er, seeing as our evening got cut short, don't suppose you fancy trying again?' He looked so hopeful that Marge smiled.

'All right. What did you have in mind?'

'Well, a bloke just asked me if I'd like to play in a football match against the navy next week and I thought you might like to come? Then we could go for drinks after?'

Marge wrinkled her nose. 'Look, Phil, I like you, but standing in a freezing wet field watching a load of blokes kicking a ball about isn't really my thing. But if I'm free, I'm happy to do the drinks after bit.'

Philip laughed. 'Fair enough. It was a bit of an ask. Match is next Thursday afternoon in the field behind the garage. How about I meet you at seven in the canteen and we'll take it from there.'

'Looks like you've got yourself a date, Padre. I'd love to stay and chat, but my shift starts in five.' She blew him a kiss and hurried towards the plotting room.

Philip turned to go back the way he had come, saluting smartly as he passed a naval officer and earning a dirty look in return. It was only after he'd passed him that he realised it was Rodney Castle. The man who'd been searching for Marge during the air raid the other day. He smiled to himself. *Bad luck, buster*, he thought with a smirk. *I asked first.*

Rodney blew out a sigh as he watched the padre's back retreating down the tunnel. Last night, as he'd walked back down the hill after Marge had called him, he'd felt nothing but dread. Since the war had started the burden of being the eldest had weighed more heavily on him than at any time since his father had died. But with Marge by his side, he realised, his problems never felt quite as onerous. Edie had been right: if he wasn't careful, he'd lose her. Maybe he already had.

# Chapter 49

It was just as well Edie was so furious, because it distracted her from the cold drizzle that was slowly working its way between her hat and coat collar. 'Bloody men,' she muttered. 'Leave a woman to walk miles in the rain because you don't like the fact they had an affair ages ago. Well, he can bugger off if he thinks I'll help him anymore.'

Her thoughts circled round and round as she trudged on, unsure how much further she had to walk. She'd probably only been going for ten minutes, but the road was steep, and she was so tired, it was a struggle to keep putting one foot in front of the other. 'Would he have done this if he knew I was pregnant?' she grumbled. 'Ha! Probably. Cos he wouldn't approve of that at all! What gives him the right to judge me? I bet he's been up to all sorts in Scotland. Swanning around in his pilot's uniform like it gives him some sort of right to any girl that takes his fancy.'

With her head down against the rain, she was so deep in her thoughts that she didn't notice the car idling at the side of the road until it tooted its horn. She looked up and scowled. Right. So the fact that he came back for her made it all better, did it? If she weren't so cold and miserable, she'd ignore him. But there was no point in cutting off her nose to spite her face.

Bill pushed open the passenger-side door. 'Get in!' he rapped.

Edie bent down to look at him. 'Why?'

'Because it's cold and wet and I don't want you walking all that way on your own.'

She raised an eyebrow at him.

He huffed. 'And because I'm sorry.'

'You don't sound very sorry,' she grumped as she got in.

'Well, I am. I shouldn't have said those things.'

'No, you shouldn't. Anyone would think you'd never made a mistake.' She shivered as another icy drop of water slid down her back. 'And I'm only getting in because I'm freezing. *Not* because I want to be in this car with you, helping find out what happened to *your* uncle.'

'I know.' He turned and took her hands in his. 'Look at me, Edie.'

Reluctantly, she turned to stare into his brown eyes.

'I really am sorry. After everything you've been trying to do for Uncle Clive, I should never have gone off at you like that. Will you forgive me?'

She tightened her lips.

'Please?'

'I'll think about it.'

'I suppose that'll have to be good enough for now. But I still don't know what our next move should be.'

'Well, if you hadn't thrown me out of the car in a fit of temper, we'd have been on our way to see Mr Wainwright, the lawyer I mentioned.'

'Fit of temper? You were the one who said you wanted to get out!'

'And why was that? Because you were being an idiot. So, if you truly meant your apology, you won't try to blame me again. Now drive. I'll direct you when we get to town.'

She sat back in her seat, wrapping her arms around herself and closed her eyes.

With a sigh, Bill put the car into gear and set off again.

As they neared Drop Redoubt, they were stopped by a sentry who demanded to see their papers.

Edie stuck her head out of the car. 'It's me, for God's sake!' she said to the soldier who she recognised as one of the men Bert had been with at the pub when she'd met up with Susan. 'Bert's sister.'

He squinted at her through the driver's side window. 'Edie, in't it? Who's this then? Don't look like the bloke I saw you with at the Christmas party.'

If she'd been closer, Edie would happily have thumped him one. 'That's cos it's not. Now, are you gonna let us pass?'

He stood back and waved them on.

Bill looked over at her and opened his mouth.

'Don't say a bloody word, Bill Penfold! Not one word!'

'I wasn't going to say anything,' he said with a slight smile.

'Good. Now take a left at Market Square, up High Street, Victoria Crescent's on the left.' She stared out of the window, noticing three figures walking towards them – two small, one large. 'Hey, that's Hester with Donny and Fred,' she said. 'Wonder what they're doing up here on a day like today?'

'God knows. What do you know about her anyway?'

'Not a lot. Why?'

Bill shrugged. 'Last night she was telling me about her house in Folkestone getting shelled, and it got me thinking . . . Do you reckon she knew my dad?'

Edie nodded. 'I think they *might* have known each other.'

'Then why haven't you spoken to her?' he exclaimed. 'She might have something to do with what's going on, or at least know something. Cos don't you think it's strange that she turns up just as everything starts to happen?'

'I think it's a coincidence,' Edie said. 'Because I bet Hester didn't mention what she used to do in Folkestone?' She smiled slyly at him.

'What difference does it make?'

'She ran a brothel.'

Bill's head whipped round and he stared at her in astonishment. 'Oh . . . *Oh!* So you think my dad was a client?' he asked with a grimace.

'Exactly. And what possible reason could Hester have for wanting to harm your uncle? Everyone likes her and she just doesn't seem the

276

nasty sort.' *And,* Edie thought silently, *I really need her right now. If she disappears, then what will I do?*

Bill shrugged. 'Maybe she doesn't, but something's going on.' He thought for a moment, then said, 'You don't know her address in Folkestone, do you?'

'No, why?'

'I wanted to see if it was near where my dad used to live. Can you ask her? Or find out somehow?'

'I suppose . . . though if she and your dad are involved she might get suspicious if I ask outright. But I'll see what I can do.'

Bill nodded. 'And then maybe we should go there to check it out.'

'Why?'

'I just have a feeling . . .'

'About?'

Bill shook his head. 'Just find the address, then we'll see.'

They lapsed into silence and soon they arrived in Victoria Crescent. When they knocked on Mr Wainwright's door, it was answered by a small, rotund man with a bald head and glasses perched on the end of his nose. 'Can I help you?' he asked.

'Mr Wainwright? I'm Edie Castle, I left a message with your secretary while you were away.'

'Ah yes. I did see that. Come in, come in.'

He led them into a comfortable office with a large walnut desk covered in papers, in front of which were two hard-backed chairs. Gesturing for them to take a seat, he went and sat down behind the desk.

Edie made a beeline for the fire that was burning in the grate, holding out her hands and groaning with appreciation. When she noticed the two men staring at her, she blushed and went over to a chair. 'Sorry,' she mumbled. 'I'm a bit cold.'

'It's very nice to meet you, Miss Castle.' Mr Wainwright smiled kindly. 'Though I must say I wasn't expecting to see another member of your family so soon. You Castles do tend to get yourselves into pickles, don't you?'

'Well, it's not me. It's—'

'Clive Pearson. Yes, I heard all about it. Couldn't believe it – I've always liked the Pearsons. So after I got your message, I decided to make a few calls to see what I could discover.' His gaze switched to Bill. 'And you are?'

When Bill told him, Mr Wainwright's eyes sharpened. 'Is that so? Is that really so?' he muttered. 'I executed your mother's will, you know? Nasty affair.'

'Do you know what's happened to him?' Edie asked before he could go off on a tangent.

The lawyer sighed. 'Yes, as it happens, I did manage to find out something. And I'm afraid I'm not sure what I can do.' He was silent for a moment.

'Go on,' Bill urged.

'Clive Pearson has been arrested under Section 2(A)1 of the Defence Regulations.'

When the couple on the other side of his desk stared at him blankly, he elaborated. 'Basically, he has been charged with encouraging members of the British public to listen to a wireless station, which is based in Germany but broadcasts in English, by communicating the bandwidth of the said station.'

Bill shook his head. 'I don't understand. What radio station?'

'It calls itself the NBBS – National British Broadcasting Service. And it seems Mr Pearson had certain items relating to it in his property. Just a day after several sticky-backs started to appear in Dover. There's very little I can do for him, I'm afraid.'

'What are you talking about?' Edie asked.

'Someone has been sticking up signs advertising the radio station's bandwidth. They found a pile of them hidden in the Anderson shelter at the garage.'

Edie looked back at him blankly.

'You've never seen them before?'

'Of course I haven't!' Edie exclaimed. 'And where would he get them anyway?'

Mr Wainwright shrugged.

'But where is he now?' Bill asked desperately.

'At a secure prison in London where he is awaiting trial.'

'Surely you don't believe he'd do something like this?'

'It doesn't matter what I believe,' Mr Wainwright said. 'It's what the government and MI5 believe – they are the ones in charge of unearthing people who may not have the country's best interests at heart.'

Bill got up and started to pace. 'This is mad! My uncle would never do this! You know him, you *know* he wouldn't.'

'Do you have evidence to support your theory?' Mr Wainwright asked bluntly.

'We think someone's set him up.' Edie explained what had happened on the night of the fire, then handed over the letter she'd found at the garage earlier that morning. 'And we think it might be Bill's dad who's behind it.'

Mr Wainwright frowned as he looked at the letter. 'Yes, yes,' he mumbled. 'This does seem very suspicious. Especially considering what happened when your mother died . . .'

'What did happen?' Bill asked.

Mr Wainwright waved his hand. 'Can't say, I'm afraid. Client confidentiality and all that.'

'Can you help?' Edie urged.

Mr Wainwright took off his spectacles and leant forward over the desk. 'I think it's unlikely. Your uncle will be charged and his trial will be held *in camera* – behind closed doors.'

'But that can't be right! Doesn't everyone have the right to a fair and public trial?' Bill exploded.

'Not if they've betrayed their country.'

'By sticking up some notices?!' Bill shouted. 'And what sort of sentence can he expect if they find him guilty?'

'Last one I heard of was twelve years' hard labour. But death is also a possibility.'

Edie gasped in dismay while Bill dropped into the chair and put his head in his hands. 'Oh, God. Poor Uncle Clive.'

Edie patted him on the shoulder in a futile attempt to comfort him; though in truth, she felt the same despair.

'What about the garage?' Bill looked up.

'It's been confiscated until this matter has been dealt with. Then it'll be returned, I suppose. But I can't guarantee it.'

'But Walter Penfold's letter,' Edie said. 'Surely that proves Mr P's been set up. And there's the fact that we think it was Walter who tried to kill him and set fire to the garage.'

'But that is pure speculation on your part, Miss Castle, so unless you can give me proof, it doesn't help matters. Where is your father now?' Mr Wainwright asked Bill.

'He's working for the Fanshawes up at Hawkinge. We just went to try and see him, but he wasn't there. But we did find fascist literature in his room. Then we got thrown out by Elspeth Fanshawe.'

'*Oh!* Now that is very, very interesting. In fact, that shines a whole new light on the matter.' Mr Wainwright sat and thought for a moment. 'Right, here's what I can do. I will get in touch with my contact at MI5 and put forward your testimony.'

'Oh, *thank*—'

Mr Wainwright held up his hand before Edie could finish. 'This won't necessarily get him released, but it might introduce doubt.' He stood up. 'Now, on you go.'

Bill and Edie got up and allowed the lawyer to shepherd them to the front door. 'Will you let us know what happens?' Edie asked as they stepped outside.

'Most assuredly. Do send my regards to your mother and sisters. And Jasper, of course. I heard his sight has returned and he discharged himself last night. Such a relief.'

Then he shut the door before they could say any more.

'How the hell did he know that?' Edie asked in bewilderment. 'I mean, I bet even Lou Carter doesn't know yet!'

Bill smiled. 'It seems there's more to him than you'd think. Contacts at MI5? Knows all about these secret trials? I think we've found exactly the right person to help.'

'*We?*' Edie said, arms folded.

'All right, *you*. Thank you.'

Edie nodded. 'That's better. And one day I'll tell you how you can make up for it. But now I need to get home and go to bed.'

'Are you ill?' Bill was suddenly solicitous.

'No, of course not. Just tired after last night.' Edie didn't like to admit she felt absolutely terrible, exhaustion dragging at her and her stomach nauseous. While so much had been happening, she'd been able to push the symptoms aside, but she wasn't sure how much longer she'd be able to.

Bill put an arm around her shoulder, hugging her close, and she couldn't resist leaning in to him. He was so warm and comforting. She lay her head on his shoulder and closed her eyes as he dropped a kiss on her hair. 'I really am sorry about our argument,' he said quietly.

'Me too,' Edie sighed. 'Sometimes my temper gets the better of me.'

He chuckled. 'I remember. But it doesn't mean I don't like you.'

She opened her eyes and looked up at him. 'I like you too,' she murmured with a small smile.

Bill stared into her eyes for a long moment, before clearing his throat and looking away.

'Right,' he said. 'You go and rest, then see what you can find out about Hester's address.'

Flustered, Edie pulled away from him and opened the car door before he could do it for her. She had no business feeling like that about Bill, she thought angrily, resolving to keep a little more distance between them in future.

# Chapter 50

The café was frantically busy the following day, for which Marianne was grateful because it distracted her from the fact that in just a couple of days it was Mr Fanshawe's funeral, and she couldn't help worrying that when she didn't show up, Henry's brother Rupert would come to find her. She supposed she wouldn't mind that so much, just as long as Henry's wife didn't accompany him. She would not allow that woman to unleash her venom on poor Donny.

'Where's Edie?' Nellie called as she picked up some orders from the hatch. 'We could do with a hand.'

'She's asleep, Mum,' Marianne said. 'She had another bad night so leave her be.'

'She's been in bed since she got back yesterday! What that girl needs is a kick up the backside.'

'Leave her, Mum. She really doesn't seem well.'

'I'll go up and see her,' Gladys said.

Nellie eyed her suspiciously. 'None of your mumbo-jumbo medicines, mind.'

Gladys rolled her eyes. 'All right. No tea. But I'm worried about her. Poor lamb's not been right for a while.'

'It's all right, Glad, I'll go,' Hester said, coming out of the pantry and wiping her hands on her apron. 'Take over here for me, will you?'

Gladys opened her mouth to protest – Hester had no business giving her orders! But she was too late, because before she could splutter out a protest, the blasted woman had already sped away.

Upstairs, Hester tapped on the girls' bedroom door and went in. 'It's only me, love,' she said as she walked over and sat down on the side of the bed. 'I've brought your medicine.' She placed a brown paper bag on the eiderdown with a clink.

Edie sat up. 'Sounds like you've got a few bottles of gin in there,' she joked, opening the bag. Inside were five large bottles filled with a cloudy liquid flecked with brown and purple specks. She opened one of the stoppers and sniffed. It smelt faintly minty, medicinal.

'What is this?'

'Don't worry, it's just herbs. I've mixed it for you cos I know the doses. All you need to do is take four spoonfuls every three to four hours.'

Edie raised the bottle to her lips and took a mouthful, swirling it round in her mouth. It wasn't terrible, she realised, raising it to her lips to take another swig.

Hester snatched the bottle back and put it in the bag. 'Hey. Don't mess around with this stuff.'

'How quickly does it work?'

Hester shrugged. 'If it's going to work it might take three to four weeks. But I've known it work quicker and I've known it not work at all. But it's better than the alternative. How far gone do you reckon you are?'

Edie counted back in her head. 'About eight weeks,' she said.

'Good. The earlier the better.'

'What happens when it does work?' Edie contemplated the bottles, thinking she might just drink the lot now.

'You'll get bad cramps, like your monthly but worse. Then, if you're lucky, you'll start to bleed. Mind, the bleedin' can get out of hand, so be careful. But word of warning, don't, whatever you do, drink it all at once.'

Edie coloured.

'You think I couldn't see the look on your face? Amount of girls I've helped in your situation, I know exactly what's going through your mind.'

283

Edie nodded. 'Thanks, Hester, I owe you for this.'

'Yes, you do. You owe me a pound.'

'How much?!' That was a good chunk of her monthly wage.

'I've taken a risk for you, so it's only fair I get proper payment.'

Edie sighed and nodded. 'I'll get it to you by tomorrow.'

'Can you give me a little deposit?'

'Don't you trust me?' Edie asked, offended.

'After the life I've led, I don't trust no one. Not even your mum.'

Edie reached for her bag and took out her purse. Emptying the coins onto the blanket, she handed them to the other woman. 'Here's five shillings. I'll get you the rest as soon as I can.'

Hester nodded and pocketed the coins. 'That'll do nicely for now. And if you need a doctor, for gawd's sake don't mention my name.'

When Hester had left, Edie took one of the bottles out of the bag, staring at it for some time, before lifting it to her mouth and drinking some more.

'What's that?'

Edie jumped as Marianne came into the room. 'Just a tonic Gladys gave me to help settle my stomach and calm my nerves,' Edie said hurriedly.

Marianne picked up the bottle and sniffed. 'Don't tell Mum, whatever you do! She's got it in for Gladys and her herbals. Although, this sounds like exactly what I need.' She lifted it to her mouth.

'No!' In a panic Edie lunged forward and grabbed the bottle from her.

Marianne stared at her. 'Why?'

'Because . . . Well, you don't know what's in it.'

'Neither do you. Besides, it's only a few herbs, isn't it? Look, I can see the purple of the flowers. And I really need to settle my nerves.'

'Is this something to do with Mr Fanshawe dying?' Edie asked, hoping to distract her. She'd not yet confronted her sister about this because she'd not been able to speak to her alone.

'How do you know about that?'

Edie explained what had happened the day before.

Marianne plumped down onto the wooden chair beside Edie's bed, astonished. 'So you think Bill's dad is somehow involved in the fire and set poor Mr Pearson up by making it look like he was a traitor or something?'

'Why else do you think the military police have been crawling all over the garage and I'm now stuck here. Anyway, Mr Wainwright's looking into it now.'

'Well, if anyone can sort this out, he can, bless him. By the way, can you keep the whole Mr Fanshawe stuff to yourself? If Mum finds out she'll insist I take whatever they offer. But I don't want their stinking money.'

'I'll have it,' Edie joked, thinking about the money she now owed Hester and the fact that if Mr Wainwright couldn't help Mr Pearson, then she might be out of a job – and if Hester's medicine didn't work, she might never be able to find a job again.

Marianne shook her head. 'I don't think they'll give him money. I think it'll be something complicated like a share in the business. In which case, we might not see a penny. Which suits me just fine. Hopefully, if I don't go to the funeral, maybe they'll just forget about us and we can live our lives in peace.'

'Marianne! Where the devil are you?'

'Christ!' Marianne jumped up, then swayed slightly as the room spun around her and she sat down again. 'You know, I almost wish this pregnancy was the same as last time when I didn't even know about it until my waters broke.' Marianne took a deep breath, then stood up more slowly. 'You gonna get up?'

Edie sighed. 'I suppose. Hey, you don't remember Hester's address, do you?' she asked hopefully.

'Somewhere off The Leas, I think. We ran there from the Grand Hotel. Why?'

Edie shrugged. 'Bill was wondering whether she lived near his dad.'

'You and Bill seem to be getting on well,' Marianne remarked slyly.

'You wouldn't have thought that yesterday if you'd seen the row we had.'

'Seems you've made up though.'

'Yes. Because we need to work together to help Mr P,' Edie responded irritably. Although she couldn't deny how good it had felt to have his arm around her yesterday. It had been safe and comforting, and when he'd looked down at her . . . She shivered. What was she thinking? Here she was, jobless and pregnant by another man – the last thing she needed was to allow herself to have feelings for someone else.

'If you say so,' Marianne replied, her eyes dropping briefly to the brown paper bag on Edie's lap.

Edie gathered it closer to her and glared at her sister, waiting for her to leave.

Marianne took the hint, and once she'd gone, Edie leapt out of bed, contemplating where she could hide the bottles and wishing she'd made up another ailment – like bad monthlies, or something – perhaps then Marianne wouldn't have been so eager to try the concoction. Finally, she hid the bottles in the gap between the wall and the large wardrobe. She'd find somewhere better later, but for now this would have to do.

Once she was dressed, she crept out and listened at Hester's door, wondering whether there'd be anything in there with her address on, but the woman had arrived with virtually nothing, so it seemed unlikely. Unless . . . an image of the suitcase she'd lugged down the hill came to Edie. The handle had had a brown address tag tied to it with string.

Just then there was a thump and a muffled curse from inside the room and she leapt away from the door. She'd try again later.

When she got downstairs, she was surprised to see Bill sitting at a table in the café, drinking tea. He smiled as she entered. 'Morning, sleepyhead. I popped in to see if you'd had any luck with the address?'

Edie shook her head. 'Not yet,' she murmured. 'But Marianne said she thought it was off The Leas, near the Grand.'

Bill reached into his jacket pocket and took out a small address book. 'My dad lived at three Clifton Gardens.' He tore a spare page from the back and wrote the address down for her. 'Just in case you forget.'

Edie nodded and put it in the pocket of her trousers. 'So what do you think we should do today?' she asked.

'Well, seeing as there's not much we can do till you find that address, how do you fancy lunch out? Or maybe the pictures? Or both?' He smiled at her and Edie's heart leapt with pleasure.

'I'd like that.' For a moment, they stared into each other's eyes.

'Edie, are you gonna sit there all day taking up room, or are you gonna help out?' Nellie called, her eyes moving from Bill to her daughter speculatively.

Edie stood up. 'I'm gonna leave,' she said shortly, heading into the kitchen to grab her jacket.

As she and Bill walked towards the front door, Ron Hames called out to her. 'Edie, do you have a moment?'

'What?' she asked shortly.

'I might have some news.' He looked at Bill enquiringly.

Curious, she sat down at the table, gesturing to Bill to take the other seat.

'This is Bill Penfold,' she explained. 'Mr Pearson's nephew.'

'And Walter Penfold's son?'

Bill nodded warily.

'I think you should know that your uncle is in deep, deep trouble,' he whispered.

'How do you know that?' Bill asked.

'Is it true?' he asked, ignoring the question. 'About him being the one behind the sticky-backs?'

'No, it's bloody not!' Bill exclaimed.

'Really? They don't arrest people on a whim, you know.'

287

Edie leant across the table. 'He's been set up,' she hissed. 'And if you think you're so bloody clever, maybe you can find out who it was. Come on, Bill, let's go.'

'Maybe I already know,' he called out after them.

Edie stopped and turned to look at him. 'Do you?'

'I might,' he said evasively.

'Sounds to me like you don't have a clue,' she said scornfully. 'In which case we won't waste any more of your time.'

Ron Hames watched them leave with a shake of his head. 'Oh, I have a clue all right,' he murmured. Then he looked over to the counter where Nellie was watching him with a frown. He grinned and held his hands up. 'It's all right, Mrs C, we was just having a friendly chat.'

Nellie pursed her lips. 'I hope you weren't accusing my daughter of shining the torch the other night.'

'I wouldn't dare.' He grinned. 'But I have my suspicions.' He got up and put his coat on, then walked over to the counter. 'And if I were you,' he said quietly, 'I'd be more careful about who I let in here.'

'What do you mean by that?'

He tapped his nose. 'You'll find out soon enough,' he said.

Nellie felt a flicker of anxiety as she watched him leave.

⁓

Outside, Bill caught Edie's arm. 'We should have asked more questions. He might know something.'

'No, he was trying to find out what *we* know,' she said with a huff of frustration. 'Tell you what, let's go to the pictures. Take our minds off things.' She gestured up Castle Street towards the Granada Cinema where a poster for *Dark Victory* was displayed.

Bill grimaced. 'Bette Davis? Never liked a single one of her films.'

'Bet it can't be worse than real life, though,' Edie said with a smile. 'Come on.' She took his hand and led him into the grand foyer of the cinema with its black-and-white-tiled floor and duck-egg-blue walls with gold cornicing.

By the time the film ended, Bill found himself holding Edie close as she sobbed against his chest. 'Hey, it wasn't real,' he murmured, dropping a kiss on her hair.

'But it could be,' Edie wailed. 'Why did she have to die? It's not fair! He loved her and it's not fair that he lost her.' In truth, Edie wasn't just crying about the film. She was crying because her life had turned into a nightmare and Bill had become the only bright spot in it. They'd known each other for most of their lives, so why was it only now, when there was no hope that anything could come of her feelings, that she'd realised how much he actually meant to her? But if Hester's medicine didn't work, in just a few short months he would know the truth, and she would lose him, just as Dr Steele had lost his Judy in the film.

Bill chuckled and pulled her tighter against him. He'd found the film tedious and melodramatic, but if it meant he could sit in the dark and hold Edie like this, then he'd happily watch it ten times over.

# Chapter 51

Late that night, Nellie crept down the stairs, her shoes in one hand. As she neared the kitchen, she was surprised to hear a man's voice. Hester better not be entertaining, she thought fiercely. Opening the door at the bottom of the stairs quietly, she peeped round and spotted Hester sitting at a table, a wireless beside her while she wrote furiously in a notebook.

'Why don't you just sit and listen to the radio upstairs with me?' she asked.

Hester didn't look up. 'Shhh.'

'What you listening to?'

Hester held up one finger and continued to write as the man's voice intoned: 'A message from Private Nicholas Stuart for Mrs Anne Stuart of 59 Shakespeare Road, Derby. "Dear Mum, I am safe and well. Please don't worry."'

'What's that?' Nellie asked.

'In a minute, Nell,' Hester hissed.

Finally, the National Anthem played and Hester sat back, shaking out her hand dramatically.

'Can you tell me now?'

'One day, not long after I got the news about Tommy, I heard about this radio station that broadcasts names and addresses of prisoners of war. I used to tune in every night in case they mentioned him, until I realised it was pointless. But I've kept on listenin' to the news reports cos it tells you all sorts of other stuff you don't hear

290

nowhere else. Then when I met Mary, I promised to listen for news of Colin and it got me thinkin' about all those other mothers, wives and girlfriends sufferin' around the country and I decided to make a note of every name and address read out and write to them.'

'I thought you said Tommy was dead?' Nellie said.

Hester shrugged. 'They said he were missin'. But what are the chances of surviving in a submarine? So I tell meself he's dead because I can't live with the hope. Whereas for Mary, hope's the only thing that keeps her goin'. We all grieve in our own way, and if this helps others a little, then that helps me.'

Nellie sat down opposite Hester and put her hand over hers. 'Bless you for doing this kindness, love. But . . . has this got anything to do with that radio station Roger Humphries and Ron Hames was getting their knickers in a twist about?'

Hester shrugged. 'I don't know nothin' about that. But how can it be illegal to listen to the radio, eh? Unless the government don't want us to hear the truth.'

'Is it the truth though?'

'It's a sight more truthful than what you hear on the BBC, Nell. It's opened me eyes.'

'But if it's illegal . . . if it's that station on those sticky whatsits—'

'Pah! How can it be bad when it helps people know what's goin' on with their loved ones?'

Nellie could see her point, but she was worried. 'But—'

Hester held up her hand. 'No, Nellie, I'm tellin' you, this is legit. Just not government legit, if you see what I mean. An' if they're lockin' people up just for findin' out stuff they don't want us to know, then what does that say about the country, eh?'

Nellie sighed. 'If you bring trouble to my door cos of this, then you'll be shacking up with Mr Evans. And don't think I won't do it.'

'Fair enough.' Hester nodded. 'But it won't, love. You've got nothing to worry about.'

Nellie wasn't convinced, but she didn't have time to argue right now; she had an appointment to keep. She stood up and slipped her shoes on.

'Late night visit to Jasper, is it?' Hester asked slyly.

Nellie stuck her nose in the air. 'No. I'm off to . . . restock.'

'Terence Carter. An' you sit there lecturing me about listenin' to the wireless!'

'This is different,' she said defensively.

'No, it ain't. You break the law to provide a service. And I'm doin' the same.'

Nellie hadn't thought of it like that, but she supposed she was right.

Hester stood up. 'I'll come with you.'

'No. You might get in trouble.'

Hester let out a cackle. 'Trouble's me middle name. Me and the old Bill have a long acquaintance – I'm not scared of them.'

Nellie nodded. If she was honest, it would be nice to have someone with her.

The two women went out into the backyard where Nellie extracted the bike from the shed and attached the trailer. Then she led the way out on to Church Street.

'Where we goin'?' Hester whispered.

'You'll see. Terence tends to move around these days after his place up Houghton got raided.'

'How do you know where then?'

'Lou passes a message.'

Hester snorted. 'Might have known she'd be involved. She were always crooked that one.'

'And here was me thinking you'd made friends.'

'We have, don't mean I'm blind to her faults, though.'

'Keep your voice down,' Nellie said irritably.

'Nell, that bloody trailer makes enough racket to wake the Jerries over the water.'

Nellie grunted. She was probably right, but how else was she going to carry everything back?

They walked through the dark back streets in silence for a few minutes then turned left down Cherry Tree Avenue. As they crossed London Road, they both became aware of a familiar droning above them.

'Nellie, seriously, where we goin'?' Hester looked up nervously, it was another clear, frosty night, the moon a sliver of light in the sky.

'It's just across the road. Railway arches on Union Road.'

Hester stopped dead. 'I don't like it, Nell. Them planes love a railway.'

'You stay here then.' Nellie continued on, her heart beating a little faster. Hester had made her nervous.

The droning got louder, but Nellie didn't stop, so Hester ran after her and caught her arm. 'I mean it, Nell. I don't like it. I got a sixth sense when it comes to trouble, we gotta get out of here.'

They were standing at the junction of Union Road now and the noise was getting louder.

'Terence Carter, get out of there!' Hester shouted suddenly, simultaneously pulling Nellie away so violently that she dropped the bike in the middle of the road.

'Oy!' Nellie screamed. 'What do you think you're doing?'

But Hester didn't loosen her grip, hustling Nellie back up Cherry Tree Avenue, the ruins of bombed houses standing out starkly in the moonlight. Moments later, an enormous crash from behind them sent them scuttling into the nearest doorway.

'Hell's bells!' Nellie exclaimed, the lost bike forgotten. 'You were right!'

'Like I said, sixth sense.' Hester was breathing heavily beside her.

'We should make sure Terence is all right.'

'No! We gotta keep going.'

The two women ran through the streets as the air raid siren started to wail through the town. Somehow they managed to avoid being seen by anyone and made it safely back into the café, where they tumbled down the basement steps.

'Where the hell have you been?' Edie demanded as they staggered in. The three girls and Donny were gathered around the table, a pot of tea in front of them.

'Gran!' Donny rushed to his grandmother and threw his arms around her waist. 'Where were you? We was worried.'

Nellie ruffled her grandson's hair, then collapsed into a chair, too out of breath to answer.

'Well?' Lily said.

'They'll tell us when they're ready,' Marianne said more mildly. She raised her eyebrows at her mother in silent question, and Nellie shook her head.

'We was just on our way back from the caves,' Hester said eventually.

'You should have gone back to them, then,' Edie said.

'We was caught in the middle,' Nellie responded, grateful for Hester's quick thinking.

'The only thing that matters is that they're here safe and sound,' Marianne interjected. 'Now, how about I pour you both some tea. You look like you could do with it.'

Hester gave Nellie a quick wink, then shooed Marianne back into her chair. 'I'll do it, love. A woman in your condition needs to look after herself.'

Nellie watched her friend closely. How exactly had she known where the planes were headed? She put her head on the table and closed her eyes as her thoughts whirled round and round. But what was uppermost in her mind were Ron Hames's words just a few nights before when the Hippodrome had been bombed. *Things have been strange in Dover recently.* She'd dismissed him at the time. But together with what he'd said earlier today, now she was beginning to think he might be right. Maybe someone *was* out to cause mischief in the town. And maybe they were living under her roof.

But as she watched Hester bustling around making sure everyone was comfortable, she just couldn't believe it. Surely a woman who painstakingly wrote down names and addresses of POWs so that she could write to their families would never knowingly put anyone in danger?

# Chapter 52

'Bloody hell,' Lou Carter exclaimed as she walked into the café next morning.

'Everything all right, Lou?' Nellie asked, trying to keep her tone light, while inside her stomach twisted itself in knots of anxiety.

Lou walked over to the counter, leaning over it confidentially. 'It's my Terence,' she whispered.

Nellie went cold. 'Is he all right?' she asked faintly.

'You were due to meet him, but you didn't show.'

'I was on me way when the bloody planes came, so I turned round and came back.'

'Well, the way he tells it, he were under the arches waitin' when he hears a voice.' She leant closer. 'An' the voice says, "Terence Carter, get out of there!" An' the thing about my boy that you might not know, is he's a bit superspicious.'

'Superspicious?'

'Yeah, you know, believes in signs and stuff like that. Gets it from me mum, who swore she used to speak to me dad long after he'd passed. Anyway, so he hears this voice, and he pegs it. Leaves his stuff and runs. An' you'll never guess what?'

Nellie shook her head.

'Ruddy great bomb lands on the railway line, bringin' bricks and all sorts down on the exact spot he'd been standing. He'd have been a goner for sure if he hadn't moved.'

'Bleedin' heck,' Nellie breathed. 'Lucky I turned back an' all.'

'Weren't it just. I'm that wound up about it, don't even know if I can manage any breakfast.'

'How about I bring you over a nice slice of toast,' Nellie said. 'Go and sit down, love, I won't be two ticks.'

Lou regarded Nellie suspiciously. 'What's brought this on?' she asked.

'Just, I know how you must be feeling,' she said hastily. 'About nearly losing your son and all.'

Lou nodded and smiled. 'See, underneath it all, you're not so bad.'

'Some toast for Lou, Marianne. Quick as you can.'

Gladys and Marianne both stared at her in astonishment – since when had Nellie been so solicitous of Lou Carter? Nellie pretended not to notice as she turned back and poured a cup of tea and pushed it over the counter to Lou. 'There you go, love. Tea's on the house.'

'And the grub?'

'Don't push your luck,' she said sternly.

Lou laughed and went to sit down at her table.

The door opened again and a woman wearing a flowery turban came in.

'All right, Mavis. Don't often see you up and about at this hour. Opening the Oak early, are you?' Nellie asked.

Mavis shuddered as she walked up to the counter. 'No chance. Ruddy great fight in there last night between the soldiers and the sailors. Something about a football match. And guess who was in the thick of it?'

Nellie sighed. 'Bert. I hope you gave him a thick ear.'

Mavis laughed. 'Let's just say he won't be fighting in my pub again any time soon. Which reminds me, guess who was with him? Mary's niece, Susan. Remember her? Nice little thing she used to be, but if the way she was behaving last night's anything to go by, she's changed.' She turned to address the other customers. 'Any of you hear about the railway?' she asked. 'Bomb dropped right on the bridge up by Union Road.'

Ron Hames, who though he'd pretended not to notice, had been watching Nellie and Lou's exchange with curiosity, perked up at that. 'Luckily no casualties, though. It's a bloody miracle.' He turned to look at Lou with raised eyebrows. He had known that Terence Carter had been dealing from there last night and was curious how he'd not been caught up in it. When she didn't respond, he went back to scribbling in his notebook.

'Couple of fried-egg sarnies to go, if you don't mind, Nell. You all right, Marianne, love?' Mavis called through the hatch. 'I heard the happy news, and I'm right glad for yer.'

Marianne poked her head through. 'Thanks, Mrs Woodbridge. I'm surviving – you know how it is.'

'Don't I just.' Mavis laughed. 'Here, Nell, you heard anything more about Clive Pearson? Or maybe Edie has?'

'She don't share much with me, that one. She's either wandering around like a wet weekend or she's running off with that Bill Penfold, so I'm guessing she don't know more than us.'

'So the Canadian pilot's no more, eh? I thought there might be some funny business going on there when she came in for the phone call a while back.'

'She called Bill?'

'Or he called her; I don't know the details, but they definitely talked.'

Nellie shrugged. 'Like I said, I've got no idea what goes on in that girl's mind.'

'But she must have some idea where Clive's got to? And if she don't, Bill will. I just don't understand it. Thrown into jail just like that.'

'Well, whatever they're saying he did, I'd bet my life it's not true,' Nellie replied. In truth she was burning with curiosity about what Bill and Edie were up to. Jasper clearly knew something but he wasn't telling and she knew better than to question her daughter, who'd probably tell her to get lost. She glanced over at Jasper's table and sighed.

She'd been up to see him again yesterday, but he'd still stubbornly refused to come to the café.

Just then, Mavis exclaimed, 'Jasper Cane! Bless my soul, I were going to come and see you later. Saved you a few bottles of Fanshawe's brown ale – two a week, just like you always drink. So you're all set for the next few months. When you comin' back to the Oak?'

Nellie's heart leapt as she turned to see Jasper standing in the kitchen doorway, Hester by his side. She raised her eyebrows questioningly, and Hester grinned and winked at her. How had she persuaded him to come? Nellie thought, a touch resentfully. Still, what did it matter as long as he was back at his table eating breakfast.

'Soon as I can walk further than ten yards without wantin' to collapse,' Jasper said to Mavis. 'Hey, Don.' He gestured to the little boy who was hovering around, eager to spend time with him. 'You couldn't take this message up to Edie.' He handed an envelope to the boy. 'There'll be a penny in it for ya.' He smiled and ruffled the boy's hair.

Donny grinned. 'You don't have to pay me, Jasper. I'm just happy to see you,' he said as he turned to go. 'But, if you want to, then that's all right too . . .'

'Cheeky monkey,' Jasper chuckled.

The bell above the door tinkled and Bunny Whittaker burst in and sat down at Lou's table. 'That were a hairy night and no mistake,' he said, loud enough for everyone to hear. 'There were an angel watching over me last night, Lou. If I'd have left the station a few minutes later, it would have been curtains for me. And not just me, but the whole of Union Road could have been blown to smithereens, considering what was in the wagons . . .'

The journalist looked at him with interest. 'Mr Whittaker, isn't it?'

'Who wants to know?' the man asked suspiciously.

'Ron Hames, *Dover Express*.' He patted the table. 'I'd love to hear all about it. Come on, there's a free breakfast in it for you.'

'Stop harassin' my customers, Ron,' Nellie called, the memory of his words making her nervous all over again.

'You're all right, Mrs C, I don't mind havin' a chat if there's free grub involved.'

The train driver moved to the other table and soon the two men were deep in conversation, their heads bent close together.

Nellie frowned. 'Ain't that Hester's mate?' she asked Gladys as she walked by.

Gladys nodded. 'Yup. Used to be neighbours when they were kids.'

Nellie watched the men, wondering what on earth the journalist could be so interested in. Bombs and shells fell every day and it wasn't the first time the railway had been targeted. But her mind went back again to what Ron had said. *Things have been strange in Dover recently.* She looked over her shoulder into the kitchen where Hester was tying on an apron and sharing a joke with Marianne. She shook her head; she was being ridiculous. Dover was Hester's hometown. And though she'd left under a cloud, since she'd been back, she'd slotted right in. There was no way she would put them all in danger. But despite what her heart was telling her, her head was shouting something very different.

# Chapter 53

In the bedroom, Edie took out one of the bottles and frowned slightly as she noticed how little there was left. Surely she'd not had that much? She needed to measure the doses out more carefully, she realised, because if she carried on like this, five bottles wouldn't be enough.

A knock on the door startled her and she hastily concealed the bottle under the bed. 'Who is it?' she called.

'It's only me, Auntie Edie,' Donny said, coming in. 'Jasper asked me to bring you this.' He held out the envelope to her.

Recognising Bill's writing, she snatched it eagerly. They'd had a lovely time yesterday and he'd been so sweet. She couldn't imagine Greg sitting patiently through that film and then being happy to hold her while she wept all over him. Bill had taken her for lunch afterwards, and they'd reminisced about when they were younger and how impatient Mr Pearson used to get at their bickering.

'We'll get him back, you know,' Edie had said comfortingly, putting her hand on Bill's.

He'd squeezed it gently. 'With you on his side, then I don't doubt it.'

'Aren't you going to open it?' Donny asked, interrupting her thoughts.

Edie nodded and ripped open the envelope.

*Sorry our date yesterday made you so sad. Next time, let's choose a comedy.*

*Bill xx*

Edie smiled sadly, her eyes focused on those two kisses. There wouldn't be a next time. Because once Mr P was free, she wouldn't see Bill again – it was the only way she could protect her heart.

'Who's it from?' Donny asked curiously.

'Never you mind, nosy,' she teased.

Donny grinned as he walked to the door. 'It must be from someone special, cos you look happier than normal.'

'Yes,' Edie replied softly. 'It is from someone special. Hey, have you seen Hester?'

'She's downstairs helping with breakfast,' Donny replied. 'And then she promised that me, Fred and her could go on one of our adventures. Today we're gonna go up Pudding Hill and if we're lucky the soldiers'll give us a lift up in one of their trucks.' He grinned. 'Although Hester thinks they won't want to take her, but I bet me and Fred can make them.'

'Sounds like fun,' she said, wondering how Hester had the energy to run around with the boys every day.

'It is!' Donny slammed the door as he left, and Edie waited until she'd heard his footsteps fade, before going out into the hall. Then taking a deep breath, she turned the handle of Hester's bedroom door and crept in.

She spotted the suitcase on top of the wardrobe almost immediately and after pulling it down, she turned the label over and gasped. 'Three Clifton Gardens . . . What the hell is going on?' she murmured to herself.

Putting the case back, she went back to her room to throw on some clothes and hurried out.

# Chapter 54

Bill answered the door at Edie's knock, wearing his uniform trousers and a white vest. His hair was wet and he smelt of Pears soap.

'Edie!' he exclaimed with a broad smile. 'You get my note?'

'I did. Thank you,' she said, trying to keep her tone cool. 'But I'm not here to go to the pictures again. It's about Hester.'

'You've got some news?' he asked anxiously.

Edie nodded and pushed past him; who'd have thought Pears soap could smell so good, she thought. Then gave herself a mental shake.

'Hester's address was three Clifton Gardens,' she said.

Bill rubbed the back of his neck. 'Bloody hell, the plot thickens.'

'So it wasn't a coincidence that she arrived here the same day your dad did. Question is, what are they up to? I mean, she has some funny ideas about the war and stuff, but I just can't see her doing anything bad.'

'Doesn't mean she wouldn't though. So what do we do now?'

'We tell Mr Wainwright,' Edie replied. 'And maybe talk to Hester.'

'No. She might run off if we start asking her questions.'

'You're probably right,' Edie agreed. 'So hurry up and get dressed and let's go.'

∽

Outside Mr Wainwright's house, Bill and Edie took a moment to catch their breath before knocking. The door was answered by the same fearsome secretary they'd met before.

303

'Do you have an appointment?' she asked before they'd got a word out.

'No. But he'll want to see us.'

'Sorry, no appointment, no meeting. Anyway, Mr Wainwright is on the telephone. Come back tomorrow morning at nine a.m. I will put it in the diary.'

Bill pushed past her. 'I'm sorry, this is urgent. We'll wait for his call to end.'

The secretary gasped in outrage.

'Who is it, Mrs Frobisher?' a voice called through the door of the office.

'It's Bill Penfold,' Bill replied.

'Give me five minutes and I'll be right with you,' he called back.

Edie smiled smugly at Mrs Frobisher. 'See? We told you he'd want to see us.'

The woman huffed and gestured to a couple of chairs against the wall. 'Please sit quietly. Mr Wainwright is on a *very* important call.' Then she disappeared into an adjoining room from where they soon heard the click-clack of a typewriter.

It wasn't long before Mr Wainwright appeared wearing an old-fashioned red velvet smoking jacket. 'Bill, Edie,' he said jovially. 'Funny you should turn up now. I was just having a most intriguing conversation. Come in, come in.' He ushered them into his office. 'Apologies for Mrs F. Her heart's in the right place, but dear me she's a stickler. Life was much simpler when Marge worked for me.' He sighed and plumped down on his chair.

'Right, well, what can I do for you?' he asked.

'We've just found out that Walter Penfold lived with Hester in Folkestone,' Edie burst out.

Mr Wainwright's eyebrows rose. 'Hester? I take it you mean the woman who's currently lodging at the café?'

At Edie's nod, he murmured, 'How fascinating. Do you have any other information?'

'We were hoping you would have some for us,' Bill said. 'About my uncle?'

'Patience, lad. Things are happening, but what you've just told me is very useful.'

'We were thinking of going there to see if she lied about her house being destroyed by a shell,' Edie said eagerly.

Mr Wainwright sat back and smiled slightly. 'I really do admire your persistence and enthusiasm, but there's no need. I suggest you go home and wait. Like I said, everything's in hand.'

'But what about Hester?' Edie exclaimed.

'Don't breathe a word to her. Act completely natural. Please, Edie, Bill. If you say anything about your suspicions, you could ruin everything. Do you trust me?'

They nodded.

'Good.' He slapped his hands on the table. 'Off you go, then.' He opened the door and ushered them out. 'And here's hoping that next time I see you I have more news for you.'

'What do you think he meant that it could ruin everything?' Edie asked once they were outside.

'I don't know, but it sounds to me like we were right. Hester is involved somehow, and maybe things are moving at last and Uncle Clive will be free soon.'

'Please God you're right,' Edie said softly. 'I hate the thought of what he's going through.'

Bill put his arm around her shoulder. 'Me too,' he said. 'But I'm sure he knows you'll be doing your best to help him, so I'm sure that gives him comfort.'

'I hope so.' Edie kicked the pavement despondently. 'So what now?'

Bill sighed. 'I don't know. I want to go see Dad again, but after last time I don't think they'll even let me in the drive . . . Anyway, from what Mr Wainwright said, it might be a bad idea. So how about I treat you to a cup of tea and a bun in the Pot and Kettle? Hopefully that won't make you cry.' He grinned and held out his arm.

Edie hesitated. She knew it was a bad idea to spend too much time with him, but surely a cup of tea couldn't do any harm, she thought, taking his arm with a smile.

They'd walked only a little way when a voice called out behind them. 'Oy, Edie! Wait up!'

Edie turned to see Susan running towards her. 'Oh no ...' Edie murmured. She'd purposely avoided seeing the girl since New Year – she had enough to deal with without being reminded about the dilemma she had about Charlie and Lily.

'Hello, Susan,' she said.

'And who's this?' Susan said archly, looking Bill up and down.

'This is Bill Penfold. Mr Pearson's nephew.'

For a moment, Susan looked surprised, but then she smiled prettily. 'A pilot? I didn't know you were walking out with anyone, Edie.'

Edie glanced at Bill and blushed. 'I'm not. It is possible to walk down the road with a man who's not your boyfriend, you know.'

Susan laughed. 'Maybe it is. But it's much more fun if they are. Anyway, I'm glad I've caught you. I wanted to ask you if you'd come to Bert's football match with me.'

At Edie's blank look, she elaborated. 'Didn't you know? He's arranged some match between the army and navy up in the field by the castle next week. Please say you'll come. Oh, I do love seeing men running around in shorts.' She giggled and Edie resisted the impulse to roll her eyes.

'What happened to Charlie?'

Susan waved her hand dismissively. 'Charlie who? I don't know why I wasted so many tears on the man. Bert's much better-looking and he's funnier. Just think, we could be sisters one day!'

Edie's eyes widened. 'It's a bit soon to think like that, isn't it?'

'It only takes a minute to fall in love. And this time I really think he loves me back. In fact, I'm off to see if he's free now.'

'What, you hang around the barracks?'

'Of course not, silly. The boys in the sentry box let me sit with them and give me tea. Aren't soldiers just lovely? So I'll see you next week? Please say you'll come.'

'All right,' Edie said, although she had no intention of going.

'Blimey,' Bill remarked. 'She seems like the type that once she gets her teeth into you, she never lets go.'

Edie giggled, watching Susan skip down the road, her red coat bright against the muted colours of the other passers-by. 'I know, terrible, isn't it? Poor Bert.' But Bill's comment reminded her of what Charlie had said about how Susan had followed him around and pestered him. Maybe he'd been telling the truth ... And if he had, then as long as Lily never found out, it looked like one of her problems at least was over. It had been a stroke of genius to get Bert to seduce Susan away. Edie grinned to herself. She'd buy him a pint next time she saw him.

At that moment she noticed a car stop on Cannon Street and Susan walk over to it, bending to look in at the driver.

Edie frowned. 'You see that car next to Susan?'

Bill looked over. 'The black Ford Coupe? What about it?'

Edie shook her head, she was being stupid. There were a lot of Fords around after all, but in her mind's eye, she pictured another black Ford Coupe, looking insignificant next to the shiny Bentley beside it. 'Nothing,' she said. But something was niggling at the back of her mind about Susan, but for the life of her she couldn't work out what it was.

⁓

'You wouldn't mind if I took a quick break, Mum?' Marianne asked later that morning after the breakfast rush had died down.

Nellie poked her head through the hatch. 'You all right, love? You look a bit peaky. You're not about to faint again, are you?'

'I'm fine, just a bit tired,' Marianne replied. Though in truth, with things quieter in the kitchen, her thoughts had turned once again to what might happen tomorrow and the anxiety was making her feel shaky.

'Go on, then. We can manage.'

In the bedroom, she crouched down by the wardrobe and took out one of the bottles Edie had tried to hide. With so much to worry about, she hadn't been able to resist trying some of the medicine the day before, and she'd found it had soothed her stomach beautifully. Gladys had always been clever with herbs and plants. She opened the stopper and took a gulp, then sat back and closed her eyes. After a moment, she took another large mouthful, feeling her heartbeat quieten. She knew it was bad, stealing Edie's liquid, but if it kept this feeling of impending doom at bay, she was willing to risk her sister's wrath.

She stoppered the bottle and put it back where she'd found it, then lay on the bed, rubbing her hand over her stomach. 'Don't worry, Daisy, one day you, me, Daddy and Donny will be living in our own little house and it will be the most perfect life you can imagine.' She closed her eyes and pictured herself walking along a sun-drenched beach, Donny racing in and out of the water, while a sweet fair-haired little girl squealed with delight as she and Alfie swung her between them.

# Chapter 55

The next day, though, Marianne's anxiety was back a hundred-fold. Today was Mr Fanshawe's funeral and she was on tenterhooks in case one of the family turned up at the café to find out why she hadn't attended the will reading.

The atmosphere at home didn't help, either. The evening before had been strange and tense, with her mother and Edie both staying in their rooms. And when Hester had gone to ask Nellie if she would like a cup of tea, she'd had her head bitten off.

Lily and Marianne had exchanged a glance but knew better than to disturb their mother when she was in one of her moods. Marianne had noticed a cooling in her mother's attitude towards Hester throughout the day, though she couldn't work out why. Especially as Hester had made a special effort to bring Jasper over for breakfast.

'Don't worry, Hester,' Donny had said. 'Gran gets like that sometimes. It'll blow over.'

Hester had chuckled and ruffled his hair. 'Oh, I don't mind, Don. I get like that too sometimes. Long as you an' me are still mates?'

'Course we are. Can we go out again soon?'

'I was thinking we should explore Crabble next,' Hester replied. 'It's been ages since I been there.'

'Oh, there's lots to see up there. How about tomorrow?'

'Let's make it the day after, eh?'

Donny had nodded happily, returning to his schoolwork.

Now, with the lunchtime service over and the kitchen cleaned, Marianne felt too anxious to relax, so she distracted herself by making some bread and butter pudding for the next day. Considering her mother's failed attempt to get more supplies, she could only use a sliver of margarine, making up the difference with a little lard and some water and using golden syrup instead of sugar, then she added plenty of nutmeg. After that, she made some dumplings with potato, eggs and cheese to help the left-over rabbit stew from lunch stretch a little bit further for the family's dinner that night.

She glanced at the clock. Three thirty. All day she had been picturing what might be happening up at The Gables, the Fanshawes' Victorian mansion. The funeral would be over now, she realised. No doubt it had been a fancy affair with lots of mourners from the village and a mahogany coffin with brass handles. Nothing like the funeral of those poor people in Coventry just a couple of months before, who had been buried in two mass graves. At the time her mother had complained that if things went on as they had been, the entire population of Dover would end up buried together in a field somewhere.

With the dumplings in the oven she rubbed her back and slumped down at the small kitchen table.

'You all right, love?' Hester asked, coming in with another tray of dirty cups and saucers.

'Back ache,' she said. 'It's been on and off all day.'

Hester eyed her with concern. 'You want me to get you some aspirin?' she asked.

'We've run out.'

Hester dumped the tray in the pantry then put her coat on. 'I'll nip out and get some, love. Can't have you in pain.'

'You don't have to . . .'

'It's no bother. I need a bit of air, and I've got some letters to post.'

'What you need is some camomile and ginger tea,' Gladys remarked from the pantry. 'I can make you some if you like.'

'Aspirin will be fine. By the way, Glad, that stuff you gave Edie for her nightmares and anxiety, what's in it? I've been taking a few nips of it myself, and it really does help settle my stomach.'

Gladys looked confused. 'But I never—'

She was interrupted by Hester exclaiming, 'You shouldn't drink anything if you don't know what's in it! Not in your condition.'

'But it's only a few herbs and things,' Marianne said.

'It don't matter. You mustn't drink it.'

'Drink what?' Nellie asked from the hatch.

'Glad was just recommending ginger and camomile tea for Marianne's backache. But I reckon aspirin'll do the job quicker, so I'm popping out to get some. But I mean it, love,' she said to Marianne. 'Only take stuff if you know what it is.' Then she hurried out of the door.

'Hester's right. Camomile and ginger indeed. I've told you before not to bring your potions here, Glad. And where's Edie?'

Marianne shrugged. 'Out. Think she's gone up to the forge to visit Bill.'

'Again! She's only just got rid of that Greg bloke, and now she's running around with another man.' She shook her head. 'That girl'll get herself into trouble if she's not careful.'

'Leave her alone, Mum,' Marianne said. 'They're trying to sort out poor Mr Pearson.'

Nellie sniffed, feeling aggrieved. If she'd been the one arrested, would Edie have lifted a finger to get her released? she wondered. Somehow, she doubted it.

∞

Hester had got no further than the corner of Church Street when a long black car stopped beside her and a young man with thick, black-rimmed spectacles and wearing a homburg and smart blue overcoat stepped out. Briefly she thought he didn't look old enough to be wearing those clothes. But when he spoke, she realised that he was a lot older than he looked.

'Hester Erskine?' he asked in a broad Liverpudlian accent.

Hester eyed him warily. 'Who's asking?'

'Would you come with me, please?' He grasped her arm and before she could protest, bundled her into the car. She didn't even have time to catch her breath before the man had shut the door and they were speeding through the streets of Dover.

'Oy!' she said. 'You can't just shove me in a car and drive off!'

'Actually, I can,' the man replied. He reached into his inside pocket and brought out an ID card. 'Peter Holmes, MI5.' She stared back at him blankly, so he elaborated. 'Counter-espionage.'

Hester's stomach flipped. 'What's that even mean?'

'It means that I investigate people who we think are betraying the country. And from the information we've gathered about you, it seems you are one of them.'

Hester's lips trembled as the reality of her situation hit home. 'I never hurt anyone,' she whispered.

'Maybe not personally, but your actions have caused severe damage. And that little trick at the Hippodrome could have resulted in multiple casualties. As could the railway.'

'No! No, those things had nothin' to do with me. I mean, I only mentioned a couple of things to someone. I didn't know that would happen.'

'In which case, you need to tell us who it was. And if you cooperate, you might get a more lenient sentence. Because as it stands you could be facing a firing squad.'

Hester paled. 'You can't be serious?'

The young man smiled grimly. 'I don't joke about things like that. So, we're going to take you to Dover Police Station, where you'll be able to tell me all about it.'

Hester stared blindly out of the window, thinking about the last couple of weeks. She'd known they were using her, but it had suited her to go along with their plans. What did she have to lose, after all? And if she could inflict some damage on the people who had caused the death of her son, then so much the better. She leant her head on the cool glass, feeling the tears gather; she'd made some stupid decisions in her life, she thought, but listening to those people took the biscuit. Well, if this man wanted information, she'd give it to him. She owed them nothing.

# Chapter 56

Despite Hester's dire warning, Marianne was considering sneaking up to the bedroom for another sip of the medicine, when Nellie's voice drifted through to the kitchen.

'What the *bloody hell* are *you* doing here?'

Then a voice Marianne remembered all too well replied, 'And a very good afternoon to you too, Mrs Castle.'

With a feeling of dread, Marianne slowly went to the kitchen door, watching with her heart in her mouth as Elspeth Fanshawe, as beautiful as ever, her blonde hair swept into a bun under a fur hat, her lips bright red, sauntered towards an empty table by the window, unbuttoning her fur coat to reveal a full-skirted black satin dress. 'I'd like a cup of tea and one of those delicious-looking scones, please?' she said to Gladys, who'd rushed to the table to serve her.

'I don't think so,' Nellie said, folding her arms.

A silence descended on the room as the customers looked between Nellie and the glamorous stranger in bewilderment.

'Are you refusing to serve me?'

'Yes. And now I'd like you to leave.' Nellie went and opened the door, but Elspeth ignored her as she slowly drew off her black satin gloves, one finger at a time, seemingly unconcerned; Marianne doubted that anything ever scared her.

The back door opened and she turned to see Edie walk in, her nose and cheeks bright red from the cold. 'Get out!' Marianne hissed.

Edie frowned in confusion. But then Elspeth's voice floated into the kitchen, and with a gasp, Edie turned around and left, running full tilt back up to the forge where she'd just left Bill and Jasper playing cards.

Marianne took a deep breath and went to stand behind the counter. 'Mrs Fanshawe, I'm sorry that I—' she began, but the other woman held up a hand.

'Leave it.' She took a black handkerchief from her bag and dabbed at her eyes. 'I shouldn't have been surprised that someone like you would totally disregard a sick old man's dying wish, but I had hoped you would at least allow his grandson to attend his funeral.'

Nellie looked round sharply at Marianne. 'What's she talking about?' she snapped.

'Didn't she tell you? It was dear Mr Fanshawe's funeral today. All the family was there. Apart from his much-adored grandson.'

Nellie shot one of her terrifying 'I'll-deal-with-you-later' looks at Marianne and was about to shut the front door in defeat, when it was pushed open by Lou Carter who stopped short at the sight of the elegant woman sitting at her table.

'Usual, Lou?' Nellie asked.

'If you don't mind, love.' She nodded in Elspeth's direction and mouthed, 'Who's that?' But Nellie just shook her head.

Gradually, the hum of conversation resumed as Nellie, realising that short of manhandling the woman out of the door, there wasn't much more she could do, went back to stand behind the counter.

In the kitchen, Marianne couldn't concentrate on anything, it felt as if Elspeth's steely gaze was on her all the time, even though she knew that wasn't possible. She just hoped Donny didn't arrive home while she was here.

Finally, unable to leave someone sitting at a table without even a drink, Gladys went over to Elspeth again.

'I said no, Glad. She's not staying.'

There was a brief hush as once again people's eyes were drawn to the stranger, who smiled around at them sweetly.

315

'She's right, you know. I'm not staying. I just wanted to warn you about the sort of place you're frequenting.'

From her bag she took out a copy of the *Dover Express*. 'This evening's copy,' she said. 'Hot off the press and not yet available. So useful when your family owns the newspaper, don't you think?'

Now she had the room's attention, she smiled again. 'Would you like me to read the highlights?'

Bemused, Gladys went to stand next to Marianne in the kitchen doorway, while Nellie stood stock-still by the counter, a feeling of dread washing over her. She glanced over to the table where Ron Hames usually sat, but he was absent today.

Elspeth sauntered towards Nellie, then turned to face the room, leaning against the counter casually. Then she cleared her throat.

'The headline, ladies and gentlemen.' She held it up and there was a collective gasp.

'"Café gossips put Dover in danger",' Elspeth read in her cut-glass accent. She looked around, one eyebrow raised. 'I'm guessing he means *this* café. Shall we find out?' She shook out the paper and started to read.

'"Castle's Café sits on the corner of Market Square and Castle Street. With its mock-Tudor frontage, it is a Dover landmark and has served food to the townspeople for over one hundred and fifty years. If any of you have read *Great Expectations* by the late, great Charles Dickens, an habitué of Dover . . ."' Elspeth paused and looked up. 'That means he came here a lot, in case anyone was wondering. ". . . then you may remember that Pip collapsed on the steps of this very building." Gosh, how interesting, I never knew that.' Elspeth smiled condescendingly.

Nellie finally found the power to move again and tried to grab the paper from the woman's hands. But Elspeth held it away from her. 'Patience, Mrs Castle, I'll get to the good bit very soon.'

Nellie glanced around at the customers, all of whom were sitting staring at Elspeth, their eyes wide. She desperately wanted to leave, but she couldn't; whatever Ron Hames had written, it clearly wasn't good, so she needed to stay. She turned to look at Marianne whose face was paper white, while Gladys stood with a protective arm around her shoulders. She wished with all her heart that Jasper was here right now; he was probably the only person in the world who might be able to avert the trouble she could sense was about to engulf the café.

As if in answer to her prayers, the back door crashed open and Jasper walked in, Edie and Bill each holding an arm. He stopped in the kitchen doorway and grinned round at everyone.

'Afternoon all,' he said chirpily, then dropped into his usual seat. 'And look, here's Mrs Fanshawe, all dressed in satin and fur. Nice of you to come eat with the peasants.'

A few of the customers laughed at that, but most kept silent as they tried to work out what was going on.

Elspeth glared at Jasper. 'I have no idea who you are,' she said. 'But I'm so happy you could join us for this little reading.'

'Oy, Glad, get us a cuppa,' Jasper called loudly. 'And, Marianne, sort us out a cheese sarnie, will ya?'

They both looked at him as if he were mad. 'An', Polly! How goes it today?'

On the counter by Nellie's arm, the bird started to flap her wings. 'Hello, Jasper,' she squawked. 'Jasper's a hero. Hello, Jasper.'

For the first time in her life, Nellie wanted to kiss the bird. 'How's Hitler today, Polly?' she asked, catching on quickly to Jasper's tactics.

'Bloody man!' she squawked.

'Do you want some food, Polly?' Nellie stuck her fingers through the cage.

'Get a move on!'

'Oy, Polly, what do you think of Mrs Fanshawe?' Lou Carter shouted.

When the parrot didn't say anything, Nellie said, 'What are you?'

'Bloody bird!' Polly squawked.

The comment caused a ripple of laughter, and Elspeth's face reddened. 'Quiet please!' she shouted above the noise. 'I haven't finished.'

'Get a move on!' Polly said obligingly.

'This café is a hotbed of gossip and has been harbouring a traitor! A traitor that *this* woman' – she pointed at Nellie – 'allowed in. You have to ask yourself whether Nellie Castle knew what was going on! Or worse, was she in on it?!'

Once again the room fell into shocked silence.

Suddenly, Lou Carter stood up and stalked over to Elspeth. '*This* woman,' she snarled into Elspeth's face, 'does more for this town than just about anyone else I know. Whereas, none of us know who the hell you are.' She looked her up and down scathingly. 'With yer posh togs and yer plummy voice, you think we'd trust the likes of *you* over her. The woman what risks it all to feed those in need. Do ya? Well, do ya?' She grasped Elspeth's arm and marched her to the door. But her passage was blocked by the stocky figure of Walter Penfold standing, arms folded, at the door.

'I'd take yer hands off her, if I were you, Lou Carter,' he said.

'Oh, you would, would yer?' she sneered. 'Well, you're welcome to her. Don't think anyone's ever forgot how you left poor Iris to die alone.' She glanced over at Bill. 'Abandoned yer boy. An' now look, you come in here thinkin' we'd welcome you. Well, we don't. And whatever's printed in that rag, it's a lie.' She shoved Elspeth towards Walter. The suddenness of the movement made the woman stumble on her high heels as she fell into her chauffeur's arms. 'Now, get out, the both of yer, and don't come back!'

'You better do as she says,' Jasper called. 'Or we'll set the parrot on yer. What do you think, Polly?'

'Get a move on!'

Over the laughter, Elspeth pointed a shaking finger at Marianne, and screamed, 'If you think that you or your revolting brat will ever get a single penny out of the Fanshawes, you can think again.' She shook the newspaper. 'Because *this* will put paid to any dreams you

318

might have. Your family are nothing but traitors and sluts.' She glared at Edie, threw the newspaper on the floor and flounced out, followed swiftly by Walter.

Bill rushed after them, threading his way through the tightly packed tables, Edie following close behind. He reached the pavement just as Walter was pulling the door of the beautiful sky-blue Alvis shut.

Bill grabbed it. 'Dad! We need to talk.'

Walter Penfold shook his head. 'We got nothing to talk about, son. You've been stickin' your nose where you've got no business to. As for you' – he looked at Edie – 'your loyalty to Clive is touching, but just so you know, I never lied to you. Just left out a few facts.' Then he winked at her and slammed the door shut.

Bill and Edie watched the car screech away in a cloud of fumes. 'He's got to be lying,' Edie said faintly.

'Of course he is.' Bill's face was pale and a muscle jumped in his cheek. 'It's all he knows how to do.' He grabbed her hand and began to run.

'Where are we going?' Edie shouted.

'To see the only person who might know what the hell is going on!'

# Chapter 57

A shocked silence descended on the café after Elspeth and Walter had left, broken only by the tinkling of the bell over the door. Marianne stood frozen in the kitchen doorway, while Nellie looked around at her customers, convinced she could see accusation in their eyes.

Then Mr Gallagher, who had been sitting at the table nearest the door, bent down and picked up the newspaper. Before he could start reading, Nellie rushed forward and snatched it from him and began to read as she walked slowly back to the counter.

'What does it say?' Jasper asked as all the colour left Nellie's face.

Nellie shook her head. 'That Ron Hames will never set foot in this café again,' she exclaimed. 'Day after day he's sat there. He's sheltered in our basement, eaten our food, drunk our tea . . . And all the while he were just biding his time till he could aim his gun at us and fire!' She thrust the paper at Jasper, who skimmed it quickly.

'Gordon Bennett,' Jasper muttered. 'I thought she were just shootin' her mouth off. Is this true?'

'Yes. And when he blames the café, he blames the community!'

'Hang on a minute!' a soldier shouted indignantly. 'How are *we* to blame for putting Dover in danger. We're here to protect the town – every man jack of us has signed our lives away. The most we talk about in here is who's decked who and which bird's worth a second look.'

'I'm sure he doesn't mean you military people,' Gladys interjected. 'But we all know very well who he means, don't we, Nellie?' She glared challengingly at her friend.

Nellie refused to meet her eyes, instead turning her attention to Lou. 'I owe you one, Lou. Never expected in a million that you'd be the one to stand up and protect my honour. Not after what happened last year.' Nellie still hadn't entirely forgiven the woman for believing Lily had helped a German prisoner escape from the hospital and organising a mob to stand outside the café.

Lou looked sheepish. 'I learnt my lesson, girl. And I'm right sorry about all that nonsense. I got caught up in the moment. For all we don't always see eye to eye, I know exactly what you do for everyone. We all do.'

Nellie felt tears spring to her eyes. 'Thanks, Lou. You don't know how much that means to me.'

'Are you gonna tell us what it says?' Mr Gallagher asked.

Nellie didn't think she could bear to. But then, everyone would know soon enough, so what did it matter? She looked at Marianne. 'Is Hester back yet?'

Marianne shook her head. 'Never returned from getting the aspirin.'

Well, at least that was something, she thought. Because reading the article had clarified a lot of things for her, and she realised that she had no option but to report her suspicions to the police. That is, if they didn't come to her first.

She looked back round, noticing that several more people had come into the café – word had clearly spread that something was afoot at Castle's.

'In you come, then,' Nellie greeted them with false cheer. 'All right Brian, Phyllis, Ethel. Good to see you too, Reenie. And Miss Frost, how kind of you to grace us with your presence. Ain't seen you in here for a few weeks. Not since . . .'

'Since you took it upon yourself to harbour a sinner,' the woman said.

Nellie had no reply to that. Ordinarily she'd have leapt to Hester's defence. But never again.

'Get on with it, will you?' somebody called out.

'Get a move on, hurry up!' Polly squawked and for once Nellie didn't feel irritated. The bird had proven herself to be worth her weight in gold.

'Right, then. I'll carry on from where that witch left off, shall I?' She cleared her throat and began to read:

*For the last couple of weeks, the bomb and shell attacks have felt subtly different to this author. It started with the firebombs on 27 December, after which popular mechanic Clive Pearson mysteriously disappeared and his garage was shut up. It continued with the bombing of the Hippodrome – where this author saw someone flashing a light near the stage door on Northampton Street, minutes before just one bomb dropped through the roof of the theatre where a free concert for our brave troops was due to begin.*

*Then there was the attack on the railway … It is my belief that this was targeted for reasons that can't be revealed. And on the same night, the old Dover Electrical premises in Charlton Green was bombed. Few know what really goes on there, but it seems the Luftwaffe does.*

*In addition, there are the cases of shells falling in tight groupings round other assorted military targets. Secret places. Places essential to the defence of our gallant, besieged island.*

*So how were Dover's secrets so easily uncovered?*

*The answer is simple: they were revealed over a cup of tea at Castle's Café where on any given day you can find an assortment of people – from soldiers to sailors to railwaymen and shopkeepers – all there to relax, eat and gossip.*

*But as the events of the past weeks have proved, walls really do have ears. And so I beseech you, people of Dover, for the sake of our country, keep your mouths shut and your eyes open! Not everyone is who they seem and the chatty woman with the ready smile who serves you tea, might equally be serving up information to our sworn enemy.*

When Nellie had finished reading, Gladys said, 'Well, short of namin' her, he couldn't have been clearer who he means, could he? I warned you and warned you and warned you, Nellie. But would you listen? Pah! Nellie Castle don't listen to no one unless it suits her.'

'Steady on, Glad,' Jasper said. 'It ain't Nellie's fault.'

'Then whose fault is it?' she said shrilly. 'This is what happens when you let a *prostitute* into your house!'

'Exactly right, Gladys,' Miss Frost chimed in. 'But the woman will get her just deserts. "For the sexually immoral and all liars, their portion will be in the lake that burns with fire and sulphur."'

'Christ on a bike,' a soldier said, standing up and putting on his helmet. 'I came in here for a quiet cuppa and a fag after a pig of a day, and instead I get conspiracies, treason and a group of screaming banshees spouting fire and brimstone. Where're the bloody shells when you need 'em!' He walked out.

'You know, Mrs C,' a man in naval uniform said, as he got up to follow the other man out of the door, 'I've got no idea who this person that's been blabbing is, but maybe in future you should get all your customers to sign the Official Secrets Act before you serve 'em.'

Cheeks red with a mixture of humiliation and fury, Nellie turned on Gladys and Miss Frost. 'As if there isn't trouble enough without you two quoting the flippin' Bible at me. If you haven't got anything useful to add, then you can get out, the both of you!'

'Woe to you, Nellie Castle, for you have brought evil on yourself,' Miss Frost said as she turned to leave. 'I will not stay in a house of sin.'

Nellie ignored her as she turned to Gladys, who was stripping off her apron.

'As for you, Glad, what happened to your Christian charity?'

'I got plenty of it. But I just knew she were up to something. You shoulda listened to me, Nellie. Why do you *never* listen?' She shouted the last question and Nellie's eyes widened.

323

For a moment, the two women stared at each other and to Marianne it looked as if they were carrying out a silent conversation that had nothing to do with Hester.

'That ain't fair,' Nellie whispered finally.

Gladys shook her head. 'You would say that. You're as good at lyin' to yourself as you are to everyone else.' Then she whirled round and stormed out of the back door, not even stopping to get her coat.

After she'd left, Nellie slumped down on a chair and put her head in her hands. Jasper sat down opposite her. 'She'll come round, love, don't worry.'

Nellie shook her head. 'I'm not so sure.'

Phyllis came over and put a comforting hand on Nellie's shoulder. 'Course she will. You know Gladys – her heart's soft as butter, she'd hate to think she's upset you.'

Nellie sniffed and straightened her shoulders. She could collapse later, she thought. Right now she needed to take control. She stood up and clapped her hands. 'Right, you lot. Considerin' what's happened, I'm closing the café for the rest of the day, so please finish up and leave. As for you lot' – she looked around at her friends – 'thank you for being here. But as there's no Glad, Hester's disappeared and Edie's run off to God knows where, I got stuff to do.' She glanced over at Marianne, who looked as though she was about to collapse. 'You all right, love?' she asked softly.

Marianne shook her head. 'Sorry, Mum,' she said faintly. 'I don't think I can . . .' She gestured at the mess left by the customers.

Phyllis rolled up her sleeves. 'Don't worry, Marianne, love. Go upstairs and lie down. Me and Ethel can help your mum.'

Ethel nodded. 'The men can sort out the shops for a change. Reenie, can you start collecting the plates. We'll have this place shipshape in no time.'

Marianne smiled gratefully and disappeared up the stairs.

'I'll help in just a tick,' Reenie said. 'First I want to make sure Marianne's all right.'

Upstairs, Reenie knocked on her friend's door and went straight in. Marianne was sitting on the bed, drinking something from a bottle. Guiltily, she quickly hid it, but when she saw who was at the door, she brought it out and put the stopper on.

'What's that?' Reenie asked, walking over to sit on the bed.

'A tonic Glad made for Edie's nerves and nightmares. And if ever I needed something for my nerves, it's today.'

'Are you all right?' Reenie asked gently, worried by Marianne's pale face and red eyes.

'Not really. The baby is really taking it out of me. And now this. I'm just so bloody tired of it all.'

'Look, why don't you go to sleep. I'm going to help clean up downstairs, and later I'll pop up to Drop Redoubt and leave a message for the boys. Tell Alfie you need him.'

Marianne smiled tiredly. 'I'm not sure even Alfie could make me feel better today.'

'Course he can. That man makes your eyes light up like a Christmas tree. And just cos there's been a bit of trouble, that won't change. After all, when isn't there trouble here?' Reenie chuckled as she pulled down the eiderdown and Marianne obediently slipped underneath it.

Marianne sighed. 'You sure you want to be part of this family, Reens?'

'I'd give my eye teeth for the chance. But there's no sign it'll happen any time soon,' Reenie said regretfully, thinking of how Jimmy had never returned after he'd run off on New Year's Eve. And after what Wilf had said, she'd not felt confident enough to go and see him either. 'Sleep well, love.' Reenie tucked the eiderdown around her friend's shoulder then went downstairs to help with the clearing-up.

# Chapter 58

This time when Mrs Frobisher answered the door, she didn't bother trying to stop Bill and Edie entering the building, instead standing aside to let them rush through.

Without even knocking, Bill thrust Mr Wainwright's office door open. 'Elspeth Fanshawe has just been at the café!' he exclaimed. 'Along with my dad!' He stopped as he noticed a copy of the *Dover Express* on the desk.

'And good afternoon to you too, young Bill. And Edie. I deduce that you have some idea of the contents of the article?'

'She tried to read it out to everyone, but she was interrupted.'

Mr Wainwright held out the newspaper to them and Edie took it, curious to know exactly what the article said.

'And where is the lovely Mrs Fanshawe now?' Mr Wainwright asked.

'They drove off. I expect they're on their way back to Hawkinge, but I couldn't be sure.'

Mr Wainwright picked up the telephone. 'Dover Police Station, please.' After a moment, he said, 'Suspects on way to Hawkinge.' He held his hand over the mouthpiece for a moment. 'Can you describe the car?'

'A sky-blue Alvis,' Bill replied promptly.

Mr Wainwright relayed the information, then put the receiver down with a satisfied sigh. 'Good, that's that sorted far more easily than I anticipated.'

'Hang on,' Bill said. 'Why did you describe them as suspects?'

'Because Mrs Fanshawe has been under observation for some time now. As has your father. And just over an hour ago Hester Erskine was arrested and she's made it clear that she has not been acting alone. I was just on the phone to the gentleman from the government who arrested her.'

'You mean all this stuff is true?' Edie asked, tapping the paper, which she'd been reading with a growing sense of disbelief.

'It would seem so. And it's a blessing they've managed to catch her after such a short time. The damage she could have done here doesn't bear thinking about. Dover might be a small seaside town, but it's one of the most important places in the country right now. It's not for nothing it's known as the lock and key to the kingdom – if Dover falls, the country falls.'

'Was Hester the one shining the torch, do you think?' Edie asked.

Bill's eyebrows rose and he snatched the paper from Edie.

'She says not. But who else could it be? Unless it was your father, Bill. I really can't see Mrs Fanshawe doing any of the dirty work, can you?'

'But what about my uncle and the garage?' Bill asked.

'I don't have any clear answers on that, I'm afraid. Maybe we'll discover more once your father is in custody. What I can tell you is that he has always believed he should have received half the garage when your mother died – which I assure you he shouldn't have. This has led me to believe that he could well be the person behind the attack on your uncle. You see, if Clive were to die, the garage would come to you. And with you away flying, you'd need someone to keep it going. And of course Walter would have volunteered himself. Then, once installed, he would be able to exploit the trust your uncle had built up with the military at the castle. Just the thought that he might have been able to come and go there makes me shudder.'

'So why did he leave the sticky-backs in the shelter? Or did they really belong to Uncle Clive?'

'Ah. Now that's where my theory comes unstuck. Because, honestly, I have no idea.'

'So you think Dad tried to kill Uncle Clive, then set his room on fire to cover up the fact? I hope when he's arrested they throw away the key!' Bill said fiercely. 'And if I owned the garage, he'd be the *last* person I'd get to run it. There's really only one person for the job and that's Edie.' He looked over at her and smiled.

Edie blushed with pleasure. 'Really?' she squeaked.

'Of course. You're a brilliant mechanic and I trust you. What more could I want?'

Edie felt tears spring to her eyes. Bill's praise meant the world to her. But if he knew what her circumstances were right now . . . Well, that would be the end to any possibility of working at the garage. But worse than that, he'd probably want nothing more to do with her.

'What's going to happen to Hester now?' Bill asked, oblivious to Edie's turmoil.

'She'll be tried and probably convicted.'

'And the other two?'

'Your father will no doubt be convicted as well. As for Mrs Fanshawe, well, that's a little more complicated . . .' He shrugged. 'She has wealth and position on her side, so I expect she'll merely be interned. She may even get off scot-free.'

'But that's not fair!' Edie cried, shaken out of her reverie. 'She deserves to be thrown into prison for life!'

'Yes, I imagine you would say that. And she'd say the same about you. Did it ever occur to you why they might have sent Hester to live at the café?'

Edie shook her head.

'Hell hath no fury like a woman scorned, my dear.'

Edie frowned, then as his meaning became clear, she flushed with humiliation. 'You mean Mrs Fanshawe wanted to get revenge on me because of Henry?'

'Not just you. Marianne and Donny as well. I understand Donny's due to inherit his father's share of the business now Mr Fanshawe's died and Henry is deemed mentally unfit. She was furious about that. Furious about all of it, so she was looking to bring down your family, or at least tarnish the Castles' reputation enough to be able to argue that Donny should not be allowed to inherit. But it seems her plan's been hijacked by that clever journalist who's managed to put it all together before she got a chance to make sure that your family took the blame. You should thank your lucky stars he's so sharp.'

'Oh my God!' Edie covered her mouth with her hand as she considered what might have happened if Ron Hames hadn't had his wits about him. 'This is all *my* fault.'

'No, dear. The roots of this go much further back. To the day Henry Fanshawe impregnated your sister. So, around twelve years. I'm sure if Mrs Fanshawe had known about Donny before last year, she'd have taken her revenge sooner.'

His reassurance didn't make Edie feel any better. She glanced quickly at Bill, but he was staring straight ahead, avoiding her eyes. Was there no end to the humiliation that man had inflicted on her? And not just her – on Marianne as well. 'I hope she rots in hell!' she choked out furiously.

'From the looks of things she feels the same way about you. Now, if you don't mind, I need to be getting on.' He stood up and gestured to the door.

'But what will happen to Uncle Clive?' Bill asked anxiously as he stood up. 'Will he be released?'

'I can't say, I'm afraid. They've discovered that a few years ago he attended some meetings with your father.'

'I don't believe it!' Edie gasped.

'Nevertheless, he did. He admitted to it himself. But it wasn't illegal. So now they just need to ascertain that he's no longer involved in any of these fifth columnists' schemes. Now shoo.' He waved his hand towards the door, and they left obediently.

Outside, Edie leant against the whitewashed walls. 'I'll never forgive myself for this. My whole family could have ended up in jail if not for Ron Hames getting his article out first.'

Bill put a hand on her shoulder. 'It wasn't your fault,' he said soothingly.

'I'm so bloody stupid! Why do I pick such terrible men . . . Look what happened with Greg!'

'Come here.' Bill pulled her into a comforting hug. 'Not all men are bad, you know,' he said against her hair.

'All the ones I get involved with are,' she muttered, aware that she needed to put some distance between them, if only for her own sanity.

Bill's arms tightened around her. 'You need to stop blaming yourself. We all make mistakes.'

'I bet you don't,' she said.

Bill chuckled. 'Oh, I've made a few, I promise.'

'Tell me about them. Make me feel better.'

'No. Because then you might not like me anymore.'

Edie pulled away at that and stared at him. 'You know about my mistakes, so does that mean you don't like me?' she asked.

The humour left his expression. 'I like you very much, Edie. More than I ever thought I would. You're beautiful, clever, loyal and resourceful.' His face came closer and he brushed his lips over hers.

Edie allowed herself to revel in the sensation for only a few seconds, then she pushed him away. 'Don't!' she said.

He released her immediately. 'Sorry. After yesterday, I thought . . .' Bill's face reddened, then he gave a rueful laugh. 'Like I said, you're not the only one who makes mistakes.'

Edie's heart broke a little more at his expression. How she wished she could tell him that it hadn't been a mistake. That she liked him just as much, if not more, than he claimed to like her. But there was no point. Because so far she'd felt no effect from the medicine and with Hester now in prison, there'd be no chance of getting any more.

# Chapter 59

Reenie hurried up Cowgate Steps, glad to escape the strained atmosphere in the café. Worried by Marianne's pale face and red eyes, she'd decided the others could clear up without her. Finding Alfie was much more important.

At the top of the steps, she paused briefly to catch her breath, gazing out at the sea. After a calm, clear day, the clouds had rolled in on a stiff sea breeze and the waves had started to pick up, white horses rushing in to crash on to the shingle below. Out in the middle of the Channel she could see a small boat struggling through the waves and she sent up a prayer for it. It looked no bigger than Wilf's fishing boat and if the waves got up any more, it could easily be overwhelmed.

A gust of wind nearly blew her over, so she hurried on. At the bridge that led to the fortress she was relieved to see that she recognised the sentry. He often came into the shop and he'd been one of the men to carry the piano to the market square on New Year's Eve.

'Have you seen Alfie?' she asked. 'Marianne's ill. I think he should go to her if he can.'

'Saw Alf just an hour ago before I came on duty. Scoffing down some food after he'd finished his shift. Reckon he'll be able to get out for a couple of hours if it's urgent.' He went to the telephone and rang through to the barracks.

'Can you check to see if Jimmy and Bert are available as well? I think their mum could do with their support – bit of trouble at the café.'

'Nothing new there.' The man rolled his eyes. 'But seeing as it's you, Reenie, I'll see what I can do. Word of warning, though, don't mention I said Bert might be free to the girl in there. Managed to fob her off yesterday, but today she's refusin' to budge. I told her he was off at Fan Bay, but she reckons I'm lying.'

Reenie was intrigued. 'And are you?'

'Might be,' he said with a sheepish grin. 'Bert's left strict instructions, but this is the last time I do it. She sits there for hours sometimes and I have to get her to duck down every time an officer comes so they don't spot her, but it can't go on. Listen, you couldn't help us out and persuade her to leave with you, could you?'

'Who is she?'

'Go see for yourself,' he said with a sigh.

Curious, Reenie stepped into the sentry box and saw a pretty girl with black hair sipping tea out of a tin mug.

She smiled at Reenie.

'Oh, it's you,' Reenie exclaimed, recognising the girl Bert had been with on New Year's Eve.

The girl's eyebrows rose. 'Yes, it's me. And who are you?'

'Reenie Turner.'

'Oh, Jim's girl!'

'That's right,' Reenie said – at least she hoped she still was. But she was beginning to doubt it.

'This is perfect. We can get to know each other while we wait for our men. After all, we might be sisters one day.'

Reenie smiled politely, although inwardly she felt sorry for the girl. Knowing Bert, the poor thing had a nasty shock coming to her in the not too distant future.

The sentry came in and poured some tea into another tin mug for Reenie. 'What is it about those Castle boys?' he muttered. 'Amount of girls that come to see them. Well, come to see Bert,' he amended.

'I hope you're not implying there have been other girls dropping in on Bert recently,' Susan snapped.

332

The young man coloured. 'Oh ... no. Course not. He's a one-woman man, that one.'

Reenie raised her eyebrows at him, but he refused to meet her eyes.

'You better not be lying,' Susan fumed. 'If there have been any other women coming to see him, then I deserve to know.'

Reenie was taken aback by the girl's ferocity. Surely she'd only known Bert a couple of weeks. But the sentry looked so mortified that she stepped in to help him. 'I'm sure he hasn't,' Reenie lied. 'But he's so good-looking, the girls follow him everywhere. You should watch out – if they know you're his girl, they'll want to scratch your eyes out.'

Susan smiled smugly and tossed her black hair. 'It wouldn't be the first time. Girls are always jealous of my looks, you see. But you don't seem like the type to hold a woman's beauty against her. And Jimmy's ever so nice. Although, I am surprised he went for someone as old as you ...'

There was nothing Reenie could say to this, so she kept silent, but inside she felt the familiar burn of humiliation.

Finally, she put down her mug. 'Actually, I think I'll just go. If you could pass on my message. Nice to see you again, Susan.' Then she bolted out into the rain, and putting her hands in her pockets and her head down, she marched back the way she had come.

She was making her way carefully along the clifftop when there was a yell behind her and she looked round to see three figures moving towards her.

'Why'd you run off?' Jimmy panted as he reached her.

'I wasn't keen on the company,' she said. 'Where is she now?' Reenie asked Bert.

'Still there as far as I know. There are other ways out of the fortress, you know.' Bert grinned cheekily.

'That's not fair. The poor girl's been waiting for ages. Plus she's giving the sentry a hard time.'

'Listen, the *poor girl* has been on at me from the minute I met her. I swear I'll kill Edie for getting me involved in her schemes.'

Before Reenie could ask what Edie had to do with it, Alfie reached her and grabbed her arm. 'Reenie! What's up with Marianne? Is it the baby?'

Reenie explained everything that had happened at the café that afternoon. 'I think she's just really tired and worried about everything. She needs you to cheer her up.'

'Flippin' heck!' Bert exclaimed. He clapped Alfie on the back. 'Come on, I'll race you. Last one swaps a night patrol.'

'You're on,' Alfie responded, sprinting off immediately.

'I'll catch you up,' Jimmy called after them, then he turned to Reenie. 'I've been meaning to see you to apologise about New Year.'

'Where did you go? I was sat waiting for you at the café like a bloody mug.'

Jimmy sighed. 'I'm sorry. Although it wasn't that bad, was it? Bert says you drank your fair share of champagne and left singing!'

'That's beside the point,' Reenie said. 'I was only there because I thought you'd be coming. Why didn't you?'

'I went to see Mary Guthrie. I shouldn't have gone. She made me feel . . . Well, let's just say, she thinks I've betrayed Colin.'

Reenie sighed. 'It always goes back to Colin, doesn't it?'

He didn't answer.

'Will you ever be happy, Jimmy?' Reenie asked.

'I don't know,' he murmured. 'I'm trying. And you help.' He smiled down at her, but Reenie didn't smile back. Instead she folded her arms and turned her head away, gazing out over the sea, hoping to spot the little boat she'd seen earlier.

'Reenie?' he asked.

She looked round at him again, eyes flashing. 'Am I just a prop then? Something to make you feel better?'

'Isn't that what love is about?' he asked uncertainly, surprised by her anger. 'You find someone who makes you feel better, makes life easier . . .' He trailed off.

'That's the problem, though, Jim. You don't make me feel better at the moment. You've left me standing in the street twice and both times it was because of Colin.'

'I'm sorry,' he whispered.

His devastated expression made Reenie's heart squeeze. 'I know you are, love. But . . . well, I think maybe we should end things. You're not able to give me what I want.'

'What do you want?' he asked.

'I want all of you,' she said tearfully. 'I want you to leave other people standing in the street because you need to be with *me*. But I don't have that.'

'I just need a bit more time,' he said weakly.

'And I'm going to give it to you. You take all the time you need, and if you ever feel that I can be enough for you, come and see me. But for now I'm tired of just being the support. I'm tired of comforting you. I want us to be equals. And frankly, Jim, I feel more like I'm your mother sometimes.'

Despite the serious conversation, Jimmy let out a splutter of laughter. 'God forbid,' he said, pulling her into him. Then, tilting her head up, he kissed her deeply.

'Does that convince you that I don't think of you as my mother?' he asked as he pulled away.

She smiled dreamily. 'You're very good at that.'

'So I've been told.' Jimmy smirked. He bent his head to kiss her again, but she dodged out of the way.

'Who by?' she asked, arms folded.

Jimmy shuffled his feet, embarrassed. 'You didn't think I'd got to this age and never kissed anyone, did you?'

Reenie huffed. 'I suppose not.'

'So do you forgive me?' he asked, not sure why he was trying to persuade her, other than, without her, he wasn't sure what he'd do. Reenie anchored him, made him feel more secure – made him appear to be just like all the other men.

Reenie studied his face. His long dark lashes were wet and spiky, emphasising the beautiful blue of his eyes; it would be so easy, she thought, to say yes. To carry on as they were. But she needed more.

'Yes, I forgive you. But it doesn't change anything.'

Jim sighed. She was right, he knew. Even before Mrs Guthrie's brutal words, he'd been thinking along the same lines. But even so, he hadn't been able to let go of the hope that one day he might develop deeper feelings for her and he could embrace this new life – a life without shame or fear. But then Mary Guthrie's words echoed in his mind: *You're not worthy of him.* He wasn't. She was right about that. And he wasn't worthy of this wonderful woman either. He didn't deserve any of it.

Nodding regretfully, he touched her cheek. 'I meant what I said, Reens. I really do love you.'

Reenie shook her head. 'But not enough, Jim, and not in the way I love you. Go on, now. Go help your family.'

Jimmy nodded. 'I'm sorry,' he said, then turned and headed towards town.

Reenie stayed where she was for a long time, the tears on her cheeks mixing with the rain. Wilf was right, she thought. And so was Marianne. She was a fool to have imagined a man like Jimmy would ever truly be interested in a girl like her. Hadn't she learnt a long time ago that she always came out second best?

∽

Marge was sitting in the canteen eating an unappetising bowl of stew, which consisted mostly of turnip and potatoes with a couple of lumps of gristly meat in between. 'Ugh, the food gets worse,' she commented to the man opposite her. 'Still, I suppose it helps keep the weight off.'

'I can't imagine you've ever needed to worry about that,' Philip said, giving her tall, slim figure an admiring glance.

'Don't you believe it. I wasn't always the slim goddess you see before you.'

'Slim or not, you'll always be a goddess in my eyes.' He waggled his eyebrows at her.

Marge laughed. 'If you weren't a chaplain, I'd say you were trying to get into my knickers.'

Philip blushed. 'I'm not a Catholic priest, Marge.' He looked into her eyes meaningfully. 'I'm just a normal man with—'

'Have you seen this?' Philip's moment was ruined as Rodney Castle appeared beside them and slapped down a copy of the *Dover Express*.

Marge looked at the newspaper and then back up at Rodney with a frown. 'And hello to you, too, Rodney. As you can see, I'm in the middle of a conversation,' she said.

Rodney looked briefly at Philip. 'Sorry,' he said shortly. 'Read it, Marge.'

With a huff, Marge picked up the paper and read the article quickly. 'Blimey. They can't seriously be suggesting that these attacks have something to do with your mum!'

'Of course not,' Rodney snapped. 'It's that woman – Hester whatever her name is – who Mum's got some misplaced sense of loyalty to since she helped Donny.'

Marge remembered the cheerful woman with brassy hair she'd met at New Year. 'But she seemed so nice.'

'Of course she seemed bloody nice. Not as if she was going to announce her intention to give away military secrets, is it? Come on. We need to get down there.'

Marge raised an eyebrow at him. '*We?*'

Rodney glanced at Philip, then looked back at Marge. 'You don't want to come?'

'No, I don't. Like I said when you so rudely interrupted, I'm talking to someone. And frankly, I have better things to do with my time.'

Rodney narrowed his eyes. 'Fine. I understand perfectly. See you around, Marge.'

Marge watched him go with mixed feelings. On the one hand, she hated pushing Rodney away. No matter how hard she tried, she just couldn't shake off the feelings she had for him. But on the other, Rodney couldn't keep using her like this. She was not the sort of woman a man could pick up and put down depending on their mood. It was all or nothing as far as she was concerned.

'You can go if you want.' Philip broke into her thoughts.

Marge smiled distractedly at him. 'I know. But I'd rather stay here and listen to you telling me all the reasons you think I'm a goddess.'

Philip didn't smile back. 'Listen, if you and Rodney are more than just friends you need to let me know. I don't want to tread on anybody's toes.'

Feeling guilty, Marge focused her attention on him. 'The only toes you'll be treading on are mine when we go dancing.'

Philip laughed, relieved, and took her hand. 'That's the best offer I've ever had. Shall we make a plan for when this wondrous evening will be?'

# Chapter 60

Phyllis was sweeping the floor of the café when she was surprised by a knock at the window and a young man pointed to the door, which Nellie had bolted as soon as the last customer had left.

'Can't you see the sign?' Phyllis said as she opened the door.

'I'm not here for food.' He dug in his inside pocket and drew out an identity card, which he held up to show her. 'Peter Holmes. I'm here on government business. Are you Mrs Castle?' he asked.

'Mrs Castle's upstairs. Is this about all that stuff in the papers? I tell you now, the Castles are the heart of this community. No way they'd be involved in anything shady. Would they, Ethel?'

'Of course they wouldn't. You're wastin' your time.'

'Either show me upstairs, or I will go by myself,' he said sternly.

'I beg your pardon!' Phyllis said indignantly. 'A few manners wouldn't go amiss, young man. How do we know you are who you say you are? You can't be too careful, you know.'

The young man raised his eyebrows. 'Perhaps if Mrs Castle had abided by that, I wouldn't be here now.'

Ethel huffed. 'Of all the cheek!'

'Who's at the door?' Jasper asked, coming into the café.

'This young man says he's here to see Nellie on *government business*,' Phyllis said with disdain.

'What do you want, lad?' Jasper eyed the man suspiciously.

'My name is Peter Holmes.' He flashed his identity card again. 'I need to ask Mrs Castle some questions about Hester Erskine, and if you continue to obstruct me, I'll arrest the lot of you.' He glared round at them in irritation.

'All right, all right, I'm bloody comin',' Nellie called from the bottom of the stairs where she'd been hovering, listening to the conversation.

'Do you want us to stay, Nell?' Ethel shouted, keeping her eyes on the man.

Nellie came into the café, her bright orange jumper and green skirt clashing with the fuchsia-pink cardigan she'd wrapped around herself. 'No, you're all right, love. I think I can handle this one.' She looked around at the gleaming café and smiled tiredly. 'Thanks for doing this, girls. I'll make it up to you, I promise.'

After the two women had left, Nellie sat down and gestured for the young man to do the same. Jasper also pulled up a chair.

'Jasper Cane,' he said. 'Nellie's friend.'

Nellie smiled at him and put her hand on his.

'Jasper's a hero,' Polly squawked from where she'd been left, forgotten, on the counter.

Peter Holmes glanced at the bird in alarm.

'That's Polly,' Jasper supplied helpfully.

'What do you want to know?' Nellie asked.

'I need you to tell me everything, Mrs Castle. From how you know Hester Erskine, where she's been, who she's been speaking to, what she did all day. Everything. And after that, I need to search her room.'

Nellie regarded him balefully. 'What do you take me for? Her jailer? She lived here, helped out with the customers, and sometimes she went out. I never asked where cos it weren't my business. But I swear to God, I knew *nothing* about what she were up to! None of this is my fault. All I did was offer a helping hand to a woman in need.'

Peter Holmes was busy scribbling in his notebook. 'Lucky for you, Mrs Castle, there are plenty willing to vouch for you. But tell me, did you ever see any of these around the place?' He placed a piece of card on the table. Nellie picked it up and frowned at it. '"Hear the truth . . ."' she murmured. 'Yes. Roger Humphries came in with these a while

340

back. And—' She shut her mouth, wondering if she'd get in trouble if she admitted that she knew Hester listened to the radio station.

'And?' Peter said.

Nellie sighed. 'And I know Hester listened to it. I caught her at it one night.'

'You knew she was listening to an illegal radio station, yet you didn't report it?'

'For God's sake!' Nellie exclaimed. 'No, I didn't! This ain't the sort of place we dob in our neighbours for listenin' to the wireless. And anyway, she'd take down all the names of these prisoners and write to their families to tell 'em they were safe. I thought it were a kind act.'

Peter nodded. 'They reel people in that way. It's very effective. Did you ever see her with any of the sticky-backs?' he asked.

Nellie shook her head.

'And what about her movements. I want you to tell me everything you can about what she did while she was here.'

For the next few minutes, Nellie told him what she knew about Hester, which, she realised, wasn't that much. 'But she never hid the fact that she were very angry,' Nellie said finally. 'Angry about her son dying, angry about losing her house. Angry that we have to go through all this again.' Nellie sighed deeply. 'And when I put it like that, I suppose I am too.'

'No one's happy about it. Doesn't mean we all go out and try to sabotage the war effort, though, does it?' Peter Holmes said, unmoved by Nellie's argument. 'Now, I need to speak to your daughter – Edith. And Bill Penfold, who, I understand, has been staying with you, Mr Cane.'

'Why?'

'Because they've both been very helpful up to now and they might have more information.'

'Helpful with what? And since when did you meet her?' Nellie realised that she and Edie had barely spoken about anything in the last week or so, even though they saw each other every day. Although

341

that was nothing new, she supposed. But if Edie had known about Hester, then she should have said something!

Peter Holmes smiled. 'I haven't. She knows an acquaintance of mine.'

'Well, she ain't here. Ran off as soon as Mrs Fanshawe left. And if I were her, I wouldn't come back cos I'll tan her hide when I get my hands on her. It's her fault that evil Fanshawe bitch is in our lives. If she hadn't got involved with that man, Donny wouldn't have been kidnapped, I'd not have found Hester, and that posh cow would never have darkened our door.'

'Stop it, Nellie,' Jasper said firmly. 'Don't go blamin' Edie. You two have enough trouble between you without that. If you want to blame someone, you should start with Henry flippin' Fanshawe! It were him that seduced two innocent young girls. Him that betrayed his wife. And it were him that kidnapped Donny.'

Nellie huffed and folded her arms across her chest. She knew he was right, but it didn't stop the simmering anger that was rising within her.

Peter Holmes stood up. 'While we wait for your daughter to return, can you show me Hester's room?'

Upstairs, Nellie opened the door to Hester's bedroom and looked around. 'Hell's bells,' she muttered, picking up a pair of knickers that were lying in the middle of the floor, along with some woollen stockings and the scuffed, high-heeled red shoes that Hester had arrived in. The eiderdown that had covered the bed she'd been sleeping in was in a heap on the floor, and the sheets and blankets were half on and half off. The few clothes that Hester possessed were flung over the other two beds, along with Nellie's yellow shirt. Hester's towel was hanging off one of the open wardrobe doors.

'Help yourself.' Nellie gestured around the room. 'Not sure you'll find anything in this lot though.'

The young man didn't answer as he began to search through the chest of drawers. Apart from a few toiletries, there was very little in them, considering most of Hester's possessions were lying around on the floor.

'Mum?!'

'Oh, Jesus, it's Donny's back again. Jasper go and head him off, and keep him occupied, will you? He don't need to know about this.'

Jasper left obediently, while Peter Holmes took down the suit-case from the top of the wardrobe, laying it on one of the beds before opening it. The first thing he took out was a pair of wire-cutters, which he examined carefully, then put aside.

'Why's she got them?' Nellie queried.

'She's been cutting telephone wires,' he said.

'What? Where?'

'There've been a few reports from Drop Redoubt and the Citadel.' He reached back into the case and pulled out a sheaf of papers and flicked through them. 'Christ,' he murmured, 'how did she manage to wander around so freely?'

'What are they?' Nellie asked again.

'Drawings, Mrs Castle. Maps, locations, gun placements . . .' He shook his head.

'She used to go walking on the cliffs with my grandson and his friend sometimes,' Nellie offered. 'She said she loved bein' with them cos they reminded her of her son.'

'Maybe they did. But I bet you any money she wouldn't have liked them half so much if they hadn't suited her purpose.'

'Are you sayin' she used my grandson as cover for her activities?' Nellie could feel her temper rising further. 'And here I was feeling sorry for her when all the while she was puttin' Donny and Fred in danger. If they'd been caught . . .' Another thought occurred to her. 'You don't think she got the boys to do any of her dirty work, do you?'

'Let's ask them, shall we?' Peter tucked the drawings and the wire-cutters into his briefcase.

'You will not question my grandson!' she cried.

'I can question who I like,' he replied. 'Now, where is he?'

'Downstairs with Jasper, I suppose,' she said reluctantly.

As the man left the room, Marianne opened her bedroom door. 'What's going on, Mum? And who's he?' She gestured towards Peter Holmes's retreating back.

'Just someone asking questions about Hester. Go back to bed.'

'But I heard him mention Donny.'

'He wants to ask Don about the walks he went on with Hester.' She hustled Marianne back into the room and helped her into bed. 'You take care of the baby and I'll take care of Donny, all right?'

Marianne nodded tiredly. 'Thanks, Mum.' She caught her mother's hand and gave it a squeeze.

Nellie stared down at her with concern. She looked even paler than she had that afternoon. 'Does anything hurt, love?'

'My back,' Marianne whispered. 'And it feels like I'm having my monthly.'

Nellie's heart lurched slightly at that. 'I'm going to get Dr Palmer to come and have a look at you. Just to make sure, all right?'

Marianne nodded and shut her eyes.

Downstairs, Peter Holmes was chatting to Donny, who, though he seemed surprised at the questioning, clearly wasn't aware of its seriousness as he cheerfully described the walks he'd gone on with Hester. 'She's a good laugh. We used to play spies and creep through the bushes to see if we could sneak into the Citadel, but we never could. Then at other times, she'd ask us where the big guns were hid, an' we knew cos we'd watched them setting them up,' he said proudly.

After asking Donny to show him exactly where they'd walked on a map, Peter thanked him for his help. 'Did Hester ever ask you to stick up notices around the town?' he asked.

'No. She never asked us to do anything, 'cept show her stuff.'

'I need to go out,' Nellie interrupted the conversation. 'Will you be all right to stay, Jasper? Marianne needs the doctor.'

'I'm just about finished here, Mrs Castle. I think I have everything I need.'

'I thought you wanted to speak to Edie,' she said.

344

'And I will, but for now I think I have enough.'

'Good. So you can get out of our hair.'

'Oh, by the way, Hester asked me to give you this.' He handed her an envelope with Nellie's name scrawled on the front. 'Strictly speaking, it's against the rules, but I've read it and I can't see any harm. I'll see myself out.'

After he'd left, Nellie stared at the envelope in silence, not sure she wanted to read any of Hester's self-justifications.

'Why was that man asking so many questions about Hester, Gran?' Donny asked.

Nellie sighed. 'Because it looks like she's been doin' bad things. And she used you so she could wander round with no one batting an eyelid. So now she's been arrested.'

Donny gasped, his eyes round. 'But Hester wouldn't do anything bad!' he protested.

'I'm afraid she did, son,' Jasper said more gently. 'I know you was fond of her, but turns out she's been causin' trouble.'

'Is this all mine and Fred's fault then?' he asked, his voice trembling with fear. 'Will we get arrested too?'

'No, this is all Hester's fault, love. And you've got nothing to worry about. Now, your mum's not feeling too good, so I need you to run to Dr Palmer and ask him to visit as soon as he can.'

Donny jumped up. 'I need to go see her.'

'No, love, not now,' Nellie said sharply. Then in a softer tone, 'The best way you can help is to get the doc here soon as you can.'

Once he'd gone, Nellie dropped onto her chair, laying her head back on the lace antimacassar with a sigh.

'She'll be all right, love,' Jasper said sympathetically. 'It's just all the stress and worry gettin' to her. A woman in her condition needs to take it easy.'

'This is all my fault. She never complains, so sometimes I forget how hard she works. And then all this with Hester ... I've been a fool. I should have listened to my instinct when she first arrived and turned her away.'

'You couldn't have though, could you? It ain't in your nature to turn anyone in need away.'

'I knew then, though. I knew she'd cause trouble. But I let her in. An' she played a good game, I'll give her that. She wormed her way into the household, into the community . . . But she were a viper waiting to strike. She used us all, Jasper, and I'll never forgive myself for allowin' it. Never.'

'Come on, Nell. Don't blame yourself. It were that Mrs Fanshawe and Walter Penfold's fault. Not yours.'

'I let a serpent into the garden,' Nellie wailed dramatically.

Jasper guffawed. 'You sound like Gladys. Serpent into the garden, indeed. You looked after someone in need, and no matter what else she's done, she did need you. Your conscience should be clear.'

Nellie sat up. 'Well, it's not. As for Gladys, I need to apologise to her for throwing her out.'

'*Another* apology? Are you gettin' soft in your old age?'

Nellie huffed. 'Not likely. Anyway, the last apology I made didn't go so well, so maybe I shouldn't bother.' She gave him a pointed look.

'I'm here, aren't I?'

Nellie reached over and took his hand. 'You are. Does that mean you've forgiven me?'

Jasper cleared his throat and looked away. 'It's like it says in the Bible – I were blind but now I see.'

Nellie gaped at him. 'Flippin' heck, Jasper, don't tell me you've been goin' to the prayer meetings an' all!'

'But it's like a miracle I was cured, dontcha think? God were watchin' over me. An' I took it as a sign. A sign not to hold grudges, to let bygones be bygones. Life's short, there's no point livin' in anger.'

Nellie stared at him in stupefaction, until she noted the twinkle in his eye.

'You little bugger, you nearly had me there!'

Jasper grinned and tried to withdraw his hand, but Nellie tightened her grip and they sat for a while in silence, their hands clasped.

# Chapter 61

'Mum!' Edie yelled as she stomped up the stairs. 'What's happening?'

Jasper and Nellie jumped apart guiltily, Jasper settling into the armchair opposite Nellie just in time before Edie rushed in.

'Oh, so you've decided to make an appearance, have you?' Nellie said waspishly.

'That's not fair!' Edie exclaimed. 'Me and Bill have been up at Mr Wainwright's.'

Nellie raised her eyebrows. 'And what's he got to do with anything?'

'He's been helping me with my uncle, Mrs C,' Bill said placatingly, following Edie into the room. 'Also, you'll be happy to know that I think they're going to arrest Mrs Fanshawe and my dad.' He looked away, embarrassed at having to admit his father was a criminal – worse, a traitorous one.

'Well now, that is good news,' Jasper said. 'So Clive'll be released soon?'

Bill shrugged. 'I hope so. But what's been happening here?'

Nellie started to explain about Peter Holmes's visit, but she was interrupted by the sound of yet more footsteps on the stairs.

'Well, I'm relieved to see you haven't been arrested.' It was Bert. Behind him, Alfie's figure could be seen racing upstairs to the top floor.

'Oh, a visit from my son. How lovely.'

'And Rod's here too. Met him at the door.'

'For God's sake, Mum, can't we go more than a few months without this family being at the centre of some scandal or other.' Rodney walked in looking harassed.

'Hey,' Jasper said. 'This ain't your mum's fault.'

'Not her fault? Do you know how I got to see this article?' He waved the newspaper around dramatically. 'The admiral, Mum! Yes, him. He'd been shown it by the bloody MPs! And you shoulda seen the look they all gave me when I was called in!'

Jasper stood up and put his arm around Rodney's shoulder. 'Rod, please. It's been a bad day for all of us. Calm down and listen.'

Rodney swallowed and ripped off his cap, running his hand through his hair. 'Sorry, sorry. It's just after what happened at the garage with Mr Pearson being arrested and now this? When's it all going to end? And why is it always *this* family that has to be involved? Why can't we just be quiet and normal like . . . like the Perkins or something. You don't see the fish shop being picketed by an angry mob, or the Turners being accused of harbouring a traitor!'

'You should have just brought the MPs with you and have us all arrested,' Edie said snidely. 'Then all your troubles would be over and you'd never have to see us again.'

'I was right about that, though, wasn't I? Mr Pearson was up to something, otherwise why would they have arrested him?'

'Hang on a minute! My uncle's done nothing wrong!' Bill only just managed to restrain himself from hitting Rodney.

'If you want someone to blame, Rod, then look no further than your sister!' Nellie pointed at Edie. 'If it weren't for her that woman would never have known this family even existed, let alone tried to ruin us!'

Edie was shocked by her mother's attack – it was no more than what she'd been thinking herself, but to hear her mother say it was devastating. 'Is that what you really think?' she asked tremulously.

'No, she doesn't!' Jasper interjected. 'Nellie, shut up. Rodney, sit down. Bill, we know your uncle's not to blame. Edie, take no notice.

And, Bert, go and get the sherry and some glasses. I think we could all do with a drink.'

'It's not my fault,' Edie said tearfully.

'Funny how it all comes back to you, though, ain't it?' Nellie responded harshly. 'You brought Hester here. You were at the garage when it caught fire. And *you* are the one what had an affair with a married man, putting us in that sour-faced bitch's firing line.'

'WHAT DID I SAY, NELLIE!' Jasper roared.

The room descended into sudden silence as everyone stared at him in astonishment. They'd never heard him shout like that before.

'Right, sit down and shut up. And once Bert's got us all a drink, Nellie can read Hester's letter. Then maybe you can all stop blaming each other. For God's sake, as long as I've known you, you lot have always stuck together. Are you really going to let that woman change that?' He sat down with a huff, exhausted from the effort of keeping them in check. But he knew from experience that if you didn't rein the Castles in at the first sign of trouble, then it might be weeks before they sorted themselves out.

Bert came in with a tray of glasses and the bottle, and after pouring some sherry for each of them, he handed the glasses round.

Nellie drank her glass down in one, then picked up the envelope, pulling out two sheets of paper scrawled with large round letters.

'Go on then, Mum,' Bert urged.

Nellie sighed and started to read.

*Dear Nellie,*

*Mr Holmes has promised to give this letter to you, and I hope he does. Cos I owe you an apology. I want you to know that none of this is your fault. I thought I were helping to end the war. Please believe me when I say I didn't mean to hurt no one.*

*All I ever wanted, was for it all to stop. And when my Tommy went missing, I had nothing left to lose. That was when Walter upped and left and went to work at Mrs F's. Turns out he's a bad 'un –*

there's no fool like an old fool, eh? Cos I believed him when he came back. Told me he were sorry and that he loved me. It were him that gave me the radio, said I could listen out for news of Tommy. Said that he and some others were working to end the war and to make a better world. He said to let him know if I wanted to join the movement. I'd seen his scars from the last war and I knew how he'd suffered, so I believed him. I thought it were a noble cause. And when I listened to all the talk of a fairer world on the wireless, it made sense to me.

But it don't anymore, not when it puts my mates at risk, kills even more young men. I never realised that woman were usin' me to get revenge on you; if she'd had her way, you'd be sittin' in the cell next to me. So I'm glad I got caught. Cos that woman and Walter need to be locked up, so I've told them everything. It's the only way to make up for the trouble I've caused all of you and poor old Clive Pearson. Cos that were my fault too.

I got the bus late when I come over from Folkestone an' it dropped me up near the castle cos the road was damaged. I didn't want to come to the café so late, so I found Mr Pearson's shelter and stayed there. But the next mornin' I left the sticky-backs Walter had given me under the bed. I woulda gone back, but Walter and that woman were hovering around watching to make sure I went to the café like I'd said I would. I thought I'd just get 'em later, but I never got the chance. But I never thought Mr Pearson would get in trouble. I swear, though, that fire had nothing to do with me. If you ask me, that were all Walter. So maybe I did everyone a favour leaving those things there if it meant he didn't get his hands on the garage like he planned.

Mr Holmes told me I could get the death sentence for what I done, and I don't care, because my life ended the day my Tommy was taken. I'm just sorry that you and your family got dragged into it. I'll never forget how kind you've been. Ask Gladys to pray for me. I know she'd love to hear that I'm a repentant sinner.

Love, Hester

Nellie's voice trembled as she read the last couple of paragraphs, her eyes blurred with tears. She set the letter down and looked around. Jim had crept in while she'd been reading, and was standing beside Bert, his hair wet and clinging to his face. All her children under one roof – well, apart from Lily, but she'd be home soon. Just the thought of one being missing made her want to curl up and die. But poor Hester had had her only child taken from her ... How could she blame the woman for her actions when she'd clearly been driven mad by grief?

'Is it true about the death sentence?' Bert asked.

Rodney nodded. 'Afraid so. But I doubt they'll do that. Especially as she's confessed and is testifying against the others. It'll probably be a few years' hard labour.'

'She deserves it,' Edie said fiercely. 'How could she be so stupid? I mean, I thought something was going on but not this! She says she didn't want to hurt anyone, and yet I bet it was her standing outside the Hippodrome shining a torch into the sky. And what about her so-called *friend*, Bunny Whittaker. She knew he were driving that train and she nearly got him killed!'

'But no one did die, did they?' Nellie responded. 'And didn't you hear a word of what she said? You have no idea what the loss of a child can do to you.'

Edie winced inwardly at that. She would soon, she hoped. And she certainly wouldn't grieve when it happened. 'Neither do you,' she snapped.

'But I can imagine. And the life she led ... She gave up everything for that boy. She could have just left him at the workhouse. But she didn't. She cherished him.' Nellie started to weep. 'Every child is a gift,' she gasped.

Jasper put an arm around her. 'All right, Nellie. No need to upset yourself.'

Nellie pulled a handkerchief from her sleeve and blew her nose. 'I hate this war!' she cried. 'I hate it, I hate it, I hate it! How soon before I lose one of you?'

351

'Mum.' Rodney knelt down in front of her and took her hands. 'I'm not going to pretend that might not happen, but you are the strongest woman I know. You'll cope. And cos there are so many of us, you're never gonna run out of kids.'

She laughed through her tears and cupped his cheek. 'I never did know when to stop,' she said.

'Nellie.' Alfie stood in the doorway looking pale and shaken. 'Where's the doctor? Marianne's bleeding!'

Edie leapt up from the sofa, her hand to her mouth. 'Is it the baby?' she whispered.

'I don't know,' Alfie said, wringing his hands. 'I just need someone to make it stop.' He rushed back upstairs to sit with his stricken wife.

Nellie stood up, all emotion set aside in the face of this new crisis. 'Edie, get the kettle on. Rodney, go get all the clean towels from the linen cupboard. Jim, go get the brandy from the pantry. Bert, go stand by the back door and when Donny gets back, take him out for fish and chips or something. Anything. Just don't let him come upstairs.'

'Can I help?' Bill asked.

'You and Jasper stay down here in case we need anyone to go out for anything.'

'I need to see Marianne first,' Edie said through trembling lips.

'No. She don't need no one except Alfie, her mum and the doctor right now. Hopefully it's nothing. I had the same with at least a couple of you lot.'

But Edie wasn't listening. Her mind was full of the image of the nearly empty bottle. She knew she hadn't drunk that much ... Stomach swirling with fear, she brushed past her mother and took the stairs two at a time. This was her fault. She knew it as surely as if she'd fed the stuff to Marianne herself. Why hadn't she hidden the bottles more carefully? There wasn't a nook or cranny in that bedroom that her sisters didn't know about.

Thrusting the door open she rushed to the bed where Marianne was curled into a ball, groaning, her face paper white. Alfie was sitting beside her looking helpless as he stroked her damp hair back from her face.

'Alfie,' Marianne gasped. 'Please don't let anything happen to Daisy.'

'I won't, love,' he said soothingly. 'The doctor will be here soon and you're both going to be just fine.' But when he looked up at Edie, his eyes were bleak.

Edie knelt beside the bed. 'Marianne,' she whispered. 'It's going to be all right. Just hang on, love. The doctor will sort you out.' But she had no idea if he could. She bent lower. 'Marianne, how much of that stuff did you drink?'

'What?' Marianne moaned.

'Those bottles, how much did you drink?'

For a moment, Marianne's eyes opened and focused on her sister. 'Is that why this is happening?' she gasped. 'Is it my fault?'

'No! No, this isn't your fault.' Alfie threw Edie a furious glance. 'How could it be?'

'I drank it. I shouldn't have but I did. Hester told me I shouldn't . . . She said it today . . .'

'What did you drink?'

'It was nothing, love. Honest. Just herbs, like you thought. Nothing that could harm you.'

'Do you promise?' she whispered.

Edie swallowed and nodded. 'I promise.'

'What is she talking about?' Alfie hissed at Edie.

'I don't know.'

'You're lying. But I don't have time to deal with this now. I think you should leave.'

Edie had never seen Alfie angry before. Had never guessed that he was capable of looking at anyone with such fury. Feeling even worse, she did as she was told and went downstairs to put the kettle on.

The doctor arrived and went straight upstairs, but before Donny could follow him, Bert sprang into action. 'Donny! My favourite nephew. Why don't you and me go get a spot of fish and chips?'

Donny regarded him suspiciously. 'I want to see how Mum is.'

'No need for that. Alfie and the doctor'll look after her. Come on, mate, how about we make it into a boys' outing with all your uncles, plus Bill and Jasper?'

Donny grinned. 'Can Freddie come?' he asked.

'Of course he can. The more the merrier.'

As Edie watched the six of them troop out, she wished with all her heart that she could join them. But she needed to stay and make sure her sister was safe. And if anything happened to the baby, she would never ever forgive herself.

# Chapter 62

Lily pushed open the door of the staff cloakroom, her hand in the pocket of her apron, fingering the envelope that rested there. Her very first letter from Charlie. She smiled in anticipation. When she'd found it in her pigeonhole, she'd been so tempted to read it there and then, but she'd resisted. There was no way she could wait until she got home to open it, though.

Hurrying into one of the toilet cubicles, she slit the envelope open. But as she started to read, the smile died on her lips.

*My Lily,*

*Here, as promised is my first letter. The first of many. Possibly thousands. I know I've said it in the telegrams, but I hope you understand how much I love you. How I can't wait for us to be married, maybe even working together at a hospital. Dr and Dr Alexander! That has a ring, don't you think?*

*But first, I need to tell you something. Because if you find out from someone else you might hate me and if I lost you, I don't think I could carry on. Before I start I want to promise you that you are my first and last love. I have never even slightly loved anyone before I met you. You are the first and last person I will ever propose to. The first and last person I will ever marry. The only woman in the world for me . . .*

*My parents' butcher's shop is next door to a hardware store. Not that that matters, but still. The people who run it, Mr and*

Mrs Blake, have a daughter called Susan. She's a bit older than you. Maybe Edie's age. Anyway, I think she's in Dover. And I think she's telling people that she is engaged to me. I swear to you that she is not! Never has been, never will be. But she sort of latched on to me. And maybe I was too nice to her, but I felt sorry for her. So I did nothing to discourage her. I should add that I did nothing to encourage her either.

Since then she's been writing to me. But I never reply. So many bloody letters. I've stopped opening them. I just throw them away now.

Lily put the letter down and rubbed her eyes. What the hell was he talking about? And how did he know this Susan was in Dover unless he'd seen her? She thought back to the night when she'd finally accepted his proposal; had he come from seeing *her*? Or did he visit her after he left? Her stomach felt hollow, but she steeled herself to read on.

Lily, it's you I love. I have never even asked this woman out. The most I've done is speak to her when her family came for lunch every so often. When the invitation was returned, I would always make an excuse not to be there. Please believe me, sweetheart. I feel helpless being so far away, not being able to see your beautiful face, or kiss away the tears I know will be falling. God, Lily, if I could, I would jump on a train and risk getting court-martialled just to reassure you. But I can't. I can't say where I'm going, but put it this way, I have had to post this hastily before boarding a ship.

Write to me, my darling. Please write. Tell me that you don't believe her. That you still love me. That this woman won't rip us apart.

Please, put me out of my misery as soon as you can.

All my love (and I mean ALL of it)

Charlie xxxx

Wiping away her tears, Lily put the letter down. Was he telling the truth? Or had she just been taken in by the best liar she'd ever met?

No. This was Charlie, for goodness' sake. Just five minutes ago, she'd have sworn she trusted him with her life, so she shouldn't stop that now, surely. She pictured him staring down at her on the last night they'd spent together. His eyes had been full of love. She refused to believe he would do something like this to her – or any woman.

Suddenly a thought occurred to her. Bert had been kissing someone called Susan at New Year and Alfie had asked whether that was the woman he'd hit somebody over . . . she thought hard, trying to remember the conversation. Alfie had said 'Ch—' before Bert had interrupted him . . . had he been going to say Charlie? And that girl in the café with Hester, Edie's friend Susan!

She put her hand over her mouth. She'd said it many time before, but this time she absolutely meant it. She would kill them! They'd known and hadn't said anything? How dare they keep something like this from her? She wasn't a child!

In a rush, she stood up and slammed open the cubicle door, startling Vi, who was putting on her cloak.

'Everything all right, Lily?'

'No, it bloody well isn't!' she shouted, stuffing the letter in her pocket and putting on her cloak before rushing out the door.

# Chapter 63

Edie sat hunched on the sofa biting her nails, listening out for any sound from upstairs. But all she could hear was the loud ticking of the clock on the mantelpiece. By the fire, Nellie sat with her eyes closed, her fingers clasped on the arms of the chair, knuckles white. Alfie paced the room, hands in pockets, head down. Every so often, he'd light a cigarette, take a few puffs, then put it out, too tense even to smoke.

They all jumped when the back door downstairs slammed. Loud footsteps thumped up the stairs and Lily burst in, her cheeks red from the cold, her hair dishevelled and falling out of its pins and her eyes sparkling with rage.

'I need to talk to you!' she shouted, pointing at Edie.

Edie stared at her in bemusement, her first thought was that her sister had heard what was happening and had drawn the obvious conclusions – that it was Edie's fault Marianne might lose her baby.

Nellie saved her from answering when she hissed, 'Keep your bloody voice down.'

For the first time, Lily noticed Alfie standing by the table, cigarette in hand, face pale.

'What's going on?' she asked.

'It's Marianne,' he whispered. 'We think she's losing the baby.'

'What?' Lily gasped.

'Dr Palmer's with her now,' Nellie said.

Lily's gaze flew to Edie. 'But how? Why?'

Edie just shook her head, refusing to meet her eyes.

Lily stayed where she was for a moment, staring at her sister, before she turned and ran up the stairs.

The room returned to silence, as the three continued their vigil, but Nellie had noticed the exchange between the sisters. 'What was that about?' she asked Edie.

Edie shrugged. 'Anyone for more tea?' she said, standing up and picking up the teapot from the table, before walking hastily to the small galley kitchen across the hall. It was the last thing she wanted – just the thought of eating or drinking made her feel sick – but she couldn't bear the weight of her mother's gaze. Because she knew that soon she'd have to confess to her part in this.

Not long after she'd poured everyone more tea, which no one drank, they heard Dr Palmer's footsteps on the stairs.

'Is she going to be all right?' Alfie asked anxiously before the doctor had even walked in the door.

Dr Palmer nodded. 'I hope so, Private Lomax. She's resting now and the bleeding has stopped. But she needs complete bed rest for the next couple of weeks.' He looked at Nellie. 'That means she can't work at all, Mrs Castle. Do you understand?'

'I understand, Doctor. And don't worry. We'll take care of her.'

'Is the baby all right?' Alfie asked, a catch in his throat.

'It's still there, at least, so hopefully all will be well. You can go up and see her if you like.'

Alfie rushed out of the room, taking the stairs two at a time.

Sitting on the sofa by the window, Edie sagged with relief.

'One thing puzzles me, though. She kept muttering that she shouldn't have drunk it. Do you have any idea what she means? Because if this was caused by a substance, I need to know.'

Nellie looked at Edie. 'Any idea, Edie?' she asked, narrowing her eyes as she noticed the girl's expression – it was the same one she'd had when she'd been caught stealing sweets from Woolies once. 'Edie?' she repeated when she didn't receive an answer.

'No,' Edie said.

Nellie knew without a shadow of a doubt her daughter was hiding something. 'I'll look into it, Dr Palmer. And don't worry, we won't let her lift a finger.'

'I'm pleased to hear it.' He put his hat on. 'Don't hesitate to call me if the bleeding starts again.'

After he'd left, Edie shifted uncomfortably on her seat, aware that her mother's eyes hadn't left her.

'Edie, so help me God, if you know something about this, then you better tell me.'

Finally, Edie managed to look at her mother. 'I promise, Mum. There's nothing.'

Her mother grunted. 'You forget, I always know when you're lying. So don't think you'll be able to hide whatever it is from me for much longer. But right now your sister needs me more.'

As her mother went upstairs, Edie put her head in her hands. She needed to get those bottles out of the bedroom and hidden somewhere else, but there was no chance now. How could she have been so stupid?

Slowly, she got up and followed her mother upstairs.

In the bedroom, Marianne was propped up on the bed. She was still pale, but she looked a little better. Alfie sat beside her, clutching her hand tightly. Lily and her mother were sitting next to each other on Edie's bed.

'Marianne says she doesn't know what the doctor means,' Lily said.

Edie looked at Marianne, who smiled slightly. 'I must have been delirious from the pain and worry.'

'But I heard Edie ask you,' Alfie said, glaring at his sister-in-law.

'And I heard Hester telling you not to drink something just before she left to get you aspirin,' Nellie chipped in.

'It was nothing. Just some herbal mixture Gladys made to help settle my stomach,' Marianne said.

'What the—' Nellie stood up quickly. 'I have *told* that woman a million times not to bring her quack remedies into my house! And to think I was going to apologise to her. Well, she'll be hearing from me, that's for sure. But it won't be an apology.'

She stormed out of the room, her colour high.

'Oh God.' Marianne put her hand to her head. 'I shouldn't have said anything. Now look what I've done.'

'*You* haven't done anything, love,' Lily said soothingly. 'But someone else might have.' She looked over at Edie again. 'Was it yours?' she asked challengingly.

Edie swallowed and looked away.

'*Was it?*' she shouted.

Finally, Edie nodded.

'Please stop it,' Marianne said weakly. 'Edie told me not to take it, but I was so anxious, and it helped.'

'Shh. It's fine, love. None of this is your fault,' Alfie soothed. 'And all's well that ends well, eh? So how about we all just calm down. Marianne needs peace and quiet if she's going to get better.'

But Lily ignored him as she went up to Edie. 'Where is it?' she hissed.

Instinctively, Edie looked towards the wardrobe and Lily immediately went over, reaching behind it and extracting the bag. Then, without even looking inside, she marched out of the room.

Edie followed. 'Lily, please don't.'

Lily whirled around. 'Do you realise what could have happened? *Do you?* And you want to keep this stuff here?'

Helplessly, she watched as Lily went into the bathroom and emptied Edie's last hope of getting rid of her pregnancy down the sink, running the taps to wash away the residue.

'How could you?' Edie wailed. 'What will I do now?'

'You're just going to have to take responsibility and face up to it,' Lily said, unmoved by her sister's devastation. 'And later you can tell me all about Susan.' She put the bottles back into the bag and thrust it at Edie, then walked back to the bedroom.

361

Edie stood with the empty bottles, tears pouring down her face. She'd known her problems hadn't ended with the arrest of Elspeth and Walter, but at least she'd still had a small sliver of hope. But now it was all gone and she was stuck with a baby she didn't want, a sister who hated her and another who had nearly lost her much-wanted baby because of her – she wasn't sure how she'd be able to look Marianne in the face again. As for Lily, when she told her about Susan and what she'd done, no doubt she'd hate her even more.

She crept back to the bedroom and peeped in.

'What?' Lily was exclaiming. 'How have I missed all this?' In her hands was a copy of the *Dover Express* and Marianne was explaining what had happened earlier that day.

Edie left them to it and went back downstairs, just in time to see her mother come out of her bedroom, her purple coat on.

'Where are you going?' Edie asked.

'To see Gladys,' her mother responded angrily.

Edie closed her eyes. And now this. None of this was poor Gladys's fault, and yet she'd take the blame. She should follow, she thought. Confess. Take responsibility like Lily said. But she was so tired. She lay down on the sofa, pulling her knees up to her chest and closed her eyes.

362

# Chapter 64

Not needing any light to show her the way, Nellie's anger took her storming up Cannon Street to Pencester Road where Gladys lived in a couple of rooms above a newsagent's. She banged her fists on the door until the window above opened and Gladys looked down.

'Who's there?' she called querulously.

'Let me in!'

'What do *you* want?'

Nellie responded with another loud bang on the door.

Finally, Gladys came down and opened the door, her grey hair loose around her face and a pink crocheted shawl around her shoulders. 'This better be good,' she grumbled.

Nellie brushed past her into the dingy hall, and made straight for the stairs, which were covered with a fraying brown carpet.

'What's this about, Nellie?' Gladys called after her. 'I was hoping you'd come to apologise, but from the look of you, you're as stubborn as ever. Never could admit a wrong, could ya?'

Nellie didn't reply as she walked into Gladys's sitting room and looked around. Unlike the hall, Gladys's room was neat as a pin, every surface covered with plants and flowers. And in the centre of the small dining table, on a lace tablecloth, was a pot of blue hydrangeas. Nellie picked it up and threw it at the wall, leaving a brown stain just below the crucifix that hung there.

'What did you do that for?' Gladys gasped, slamming the door shut. She rushed over and carefully lifted the flowers, their roots bunched up in soil, and took them into her small kitchen where she put them in the sink. 'How dare you, Nellie!' she wailed.

'How dare I?' Nellie responded. 'How *dare* I? You're gonna need a sight more bloody blue flowers than that to apologise to *me*!'

Gladys paled and put her hand on her chest.

'Do you know what's been happening at my house? Do you?'

'Yes I do, and it's no more than you deserve! You let that woman into your home. You treated her as if she were your long-lost best friend. You didn't listen to me!'

'I'm not talking about Hester!' Nellie screamed back. 'Hester's the bloody least of my problems. And you only disliked her cos you felt she was takin' your place. And do you know what? I'd rather have a million Hesters than one of you!'

Gladys gasped. 'What do you mean?'

'My daughter ... my Marianne nearly lost her baby today. And it's all *your* fault!'

Gladys slumped down on a chair. 'Is she all right?'

'Yes. No thanks to you!'

'Why is this my fault? I'd say it's yours. Working that girl half to death, and then Hester bringing all that trouble to your door. It's no wonder she nearly miscarried!'

'You have the cheek to blame me, when it was *your* concoction that did it! Just like with Donald!' She looked around at the pots of flowers and herbs. 'Well, this time I won't keep quiet!'

'Keep quiet about what?'

'About the muck you gave Marianne and what it's done to her. Did you learn nothing after what happened to Donald?' Nellie stormed at her.

At that, Gladys's cheeks flushed. 'I gave *nothing* to Marianne. And don't you DARE blame me for Donald! I only did what you asked of me, Nellie Castle. Because I loved you. And let's remember, I weren't the one holding the gun!'

Nellie stared at her, stunned. Then she shook her head. 'You have no idea what you're talking about,' she said in a low voice. 'And I swear to you, Gladys, if you set one foot in my house again, so help me God, I will tell *everyone* what you did!'

She stormed past her, stumbling blindly down the stairs, her heartbeat loud in her ears.

As she emerged on to the street, the first-floor window opened. 'God sees everything, Nellie. And may he have mercy on your soul!'

Gladys slammed the window shut and threw herself onto the floor in front of the crucifix, tears pouring down her face as she whispered over and over again, 'Forgive me, Father, for I have sinned.'

∞

Out in the street, Nellie slumped down on the pavement, all her anger and bravado gone. She put her head between her knees as nightmare images from the day her husband had died replayed over and over in her mind. She squeezed her eyes shut, willing the memories away. But one in particular refused to leave: Edie, her sweet, happy little girl, standing in the doorway screaming. And she wouldn't stop, no matter how tight Nellie held her. When she finally did, she'd looked up at her through tear-drenched blue eyes, so like her father's. 'Why did you kill Daddy?'

# Chapter 65

The thunder of footsteps on the stairs woke Edie and she sat up, rubbing her eyes and smoothing down her hair.

'How's Mum?' Donny ran into the room. 'Is she all right?'

He was followed by his uncles, Jasper and Bill, who all looked at her tearful face anxiously. 'She's fine.' Edie tried to smile but her lips wouldn't obey.

'Why've you been crying then?' Donny asked.

'Happy tears, Don, that's all. Go see for yourself. Alfie and Lily are with her, but I bet she'd be pleased to see you.'

Donny ran out of the room and Jasper plumped down on the sofa beside her, putting his arm around her shoulder. 'Is it really good news?' he asked. ''Cos your face is telling us something different.'

'It really is.' She lay her head on his shoulder.

'Thank Christ for that,' Bert said, dropping down onto his mother's chair and rubbing his hand over his face.

'And where's Nellie?' Jasper asked.

'Gone to see Gladys.'

'Ahh, good. She's gone to apologise. You know, I have a feelin' your mum is starting to learn.' He chuckled.

Edie didn't reply. She wasn't going to tell him what her mother was really doing over at Gladys's because that would only lead to more questions.

'Well,' Rodney said, rubbing his hands together. 'Looks like the crisis is over – and not just for us. The baddies have been caught,

Marianne's going to be fine. And Dover can go back to being bombed and shelled in the regular way.'

'Ain't that a relief,' Jimmy said sarcastically. He'd been unnaturally quiet through the whole afternoon.

'You all right, Jim?' Rodney asked.

'Yeah,' he said. 'Like you said, we can all go back to normal.' He looked distracted as he put his cap back on. 'If you don't mind, I think I'm gonna head back.'

'What's eating him?' Rodney asked after Jim had left.

'Woman trouble,' Bert replied. 'Him and Reenie were having intense conversations earlier. He should take a leaf out of my book – love 'em and leave 'em. Speaking of, Edie. What about that other thing?'

Edie sighed. 'I think she knows.'

'Who? Lily?'

Edie nodded and Bert cursed quietly.

'If you're talking about Charlie and Susan, then, yes I do know.' Lily stood in the doorway, waving an envelope. 'He's told me everything. And very soon you two are going to explain yourselves!' She looked between them. 'You're just lucky I got distracted tonight, cos I had plans for you. And they weren't good. How could you believe that of him?'

'You mean she lied?' Bert glanced at Edie, eyebrows raised and Edie shrugged.

'Of course she bloody lied!' Lily practically shouted this last. 'I'm not stupid, Bert. You really think I'd fall for a man who'd do something like this? You're confusing me with Edie.'

'Hey, that's unfair!' Bill said. He'd been watching the interaction in consternation. Not having brothers and sisters he'd had no idea they could talk to each other like this.

'And what would you know about it?' Lily asked heatedly.

'Me and Edie have known each other for years,' he retorted. 'And yes, she's made some mistakes, but she's brave, loyal and kind, and I won't have you throw 'em in her face like that.'

Edie looked at Bill in surprise and he grinned back at her. 'Nellie isn't the only one who's learnt their lesson,' he said.

She smiled slightly at him. 'Thank you,' she said softly. But inside she felt her heart break a little more. Because Bill had no idea about her biggest mistake of all. The one that was sitting like a stone in her belly and was the reason nothing could ever come of their growing feelings.

'Hang on, hang on.' Rodney held his hand up. 'What's this all about?' He looked between his brother and sisters.

'Nothing,' Edie and Bert said at the same time.

Rodney sighed. 'You know, I give up. I'm going back to the castle where things make a lot more sense.'

'You do that, Rod,' Bert said. 'God forbid you get caught up in something as messy as real *feelings*. How's Marge, by the way?'

In response, Rodney clapped his hat back on and left without another word.

Bert grinned. 'Oops, looks like I hit a nerve.'

'You should know better than to tease your brother like that,' Jasper admonished. 'That boy has more feelings than he knows what to do with. That's his whole problem. Anyway, I'm too tired to listen to you lot squabble. You couldn't help this old bag o' bones back home, could ya, Bill?'

Bill came and helped Jasper up from the sofa. 'See you tomorrow?' he asked Edie. 'Maybe we can go pester Mr Wainwright till he gets Uncle Clive back home.'

Edie nodded. 'Yes. Tomorrow. Thank you, Bill.' She held his gaze for a moment and he nodded, before helping Jasper out of the room.

'And then there were three,' Bert said. 'Soon to be two, cos I've had enough of all this drama.'

'That's right, Bert, run off at the first sign of trouble,' Lily sneered.

Bert whirled round to face her. 'You have no idea what I've been through for you! It were Edie's idea when that Susan flashed her ring round saying she were looking for Charlie. She dragged me into her plan, and cos I played my part so well, that girl has sunk her claws into me and won't let go! Everywhere I bloody go, she turns up. And I did this for you, Lily! My little sis who I didn't want to see get hurt! So don't you come laying your anger at our door. Go have it out with Susan. Cos we only did this to protect you. And now I'm lumped with a crazy girl who won't leave me alone, and you're there shouting your mouth off as if *I'm* the one what did something wrong. Well, I won't stand for it. When you want to apologise, come see me. But until then, I'm bowing out of this little pantomime.' He stalked out of the room.

'Well, that told you,' Edie said mildly.

Lily blew out a breath. 'All right,' she conceded. 'I can see you did this for me. But that doesn't change the fact that you should have come and told me! It's not fair to keep something like that secret. I'd tell you if I knew Bill was doing the dirty.'

'It wouldn't be my business if he was,' Edie responded tiredly.

'Ha! Don't look like he feels that way. But you're right. You can't get involved now, can you?'

Edie jumped up. 'No, I can't. And that's your fault. I had the chance to put this all behind me, but I'm stuck now. So thanks very much for ruining my life, Lily!'

Lily shook her head. 'You ruined your own life,' she said softly. 'That has nothing to do with me.'

Edie could feel the sobs gathering at the back of her throat and not wanting Marianne to hear her crying, she went into her mother's room, where she curled into a ball on the eiderdown, stuffing her fist in her mouth to try to keep from wailing. Lily was right, she thought miserably. She *had* ruined her own life. And there didn't seem to be anything she could do to put it right.

# Chapter 66

Unable to face seeing her family, Nellie wandered into Pencester Gardens. She wished she could talk to Jasper, ask his advice. But if he found out the truth, there was no doubt that she would lose him forever.

She walked towards the low stone wall that separated the church from the park, staring sightlessly into the dark graveyard. Finally, she turned away. She couldn't go in. Instead, she walked around the park until she found a wooden bench, where she sat with her head bowed, silent tears falling down her cheeks.

It was late by the time she roused herself to leave. The day had been an endless string of dramas, each one coming hot on the heels of the last. But it was the scene with Gladys that wouldn't leave her mind.

Walking quietly into the sitting room, she went over to the fireplace and touched one of the bright yellow flowers on the wallpaper by the fireplace. Underneath it was the evidence of her guilt. That awful red stain that no amount of scrubbing could remove. In the end, she'd covered it with a picture so the children wouldn't see it, and as soon as the funeral was over, she'd spent more than she could afford on redecorating the whole place in the brightest colours she could find.

'I'm so sorry, my love.' She rested her forehead against the wall and let the tears fall again. Jasper's words came back to her. *I don't want to end up like Donald . . . The longer he was home, the worse he got.* And it was true. And no matter what Gladys said, they shared the blame for that equally.

Shoulders sagging, she went into her bedroom and stopped short at the sight of Edie lying on her bed, her knees pulled tight to her chest, just as she'd slept when she was a tiny baby. She tiptoed over and stared down at her. Edie's cheeks were tear-stained and every so often she'd hiccup. Sitting down beside her, Nellie stroked the hair back from her face and stared at her profile: the long lashes fanned out against her pale cheeks, the straight nose, the determined chin . . . Just like Donald's.

She bent to kiss her forehead, then undressed quietly, slipping in bed beside her daughter and pulling her into her arms. What damage had she done to her girl? she wondered. She kissed the back of her neck softly. 'I'm sorry, Edie. I'm so sorry.'

After a while, the day caught up with her and she fell asleep, only to be woken a short time later by Edie thrashing around. 'Mummy!' she called. 'Mummy!'

'I'm right here, love. I'm right here.'

Edie turned over and snuggled into her and Nellie stroked her hair. 'Shh, sweetheart. Everything's going to be all right.'

Suddenly, Edie sat up. 'Mum?' She looked around her. 'Oh, sorry. I fell asleep.'

'It's all right, love, lie down. You were having a nightmare. Was it the same one you used to have when you were younger?'

Edie didn't reply.

'Lie down. Let me comfort you.'

Edie lay down stiffly on her back, staring at the ceiling.

'Tell me about the dream,' Nellie whispered.

'Why? You've never been interested before.'

'I've always been interested. I just didn't want to know. Tell me,' Nellie urged, holding her breath. Would she talk to her? she wondered. She wouldn't blame her if she didn't, not after the number of times she'd refused to answer her questions about her father in the past.

Finally, her patience was rewarded as Edie, soothed by her mother's caress and feeling safe for the first time in she didn't know how long, started to talk.

'I don't see much. I'm scared, that's all I really know. So scared, Mum. And then there's a bang, a scream, a splash of red on the wall.' Edie shuddered.

Nellie's heart broke at her words. All these years, she thought, her daughter had wrestled with her nightmares alone because her mother was too much of a coward to face hearing about them.

'I think it's from when Dad died,' she whispered.

Nellie sighed. 'It is, love.'

'Did I see it?'

'No, sweetheart. You came in after . . . after it had happened.'

Edie sat up. 'I knew it!' she said fiercely. 'I knew it! Why would you never tell me anything?'

Nellie sat up too. 'Because I didn't want you to know.'

'Did you do it? Rodney said something about Dad trying to kill you. So after that was it a case of him or you?'

'No! No, Edie. It wasn't like that! Your father was half-crazed when he died, but I didn't kill him. But . . .' She paused and took a deep breath. 'But his madness, that was down to me. To the drink we gave him.'

'The drink? The one *I* used to give him?'

'Gladys's poppy head tea. It used to calm him. But then it stopped working, so I asked Gladys to make it stronger. She warned me it was dangerous, but . . .' She sighed deeply. 'I just didn't know what else to do to help him,' she said finally.

Edie sat in silence, digesting this piece of information. Remembering how her father would only ever read to her or play with her after he'd had his drink. 'So I killed him?' she whispered.

'No! No, Edie! He killed himself. You were just a child. A child who loved her father – you are entirely innocent.'

Edie sat for a long time in silence, her eyes squeezed tightly shut and suddenly she began to rock back and forth, her body trembling.

372

'Oh God! I saw him dead!' she wailed. 'All that *stuff* splattered over the wall!' The images were coming thick and fast. 'It was everywhere. And his face was gone. *His face was gone!*' She clapped a hand to her mouth. 'I'm going to be sick!'

Nellie hurriedly reached under the bed for the old chamber pot she still kept there. She managed to get it to Edie just in time before she threw up the contents of her stomach, eyes and nose streaming and her body wracked with sobs.

Nellie's heart broke. This was her doing. All this pain her daughter was suffering was on her. She was meant to love and protect her children. But look what she'd done.

When Edie finally stopped being sick, Nellie took the bowl away and then pulled her back into her arms. 'I'm sorry. I'm so sorry. I should never have hidden the truth. I love you so much, my little girl. But I lost you after your dad died. And I didn't know how to get you back.'

'You should have told me the truth!' Edie said, her voice husky. 'Maybe not when I was so young, but later. When I asked. When I had nightmares every night. Why didn't you tell me, Mum? You could have stopped it. Because it wasn't just you who lost something that night. I lost my dad, but I lost you too. Nothing was ever the same.' She pushed Nellie away and pulled her knees to her chest and lay her head on them, sobbing until there was nothing left.

Nellie watched her helplessly, unsure what to do. She'd made so many mistakes in her life. But this, this was probably the one she regretted most. She'd driven her daughter away. When Edie had needed her most, she'd let her down. Such a sweet, loving little thing she'd been with her dark hair and blue eyes, so trusting and happy. But since that day, she'd been neither.

Edie got off the bed. 'You know what, Mum, you might not have shot him, but you *did* kill him! And you made *me* give him that poison. I was just a child. How could you have done that to me?' Her voice broke. 'I can't bear to be near you right now,' she muttered as she ran out of the room.

373

Nellie stared after her bleakly. Edie was right. She had killed Donald. She might not have intended to, but her actions had led to his death. And now she might never get her daughter back. If she were in Edie's position, would she be able to forgive and forget? she wondered. She didn't need to think too hard to know the answer to that, because she wouldn't. And of all her children, Edie was perhaps the most similar to her in temperament.

She listened to her daughter's feet thump downstairs, and not long after, the back door slammed. Her heart physically hurt at that. Because she knew where she was going.

To Jasper.

The person they all went to when they were in trouble. Not her. Jasper. Well, at least she'd be safe there, and that was all that mattered.

Would Edie tell him? she wondered fearfully. Would she tell him what she and Gladys had done, however inadvertently, and drive him away from her once and for all?

If she did, it was no more than Nellie deserved.

# Chapter 67

Without stopping to put on a coat, Edie ran down Church Street. The night was pitch-black and it was pouring with rain, but she barely noticed. All she knew was she needed to speak to her father. Her poor dad, who'd trusted his wife to care for him, to love him. And instead she'd betrayed him and poisoned him.

In the churchyard, she threw herself down on her father's grave, her arms going round the cold, wet gravestone. 'I didn't know, Daddy! I didn't know what I was giving you! I'm sorry! I'm sorry! I'm sorry!' She raised her head, kissing the cold marble over and over, but in her head, it was her father's face she saw. Her father's cheeks she was kissing. Just as she had when he sat, relaxed and calm after drinking his tea. But then another image came to her. Her father's body in the chair, his face blown away. No cheeks to kiss. No eyes to wink at her. No mouth to smile at her.

She felt the nausea rise again, but she swallowed it back. 'Forgive me! Please forgive me!' She started to cry again as the rain poured down, soaking her clothes. 'I didn't know!' she said again. 'I didn't know!' She knelt up and leant against the stone, putting her arms around it again, hugging it close. 'I loved you so much, Daddy. So much.'

She stayed like that for a long time, her face pressed against the words her mother had chosen. *To live in the hearts of those we love is not to die.* 'Not a lie after all,' she whispered. 'You are in my heart. I will always love you.'

Edie didn't know how long she stayed like that, but soon, her arms grew tired, and she curled up on the wet grass in front of the stone and fell asleep, her dreams full of visions of her father as only she remembered him.

# Chapter 68

To Nellie's surprise, she fell asleep soon after Edie had slammed out of the house. She woke early though, her head throbbing, her eyes scratchy from all the tears she had shed the night before.

Stopping only to double-check that Edie still wasn't there, she dressed quickly, throwing on her warmest clothes and left. It was barely six a.m., but she couldn't wait any longer. The café would remain closed today, she decided. She couldn't face everyone, let alone muster the energy to do all the cooking, and she doubted Gladys would come to work. In fact, after last night, she wasn't sure if she'd ever return, or if she wanted her to.

There was no answer when she banged on the door of the forge, so she used her key to let herself in. She entered quietly and turned on the light. But the sitting room was empty – no Edie lying on the sofa or sitting in the chair. She went to Jasper's bedroom door and knocked. When there was no reply, she crept inside. Jasper was fast asleep, his snores echoing round the room. 'Jasper,' she whispered. 'Wake up.' He stirred but didn't wake so she plumped down on the side of the bed and shook his shoulder.

'Wha—' Jasper's eyes flew open and he stared at Nellie in incomprehension for a moment, his hair a bushy white bird's nest around his head, his chin bristly before his morning shave.

'Nellie?' he said hoarsely, sitting up. 'What's wrong? Is it Marianne?'

Nellie shook her head wordlessly.

'What's happened? Is anyone hurt?'

She shook her head again and opened her mouth to speak, but the words stuck in her throat.

'Jesus Christ, woman, just tell me!'

'I-i-it's Edie. She's disappeared. I thought she'd come to you, but she's not here.'

His eyebrows shot up. 'Disappeared? What do you mean, disappeared?'

'Oh Jasper . . . It's all my fault. I t-t-told her what happened. I told her what happened and she ran away from me.'

Alarmed at the tears that were pouring down Nellie's face, Jasper sat up and pulled her head to his shoulder. 'All right, love. All right. Now, what did you tell her?'

'I told her about Donald . . . Did she come here?'

'No. I ain't seen her. But what did you tell her?'

Nellie shook her head and stood up. 'I have to find her,' she said, going back into the sitting room. 'Where would she go?'

Bill popped his head out of his bedroom. 'Mrs Castle? What's happened?'

Jasper had managed to get out of bed and was leaning against his bedroom door, watching Nellie pace with growing alarm. She was always so strong, so confident and bullish. But this Nellie . . . He'd only seen her once. On the day Donald had died.

'She says Edie's gone missing,' he rasped.

Bill paled. 'When? Why?'

Nellie didn't answer, so Jasper said, 'She doesn't know. She told her something about her dad . . .' He thought for a moment. 'Did you try the church? She might have gone to his grave. I know she goes regular. And if this is about Donald, then I lay good money that's where she is.'

'Yes! Yes, of course,' Nellie muttered, hurrying out.

Bill went back into his room, emerging a few minutes later fully dressed.

'Where you going, lad?' Jasper asked from the kitchen where he was putting the kettle on.

'To find Edie,' he said.

∞

By the time Bill reached the churchyard, Nellie was already there, kneeling in front of a gravestone, her head bowed.

'Mrs Castle?' Bill approached her carefully. 'Have you found her?'

Nellie shook her head, then held up some blue flowers, soil clumped in the shape of a pot around their stems.

'Glad's been,' she said, tears in her eyes. 'But no Edie. Where is she, Donald?' she murmured. 'What have you done with her?'

Bill looked around him in agitation, it was still dark, and the graveyard felt haunted by the spirits of all who lay beneath them. He hated this place. He'd been only twice: to bury his mother and to bury his aunt. Two of the worst days of his life.

'This isn't helping to find Edie,' he said, reaching down to help Nellie to her feet. 'Where could she have gone?' He paced over to the church door and went in. 'Edie?' he called. But there was no answer. Shivering slightly, he walked down the aisle to the back of the church and through the door that he knew led to the vicar's office. 'Edie?' he said again.

He went in, switching on the light. The first thing he saw was Edie's jumper, lying in a crumpled heap by the fireplace. Breathing a sigh of relief, he picked it up. It was still wet. She must have run out into the rain last night. He felt a surge of anger towards Nellie. What the hell had that woman said to her to make her this upset? He'd always known of the tension that simmered between them – why else would she have spent so much time at the garage, moved in – but before he'd got to properly know her these last few days, he'd assumed it was two strong-headed women who couldn't get along. But now, he wasn't so sure. Now he was beginning to wonder whether Nellie was the one responsible for their strained relationship.

379

He walked back out to find Nellie sitting on the front pew staring into space.

'She was here, Mrs Castle. What did you argue about?'

Nellie just shook her head. He threw the jumper at her in frustration, and walked back out of the church, striding across the road to the vicarage, where he knocked on the door.

It was opened by Reverend Johnson, who looked exhausted and careworn, and no wonder. The number of funerals he'd had to officiate in the last few months – many of them people he'd known for years – would wear down even the most robust person.

He squinted at him. 'Bill Penfold, isn't it?'

Bill nodded, impressed that he remembered him. 'Is Edie here?' he asked.

He nodded. 'She's sleeping. I found her distressed at her father's grave.'

'Will you wake her?'

'She needs rest. When she wakes, I'll tell her you called.'

Nellie appeared behind Bill then. 'She's here? Oh, thank God! Thank God.' She searched the vicar's face for signs of accusation, but there were none.

'Would you like to come in and talk, Mrs Castle?' he asked.

Nellie hesitated.

'You may find it helps.'

'I don't think anything will help,' she said miserably. 'I let her down. She needed me and I thought only of protecting myself because I couldn't face the truth.' Her face crumpled and Reverend Johnson stepped forward to put his arm around her shoulders. 'Come on. I have half an hour before I need to be at the church. And, Mr Penfold, try not to worry about Edie, I'm sure she'll talk to you when she's ready.'

He shut the door, leaving Bill feeling frustrated and helpless on the doorstep. If Edie was in pain, he wanted to help her. He'd known her almost all his life, but after these last few days, he finally felt he'd got to *know* her. Her loyalty, her courage, her dogged determination to help his uncle – all of these things had opened his eyes. When they were children hanging around the garage, he'd found her irritating, and he couldn't deny he'd been jealous of the attention his uncle paid her. But later, as she'd grown up, he couldn't help but notice how pretty she was. Even then, though, he'd held back, intimidated by her sharp tongue. But it had always been there, this little spark in his heart that had been fanned to life since he'd been back. What he didn't know, though, was whether Edie might feel the same. Sometimes, it felt as if she might. But she'd drawn away when he'd tried to kiss her, so maybe she didn't.

He needed to know, though. He was heading off for his operational training in a few days and knew the odds were stacked against him coming back alive – he'd stopped counting the number of friends he'd lost, they all had. It was the only way any of them could face getting back into a plane.

But he didn't want to die not knowing whether Edie might love him, as he was beginning to realise he loved her.

# Chapter 69

Bert looked at his watch. After yesterday's drama, he was relieved he had a full day off, and though it was the last thing he wanted to do, he knew he should visit the family. Make sure they were all right.

In the bunk next to him, Jim was lying staring up at the ceiling.

'You wanna come home with me today? Feel we should check on everyone.'

Jimmy sighed. 'Not really.'

'What's eating you, Jim? I mean, I know you had a bit of a tiff with Reenie yesterday, but it's not just that, is it?'

Jimmy shook his head. 'No, it's not just that.'

'What then?'

'Nothing I want to discuss with you.'

Bert stared hard at his brother. 'Colin,' he said finally.

When there was no response, Bert continued, 'Are you ever gonna forgive yourself? It weren't your fault, Jim. It was mayhem over there. There was nothing you could have done.'

'Just leave it, will you?' Jimmy grated, getting out of bed. 'Let's get breakfast, then go down to see what's what.'

'So are you and Reenie off?' Bert persisted.

Jimmy shrugged.

'Are you?' Bert pushed.

'Yes! I think so. I mean . . . I'm not right for her.'

Bert's eyebrows rose. 'Well, we all knew that. But if she makes you happy then it doesn't matter, does it?'

The bugle sounded the 'Reveille' then, and the rest of the barracks started to stir, so the conversation ended there.

But Bert was worried. He didn't want his brother returning to the deep depression he'd suffered in the weeks after they'd returned from Dunkirk.

'Oy, Alf,' he called over to his brother-in-law, who had come in late last night, so Bert hadn't had a chance to speak to him. 'How was Marianne when you left her?'

Alfie smiled and sent him a brief thumbs-up.

Satisfied, Bert carefully Brylcreemed his hair, then blew himself a kiss in the mirror. Apart from visiting his family, today he was determined to get Susan off his back once and for all. And now he knew Lily's heart wasn't in danger, he didn't care how brutal he needed to be about it.

∽

'So?' Marge asked as she sat down in the canteen opposite Rodney.

He looked up at her briefly and frowned. 'So, what?' he said moodily.

'How'd it go yesterday? You know, with all that stuff in the papers.'

Rodney's eyebrows rose. 'I didn't think you were interested,' he said tonelessly.

'Of course I'm interested.'

'If you must know, that was the least of it. Marianne nearly had a miscarriage.'

Marge gasped. 'Are you serious?'

Rodney paused with a piece of toast halfway to his mouth and gave her a baleful stare.

'I know, I know. You wouldn't joke about that sort of thing. Or anything else, for that matter,' she muttered under her breath.

'And I just bet your padre is a laugh a minute,' he said. 'What with all the Bible quotes and hymns.'

'Oh, shut up, Rodney.' Marge picked up her plate and cup. 'You know, your problem is not a lack of humour, it's a lack of *feeling*. You're like a great lump of wood. Solid but unresponsive.' She walked away and joined some people at another table.

With an effort, Rodney resisted the temptation to go over and shout at her. If that was what she thought, then he knew where he stood. There was no point pining over someone who didn't love you. His father had taught him that lesson. He looked round briefly to see whether anyone else had seen Marge getting up and leaving him. And his eyes met the sympathetic gaze of Philip, the bloody padre. It seemed he couldn't go anywhere these days without running into him.

It was time to put in for a transfer, he decided. He needed to get away from Dover, away from his family, but most of all, away from Marge and her saintly new boyfriend.

# Chapter 70

Nellie sat by the fire in Reverend Johnson's front room, a cup of tea in front of her, and stared into the flames, avoiding looking at the vicar who had sat for the last ten minutes watching her in silence.

Finally, she couldn't bear it any longer, so she spoke. 'She told you then?'

Reverend Johnson tilted his head in acknowledgement. 'She told me her version. Perhaps you'd like to give me yours.'

Nellie took a sip of tea. 'Not really,' she muttered like a sulky child. She wasn't used to explaining herself to anyone, and the feeling she had now was very much the same as when she'd been called in to see the headmistress after some transgression or other at school – and there had been a few.

'I won't judge you, you know. Edie thinks you killed Donald, but that's because she's angry at you for not telling her what happened sooner. And to be honest, Mrs Castle, I can't blame her.'

'Yes, well . . . It's not an easy thing to talk about with your daughter. How could I tell her that she saw her father's brains splattered all over the wall? When I realised she didn't remember, I thought it best to leave it that way. But that day has always been between us. She didn't know it, but I did. I should have cleared it away. It was my responsibility, and I shirked it.' Nellie wiped away a tear angrily. She was not going to cry anymore. What use were tears, after all?

'So, what are you going to do about it?' the vicar asked.

Nellie looked at him in surprise. 'Do? What can I do? My daughter thinks I killed her father – worse, she thinks I used her to kill her father. But it wasn't like that. It really wasn't like that. I just wanted him to have some rest. Some peace. And laudanum had been the only thing that did that. So when they banned it, Gladys made a version for him from poppy seeds. I never meant him harm. I thought if his mind could rest, if it could stop replaying those horrific images, then maybe one day they would stop altogether, or if they didn't stop, just . . . I don't know . . . stop tormenting him.'

'Did you love him?' he asked.

Nellie sighed, unwilling to answer. She *had* loved him. She'd loved him more than life. But it was so hard to live with someone who thought you were the enemy, who sometimes greeted you with a smile and sometimes threw their plate at you because they thought you were there to do them harm. Yes, she'd loved him. But little by little, drip by drip, the love had drained away. How could she still love him after he'd tried to kill her? After he'd thrashed poor Rodney for waking him up, for laughing too loudly, for spilling his drink . . . for just being Rodney. The eldest, the one who needed to grow up, to be a *man*! And if that hadn't killed her love, then his *bastard* turning up at their door last year would have seen to it. His filthy little secret that showed that even when she had loved him, she couldn't be certain he loved her back.

'No,' she said quietly. 'No, I didn't love him by the time he died. But I loved him when I married him. And I tried to stay faithful to the vows I made. I tried, Reverend, I really tried.'

Nellie started to cry again and the vicar sat quietly, not offering comfort, just waiting for the storm to pass.

'And if you believe that you'll believe anything,' a harsh voice said from the doorway.

Nellie looked up and even through the fog of her tears she could see the hatred on her daughter's face.

Reverend Johnson stood up. 'Come in, Edie. Sit down. Speak to your mother with an open heart.'

'I've heard every word of what she just said. And frankly, it makes me sick. I don't want to hear any more. Thank you, Reverend Johnson, for letting me stay. But I'll go now.' She threw a hard look at her mother.

The vicar sighed and followed Edie out of the room. 'Don't be so hard on her,' he whispered.

'Are you serious? I have asked her and asked her, but not once has she told me what happened. Rather than trying to help me, she chose to protect herself! To keep her guilty secret.' She stormed back to the front room and stood in the doorway. 'Well, guess what, Mum? You're not the only one who's got a guilty secret. I'm pregnant, and Hester had given me something to get rid of it! *That's* what Marianne drank. So it's my fault she nearly lost the baby.'

Nellie, who had been staring at her hands through the whole of this tirade, looked up at that, startled.

'It was you . . .' Nellie whispered.

'Yes. It was me. Not Gladys. ME! But don't worry, you won't have another little bastard in the café, because I'm never coming back. I don't care if I have to live on the streets. I'll put the baby up for adoption and I never, ever want to see your face again.'

She turned and ran to the front door, wrenching it open.

'Edie . . .' Reverend Johnson called. 'Come back.' He ran out after her. 'Edie,' he said again. 'Bill Penfold was asking for you.'

'Well, Bill Penfold can go to hell too!' she shouted. 'Because he won't want anything to do with me when he finds out I'm pregnant! No one will.'

She carried on walking blindly, then turned into Castle Street. There was only one place she could think to go now. The only place she had ever felt content and valued.

Across the street, Bill's stomach dropped. He'd been standing in the cold waiting for her to come out. But hearing those words shattered his dreams.

Shoulders slumped, he waited until Edie was out of sight, then made his way back to the forge. He would pay a visit to Mr Wainwright to see what more he could do for his uncle, then he would leave Dover. There was nothing for him here now.

# Chapter 71

When Reverend Johnson returned to the house, he found Nellie putting on her coat.

'Are you all right, Mrs Castle?'

Nellie's face was creased with pain. 'You reap what you sow, that's what it says in the Bible, isn't it? Next time you preach about that, keep me in mind, Reverend. Cos that's exactly what's happened.' She did up her buttons. 'Will she ever come back to me?' she asked plaintively.

'Give her time. Time and understanding.'

Nellie nodded. But as well as feeling full of remorse and guilt, there was anger too. Anger at what her daughter had just told her. But overriding that, white-hot fury at Hester for putting both her girls in danger with her concoctions. Why hadn't Edie just told her? She'd have been angry, of course, but didn't she know she'd do anything for her children? She would never turn her away. And every grandchild, no matter how difficult the circumstances, was a joy.

Reverend Johnson regarded her sympathetically. 'Don't be too harsh on her, will you?'

Nellie let out a small laugh. 'I doubt I'll get the chance. She's as stubborn as a mule. If she says she's not coming back, then she's not coming back. And I don't blame her.'

When the vicar didn't disagree, she walked towards the door. 'Thank you for looking after her. And me. I won't trouble you again.'

Standing on Church Street, Nellie knew she should find Edie. Talk to her. But she couldn't face it. Instead, she went over the road to the churchyard and knelt down in front of Donald's grave, running her fingers over the words – words Jasper had chosen for her because she'd not known what to put. Her eyes fell on the hydrangeas and she picked them up, kissing the petals. Then she put them down and began to dig in the cold grass, pulling up clumps and tossing them aside, oblivious to everything but the task she'd set herself.

Suddenly another pair of hands joined hers, and she looked up in surprise. Gladys, her face set, was kneeling on the other side of the grave. Briefly their eyes met. 'I'm doing this for Donald,' Gladys grated. 'Not for you. I made that tea to help you both, Nellie.'

Nellie gave a short laugh, returning to her digging. 'Well, it helped all right. It helped him get so out of his mind that he shot himself. And you know it, too! That's why you've been putting these flowers on his grave all these years. As if that makes up for what that stuff did to him!'

'He didn't shoot himself, though, did he? His death is on you. I might have made him the tea. An' I might have increased the dose – at *your* request. But *I* weren't the one holding the gun. And neither was he.'

Nellie opened her mouth to speak, but found she couldn't.

Gladys nodded. 'These hydrangeas aren't just for the poppy tea . . . they're for lookin' the other way. I did that for you, Nellie. And for the children. Out of love and loyalty. But the guilt of it . . . It's been eatin' away at me. And every year, it gets worse.'

'You really believe that?' Nellie exclaimed. 'You really think I did that?' She slammed her hand down on to the mud.

'I know what I saw. But I've never told a living soul.'

'How could you think I would do something like that?' As she dug, Nellie's fingers scraped against a stone and she picked it up, resisting the temptation to throw it at Gladys, before tossing it aside.

'You'd do anything for your kids. And he were horrible. He hit the boys, he nearly killed you; he were a millstone round all of your necks. Apart from poor Edie . . .' Gladys put a trembling hand to her head.

'I didn't shoot him.'

'Even if you didn't, you didn't mind drugging him.'

'I didn't know it would make him kill himself!' Nellie screamed. 'All I knew was that it calmed him down. And when it didn't anymore, I thought if we just made it stronger . . .'

'I warned you though. I warned you what might happen. Just like I warned you about Hester. And you went ahead anyway. Making poor little Edie give it to him.'

'He wouldn't take it from me,' Nellie sobbed. 'And it were the only thing that made him quiet.'

'They didn't ban laudanum for nothing. It can be lethal. Or it can drive you mad. I told you that.'

'But you still made it, didn't you?' Nellie retaliated. 'You still made the tea, knowing what you knew.'

Gladys nodded and made the sign of a cross on her chest. 'God forgive me for it, I did. But that wasn't what killed him. That was you.'

Nellie shook her head. 'I didn't. I took the gun from his hand. I didn't fire it . . . But all these years, Glad . . . all these years, you thought I was a murderer, yet you stayed with me . . .'

'Yes, I stayed. There was a stain on your soul, but I understood. He woulda killed one of you one day, I was sure of it.'

'But I didn't kill him. It was the poppy tea. We used too much. That's what drove him to shoot himself. And I swear on the kids' lives, he did it to himself.'

Gladys sat back, her muddy hands in her lap and looked at her friend for a long time. Nellie's eyes glittered with tears of regret and grief. They had spent so many years together, helping each other, and Gladys always knew when Nellie was lying. And she knew then, without a shadow of a doubt, that she wasn't lying now. Which meant

391

only one thing. 'So it were me,' she whispered. 'It were my fault. I made it too strong.'

Nellie shuffled over the mud on her knees and clasped Gladys's hands. 'It were *my* fault. I asked you to do it. You warned me, but I insisted. And in the end the poppies made him madder. I wonder sometimes, would he have recovered if we'd not given it to him in the first place?'

'Oh God!' Gladys said, covering her face with her hands, smearing wet earth over her cheeks. 'All these years I've blamed you. I picture poor little Edie's face when she came in. Oh, that poor girl. She might not remember, but it's stayed with her, that day. It's stayed there. All them nightmares, her temper, her anger . . .' She burst into tears, rocking back and forth. 'Oh, that poor little lamb . . . And it's our fault, Nellie. All our fault.'

'No. It's *my* fault, Gladys. You have been nothing but a true and loyal friend to me.' She reached over for the clump of flowers and stuck them in the hole they'd dug. Then together, they filled it in, until the flowers sat straight and tall, a splash of colour against the white of the gravestone.

Then the two women knelt together, heads bowed, hands clasped, oblivious to the cold and damp.

# Chapter 72

Lily woke late the next morning, thoughts of Edie and the argument they'd had swirling in her mind. Yesterday all their emotions had been running high and none of them had been thinking straight. But today she was determined to make it up to her. She hated the fact that they'd been on such bad terms, and Edie needed her now more than ever.

In the bed beside her, Marianne was still fast asleep, but the other bed was neatly made. In fact, she was pretty certain Edie hadn't slept in it last night.

She got up quietly and padded through the flat. Her mother's bed was unmade, which was unusual, but Donny was in his room, packing his satchel.

'School at the caves, is it, Don?' she asked from the doorway.

He nodded gloomily. 'And after all that racket last night, I didn't get much sleep.'

Lily smiled at the grown-up way he was talking. 'We weren't that loud.'

'Not you. Gran and Auntie Edie. Then I heard Edie run away.'

'What do you mean?'

He shrugged. 'She left. Then it was quiet.'

Edie must have told their mum she was pregnant, she thought. And no doubt Nellie hadn't taken it well. She needed to find her sister. She gave Don a quick kiss on the head. 'Have a good day, love,' she said. 'I'm off to see Jasper.'

Five minutes later, she ran through the door of the forge and straight up the stairs. After knocking briefly, she walked into Jasper's flat. 'Have you seen—' She stopped short as she saw Bill sitting in one of the chairs, his head in his hands, while Jasper awkwardly patted his shoulder.

'What's happened?' she asked.

'No idea, love. He comes in here, slumps down and hasn't moved since. It's been a while, too.'

'Has Edie been here?'

'You an' all? No. Your mum was in here first thing askin' for her. She were in a terrible state. Then Bill ran out after her. And he came back like this . . .' He looked at her helplessly. 'Have you seen your mum?' he asked. 'Cos the way she was when she left, I'm worried. Do you know what they rowed about?'

Lily cast a quick glance at Bill, who had taken his hands away from his face and was looking at her.

'I can't say,' she muttered. 'But I really need to find her.'

Bill let out a short laugh. 'If you think they rowed cos Edie's pregnant, then just say so.'

Jasper's eyes widened. 'She never is,' he whispered. 'That Greg, was it? Wait till I get my hands on him. I knew he were trouble the minute I set eyes on 'im!'

'It does take two, you know?' Bill said drily.

Jasper threw him a glare. 'Oh, I see clearly now what your problem is. You were startin' to have feelin's for Edie, but now this has happened, you're thinking she's not worth the bother.'

Bill coloured slightly.

'Because all of a sudden, you're thinkin' she's not the girl you thought, am I right?'

Bill stared down at his hands.

'So now you're thinkin' she's tainted somehow. Not the same Edie you've been spendin' all the hours God sends with these last few days?'

394

When Bill still didn't answer, Jasper nodded. 'You blame her, dontcha? She's proven herself to be just another human bein' what makes mistakes, and now you feel let down, is that it?'

'Don't talk to me like that!' Bill responded heatedly. 'I never thought she was perfect! I was able to overlook her affair with a married man.'

'Oh, *able to overlook it*, were ya? What a *gentleman* you are!' Jasper said mockingly, two bright spots of colour on his cheeks. 'Tell me this, Bill, can you say with your hand on your heart that you never got a girl in trouble? Can yer?'

'Of course I haven't!' Bill said indignantly.

'An' how do you know?'

'I just . . .' He trailed off uncertainly.

'Exactly. You ain't got a clue. So don't you go blamin' that poor girl for lookin' for love in all the wrong places. Don't you bloody dare! And if you are blamin' her, then you can leave my house!'

Exhausted by this speech, Jasper slumped into his armchair and lay his head back. 'All me life, I've seen girls in trouble. Hester were one, Marianne another. Then there were poor Annie Brown what Donald left high and dry, and him a married man! And for every girl what's had her life ruined, there's a bloke walkin' around with not a care in the world!' He pointed at Bill. 'Think on it, Bill. Think on all the girls you've known and tell me that you know *for sure* that you ain't one of them blokes.'

Bill looked away.

'Course you can't. Cos that's what men have bin doin' since time began. Gettin' girls in trouble, leavin' them to pay the piper.' Jasper rubbed his face. 'It makes my blood boil. I did me best for Annie and for Hester. And for a couple of others I won't mention. An' Edie shouldn't fear – I'll do me best for her and all. But what about you, Bill? What'll you do?'

Bill stood up. 'I'm going to pack,' he muttered. 'And then I'll be out of your hair, Jasper.'

He walked into his bedroom and shut the door and Lily went to sit on the arm of Jasper's chair, putting her arm around him. 'That was quite a speech,' she said with a lump in her throat. 'I've never heard anyone speak like that about it. And the last person I'd have expected to hear it from was a *man*.'

'Yeah, well, it needs sayin'. An' the reason I feel like this is cos my mum – your gran – were one of them women, Lily. She were just a slip of a girl when some brute abused her. You have the look of her, you know. She were a beauty, too. Oh, how she'd have loved you. But she never got the chance. Instead she worked herself to the bone to keep me. She died when I were fifteen, exhausted and alone 'cept me. That's why me and Donald was such good friends. He wouldn't stand for anyone calling me names. I thought he were the best bloke in the world. Turns out, though, he were just like all the rest.'

Lily kissed the top of her father's head. Jasper hadn't had much of an education, but his compassion, how he seemed to instinctively understand people – that was something that could never be taught. 'I need to find Edie. Where do you think she'd have gone?' Lily asked against his hair.

'Only one place she will go now. The garage.'

Lily nodded. Of course that's where she'd go; she should have thought of that herself.

'I 'spect your mum's gone off somewhere to cool down after hearin' Edie's news.' Jasper sighed tiredly. 'No doubt she'll turn up sooner or later. An' when she does, you leave her to me.'

After Lily had left, Jasper sat staring into space for a long time. Why had his heart chosen this family? he thought ruefully. His life would be a sight more peaceful if he'd just kept himself to himself.

Bill came out of his room with his kitbag over his shoulder. 'I'll be off then,' he said.

Jasper nodded, his eyes narrowed. 'You're a good lad, Bill, but I can't pretend I'm not disappointed in you. I saw how you an' Edie were together – how you worked together, helped each other.

Everythin' she's done for Clive these last days, don't that mean anything to you?'

Bill looked shamefaced. 'Course it does.'

'So what's the problem?'

Bill shrugged, avoiding his gaze.

'She ain't as pure as the driven snow, is that it?'

Bill snorted. 'I already knew that. I don't care about that.'

'But you blame her anyway. You think she ain't worthy of you anymore. St Bill bloody Penfold, is that it? Well, get on yer way, then, son. But think on what I said. Think on it carefully. And try to stay safe, eh?'

Bill nodded briefly. 'You take care, Jasper,' he said. 'And thanks. For everything.'

Jasper shut his eyes after he left. There was nothing more he could do there, he realised. He just hoped that after Bill had had some time to digest his words, he'd come round. Because he had a feeling that Edie's heart would be truly broken this time if he didn't.

# Chapter 73

The flat above the garage smelt of a combination of damp and smoke when she entered and Edie went through, opening all the windows, despite the cold. Then she went into the kitchen and filled a bucket of water and took out all the cleaning utensils. If Mr Pearson ever returned, she didn't want him to come back to this mess.

For the next couple of hours, Edie managed to keep her dark thoughts at bay as she dragged out the ruined bedclothes, the destroyed bed, the burnt carpets and threw them onto the forecourt. She didn't care if anyone saw her, not now. She had nothing left to lose. If they arrested her, so much the better. At least she'd have somewhere to stay.

She'd just finished scrubbing the walls in Mr Pearson's bedroom, when she heard a noise downstairs. She stood quietly in the middle of the room, holding her breath as she waited to hear the heavy footsteps of the military police on the stairs. But instead she heard lighter steps, and she knew immediately who it was. 'Like the pitter-patter of rain' her mum had said, and turned out she was right.

She sighed and went into the sitting room. If it had to be anyone, then Lily was the best of a bad bunch, she supposed.

'Jasper said you'd be here.' Lily came into the room, her eyes taking in her sister's dishevelled figure – her face smudged with dirt, her clothes damp and the knees of her trousers black where she'd knelt on the carpet to pull it up.

Edie smiled slightly. 'Course he did. Jasper always knows.'

Lily went to hug her but Edie moved away.

'What are you doing here, anyway?' Lily asked, wrinkling her nose as she looked around.

Edie shrugged. 'There's nowhere else for me to go.'

'You can go to Jasper's?'

Edie laughed. 'I don't think so. Especially as Bill's there.'

'What's the deal between you two?'

'Nothing.'

'You like him though.' It was a statement.

Edie shrugged again. 'Doesn't matter if I do.'

'Well, it does, really.'

'Seeing as you've decided that I don't have the right to try to get rid of this baby, then no, it doesn't. Who'd want me now?'

Lily had no answer to that. Despite Jasper's speech, she wasn't sure if it would change how Bill felt.

'Why did you tell Mum?' she asked instead.

'Because I don't care what she thinks. I don't care what she says, does or even whether she's alive.'

Lily was stunned. 'Surely it can't be that bad? What did she do?'

Edie looked her square in the face. 'You'll have to ask her that because I don't want to talk about it. Now, unless you want to help me clean this place up, you may as well go.'

'Funnily enough, I don't want to help clean up. What I do want is for you to come home and talk to Mum; you're gonna need her,' Lily said.

'No, I'm not.'

'Please, Edie. At least try. And if you still feel the same, then I'll do everything I can to help. Just come. For me.'

Edie was silent for a long time. In her mind's eye, all she could see was her mother's face. The regret. The grief. The devastation. The memory of last night was bitter, but she couldn't forget the way her mother had held her either. Comforted her. Could she trust her ever again? she wondered. She put her hand on her stomach. She wasn't sure.

'No, I'm not coming. But feel free to tell her where I am. If she really wants to talk then she can come to me.'

'Look, I know how angry you are—'

'You have no idea, Lily. No idea at all. So if you're not cleaning, then just go.'

Seeing the stubborn set of her sister's jaw, Lily knew there was no point pushing it. But she'd at least got a small concession from her, so that was better than nothing.

∽

Edie sat in the cold flat for a long time after Lily had left, the cleaning forgotten as her mind went over and over everything she'd learnt the night before. She wasn't sure what to think anymore. What to feel.

And then there was Mr Pearson. She needed to know he was all right. Even if whatever had been growing between her and Bill over the last days could never come to anything, she couldn't give up on his uncle. She pushed the heels of her hands into her eyes. Lily was right in one way. She couldn't just leave home. She had nowhere to go and a baby to support. She needed her family. And if she left, she'd lose her brothers and sisters too.

A car door slammed outside and she went to the window to see Mr Pearson's little Morris Minor sitting on the forecourt, Bill walking around to open the passenger door.

She watched in astonishment as Mr Pearson's head emerged. He looked haggard, exhausted, but he was there.

Without thinking, she flew out of the room and down the stairs.

'Mr P!' she yelled, throwing herself into his arms. 'You're back! Oh my God!' She burst into tears, squeezing him tight, noting how bony he'd become.

Mr Pearson stumbled back slightly, then his arms came around her. 'Edie, love,' he said. 'Oh, Edie. Am I glad to see you.'

They clung together for a long time, Edie's tears soaking into the shoulder of his jacket. She couldn't be sure, but she could have sworn her own shoulder was a little damp when they finally drew apart.

She cupped a hand round his cheek. 'Are you all right?' she whispered. 'They didn't hurt you?'

'I'll live,' he said with a tired smile. 'But I'll never listen to a bad word about your cookin' again. Prison grub ain't for the faint-hearted.'

Edie laughed. 'That bad, eh? Not surprised you're so thin.' Her eyes filled with tears again. 'I thought I'd never see you again,' she whispered.

'Pah. It takes a bit more than the might of the government to keep *me* down, girl.' He smiled into her eyes and her heart broke at the shadows she could see in his face.

Mr Pearson cleared his throat and stepped back, looking embarrassed.

Edie looked at Bill enquiringly.

'You and I were meant to go to see Mr Wainwright today,' he said. 'But as you were otherwise occupied with the reverend and your mother, I went by myself. And look who I found, sitting by the fire in his office.'

'How do you know where I was?' Edie said fearfully, remembering what she'd shouted to Reverend Johnson as she'd slammed out of his house.

Bill shook his head, his lips in a thin line, his eyes avoiding hers.

Did he know? she wondered, her stomach sinking. Turning quickly to hide her expression, Edie walked her boss over to the stairs. 'What you need is a nice cup of tea,' she said brightly. 'Although I'm afraid the place is a bit of a mess as I haven't finished cleaning up. You'll have to sleep in my room too, because yours is ruined, but a splash of paint and a new carpet and it'll be shipshape again.' She was fully aware she was babbling, but needed to cover up her mortification at Bill's expression.

401

But then, she supposed it made no difference if he'd heard what she'd shouted at the vicar. He'd find out soon enough. As would her boss. Which meant he probably wouldn't want her to work there anymore.

Once the tea was made, the three sat together in the sitting room while Mr Pearson described the horror of the last few days. 'If it weren't for you two, I don't know what would have become of me,' he said gratefully. 'Mr Wainwright told me what you done.' He took each of their hands in his. 'And I want you to know, Edie, this place is your home as long as you want it. And, Bill, obviously it's yours too.' He looked between them meaningfully.

When neither of them looked at him, he sighed and stood up. 'Tomorrow, Edie, you and me are gonna start to rebuild the business, but right now, I'm gonna leave you young people to it and catch up on all the sleep I've missed.'

There was a long silence after Mr Pearson had left. Finally, Edie stood up. 'I'm really glad he's home safe, Bill. And if I don't see you before you join your squadron, good luck. But I best get off home now. I need to sort a few things out.'

Bill cleared his throat. 'Wait, please. I'd like to talk to you.'

Edie sat down again. 'All right.' She tapped her foot on the floor nervously.

'The thing is, Edie. You remember what I said to Mr Wainwright – that if anything happened to Uncle Clive, I'd want you to run the garage.'

She nodded.

'I meant it.'

She smiled slightly. 'It's a lovely thought – I mean not lovely if anything happened to Mr P, obviously, but that you trust me enough for that.'

'I do. I do trust you enough for that. And so does Uncle Clive. And the thing is, with the job I do, chances are I won't survive the war.'

'Don't say that!' Edie instinctively reached for his hand.

'It's true though. And that's why I have to get things in order in case I don't come back. I don't want to leave anything unsaid and undone.'

'You're not gonna die. You're gonna come back.'

'Maybe, maybe not. But, you see . . . over the past days, I've been thinking that you and me, we make a good team. And if we married, then I wouldn't have to worry about the future of the garage or who will look after Uncle Clive when he gets old.'

Edie stared at him in astonishment. 'You want to marry me so I can look after your uncle in his old age? That's ridiculous!' She couldn't lie. Her heart had leapt slightly at his words. But even if she could accept, it was hardly flattering to know he'd only married her for his uncle's sake.

'Why? It seems sensible to me.'

'And what if you do survive? I'm not sure you'd feel quite so pleased to have installed me here. I mean, you hardly know me. And what if you meet someone else? Someone you want to marry for love, rather than just to secure your family business?'

He squeezed her hand tightly. 'That's not why I'm asking you,' he mumbled. 'And I've known you for most of my life.'

She laughed slightly. 'I've known Mr Gallagher on the newsstand for most of my life, but I'm not going to marry him!'

Bill huffed. 'You know what I mean.'

'No, Bill, I don't know what you mean. We've spent these past few days together, but that's hardly time enough to really get to know each other, is it?'

'I might not have time enough, Edie.'

'Then again, you might. Marry in haste, repent at leisure – that's what they say. And I don't want you to regret your marriage, Bill. It wouldn't be fair.'

'I wouldn't regret it,' he said softly.

She looked at his face and her breath caught at his gentle expression. It hadn't been the most romantic proposal, but she still longed to say yes. To leap into his arms and kiss him. But she couldn't. 'You don't know me, Bill. If you did, you'd never ask me to marry you.'

'I do, though, Edie. I've known you forever and I know you now. All of you. You're clever, loyal, determined. And you're a really good mechanic.' He grinned.

She withdrew her hand. 'No, you don't know me. And I can't marry you.' She stood up and walked to the door.

Bill followed her and took her shoulders. 'Don't you want to marry me?'

'No! I don't want to marry you just so I can look after the garage and Mr P if you die! Are you mad? Don't you know I'd do that whether I was married to you or not?'

'That's not the only reason. What if I told you that I think I'm falling for you. *Know* I'm falling for you.'

Edie looked away. Oh God. Just two weeks ago, she'd have laughed if someone had said she'd be getting a proposal from Bill Penfold of all people. Now, though. Now . . . it was all she wanted. But she couldn't accept. She straightened her shoulders. 'The answer's still no.'

'Why?'

'Because I can't.'

He leant down and pressed his lips to hers. 'You can,' he said. 'You can.'

She pulled away. 'Stop it. I can't, and that's final.'

'Even if I said I know about the baby.'

Edie went cold at that. 'What?'

'I know,' he said gently.

'You heard?'

'Yes, I heard . . .'

'And you don't care? It's not yours, Bill. And people will know that.'

He shrugged. 'Someone very wise made me see that you having a baby by someone else doesn't change the fact that I love you. The essence of you.'

Edie whirled around to disguise the furious tears that had come to her eyes. 'I'm leaving now,' she said. 'Good luck, Bill. And know that I'll always be here to work with your uncle if he'll have me.'

She thundered down the stairs, the door slamming behind her.

Bill sat down and rubbed his hands over his face.

'You're not gonna leave it like that are you, lad?' Mr Pearson asked from the doorway. 'You know she can be stubborn, you just gotta keep trying.'

'Do you think?'

'I know. Go on, get after her. Don't give up. Cos I know that girl, and I know she wants to say yes. It's just her stupid pride getting in the way.'

Bill smiled and stood up. 'I'll do my best.'

# Chapter 74

Bert went into the Guthries' bakery, inhaling the scent of freshly baked bread. 'Mornin', Mrs Guthrie,' he said cheerfully to Mary, who stood behind the counter.

She managed a thin smile. 'Hello, Bert. What can I get you? Afraid all the loaves're reserved, but you can have a couple of rolls?'

'No, thank you. I've come to see Susan.'

Mary nodded. 'Right. She told me she were walkin' out with you.'

'Well, I wouldn't say that exactly . . .' Bert began.

'No, I bet you wouldn't. You Castles are all the same. She's downstairs helping her uncle in the kitchen right now.'

'Right.' Bert was beginning to feel uncomfortable under the woman's disdainful stare. He'd known her all his life, but she'd changed so much since Colin had gone.

'Look, Mrs Guthrie, I know you blame Jimmy for Colin's death, but it wasn't his fault.' He rubbed his hands over his chin. 'I can't describe the carnage, the chaos—' He broke off. It was something he'd never spoken about to anyone. Ever. He pushed it to the back of his mind, just like they all did.

'If that's all, Bert?' Mary said, ignoring him. 'And tell your brother not to come by here again. My Colin deserved better than him.'

'What's that meant to mean?' Bert was truly bemused at the woman's words.

'Exactly what I say. Good day.' She turned away giving Bert no option but to leave.

As he walked down Biggin Street, a voice shouted after him and he looked around to see Susan racing towards him, still wearing her white apron, her black hair tucked under a white hat and a smudge of flour on her cheek. God, she was pretty, Bert thought. Just a shame she was completely crazy.

'I heard your voice,' she said breathlessly. 'Don't mind Auntie Mary. She's taken against all you Castles since Jim started walking out with Reenie Turner.'

Bert's eyebrows raised at that. 'Why?'

'She thinks he's betraying Colin's memory,' she said blithely, putting her arm through his.

'What's it got to do with her? Anyway, she needn't worry, I think that's all over.'

'It was never gonna last, was it? Not with Jim being . . .' She waved her hand around.

Bert stopped suddenly. 'Being what?'

'You know – a nancy boy.'

Bert grabbed her arms, only just managing to restrain himself from shaking her. 'Don't you dare say that about my brother.'

'Oh, didn't you know?' she said. 'Don't worry. I won't tell. It'll be our secret.'

He stared at her, anger surging through him. Was there nothing she wouldn't lie about? 'You little bitch!' he exclaimed. 'Although I shouldn't be surprised you'd make something like that up! You're nothing but a grubby little liar,' he hissed. 'And in case you were wonderin' why I stopped by, it was to let you know that we're finished.'

Susan's face paled. 'What?'

'In fact, we never even began. I only made up to you so you'd drop Charlie. Who, by the way, is going to marry Lily and he's explained *everything* to her! You are crazy, Susan.'

Susan stepped back. 'What are you saying?'

'I'm saying I got together with you for Lily's sake. To get you away from Charlie. Because no one messes with my sisters – or my brothers, come to that. But what I don't understand is why *you* did it. Why did you lie about being engaged to him?'

Susan's lips trembled. 'I-I . . .'

Bert sighed. 'You know what, it doesn't matter. Whatever your reasons, I don't care. Because I've had enough. Bye, Susan. Have a nice life!' He whirled away from her and began to stride down the road.

'Please don't do this. Please,' Susan called after him. But when he didn't reply or stop, her expression changed. 'You'll regret this, Bert!' she called. 'You have no idea what I'm capable of.'

He turned around at that, walking backwards as he called, 'Oh, I think I've got a pretty good idea! And by the way, I regretted this almost from the moment we met.' He spun round and hurried away, feeling lighter than he had in ages.

Susan watched him go, angry tears cascading down her cheeks. 'Not half as much as you will,' she whispered fiercely, walking blindly back to the bakery.

❦

'Will you come back with me?' Nellie asked Gladys after a while. 'I think it might help if we both talk to the family.'

Gladys nodded. 'All right, love. I think it's time.'

They were both stiff from kneeling on the cold grave, but they managed to help each other up and, arm in arm, they walked out of the churchyard and on to Cannon Street.

As always, the streets were crowded and Nellie looked at the shoppers, surprised to see how life seemed to be going on as normal, while hers was lying in tatters. Again.

Lily was in the kitchen when she got back, making a tray of lunch for Marianne.

'Where've you been all day? And why are you so filthy?' she asked in surprise, staring at the brown stains on the front of her mother's coat, the mud on her hands. Then her gaze shifted to Gladys. 'You two been having a mud fight?'

'No more fighting, Lily. Me and your mum have settled our differences.'

'Have we?' Nellie asked softly.

'Yes, love. For now.'

Nellie nodded with understanding. 'Have you seen Edie?' she asked.

'She's at the garage. What the hell have you done this time, Mum? She's in a dreadful state.'

Nellie gazed at her daughter. 'She didn't tell you anything then?'

'No. She said to ask you. So are you going to tell us or is it going to be another secret to drag this family down?'

Nellie shook her head. 'No more secrets, love. I can't stand the weight of them anymore. But for now I need a cup of tea.'

Lily poured out two cups and handed them over. 'Wash your hands and go sit down, and I'll bring you a sandwich once I've taken Marianne's food up.'

After doing as they were told, Nellie and Gladys sat quietly at the café window, watching the passers-by. A couple of people knocked to ask if they could come in, but Nellie waved them all away. The way she felt right then, she wasn't sure she'd ever have the energy to open up again.

The back door opened and Jasper came in, puffing. 'Thought I might find you here. Good to see that you're friends again.' He nodded at Gladys then went to pour himself a cup of tea before joining them at the table.

'I don't suppose I'll get an explanation, will I?' he asked.

Nellie and Gladys looked at each other and a silent communication passed between them. 'Soon, love. Soon, I promise.' Nellie patted Jasper's hand.

There was a knock on the window and they looked up to see Bert grinning at them and pointing to the front door. Nellie scowled and indicated he should go to the back, but Gladys tutted and got up to unbolt the door.

As Bert stepped towards her, there was a shout.

From their vantage point at the window, Nellie and Jasper watched as a girl walked across the square and stopped right in front of Bert, her face contorted with rage.

'Ain't that Susan, Mary's niece?' she said. 'Poor love, from the looks of her, Bert's let her down,' Nellie remarked with a sigh. 'Way he carries on with girls, he'll get himself in real trouble one of these days.'

Suddenly, Gladys rushed forward to stand in front of Bert and pushed the girl back. But as she did so, there was a loud bang.

Nellie jumped up. 'What the—'

Jasper was quicker than her and ran out of the door to where Bert was kneeling beside Gladys, staring in shock at the red stain that had appeared on her stomach. He looked up. 'Someone get help!' he shouted. 'She's been shot!'

Bert stood up, his eyes frantically scanning the crowd in the square. When he spotted Susan's figure disappearing up Cowgate Hill, he went to follow her, but Jasper grasped his arm and pulled him back. 'Leave it, son. Gladys needs you more right now.'

Bert looked down in horror at Gladys. She'd always been part of his life – sometimes disapproving, sometimes irritating, but always loving. Always comforting. How was this possible? he wondered, swallowing down the nausea as the stain grew ever bigger. His eyes blurred, as other images came back to him. His mate, John, collapsed on the sand at Dunkirk, blood soaking through the jacket of his uniform. Another friend, his eyes wide open, staring sightlessly up at the grey sky, one small hole in the centre of his forehead. Another with half his leg blown off . . . Dozens and dozens of his comrades dead or mortally wounded. He rubbed at his eyes as his body started to shake, and he let out a groan of terror.

'All right, lad. All right.' Jasper pulled Bert into his arms, holding him tight as he trembled against him.

'I can't bear it, Jasper,' Bert whispered. 'I can't bear it.'

'I know, son. I know. But you have to. What other choice do you have?'

Jasper glanced to the ground where Nellie was now kneeling beside Gladys.

'Glad! Don't go, Glad! Don't go now,' she called to her friend frantically.

Gladys's eyes fluttered open. 'Did you see, Nellie? Did you see?'

'Yes, love, I saw. Please don't leave me.' She gathered Gladys to her, so her head was cradled in her lap. 'You're going to be all right.'

'I think I am.' Gladys smiled. 'Because I've made up for it now.'

Nellie bent her head over Gladys. 'Made up for what, love?'

'Donald,' she whispered. 'I'm washed clean.'

Nellie watched with a growing sense of disbelief and utter horror as her friend's eyes started to close.

'No! No, Glad. You can't! You can't go. Who's gonna do the washing up and tell me when I'm out of line?'

'Always about you, Nell, eh?' Gladys whispered with a very small smile.

'No! No, this is about you. I love you, Glad, please don't leave me.' She started to sob. 'Please, love.'

With the last of her strength, Gladys lifted her arm and rested it on Nellie's cheek. 'A life for a life, Nell,' she whispered. 'The stain has gone.'

'The stain is mine!' she shrieked. 'Never yours. Never . . .' She started to sob in earnest.

'Did you see . . .' Gladys said again, eyes closed, shivering with shock. 'Did you see?'

'Yes, I saw, love. I saw.'

'I saved him, Nellie. I saved him. It's all right now.'

'Yes, you saved him. I can never repay you for saving my son.'

Gladys shook her head. 'No,' she whispered. 'Donald. Look.' She gestured at Bert, who had knelt back down beside her, his cheeks tear-stained.

411

Nellie shuddered. Bert's expression was so like his father's when he'd come back from the war – haunted, devastated. No trace of the happy-go-lucky man he usually was. 'Take her upstairs, love,' Nellie said to him gently; he needed something to do to keep his mind occupied.

She looked around at the small crowd that had gathered, noticing Phyllis and Ethel pushing through. 'Someone call an ambulance!'

'Already done, love,' Ethel said breathlessly. 'What happened?'

'She's been shot,' Bert said in a shaking voice as he lifted Gladys carefully. 'She's been shot and she saved my life.' He ran inside and strode upstairs, laying Gladys gently on the sofa.

'Lily!' he called.

Lily came downstairs and stared aghast at the scene; she'd been sitting with Marianne in their bedroom and heard nothing of the commotion going on out in the market square. She spun round and grabbed every tea towel she could find from the drawer in the small kitchen, then rushing over, she began to press them into Gladys's stomach, but she knew already it would do no good. No one could survive a wound like this.

Marianne came down the stairs and sunk down on the bottom step, her hand over her mouth, unable to comprehend what she was seeing.

Nellie ran in and dropped down beside the sofa, grabbing Gladys's hand, the nailbeds still encrusted with mud.

For a moment, Gladys's eyes flickered open. 'D-d-did y-y-you see?' she whispered yet again.

Nellie nodded, tears in her eyes. 'I saw,' she said. 'I saw. Thank you, Gladys. Thank you.'

But she was beyond hearing now and her eyes fluttered closed as Nellie bent forward, resting her head on Gladys's, her tears trickling down over her old friend's face, like water from a baptism.

# Chapter 75

Some hours later, the devastated family sat in silence in the café – no one could bear to go into the sitting room where Gladys had died. Phyllis had collected the boys from the caves and taken them home with her. Bert had run off shortly after Gladys had died and hadn't yet returned. While Mavis had telephoned the castle and Drop Redoubt to see if the other boys could join them.

Nellie looked out of the window; though the light was fading, it was still daytime, she realised, and people were going about their business outside. Many had popped their heads in to find out what was going on, only for Jasper to send them away with a gruff word. He'd sat steadfast by her side throughout, but if he knew, Nellie thought, if he knew what she'd done, would he stay? She wasn't sure. She looked over at Edie. She probably blamed her for Gladys's death as well now. Without Gladys, she no longer had the courage to tell everyone. Would it be possible, she wondered, to just not tell at all?

Sensing her mother's eyes on her, Edie avoided her gaze. She couldn't forgive her, but in the face of Gladys's sudden and shocking death, she didn't have the heart to remain so angry either. Maybe it would be best to let the secret die with Gladys, she thought. Because what good would come of telling everyone now? Tears welled in her eyes as images of Gladys over the years played through her mind. She'd done nothing but love them all, she thought sadly. And that love and loyalty had led to her father's death. And then, ultimately, to hers . . . Surely there'd been enough pain now?

Feeling her shoulders shake, Bill dropped a small kiss on her head and she leant into him, grateful for his presence. He'd been waiting for her in Mr Pearson's Morris Minor at the bottom of Harold Passage and insisted on driving her back. They'd walked in to find Nellie sobbing in Marianne's arms and Lily sobbing in Jasper's. And poor Gladys lying dead on the sofa.

Bill had taken one look at the scene and steered her back down the stairs, whereupon he'd started to give her instructions – pour tea, cut sandwiches – anything to keep her busy, and then he'd returned upstairs to take care of the others.

Now he sat with his arm around her, his thumb stroking rhythmically over her shoulder, offering her unquestioning comfort and understanding. They'd hardly spoken a word to each other since they'd entered, but Gladys's death had once again shown her how fragile their lives were. How pointless it was to turn your back on any small happiness you could find. So she *would* marry Bill, Edie decided. Not because he was willing to marry her despite the fact that she was pregnant with someone else's child, but because she loved him, and the thought of being without him made her heart ache with loss.

She looked up at him and their eyes met. Smiling tremulously, she nodded, and the way his face lit up erased any lingering uncertainty. He wanted this too. He wanted *her*. And the thought soothed her wounded soul. He pulled her tighter against him and she snuggled into his arms, tears gathering in her eyes again. How was it possible to feel so devastated and so happy at the same time?

Opposite Edie, Jim sat with Reenie, their hands clasped tight, and beside them, Alfie held Marianne close as she wept into his shoulder. Rodney and Lily sat together, faces pale with shock, but there was no Marge. Edie felt a little sorry for her brother, but he'd had his chance and hadn't taken it. She should not make that mistake.

The door opened and Bert came in, his face chalk white, his eyes red-rimmed and all traces of his usual good humour absent. 'They've arrested Susan,' he said.

414

Edie swallowed and closed her eyes, feeling guilt settle over her once again. When Nellie had told her what had happened only Bill's strong arms around her had stopped her from dropping to the floor. Charlie had been right, she realised. He'd told her he thought Susan might be dangerous, but she'd laughed in his face. And now Gladys was dead.

She looked at Bert and his expression matched how she was feeling – guilt-ridden, haunted and bleak. 'It's our fault,' he whispered, staring at Edie.

Nellie sighed wearily. 'It's no one's fault but Susan's,' she rasped. 'Not even yours, Bert.'

Jasper put his arm around her. 'How about you go lie down, love.'

Nellie shook her head. 'I can't,' she whispered. 'I just can't.'

Suddenly a crash outside brought everyone to their feet, and through the window they watched in shock as the Market Hall exploded.

People outside started to scatter, and as another shell landed right in the centre of the square, the ground juddered and the windows of the café cracked, small shards of glass flying out despite the tape.

Everyone jumped up in shock, and while Jasper went to unbolt the door, the others raced through to the kitchen, swiftly followed by a stream of people who'd been in the square.

Only Nellie didn't move. She stayed where she was, staring out of the shattered window. It seemed fitting, she thought, that after months of being under fire, today was the day the café finally sustained damage.

Jasper took her arm and tried to urge her to move but she shook him off irritably.

'At least get under the table,' he said finally.

Nellie nodded and slid under the table, her gaze never leaving the shattered window, although the dust almost obscured the buildings opposite.

All of a sudden she sat up straighter, gasping in disbelief. 'Look,' she shouted. 'Jasper, look!'

He squinted out of the window, and his mouth dropped open in shock as, emerging through the clouds of dust, hundreds of feathers drifted across the square, twisting and turning, dancing in the breeze.

'It's the birds, Nellie,' Jasper said finally. 'All them bloody stuffed birds have been set free.'

'No, it's a sign. It's Glad telling us she's all right. Telling us that the angels have her safe.' Nellie started to cry.

'No, love. It's a sign we need to get to shelter.' Jasper tried again to get her to move.

But Nellie wouldn't budge. If the café was going down, then she intended to go down with it. So with a sigh, Jasper took her hand, and together they watched the feathers float softly to the ground.

# Acknowledgements

This one has been tough to write for many reasons, so I would like to thank my wonderfully encouraging agent, Teresa Chris, and my ever-patient editor, Claire Johnson-Creek, for keeping me calm.

And thank you as well, to my endlessly supportive family: my mother, Anne, and sister Ali. But most especially to my inspirational big sister, Sandy, who despite being so ill, was always interested and always cheered me on. This one is all for you, Sandy. Thank you for your love and encouragement, and for your unshakeable faith in me. I just wish you had got the chance to read it.

To my lovely friends, Tanita and Natacha, thank you for the encouraging messages and care packages – and for not complaining when I kept turning down invitations. You are the best.

Finally, to my children, Maddie, Sim and Olly, who were locked down with me for much of the writing of this book. Surely this has nothing to do with why you've all mostly moved out now . . . does it?

# Welcome to the world of Ginny Bell!

Keep reading for more from Ginny Bell, to discover
a recipe that features in this novel and to find out more
about Ginny's upcoming books . . .

We'd also like to welcome you to Memory Lane,
a place to discuss the very best saga stories from
authors you know and love with other readers,
plus get recommendations for new books we think
you'll enjoy. Read on and join our club!

## www.MemoryLane.Club
### www.facebook.com/groups/memorylanebookgroup

Dear Reader,

Thank you so much for reading *The Dover Café Under Fire*. As any who have read my previous books might know, I try to use as many true events from Dover's wartime years as possible, and this book is no exception. However, you must grant me some poetic licence. For example, it is true that there were concerns in Dover over some suspicious bombings. In the book, I mention an attack on the Dover Engineering Works. This did indeed happen, and it did cause concern as this was the secret site of the barrage balloon repair centre. There were other seemingly targeted attacks, too – at Wanstone Farm where some big guns were located, the Citadel, and various other sites around Dover – but no evidence of spying or sabotage was ever found. So I decided to make some up.

It was in a fascinating book called *Hitler's British Traitors* by Tim Tate that I first learnt about the Nazi radio station NBBS, and also about the sticky-backs people would stick up to advertise the station. This book taught me much about the tactics of the Fifth Column, and also the many people who worked against the country – either alone or in small groups. It is in this book that I first read about Dorothy O'Grady, who was convicted of treachery and sentenced to death during the Second World War, although this was later commuted to fourteen years hard labour. She died in 1985 and it's still not clear whether she was a genuine spy, or merely a fantasist looking for excitement. Her story inspired me to bring back Hester Erskine – who had a cameo role in *The Dover Café at War*.

What struck me about these groups was that membership depended entirely on belief and ideology, and shopkeepers, cleaners, servants, wealthy businessmen and minor royalty would all meet and correspond with each other. It was only when it came to conviction and punishment that Britain's rigid class system came back into play, and those with wealth and status would usually find themselves spending a comfortable couple of years in luxury internment, or they might be able to wriggle free altogether. While the rest would end up with hard labour or death.

In *The Dover Café on the Front Line*, I included one real character – Dr Gertrude Toland at the Casualty Hospital. This time, I have given Herbert Armstrong, the legendary manager of the Hippodrome Theatre, a small role. Despite damage, bombs and disruption to performances, he kept the place going throughout the war. And if you thought the scene at the Hippodrome Theatre seems unlikely, I promise you that this, too, is based on real events. Though it didn't happen on New Year's Eve, the theatre was bombed during a performance, but with no serious casualties, the piano was dug out and carried to a Nissen hut, where the show continued.

There is one more character to mention: Peter Holmes, the young Liverpudlian MI5 agent, is a tribute to my lovely dad. If he'd been old enough during the war, there is no question this is what he would have been doing. He always was a bit of a man of mystery.

As for the feathers in the final scene – I read about this when I first started researching *The Dover Café at War*, and it was such a striking image that I have been looking for a way to use it ever since. I am very glad it finally made it in.

Lots of love,
Ginny

# Marianne's Bread-and-Butter Pudding

While bread-and-butter pudding was a rare treat during wartimes, it's become the ultimate comfort dessert today. Why not try this delicious dish with a lovely cup of tea and a book?

## Ingredients

- 6 large slices of stale bread
- 3 oz butter/margarine/lard – whatever you have
- 3 oz dried fruit
- 3 eggs – powdered egg will do
- 3 tablespoons golden syrup
- Nutmeg
- Cinnamon
- 1 pint milk – or if you're running low, mix what you have with warm water

## Method

1. Pre-heat oven at 180°C. Spread the top of the bread with the softened butter and then cut each slice of bread into four neat squares and place buttered side up into a pie dish.
2. Sprinkle the dried fruit on top. Beat the eggs with the syrup. Warm the milky liquid, add to the beaten eggs and syrup mixture and pour over the bread and butter. Leave to stand for 20–30 minutes until the bread is swollen.
3. Sprinkle a teaspoon of sugar over the top with nutmeg and cinnamon and then bake for an hour until just firm. If you'd like a crisp top, then add 10 minutes.

# · MEMORY LANE ·

## If you enjoyed *The Dover Café Under Fire*, why not discover the previous books in the series . . .

### 1939

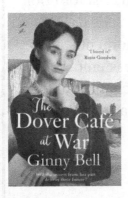

At the heart of Market Square lies Castle's Café, run by the formidable Nellie Castle and her six children. Since the scandalous birth of her son ten years ago, Marianne, Nellie's eldest daughter, has preferred to stay hidden in the kitchen. She has never revealed the identity of Donny's father – not even to her own mother.

**But with World War II just around the corner, will Marianne's past catch up with her?**

### 1940

Despite the danger of the Battle of Britain raging overhead, Nellie is determined to keep the café open, no matter what.

For Lily Castle, it is an exciting time to start her nursing career. That is until a prisoner escapes from the hospital, threating her own freedom.

Meanwhile there are strange goings-on at the café and long-buried secrets are surfacing.

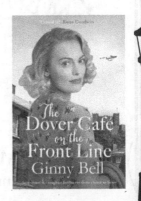

**Secrets that could tear the Castle family apart once and for all . . .**

# ·MEMORY LANE·

Introducing the place for story lovers – a welcoming home for all readers who love heartwarming tales of wartime, family and romance. Sign up to our mailing list for book recommendations, giveaways, deals and behind-the-scenes writing moments from your favourite authors. Join the Memory Lane Book Group on Facebook to chat about the books you love with other saga readers.

·MEMORY LANE·